H. J Draper

St. Bartholomew's Eve

A tale of the Huguenot wars

H. J Draper

St. Bartholomew's Eve
A tale of the Huguenot wars

ISBN/EAN: 9783337011628

Printed in Europe, USA, Canada, Australia, Japan

Cover: Foto ©Andreas Hilbeck / pixelio.de

More available books at **www.hansebooks.com**

ST. BARTHOLOMEW'S EVE

A TALE OF
THE HUGUENOT WARS

BY

G. A. HENTY

Author of " Beric the Briton," " In Freedom's Cause," " The Dash for Khartoum,"
" By England's Aid," " In the Reign of Terror," &c.

*WITH TWELVE ILLUSTRATIONS BY H. J. DRAPER
AND MAP OF FRANCE*

NEW YORK
CHARLES SCRIBNER'S SONS
1910

PREFACE

My DEAR LADS,

It is difficult in these days of religious toleration to understand why men should, three centuries ago, have flown at each others' throats in the name of the Almighty; still less, how in cold blood they could have perpetrated hideous massacres of men, women, and children. The Huguenot wars were, however, as much political as religious. Philip of Spain, at that time the most powerful potentate of Europe, desired to add France to the countries where his influence was all-powerful, and in the ambitious house of Guise he found ready instruments. For a time the new faith that had spread with such rapidity in Germany, England, and Holland, made great progress in France also. But here the reigning family remained Catholic, and the vigorous measures they adopted to check the growing tide drove those of the new religion to take up arms in self-defence. Although under the circumstances the Protestants can hardly be blamed for so doing, there can be little doubt that the first Huguenot war, though the revolt was successful, was the means of France remaining a Catholic country. It gave colour to the assertions of the Guises and their friends that the movement was a political one, and that the Protestants intended to grasp all power and to overthrow the throne of France. It also afforded an excuse for the cruel persecutions which followed, and rallied to the Catholic cause numbers of those who were at heart indifferent to the question of religion, but were Royalists rather than Catholics.

The great organization of the Church of Rome laboured among all classes for the destruction of the growing heresy. Every pulpit in France resounded with denunciations of the Huguenots, and passionate appeals were made to the bigotry and fanaticism of the more ignorant classes; so that, while the power of the Huguenots lay in some of the country districts, the mobs of the great towns were everywhere the instruments of the priests.

I have not considered it necessary to devote any large portion of my story to details of the terrible massacres of the period, nor to the atrocious persecutions to which the Huguenots were subjected, but have as usual gone to the military events of the struggle for its chief interest. For the particulars of these I have relied chiefly upon the collection of works of contemporary authors published by M. Zeller of Paris, the Memoirs of François de la Noüe, and other French authorities.

Yours sincerely,

G. A. HENTY.

CONTENTS

ILLUSTRATIONS

ST. BARTHOLOMEW'S EVE

A TALE OF THE HUGUENOT WARS

CHAPTER I

DRIVEN FROM HOME

N the year 1567 there were few towns in the southern counties of England that did not contain a colony, more or less large, of French Protestants. For thirty years the Huguenots had been exposed to constant and cruel persecutions; many thousands had been massacred by the soldiery, burned at the stake, or put to death with dreadful tortures. Fifty thousand, it was calculated, had, in spite of the most stringent measures of prevention, left their homes and made their escape across the frontiers. These had settled for the most part in the Protestant cantons of Switzerland, in Holland, or England. As many of those who reached our shores were but poorly provided with money, they naturally settled in or near the ports of landing.

Canterbury was a place in which many of the unfortunate emigrants found a home. Here one Gaspard Vaillant, his wife, and her sister, who had landed in the year 1547, had established themselves. They were among the first comers, but the French colony had grown gradually until it numbered several hundreds. The Huguenots were well liked in the town, being pitied for their misfortunes and admired for the courage with which they bore their losses; setting to work, each man

at his trade if he had one, or if not, taking to the first work
that came to hand. They were quiet and God-fearing folk;
very good towards each other and to their poor countrymen on
their way from the coast to London, entertaining them to the
best of their power, and sending them forward on their way
with letters to the Huguenot committee in London, and with
sufficient money in their pockets to pay their expenses on the
journey, and to maintain them for a while until some employment could be found for them.

Gaspard Vaillant had been a land-owner near Civray, in
Poitou. He was connected by blood with several noble families in that district, and had been among the first to embrace
the reformed religion. For some years he had not been interfered with, as it was upon the poorer and more defenceless
classes that the first fury of the persecutors fell; but as the
attempts of Francis to stamp out the new sect failed, and his
anger rose more and more against them, persons of all ranks
fell under the ban. The prisons were filled with Protestants
who refused to confess their errors; soldiers were quartered in
the towns and villages, where they committed terrible atrocities
upon the Protestants; and Gaspard, seeing no hope of better
times coming, or of being permitted to worship in peace and
quietness, gathered together what money he could and made
his way with his wife and her sister to La Rochelle, whence he
took ship to London.

Disliking the bustle of a large town, he was recommended
by some of his compatriots to go down to Canterbury, where
three or four fugitives from his own part of the country had
settled. One of these was a weaver by trade, but without
money to manufacture looms or set up in his calling. Gaspard
joined him as partner, embarking the little capital he had
saved; and being a shrewd, clear-headed man he carried on
the business part of the concern, while his partner Lequoc
worked at the manufacture. As the French colony in Canterbury increased they had no difficulty in obtaining skilled hands
from among them. The business grew in magnitude, and the
profits were large, in spite of the fact that numbers of similar
enterprises had been established by the Huguenot immigrants
in London and other places. They were indeed amply suffi-

cient to enable Gaspard Vaillant to live in the condition of a substantial citizen, to aid his fellow-countrymen, and to lay by a good deal of money.

His wife's sister had not remained very long with him. She had, upon their first arrival, given lessons in her own language to the daughters of burgesses and of the gentry near the town, but three years after the arrival of the family there she had married a well-to-do young yeoman who farmed a hundred acres of his own land two miles from the town. His relations and neighbours had shaken their heads over what they considered his folly in marrying the pretty young Frenchwoman, but ere long they were obliged to own that his choice had been a good one. Just after his first child was born he was, when returning home one evening from market, knocked down and run over by a drunken carter, and was so injured that for many months his life was in danger. Then he began to mend, but though he gained in strength he did not recover the use of his legs, being completely paralysed from the hips downward, and, as it soon appeared, was destined to remain a helpless invalid all his life.

From the day of the accident Lucie had taken the management of affairs in her hands, and having been brought up in the country, and being possessed of a large share of the shrewdness and common sense for which Frenchwomen are often conspicuous, she succeeded admirably. The neatness and order of the house since their marriage had been a matter of surprise to her husband's friends, and it was not long before the farm showed the effects of her management. Gaspard Vaillant assisted her with his counsel, and as the French methods of agriculture were considerably in advance of those in England, instead of things going to rack and ruin, as John Fletcher's friends predicted, its returns were considerably augmented. Naturally, she at first experienced considerable opposition. The labourers grumbled at what they called new-fangled French fashions; but when they left her their places were supplied by her countrymen, who were frugal and industrious, accustomed to make the most out of small areas of ground and to turn every foot to the best advantage.

Gradually the raising of corn was abandoned, and a large

portion of the farm devoted to the growing of vegetables, which, by dint of plentiful manuring and careful cultivation, were produced of a size and quality that were the surprise and admiration of the neighbourhood, and gave her almost a monopoly of the supply of Canterbury. The carters were still English; partly because Lucie had the good sense to see that if she employed French labourers only she would excite feelings of jealousy and dislike among her neighbours, and partly because she saw that in the management of horses and cattle the Englishmen were equal, if not superior, to her countrymen. Her life was a busy one; the management of the house and farm would alone have been a heavy burden to most people, but she found ample time for the tenderest care of the invalid, whom she nursed with untiring affection.

"It is hard upon a man of my size and inches, Lucie," he said one day, "to be lying here as helpless as a sick child; and yet I don't feel that I have any cause for discontent. I should like to be going about the farm, and yet I feel that I am happier here, lying watching you singing so contentedly over your work, and making everything so bright and comfortable. Who would have thought when I married a little French lady that she was going to turn out a notable farmer? All my friends tell me that there is not a farm like mine in all the country round, and that the crops are the wonder of the neighbourhood; and when I see the vegetables that are brought in here I should like to go over the farm, if only for once, just to see them growing."

"I hope you will be able to do that some day, dear. Not on foot, I am afraid; but when you get stronger and better, as I hope you will, we will take you round in a litter, and the bright sky and the fresh air will do you good."

Lucie spoke very fair English now, and her husband had come to speak a good deal of French; for the service of the house was all in that language, the three maids being daughters of French workmen in the town. The waste and disorder of those who were in the house when her husband first brought her there had appalled her, and the women so resented any attempt at teaching on the part of the French madam, that after she had tried several sets with equally bad results, John

Fletcher had consented to the introduction of French girls, bargaining only that he was to have good English fare, and not French kickshaws. The Huguenot customs had been kept up, and night and morning the house servants, with the French neighbours and their families, all assembled for prayer in the farmhouse. To this John Fletcher had agreed without demur. His father had been a Protestant when there was some danger in being so, and he himself had been brought up soberly and strictly. Up to the time of his accident there had been two congregations, he himself reading the prayers to his farm hands, while Lucie afterwards read them in her own language to her maids, but as the French labourers took the place of the English hands only one service was needed. When John Fletcher first regained sufficient strength to take much interest in what was passing round, he was alarmed at the increase in the numbers of those who attended these gatherings. Hitherto four men had done the whole work of the farm; now there were twelve.

"Lucie, dear," he said uneasily one day, "I know that you are a capital manager, but it is impossible that a farm the size of ours can pay with so many hands on it. I have never been able to do more than pay my way and lay by a few pounds every year with only four hands, and many would have thought three sufficient, but with twelve—and I counted them this morning—we must be on the high road to ruin."

"I will not ruin you, John. Do you know how much money there was in your bag when you were hurt just a year ago now?"

"Yes, I know there were thirty-three pounds."

His wife went out of the room and returned with a leather bag.

"Count them, John," she said.

There were forty-eight. Fifteen pounds represented a vastly greater sum at that time than they do at present, and John Fletcher looked up from the counting with amazement.

"This can't be all ours, Lucie. Your brother must have been helping us."

"Not with a penny, doubting man," she laughed. "The money is yours, all earned by the farm; perhaps not quite all, because we have not more than half as many animals as we had

before.   But, as I told you, we are growing vegetables, and for
that we must have more men than for corn.   But, as you see,
it pays.   Do not fear about it, John.   If God should please to
restore you to health and strength most gladly will I lay down
the reins, but till then I will manage as best I may, and with
the help and advice of my brother and his friends, shall hope,
by the blessing of God, to keep all straight."

The farm throve, but its master made but little progress
towards recovery.   He was able, however, occasionally to be
carried round in a hand-litter made for him upon a plan
devised by Gaspard Vaillant, in which he was supported in a
half-sitting position, while four men bore him as if in a
Sedan-chair.   But it was only occasionally that he could bear
the fatigue of such excursions.   Ordinarily he lay on a couch
in the farmhouse kitchen, where he could see all that was going
on there; while in warm summer weather he was wheeled outside, and lay in the shade of the great elm in front of the
house.

The boy, Philip—for so he had been christened, after John
Fletcher's father,—grew apace, and as soon as he was old
enough to receive instruction his father taught him his letters
out of a hornbook, until he was big enough to go down every
day to school in Canterbury.   John himself was built upon a
large scale, and at quarter-staff and wrestling could, before he
married, hold his own with any of the lads of Kent, and Philip
bade fair to take after him in skill and courage.   His mother
would shake her head reprovingly when he returned with his
face bruised and his clothes torn after encounters with his
school-fellows, but his father took his part.

"Nay, nay, wife," he said one day, "the boy is eleven
years old now, and must not grow up a milksop.   Teach him
if you will to be honest and true, to love God, and to hold to
the faith, but in these days it needs that men should be able
to use their weapons also.   There are your countrymen in
France, who ere long will be driven to take up arms for the
defence of their faith and lives from their cruel persecutors;
and, as you have told me, many of the younger men from here
and elsewhere will assuredly go back to aid their brethren.

"We may even have trials here.   Our Queen is a Protestant,

and happily at present we can worship God as we please in peace; but it was not so in the time of Mary, and it may be that troubles may again fall upon the land, seeing that as yet the Queen is not married. Moreover, Philip of Spain has pretensions to rule here, and every Englishman may be called upon to take up bow or bill for his faith and country. Our co-religionists in Holland and France are both being cruelly persecuted, and it may well be that the time will come when we shall send over armies to their assistance. I would that the boy should grow up both a good Christian and a stout soldier. He comes on both sides of a fighting stock. One of my ancestors fought at Agincourt, and another with the Black Prince at Cressy and Poitiers; while on your side his blood is noble, and, as we know, the nobles of France are second to none in bravery.

"Before I met you I had thoughts of going out myself to fight among the English bands who have engaged on the side of the Hollanders. I had even spoken to my cousin James about taking charge of the farm while I was away. I would not have sold it, for Fletchers held this land before the Normans set foot in England; but I had thoughts of borrowing money upon it to take me out to the war, when your sweet face drove all such matters from my mind. Therefore, Lucie, while I would that you should teach the boy to be good and gentle in his manners, so that if he ever goes among your French kinsmen he shall be able to bear himself as befits his birth on that side, I, for my part—though, alas, I can do nothing myself—will see that he is taught to use his arms, and to bear himself as stoutly as an English yeoman should when there is need of it.

"So, wife, I would not have him chidden when he comes home with a bruised face and his garments somewhat awry. A boy who can hold his own among boys will some day hold his own among men, and the fisticuffs in which our English boys try their strength are as good preparation as are the courtly sports, in which, as you tell me, young French nobles are trained. But I would not have him backward in these either. We English, thank God, have not had much occasion to draw a sword since we broke the strength of Scotland on

Flodden Field, and in spite of ordinances, we know less than we should do of the use of our weapons; even the rules that every lad shall practise shooting at the butts are less strictly observed than they should be. But in this respect our deficiencies can be repaired in his case, for here in Canterbury there are several of your countrymen of noble birth, and doubtless among these we shall be able to find an instructor for Phil. Many of them are driven to hard shifts to procure a living; and since that bag of yours is every day getting heavier, and we have but him to spend it upon, we will not grudge giving him the best instruction that can be procured."

Lucie did not dispute her husband's will, but she nevertheless tried to enlist Gaspard Vaillant, who was frequently up at the farm with his wife in the evening, for he had a sincere liking for John Fletcher, on her side, and to get him to dissuade her husband from putting thoughts into the boy's head that might lead him some day to be discontented with the quiet life on the farm. She found, however, that Gaspard highly approved of her husband's determination.

"Fie upon you, Lucie. You forget that you and Marie are both of noble blood, in that respect being of condition somewhat above myself, although I too am connected with many good families in Poitou. In other times I should have said it were better that the boy should grow up to till the land, which is assuredly an honourable profession, rather than to become a military adventurer, fighting only for vainglory. But in our days the sword is not drawn for glory, but for the right to worship God in peace.

"No one can doubt that ere long the men of the reformed religion will take up arms to defend their right to live and worship God in their own way. The cruel persecutions under Francis I., Henry II., and Francis II. have utterly failed in their object. When Merindol, Cabrieres, and twenty-two other towns and villages were destroyed in 1547, and persons persecuted and forced to recant, or to fly as we did, it was thought that we were but a handful whom it would be easy to exterminate; but in spite of edict after edict, of persecution, slaughterings, and burnings, in spite of the massacres of Amboise and others, the reformed religion has spread so greatly that even the Guises are forced to recognize it as a power. At Fontainebleau Admiral Coligny, Montmorency, the Chatillons, and others openly professed the reformed religion, and argued boldly for tolerance; while Condé and Navarre, although they declined to be present, were openly ranged on their side. Had it not been that Henry II. and Francis were both carried off by the manifest hand of God, the first by a spear-thrust at a tournament, the second by an abscess in the ear, France would have been the scene of deadly strife, for both were, when so suddenly smitten, on the point of commencing a war of extermination.

"But it is only now that the full strength of those who hold the faith is manifested. Beza, the greatest of the reformers next to Calvin himself, and twelve of our most learned and eloquent pastors, are at Poissy disputing upon the faith with the Cardinal of Lorraine and the prelates of the Romish church, in the presence of the young king, the princes, and the court. It is evident that the prelates are unable to answer the arguments of our champions. The Guises, I hear, are furious; for the present Catherine, the queen mother, is anxious for peace and toleration, and it is probable that the end of this argument at Poissy will be an edict allowing freedom of worship. But this will only infuriate still more the Papists, urged on by Rome and Philip of Spain. Then there will be an appeal to arms, and the contest will be a dreadful one. Navarre, from all I hear, has been well-nigh won over by the Guises; but his noble wife will, all say, hold the faith to the end, and her kingdom will follow her. Condé is as good a general as Guise, and with him there is a host of nobles: Rochefoucauld, the Chatillons, Soubise, Gramont, Rohan, Genlis, and a score of others. It will be terrible, for in many cases father and son will be ranged on opposite sides, and brother will fight against brother."

"But surely, Gaspard, the war will not last for years?"

"It may last for generations," the weaver said gloomily, "though not without intermissions, for I believe that after each success on one side or the other there will be truces and concessions, to be followed by fresh persecutions and fresh wars, until either the reformed faith becomes the religion of

all France or is entirely stamped out. What is true of France
is true of Holland. Philip will annihilate the reformers there,
or they will shake off the yoke of Spain. England will be
driven to join in one or both struggles; for if papacy is triumphant in France and Holland, Spain and France would unite
against her. So you see, sister, that in my opinion we are at
the commencement of a long and bloody struggle for freedom
of worship, and at any rate it will be good that the boy should
be trained as he would have been had you married one of your
own rank in France, in order that when he comes to man's
estate he may be able to wield a sword worthily in the defence
of the faith.

"Had I sons I should train them as your husband intends
to train Phil. It may be that he will never be called upon to
draw a sword, but the time he has spent in acquiring its use
will not be wasted. These exercises give firmness and sup-
pleness to the figure, quickness to the eye, and briskness of
decision to the mind. A man who knows that he can at need
defend his life if attacked, whether against soldiers in the
field or robbers in the street, has a sense of power and self-
reliance that a man untrained in the use of the strength God
has given him can never feel. I was instructed in arms when
a boy, and I am none the worse weaver for it. Do not forget,
Lucie, that the boy has the blood of many good French families in his veins, and you should rejoice that your husband is
willing that he shall be so trained that if the need should
ever come he shall do no discredit to his ancestors on our
side. These English have many virtues which I recognize
freely, but we cannot deny that many of them are somewhat
rough and uncouth, being wondrous lacking in manners and
coarse in speech. I am sure that you yourself would not wish
your son to grow up like many of the young fellows who come
into town on market-day. Your son will make no worse a
farmer for being trained as a gentleman. You yourself have
the training of a French lady, and yet you manage the farm
to admiration. No, no, Lucie, I trust that between us we
shall make a true Christian and a true gentleman of him, and
that if needs be he will show himself a good soldier also."

And so between his French relatives and his sturdy English

father, Philip Fletcher had an unusual training. Among the Huguenots he learned to be gentle and courteous, to bear himself among his elders respectfully, but without fear or shyness; to consider that while all things were of minor consequence in comparison to the right to worship God in freedom and purity, yet that a man should be fearless of death, ready to defend his rights, but with moderation and without pushing them to the injury of others; that he should be grave and decorous of speech, and yet of a gay and cheerful spirit. He strove hard so to deport himself, that if at any time he should return to his mother's country, he could take his place among her relations without discredit. He learned to fence and to dance. Some of the stricter of the Huguenots were of opinion that the latter accomplishment was unnecessary, if not absolutely sinful, but Gaspard Vaillant was firm on this point.

"Dancing is a stately and graceful exercise," he said, "and like the use of arms it greatly improves the carriage and poise of the figure. Queen Elizabeth loves dancing, and none can say that she is not a good Protestant. Every youth should be taught to dance, if only he may know how to walk. I am not one of those who think that because a man is a good Christian he should necessarily be awkward and ungainly in speech and manner, adverse to innocent gaieties, narrow in his ideas, ill-dressed, and ill-mannered, as I see are many of those most extreme in religious matters in this country."

Upon the other hand, in the school playground, under the shadow of the grand cathedral, Phil was as English as any, being foremost in their rough sports, and ready for any fun or mischief. He fought many battles, principally because the difference of his manner from that of the others often caused him to be called "Frenchy." The epithet in itself was not displeasing to him, for he was passionately attached to his mother, and had learned from her to love her native country; but applied in derision it was regarded by him as an insult, and many a tough battle did he fight, until his prowess was so generally acknowledged that the name, though still used, was no longer one of disrespect.

In figure he took after his French rather than his English ancestors. Of more than average height for his age, he was apparently slighter in build than his school-fellows; it was not that he lacked width of chest, but that his bones were smaller and his frame less heavy. The English boys among themselves sometimes spoke of him as "skinny," a word considered specially appropriate to Frenchmen; but though he lacked their roundness and fulness of limb, and had not an ounce of superfluous flesh about him, he was all sinew and wire, and while in sheer strength he was fully their equal, he was incomparably quicker and more active. Although in figure and carriage he took after his mother's countrymen, his features and expression were wholly English. His hair was light-brown, his eyes a bluish-grey, his complexion fair, and his mouth and eyes alive with fun and merriment. This, however, seldom found vent in laughter. His intercourse with the grave Huguenots, saddened by their exile, and quiet and restrained in manner, taught him to repress mirth which would have appeared to them unseemly, and to remain a grave and silent listener to their talk of their unhappy country, and their discussions on religious matters.

To his school-fellows he was somewhat of an enigma. There was no more good-tempered young fellow in the school, no one more ready to do a kindness; but they did not understand why, when he was pleased, he smiled while others roared with laughter; why when in their sports he exerted himself to the utmost, he did so silently while others shouted; why his words were always few, and when he differed from others, he expressed himself with a courtesy that puzzled them; why he never wrangled nor quarrelled; and why any trick played upon an old woman or a defenceless person roused him to fury.

As a rule, when boys do not quite understand one of their number they dislike him. Philip Fletcher was an exception. They did not understand him, but they consoled themselves under this by the explanation that he was half a Frenchman, and could not be expected to be like a regular English boy, and they recognized instinctively that he was their superior.

Much of Philip's time was spent at the house of his uncle, and among the Huguenot colony. Here also were many boys of his own age; these went to a school of their own, taught by the pastor of their own church, who held weekly services in the crypt of the cathedral, which had been granted to them for that purpose by the dean.

While with his English school-fellows he joined in sports and games, among these French lads the talk was sober and quiet. Scarce a week passed but some fugitive, going through Canterbury, brought the latest news of the situation in France, and the sufferings of their co-religionist friends and relations there, and the political events were the chief topics of conversation.

The concessions made at the Conference of Poissy had infuriated the Catholics, and the war was brought on by the Duke of Guise, who, passing with a large band of retainers through the town of Vassy in Champagne, found the Huguenots there worshipping in a barn. His retainers attacked them, slaying men, women, and children. Some sixty being killed, and a hundred or more left terribly wounded.

The Protestant nobles demanded that Francis of Guise should be punished for this atrocious massacre, but in vain, and Guise, on entering Paris in defiance of Catherine's prohibition, was received with royal honours by the populace. The Cardinal of Lorraine, the duke's brother, the duke himself, and their allies, the Constable Montmorency and Marshal Saint André, assumed so threatening an attitude that Catherine left Paris and went to Mélun, her sympathies at this period being with the reformers, by whose aid alone she thought that she could maintain her influence in the state against that of the Guises.

Condé was forced to leave Paris with the Protestant nobles, and from all parts of France the Huguenots marched to assist him. Coligny, the greatest of the Huguenot leaders, hesitated, being, above all things, reluctant to plunge France into civil war; but the entreaties of his noble wife, of his brothers and friends, overpowered his reluctance. Condé left Meaux with fifteen hundred horse with the intention of seizing the person of the young king, but he had been forestalled by the Guises, and moved to Orleans, where he took up his head-quarters. All over France the Huguenots rose in such numbers as astonished their enemies, and soon became possessed of a great many important cities.

Their leaders had endeavoured, in every way, to impress upon them the necessity of behaving as men who fought only for the right to worship God, and for the most part these injunctions were strictly obeyed. In one matter alone the Huguenots could not be restrained. For thirty years the people of their faith had been executed, tortured, and slain, and their hatred of the Romish church manifested itself by the destruction of images and pictures of all kinds in the churches of the towns of which they obtained possession.

Only in the south-east of France was there any exception to the general excellence of their conduct. Their persecution here had always been very severe, and in the town of Orange the papal troops committed a massacre almost without a parallel in its atrocity. The Baron of Adrets, on behalf of the Protestants, took revenge by massacres equally atrocious; but while the butchery at Orange was hailed with approbation and delight by the Catholic leaders, those promoted by Adrets excited such a storm of indignation among the Huguenots of all classes that he shortly afterwards went over to the other side, and was found fighting against the party he had disgraced. At Toulouse three thousand Huguenots were massacred, and in other towns where the Catholics were in a majority terrible persecutions were carried out.

It was nearly a year after the massacre at Vassy before the two armies met in battle. The Huguenots had suffered greatly by the delays caused by attempts at negotiations and compromise. Condé's army was formed entirely of volunteers, and the nobles and gentry, as their means became exhausted, were compelled to return home with their retainers, while many were forced to march to their native provinces to assist their co-religionists there to defend themselves from their Catholic neighbours.

England had entered to a certain extent upon the war, Elizabeth after long vacillation having at length agreed to send six thousand men to hold the towns of Havre, Dieppe, and Rouen, providing these three towns were handed over to her, thus evincing the same calculating greed that marked her subsequent dealings with the Dutch in their struggle for freedom. In vain Condé and Coligny begged her not to impose conditions that Frenchmen would hold to be infamous to them. In vain Throgmorton, her ambassador at Paris, warned her that she would alienate the Protestants of France from her, while the possession of the cities would avail her but little. In vain her minister, Cecil, urged her frankly to ally herself with the Protestants. From the first outbreak of the war for freedom of conscience in France to the termination of the struggle in Holland, Elizabeth baffled both friends and enemies by her vacillation and duplicity, and her utter want of faith, doling out aid in the spirit of a huckster rather than a queen, so that she was in the end even more hated by the Protestants of Hōlland and France than by the Catholics of France and Spain.

To those who look only at the progress made by England during the reign of Elizabeth—thanks to her great ministers, her valiant sailors and soldiers, long years of peace at home, and the spirit and energy of her people,—Elizabeth may appear a great monarch. To those who study her character from her relations with the struggling Protestants of Holland and France, it will appear that she was, although intellectually great, morally one of the meanest, falsest, and most despicable of women.

Rouen, although stoutly defended by the inhabitants, supported by Montgomery with eight hundred soldiers and five hundred Englishmen under Killegrew of Pendennis, was at last forced to surrender. The terms granted to the garrison were basely violated, and many of the Protestants put to death. The King of Navarre, who had, since he joined the Catholic party, shown the greatest zeal in their cause, commanded the besiegers. He was wounded in one of the attacks upon the town, and died shortly afterwards.

The two armies finally met on the 19th of December, 1562. The Catholic party had sixteen thousand foot, two thousand horse, and twenty-two cannon; the Huguenots four thousand horse, but only eight thousand infantry and five cannon. Condé at first broke the Swiss pikemen of the Guises, while Coligny scattered the cavalry of Constable Montmorency, who was wounded and taken prisoner; but the infantry of the Catholics defeated those of the Huguenots, the troops sent by the German princes to aid the latter behaving with great cowardice. Condé's horse was killed under him, and he was made prisoner. Coligny drew off the Huguenot cavalry and the remains of the infantry in good order, and made his retreat unmolested.

The Huguenots had been worsted in the battle, and the loss of Condé was a serious blow; but on the other hand Marshal Saint André was killed and the Constable Montmorency a prisoner. Coligny was speedily reinforced, and the assassination of the Duke of Guise by an enthusiast of the name of Jean Poltrot more than equalized matters.

Both parties being anxious to treat, terms of peace were arranged on the condition that the Protestant lords should be reinstated in their honours and possessions; all nobles and gentlemen should be allowed to celebrate in their own houses the worship of the reformed religion; that in every bailiwick the Protestants should be allowed to hold their religious services in the suburbs of one city, and should also be permitted to celebrate it in one or two places inside the walls of all the cities they held at the time of the signature of the truce. This agreement was known as the Treaty of Amboise, and sufficed to secure peace for France until the latter end of 1567.

GASPARD VAILLANT MAKES A PROPOSAL.

CHAPTER II

AN IMPORTANT DECISION

ONE day in June, 1567, Gaspard Vaillant and his wife went up to Fletcher's farm.

"I have come up to have a serious talk with you, John, about Philip. You see, in a few months he will be sixteen. He is already taller than I am. René and Gustave both tell me that they have taught him all they know with sword and dagger; and both have been stout men-at-arms in their time, and assure me that the lad could hold his own against any young French noble of his own age, and against not a few men. It is time that we came to some conclusion about his future."

"I have thought of it much, Gaspard. Lying here so help-less, my thoughts do naturally turn to him. The boy has grown almost beyond my power of understanding. Sometimes when I hear him laughing and jesting with the men, or with some of his school friends whom he brings up here, it seems to me that I see myself again in him; and that he is a merry young fellow, full of life and fun, and able to hold his own at single-stick, or to foot it round the maypole with any lad in Kent of his age. Then again, when he is talking with his mother, or giving directions in her name to the French labourers, I see a different lad altogether: grave and quiet, with a gentle, courteous way, fit for a young noble ten years his senior. I don't know but that between us, Gaspard, we have made a mess of it, and that it might have been better for him to have grown up altogether as I was, with no thought or care save the management of his farm, with a liking for sport and fun when such came in his way."

"Not at all, not at all," Gaspard Vaillant broke in hastily, "we have made a fine man of him, John; and it seems to me that he possesses the best qualities of both our races. He is frank and hearty, full of life and spirits when, as you say, occasion offers, giving his whole heart either to work or play, with plenty of determination, and what you English call backbone; there is, in fact, a solid English foundation to his character. Then from our side he has gained the gravity of demeanour that belongs to us Huguenots, with the courtesy of manner, the carriage and bearing of a young Frenchman of good blood. Above all, John, he is a sober Christian, strong in the reformed faith, and with a burning hatred against its persecutors, be they French or Spanish. Well, then, being what he is, what is to be done with him? In the first place, are you bent upon his remaining here? I think that with his qualities and disposition it would be well that for a while he had a wider scope. Lucie has managed the farm for the last fifteen years, and can well continue to do so for another ten if God should spare her; and my own opinion is, that for that time he might be left to try his strength, and to devote to the good cause the talents God has given him, and the skill and training that he has acquired through us, and that it would be for his good to make the acquaintance of his French kinsfolk and to see something of the world."

"I know that is Lucie's wish also, Gaspard; and I have frequently turned the matter over in my mind, and have concluded that should it be your wish also, it would be well for me to throw no objections in the way. I shall miss the boy sorely; but young birds cannot be kept always in the nest, and I think that the lad has such good stuff in him that it were a pity to keep him shut up here."

"Now, John," his brother-in-law went on, "although I may never have said quite as much before, I have said enough for you to know what my intentions are. God has not been pleased to bestow children upon us, and Philip is our nearest relation, and stands to us almost in the light of a son. God has blest my work for the last twenty years, and though I have done, I hope, fully my share towards assisting my countrymen in distress, putting by always one-third of my income for that purpose, I am a rich man. The factory has grown larger and larger; not because we desired greater gains, but that I might give employment to more and more of my countrymen. Since the death of Lequoc twelve years ago it has been entirely in my hands, and living quietly as we have done, a greater portion of the profits have been laid by every year; therefore, putting out of account the money that my good sister has laid by, Philip will start in life not ill equipped.

"I know that the lad has said nothing of any wishes he may entertain—at his age it would not be becoming for him to do so until his elders speak,—but of late when we have read to him letters from our friends in France, or when he has listened to the tales of those freshly arrived from their ruined homes, I have noted that his colour rose, that his fingers tightened as if on a sword, and could see how passionately he was longing to join those who were struggling against their cruel oppressors. Not less interested has he been in the noble struggle that the Dutch are making against the Spaniards; a struggle in which many of our exiled countrymen are sharing.

"One of his mother's cousins, the Count de La Noüe, is, as you know, prominent among the Huguenot leaders, and others of our relatives are ranged on the same side. At present there is a truce, but both parties feel that it is a hollow one; nevertheless it offers a good opportunity for him to visit his mother's family. Whether there is any prospect of our ever recovering the lands which were confiscated on our flight is uncertain. Should the Huguenots ever maintain their ground and win freedom of worship in France, it may be that the confiscated estates will in many cases be restored; as to that, however, I am perfectly indifferent. Were I a younger man I should close my factory, return to France, and bear my share in the defence of the faith. As it is, I should like to send Philip over as my substitute.

"It would at any rate be well that he should make the acquaintance of his kinsfolk in France, although even I should not wish that he should cease to regard England as his native country and home. Hundreds of young men, many no older than himself, are in Holland fighting against the persecutors, and risking their lives, though having no kinship with the Dutch; impelled simply by their love of the faith and their hatred of persecution. I have lately, John, though the matter has been kept quiet, purchased the farms of Blunt and Mardyke, your neighbours on either hand. Both are nearly twice the size of your own. I have arranged with the men that for the present they shall continue to work them as my tenants, as they were before the tenants of Sir James Holford, who, having wasted his money at court, has been forced to sell a portion of his estates.

"Thus some day Phil will come into possession of land which will place him in a good position, and I am prepared to add to it considerably. Sir James Holford still gambles away his possessions, and I have explained to his notary my willingness to extend my purchases at any time, should he desire to sell. I should a once commence the building of a comfortable mansion; but it is scarce worth while to do so, for it is probable that before many years Sir James may be driven to part with his Hall as well as his land. In the meantime I am ready to provide Philip with an income which will enable him to take his place with credit among our kinsfolk, and to raise a company of some fifty men to follow him in the field, should Condé and the Huguenots again be driven to struggle against the Guises. What do you think?"

"I think in the first place that Lucie and I should be indeed grateful to you, Gaspard, for your generous offer. As to his going to France, that I must talk over with his mother, whose wishes in this, as in all respects, are paramount with me. But I may say at once, that lying here as I do, thinking of the horrible cruelties and oppressions to which men and women are subjected for the faith's sake in France and Holland, I feel that we, who are happily able to worship in peace and quiet, ought to hesitate at no sacrifice on their behalf; and, moreover, seeing that owing to my affliction he owes what he is rather to his mother and you than to me, I think your wish that he should make the acquaintance of his kinsfolk in France is a natural one. I have no wish for the lad to become a courtier, English or French, nor that he should, as English-

men have done before now in foreign armies, gain great honour
and reputation; but if it is his wish to fight on behalf of the
persecuted people of God, whether in France or in Holland,
he will do so with my heartiest good-will, and if he die he
could not die in a more glorious cause. Let us talk of other
matters now, Gaspard, this is one that needs thought before
more words are spoken."

Two days later John Fletcher had a long talk with Phil.
The latter was delighted when he heard the project, which
was greatly in accord with both sides of his character. As an
English lad he looked forward eagerly to adventure and peril;
as French and of the reformed religion he was rejoiced at the
thought of fighting with the Huguenots against their persecutors, and of serving under the men with whose names and
reputations he was so familiar.

"I do not know your uncle's plans for you as yet, Phil," his
father said. "He went not into such matters, leaving these
to be talked over after it had been settled whether his offer
should be accepted or not. He purposes well by you, and
regards you as his heir. He has already bought Blunt and
Mardyke's farms, and purposes to buy other parts of the estates
of Sir James Holford, as they may slip through the knight's
fingers at the gambling-table. Therefore in time you will
become a person of standing in the county; and although I
care little for these things now, Phil, yet I should like you to
be somewhat more than a mere squire; and if you serve for a
while under such great captains as Coligny and Condé it will
give you reputation and weight. Your good uncle and his
friends think little of such matters, but I own that I am not
uninfluenced by them. Coligny, for example, is a man whom
all honour, and that honour is not altogether because he is
leader of the reformed faith, but because he is a great soldier.

"I do not think that honour and reputation are to be
despised. Doubtless the first thing of all is that a man should
be a good Christian. But that will in no way prevent him
from being a great man; nay, it will add to his greatness.
You have noble kinsfolk in France, to some of whom your
uncle will doubtless commit you, and it may be that you will
have opportunities of distinguishing yourself. Should such

occur I am sure you will avail yourself of them, as one should
do who comes of good stock on both sides; for although we
Fletchers have been but yeomen from generation to generation, we have been ever ready to take and give our share of
hard blows when they were going; and there have been few
battles fought since William the Norman came over that a
Fletcher has not fought in the English ranks, whether in
France, in Scotland, or in our own troubles.

"Therefore it seems to me but natural that for many reasons you should desire at your age to take part in the fighting;
as an Englishman, because Englishmen fought six years ago
under the banner of Condé; as a Protestant, on behalf of our
persecuted brethren; as a Frenchman by your mother's side,
because you have kinsfolk engaged, and because it is the Pope
and Philip of Spain, as well as the Guises, who are in fact
battling to stamp out French liberty.   Of one thing I am sure,
my boy, you will disgrace neither an honest English name nor
the French blood in your veins, nor your profession as a Christian and a Protestant.   There are Engishmen gaining credit
on the Spanish Main under Drake and Hawkins, there are
Englishmen fighting manfully by the side of the Dutch, there
are others in the armies of the Protestant princes of Germany,
and in none of these matters are they so deeply concerned as
you are in the affairs of France and religion.

"I shall miss you, of course, Philip, and that sorely; but I
have long seen that this would probably be the upshot of your
training, and since I can myself take no share in adventure
beyond the walls of this house, I shall feel that I am living
again in you.   But, lad, never forget that you are English.
You are Philip Fletcher, come of an old Kentish stock, and
though you may be living with French kinsfolk and friends,
always keep uppermost the fact that you are an Englishman
who sympathizes with France, and not a Frenchman with
some English blood in your veins.   I have given you up
greatly to your French relations here; but if you win credit
and honour I would have it won by my son, Philip Fletcher,
born in England of an English father, and who will one day
be a gentleman and land-owner in the county of Kent."

"I sha'n't forget that, father," Philip said earnestly.   "I have never regarded myself as in any way French, although speaking the tongue as well as English, and being so much among my mother's friends. But living here with you, where our people have lived so many years, hearing from you the tales from our history, seeing these English fields around me, and being at an English school among English boys, I have ever felt that I am English, though in no way regretting the Huguenot blood that I inherit from my mother. Believe me, that if I fight in France it will be as an Englishman who has drawn his sword in the quarrel, and rather as one who hates oppression and cruelty than because I have French kinsmen engaged in it."

"That is well, Philip. You may be away for some years, but I trust that on your return you will find me sitting here to welcome you back. A creaking wheel lasts long. I have everything to make my life happy and peaceful—the best of wives, a well-ordered farm, and no thought or care as to my worldly affairs; and since it has been God's will that such should be my life, my interest will be wholly centred in you, and I hope to see your children playing round me, or, for aught I know, your grandchildren, for we are a long-lived race. And now, Philip, you had best go down and see your uncle and thank him for his good intentions towards you. Tell him that I wholly agree with his plans, and that if he and your aunt will come up this evening we will enter farther into them."

That evening John Fletcher learned that it was the intention of Gaspard that his wife should accompany Philip.

"Marie yearns to see her people again," he said, "and the present is a good time for her to do so; for when the war once breaks out again none can say how long it will last or how it will terminate. Her sister and Lucie's, the Countess de Laville, has, as you know, frequently written urgently for Marie to go over and pay her a visit. Hitherto I have never been able to bring myself to spare her, but I feel that this is so good an opportunity that I must let her go for a few weeks. Philip could not be introduced under better auspices. He will escort Marie to his aunt's, remain there with her, and then see her on board ship again at La Rochelle, after which, doubtless, he will remain at his aunt's, and when the struggle begins will ride with his cousin François. I have hesitated whether I should go also. But, in the first place, my business would get on but badly without me; in the second, although Marie might travel safely enough, I might be arrested were I recognized as one who had left the kingdom contrary to the edicts; and lastly, I never was on very good terms with her family.

"Emilie, in marrying the Count de Laville, made a match somewhat above her own rank; for the Lavilles were a wealthier and more powerful family than that of Charles de Moulins, her father. On the other hand, I was, although of good birth, yet inferior in consideration to De Moulins, although my lands were broader than his; consequently we saw little of Emilie after our marriage. Therefore my being with Marie would in no way increase the warmth of the welcome that she and Philip will receive. I may say that the estrangement was, perhaps, more my fault than that of the Lavilles. I chose to fancy there was a coolness on their part, which probably existed only in my imagination. Moreover, shortly after my marriage the religious troubles grew serious, and we were all too much absorbed in our own perils and those of our poorer neighbours to think of travelling about, or of having family gatherings.

"At any rate, I feel that Philip could not enter into life more favourably than as cousin of François de Laville, who is but two years or so his senior, and who will, his mother wrote to Marie, ride behind that gallant gentleman François de la Noüe if the war breaks out again. I am glad to feel confident that Philip will in no way bring discredit upon his relations. I shall at once order clothes for him suitable for the occasion. They will be such as will befit an English gentleman; good in material but sober in colour, for the Huguenots eschew bright hues. I will take his measure, and send up to a friend in London for a helmet, breast, and back pieces, together with offensive arms, sword, dagger, and pistols. I have already written to correspondents at Southampton and Plymouth for news as to the sailing of a ship bound for La Rochelle. There he had better take four men into his service, for in these days it is by no means safe to ride through France unattended, especially when one is of the reformed religion. The roads abound with disbanded soldiers and robbers, while in the villages a fanatic might at any time bring on a religious tumult. I have many correspondents at La Rochelle, and will write to one asking him to select four stout fellows, who showed their courage in the last war and can be relied on for good and faithful service. I will also get him to buy horses and make all arrangements for the journey. Marie will write to her sister. Lucie, perhaps, had better write under the same cover; for although she can remember but little of Emilie, seeing that she was fully six years her junior, it would be natural that she should take the opportunity to correspond with her.

"In one respect, Phil," he went on, turning to his nephew, "you will find yourself at some disadvantage, perhaps, among young Frenchmen. You can ride well, and I think can sit a horse with any of them; but of the *ménage*, that is to say, the purely ornamental management of a horse, in which they are most carefully instructed, you know nothing. It is one of the tricks of fashion, of which plain men like myself know but little; and though I have often made inquiries, I have found no one who could instruct you. However, these delicacies are rather for courtly displays than for the rough work of war; though it must be owned that in single combat between two swordsmen, he who has the most perfect control over his horse, and can make the animal wheel or turn, press upon his opponent, or give way by a mere touch of his leg or hand, possesses a considerable advantage over the man who is unversed in such matters. I hope you will not feel the want of it, and at any rate it has not been my fault that you have had no opportunity of acquiring the art.

"The tendency is more and more to fight on foot. The duel has taken the place of the combat in the lists, and the pikeman counts for as much in the winning of a battle as the mounted man. You taught us that at Cressy and Agincourt; but we have been slow to learn the lesson which was brought home to you in your battles with the Scots, and in your own civil struggles. It is the bow and the pike that have made the

English soldier famous; while in France, where the feudal system still prevails, horsemen still form a large proportion of our armies, and the jousting lists and the exercise of the *ménage* still occupy a large share in the training and amusements of the young men of noble families."

Six weeks later Philip Fletcher landed at La Rochelle with his aunt and her French serving-maid. When the ship came into port, the clerk of a trader there came on board at once, and on the part of his employer begged Madame Vaillant and her son to take up their abode at his house, he having been warned of their coming by his valued correspondent, Monsieur Vaillant. A porter was engaged to carry up their luggage to the house, whither the clerk at once conducted them. From his having lived so long among the Huguenot colony, the scene was less strange to Philip than it would have been to most English lads. La Rochelle was a strongly Protestant city, and the sober-coloured costumes of the people differed but little from those to which he was accustomed in the streets of Canterbury. He himself and his aunt attracted no attention whatever from passers-by, her costume being exactly similar to those worn by the wives of merchants, while Philip would have passed anywhere as a young Huguenot gentleman, in his doublet of dark puce cloth, slashed with gray, his trunks of the same colour, and long gray hose.

"A proper-looking young gentleman," a market-woman said to her daughter as he passed. "Another two or three years and he will make a rare defender of the faith. He must be from Normandy, with his fair complexion and light eyes. There are not many of the true faith in the north."

They were met by the merchant at the door of his house.

"I am glad indeed to see you again, Madame Vaillant," he said. "It is some twenty years now since you and your good husband and your sister hid here for three days before we could smuggle you on board a ship. Ah! those were bad times; though there have been worse since. But since our people showed that they did not intend any longer to be slaughtered unresistingly, things have gone better here at least, and for the last four years the slaughterings and murders have ceased. You are but little changed, madame, since I saw you last."

"I have lived a quiet and happy life, my good Monsieur Bertram; free from all strife and care, save for anxiety about our people here. Why cannot Catholics and Protestants live quietly side by side here, as they do in England?"

"We should ask nothing better, madame."

At this moment a girl came hurrying down the stairs.

"This is my daughter Jean, madame: Why were you not down before, Jean?" he asked sharply. "I told you to place Suzette at the casement to warn you when our visitors were in sight, so that you should, as was proper, be at the door to meet them. I suppose instead of that you had the maid arranging your head-gear, or some such worldly folly."

The girl coloured hotly, for her father had hit upon the truth.

"Young people will be young people, Monsieur Bertram," Madame Vaillant said smiling, "and my husband and I are not of those who think that it is necessary to carry a prim face and to attire one's self in ugly garments as a proof of religion. Youth is the time for mirth and happiness, and nature teaches a maiden what is becoming to her; why then should we blame her for setting off the charms God has given her to their best advantage?"

By this time they had reached the upper storey, and the merchant's daughter hastened to relieve Madame Vaillant of her wraps.

"This is my nephew, of whom my husband wrote to you," the latter said to the merchant, when Philip entered the room —he having lingered at the door to pay the porters, and to see that the luggage, which had come up close behind them, was stored.

"He looks active and strong, madame; he has the figure of a fine swordsman."

"He has been well taught, and will do no discredit to our race, Monsieur Bertram. His father is a strong and powerful man, even for an Englishman, and though Philip does not follow his figure he has something of his strength."

"They are wondrous strong, these Englishmen," the trader said. "I have seen among their sailors men who are taller by a head than most of us here, and who look strong enough to take a bull by the horns and hold him.   But had it not been for your nephew's fair hair and gray eyes, his complexion, and the smile on his lips—we have almost forgotten how to smile in France—I should hardly have taken him for an Englishman."

"There is nothing extraordinary in that, Monsieur Bertram, when his mother is French, and he has lived greatly in the society of my husband and myself, and among the Huguenot colony at Canterbury."

"Have you succeeded in getting the horses and the four men for us, Monsieur Bertram?" Philip asked.

"Yes, everything is in readiness for your departure to-morrow.   Madame will, I suppose, ride behind you upon a pillion, and her maid behind one of the troopers.   I have, in accordance with Monsieur Vaillant's instructions, bought a horse, which I think you will be pleased with, for Guise himself might ride upon it without feeling that he was ill mounted.   I was fortunate in lighting on such an animal.   It was the property of a young noble, who rode hither from Navarre and was sailing for England.   I imagine he bore despatches from the queen to her majesty of England.   He had been set upon by robbers on the way; they took everything he possessed, and held him prisoner, doubtless meaning to get a ransom for him; but he managed to slip off while they slept and to mount his horse, with which he easily left the varlets behind, although they chased him for some distance.   So when he came here he offered to sell his horse to obtain an outfit and money for his voyage; and the landlord of the inn, who is a friend of mine, knowing that I had been inquiring for a good animal, brought him to me, and we soon struck a bargain."

"It was hard on him to lose his horse in that fashion," Philip said; "and I am sorry for it, though I may be the gainer thereby."

"He did not seem to mind much," the merchant said. "Horses are good and abundant in Navarre, and when I said I did not like to take advantage of his strait he only laughed and said he had three or four others as good at home.   He did say, though, that he would like to know if it was to be in good hands. I assured him that on that ground he need not fear; for that I had bought it for a young gentleman, nearly related to the Countess de Laville. He said that was well, and seemed glad indeed that it was not to be ridden by one of the brigands, into whose hands he fell."

"And the men. Are they trustworthy fellows?"

"They are stout men-at-arms. They are Gascons all, and rode behind Coligny in the war, and according to their own account performed wonders; but as Gascons are given to boasting, I paid not much heed to that. However, they were recommended to me by a friend, a large wine-grower, for whom they have been working for the last two years. He says they are honest and industrious, and they are leaving him only because they are anxious for a change, and deeming that troubles were again approaching, wanted to enter the service of some Huguenot lord who would be likely to take the field. He was lamenting the fact to me, when I said that it seemed to me they were just the men I was in search of; and I accordingly saw them, and engaged them on the understanding that at the end of a month you should be free to discharge them if you were not satisfied with them, and that equally they could leave your service if they did not find it suit.

"They have arms, of course, and such armour as they need, and I have bought four serviceable horses for their use, together with a horse to carry your baggage, but which will serve for your body-servant. I have not found a man for that office. I knew of no one who would, as I thought, suit you, and in such a business it seemed to me better that you should wait and choose for yourself, for in the matter of servants everyone has his fancies. Some like a silent knave, while others prefer a merry one. Some like a tall proper fellow, who can fight if needs be; others a staid man, who will do his duty and hold his tongue, who can cook a good dinner and groom a horse well. It is certain you will never find all virtues combined. One man may be all that you wish, but he is a liar; another helps himself; a third is too fond of the bottle. In this matter, then, I did not care to take the responsibility, but have left it for you to choose for yourself."

"I shall be more likely to make a mistake than you will, Monsieur Bertram," Philip said with a laugh.

"Perhaps so, but then it will be your own mistake; and a man chafes less at the shortcomings of one whom he has chosen himself than at those of one who has, as it were, been forced upon him."

"Well, there will be no hurry in that matter," Philip said. "I can get on well enough without a servant for a time. Up to the present I have certainly never given a thought as to what kind of man I should want as a servant, and I should like time to think over a matter which is, from what you say, so important."

"Assuredly it is important, young sir. If you should take the field you will find that your comfort greatly depends upon it. A sharp, active knave, who will ferret out good quarters for you, turn you out a good meal from anything he can get hold of, bring your horse up well groomed in the morning and your armour brightly polished; who will not lie to you overmuch or rob you overmuch, and who will only get drunk at times when you can spare his services. Ah! he would be a treasure to you. But assuredly such a man is not to be found every day."

"And of course," Marie put in, "in addition to what you have said, Monsieur Bertram, it would be necessary that he should be one of our religion, and fervent and strong in the faith."

"My dear lady, I was mentioning possibilities," the trader said. "It is of course advisable that he should be a Huguenot, it is certainly essential that he should not be a Papist; but beyond this we need not inquire too closely. You cannot expect the virtues of an archbishop and the capacity of a horseboy. If he can find a man embracing the qualities of both, by all means let your son engage him; but as he will require him to be a good cook and a good groom, and he will not require religious instruction from him, the former points are those on which I should advise him to lay most stress. And now, Madame Vaillant, will you let me lead you into the next room, where, as my daughter has for some time been trying to make me understand, a meal is ready. And I doubt

not that you are also ready; for truly those who travel by sea
are seldom able to enjoy food, save when they are much accustomed to voyaging. Though they tell me that after a time
even those with the most delicate stomachs recover their
appetites, and are able to enjoy the rough fare they get on
board a ship."

After the meal was over the merchant took Philip to the
stables, where the new purchases had been put up. The men
were not there, but the ostler brought out Philip's horse, with
which he was delighted.

"He will not tire under his double load," the merchant
said; "and with only your weight upon him a foeman would
be well mounted indeed to overtake you."

"I would rather that you put it, Monsieur Bertram, that a
foeman needs be well mounted to escape me."

"Well, I hope it will be that way," his host replied smiling.
"But in fighting, such as we have here, there are constant
changes; the party that is pursued one day is the pursuer a
week later, and of the two, you know, speed is of much more
importance in flight than in pursuit. If you cannot overtake
a foe, well, he gets away, and you may have better fortune next
time; but if you can't get away from a foe, the chances are
you may never have another opportunity of doing so."

"Perhaps you are right. In fact, now I think of it, I am
sure you are; though I hope it will not often happen that we
shall have to depend for safety on the speed of our horses.
At any rate, I am delighted with him, Monsieur Bertram, and
I thank you greatly for procuring so fine an animal for me.
If the four men turn out to be as good of their kind as the
horse, I shall be well set up indeed."

Early the next morning the four men came round to the
merchant's, and Philip went down with him into the entry-hall
where they were. He was well satisfied with their appearance.
They were stout fellows, from twenty-six to thirty years old.
All were soberly dressed, and wore steel caps and breast-pieces,
and carried long swords by their sides. In spite of the serious
expression of their faces, Philip saw that all were in high if
restrained spirits at again taking service.

"This is your employer, the Sieur Philip Fletcher. I have

warranted that he shall find you good and true men, and I hope you will do justice to my recommendation."

"We will do our best," Roger, the eldest of the party, said. "We are all right glad to be moving again. It is not as if we had been bred on the soil here, and a man never takes to a strange place as to one he was born in."

"You are Gascons, Maître Bertram tells me?" Philip said.

"Yes, sir; we were driven out from there ten years ago, when the troubles were at their worst. Our fathers were both killed, and we travelled with our mothers and sisters by night through the country till we got to La Rochelle."

"You say both your fathers. How are you related to each other?"

"Jacques and I are brothers," Roger said, touching the youngest of the party on his shoulder. "Eustace and Henri are brothers, and are our cousins. Their father and ours were brothers. When the troubles broke out we four took service with the Count de Luc, and followed him throughout the war. When it was over we came back here. Our mothers had married again. Some of our sisters had taken husbands too, others were in service; therefore we remained here rather than return to Gascony, where our friends and relations had all been either killed or dispersed. We were lucky in getting employment together, but were right glad when we heard that there was an opening again for service. For the last two years we have been looking forward to it; for, as everyone sees, it cannot be long before the matter must be fought out again. And, in truth, we have been wearying for the time to come; for after having had a year of fighting one does not settle down readily to tilling the soil. You will find that you can rely on us, sir, for faithful service; we all bore a good reputation as stout fighters, and during the time we were in harness before we none of us got into trouble for being overfond of the wine-pots."

"I think you will suit me very well," Philip said, "and I hope that my service will suit you. Although an Englishman by birth and name, my family have suffered persecution here as yours have done, and I am as warmly affected to the Huguenot cause as yourselves. If there is danger you will not find me lacking in leading you, and so far as I can I shall try to make my service a comfortable one and to look after your welfare. We shall be ready to start in half an hour, therefore have the horses round at the door in that time. One of the pillions is to be placed on my own horse. You had better put the other for the maid behind your saddle, Roger; you being, I take it, the oldest of your party, had better take charge of her." The men saluted and went out.

"I like their looks much," Philip said to the merchant. "Stout fellows and cheerful, I should say. Like my aunt I don't see why we should carry long faces, Monsieur Bertram, because we have reformed our religion, and I believe that a light heart and good spirits will stand wear and tear better than a sad visage."

The four men were no less pleased with their new employer.

"That is a lad after my own heart," Roger said as they went out. "Quick and alert, pleasant of face, and yet, I will be bound, not easily turned from what he has set his mind to. He bears himself well, and I doubt not can use his weapons. I don't know what stock he comes from on this side, but I warrant it is a good one. He will make a good master, lads; I think that, as he says, he will be thoughtful as to our comforts, and be pleasant and cheerful with us; but mind you, he will expect the work to be done, and you will find that there is no trifling with him."

CHAPTER III

IN A FRENCH CHATEAU

THE three days' ride to the chateau of the Countess de Laville was marked by no incident. To Philip it was an exceedingly pleasant one—everything was new to him; the architecture of the churches and villages, the dress of the people, their modes of agriculture, all differing widely from those to which he was accustomed. In some villages the Catholics predominated, and here the passage of the little party was regarded with frowning brows and muttered threats; by the Huguenots they were saluted respectfully, and if they halted, many questions were asked their followers as to news about the intentions of the court, the last rumours as to the attitude of Condé, and the prospects of a continuance of peace.

Here, too, great respect was paid to Marie and Philip when it was known they were relatives of the Countess de Laville, and belonged to the family of the De Moulins. Emilie had for some time been a widow; the count, her husband, having fallen at the battle of Dreux at the end of the year 1562; but being an active and capable woman, she had taken into her hands the entire management of the estates, and was one of the most influential among the Huguenot nobles of that part of the country.

From their last halting-place Marie Vaillant sent on a letter by one of the men to her sister, announcing their coming. She had written on her landing at La Rochelle, and they had been met on their way by a messenger from the countess, expressing her delight that her sister had at last carried out her

44

promise to visit her, and saying that François was looking eagerly for the coming of his cousin.

The chateau was a semi-fortified building, capable of making a stout resistance against any sudden attack. It stood on the slope of a hill, and Philip felt a little awed at its stately aspect as they approached it. When they were still a mile away a party of horsemen rode out from the gateway, and in a few minutes their leader reined up his horse in front of them, and springing from it advanced towards Philip, who also alighted and helped his aunt to dismount.

"My dear aunt," the young fellow said doffing his cap, "I am come in the name of my mother to greet you, and to tell you how joyful she is that you have at last come back to us. This is my Cousin Philip, of course; though you are not what I expected to see. My mother told me that you were two years my junior, and I had looked to find you still a boy; but, by my faith, you seem to be as old as I am. Why, you are taller by two inches, and broader and stronger too, I should say. Can it be true that you are but sixteen?"

"That is my age, Cousin François, and I am, as you expected, but a boy yet, and, I can assure you, no taller or broader than many of my English school-fellows of the same age."

"But we must not delay, aunt," François said, turning again to her. "My mother's commands were urgent that I was not to delay a moment in private talk with you, but to bring you speedily on to her; therefore I pray you to mount again and ride on with me, for doubtless she is watching impatiently now, and will chide me rarely if we linger."

Accordingly the party remounted at once, and rode forward to the chateau. A dozen men-at-arms were drawn up at the gate, and on the steps of the entrance from the courtyard into the chateau itself the countess was standing. François leapt from his horse, and was by the side of his aunt as Philip reined in his horse. Taking his hand she sprang lightly from the saddle, and in a moment the two sisters fell into each others' arms. It was more than twenty years since they last met, but time had dealt gently with them both. The countess had changed least. She was two or three years older than Marie, was tall, and had been somewhat stately even as a girl. She had had many cares, but her position had always been assured; as the wife of a powerful noble she had been accustomed to be treated with deference and respect; and although the troubles of the times and the loss of her husband had left their marks, she was still a fair and stately woman at the age of forty-three. Marie, upon the other hand, had lived an untroubled life for the past twenty years. She had married a man who was considered beneath her, but the match had been in every way a happy one; her husband was devoted to her, and the expression of her face showed that she was a thoroughly contented and happy woman.

"You are just what I fancied you would be, Marie, a quiet little home-bird, living in your nest beyond the sea, and free from all the troubles and anxieties of our unhappy country. You have been good to write so often, far better than I have been, and I seem to know all about your quiet, well-ordered home, and your good husband and his business that flourishes so. I thought you were a little foolish in your choice, and that our father was wrong in mating you as he did; but it has turned out well, and you have been living in quiet waters while we have been encountering a sea of troubles. And this tall youth is our nephew, Philip? I wish you could have brought over Lucie with you. It would have been pleasant indeed for us three sisters to be reunited again, if only for a time. Why, your Philip is taller than François, and yet he is two years younger. I congratulate you and Lucie upon him. Salute me, nephew; I had not looked to see so proper a youth. You show the blood of the De Moulins plainly, Philip. I suppose you get your height and your strength from your English father?"

"They are big men these English, Emilie, and his father is big even among them. But, as you say, save in size Philip takes after our side rather than his father's; and of course he has mixed so much with our colony at Canterbury, that in spite of his being English bred we have preserved in him something of the French manner, and I think his heart is fairly divided between the two countries."

"Let us go in," the countess said; "you need rest and

refreshment after your journey, and I long to have a quiet talk with you. François, do you take charge of your cousin. I have told the serving-men to let you have a meal in your own apartments, and then you can show him over the chateau and the stables."

François and Philip bowed to the two ladies and then went off together.

"That is good," the young count said, laying his hand on Philip's shoulder; "now we shall get to know each other. You will not be angry, I hope, when I tell you that though I have looked forward to seeing my aunt and you, I have yet been a little anxious in my mind. I do not know why, but I have always pictured the English as somewhat rough and uncouth—as doughty fighters, for so they have shown themselves to our cost, but as somewhat deficient in the graces of manner, and when I heard that my aunt was bringing you over to leave you for a time with us, since you longed to fight in the good cause, I have thought—pray, do not be angry with me, for I feel ashamed of myself now—" and he hesitated.

"That I should be a rough cub, whom you would be somewhat ashamed of introducing to your friends as your cousin," Philip laughed. "I am not surprised; English boys have ideas just as erroneous about the French, and it was a perpetual wonder to my school-fellows that, being half French, I was yet as strong and as tough as they were. Doubtless I should have been somewhat different had I not lived so much with my uncle and aunt and the Huguenot community at Canterbury. Monsieur Vaillant and my aunt have always impressed upon me that I belong to a noble French family, and might some day come over here to stay with my relations, and have taken much pains with my deportment and manners, and have so far succeeded that I am always called 'Frenchy' among my English companions, though in their own games and sports I could hold my own with any of them."

"And can you ride, Philip?"

"I can sit on any horse, but I have had no opportunity of learning the *ménage.*"

"That matters little after all," François said, "though it is an advantage to be able to manage your horse with a touch of the heel or the slightest pressure of the rein, and to make him wheel and turn at will, while leaving both arms free to use your weapons.   You have learned to fence?"

"Yes; there were some good masters among the colony, and many a lesson have I had from old soldiers passing through, who paid for a week's hospitality by putting me up to a few tricks with the sword."

"I thought you could fence," François said.   "You would hardly have that figure and carriage unless you had practised with the sword.   And you dance, I suppose; many of our religion regard such amusement as frivolous if not sinful, but my mother, although as staunch a Huguenot as breathes, insists upon my learning it, not as an amusement but as an exercise. There was no reason, she said, why the Catholics should monopolize all the graces."

"Yes, I learned to dance, and for the same reason.   I think my uncle rather scandalized the people of our religion in Canterbury.   He maintained that it was necessary as part of the education of a gentleman, and that in the English Protestant court dancing was as highly thought of as in that of France, the queen herself being noted for her dancing, and none can throw doubts upon her Protestantism.   My mother and aunt were both against it, but as my father supported my uncle he had his own way."

"Well, I see, Philip, that we shall be good comrades. There are many among us younger Huguenots who, though as staunch in the religion as our fathers, and as ready to fight and die for it if need be, yet do not see that it is needful to go about always with grave faces, and to be cut off from all innocent amusements.   It is our natural disposition to be gay, and I see not why, because we hold the Mass in detestation, and have revolted against the authority of the Pope and the abuses of the church, we should go through life as if we were attending a perpetual funeral.   Unless I am mistaken such is your disposition also, for although your face is grave your eyes laugh."

"I have been taught to bear myself gravely in the presence of my elders," Philip replied with a smile; "and truly at Canterbury the French colony was a grave one, being strangers in a strange land; but among my English friends I think I was as much disposed for a bit of fun or mischief as any of them."

"But I thought the English were a grave race."

"I think not, François. We call England 'Merry England.' I think we are an earnest people, but not a grave one. English boys play with all their might. The French boys of the colony never used to join in our sports, regarding them as rude and violent beyond all reason; but it is all in good-humour, and it is rare indeed for anyone to lose his temper, however rough the play and hard the knocks. Then they are fond of dancing and singing, save among the strictest sects, and the court is as gay as any in Europe. I do not think that the English can be called a grave people."

"Well, I am glad that it is so, Philip, especially that you yourself are not grave. Now, as we have finished our meal, let us visit the stables. I have a horse already set aside for you, but I saw as we rode hither that you are already excellently mounted; still Victor, that is his name, shall be at your disposal. A second horse is always useful, for shot and arrows no more spare a horse than his rider."

The stables were large and well ordered, for during the past two months there had been large additions made by the countess in view of the expected troubles.

"This is my charger; I call him Rollo. He was bred on the estate, and when I am upon him I feel that the king is not better mounted."

"He is a splendid animal indeed," Philip said, as Rollo tossed his head and whinnied with pleasure at his master's approach.

"He can do anything but talk," François said as he patted him. "He will lie down when I tell him, will come to my whistle, and with the reins lying loose on his neck will obey my voice as readily as he would my hand. This is my second horse, Pluto; he is the equal of Rollo in strength and speed, but not so docile and obedient, and he has a temper of his own."

"He looks it," Philip agreed. "I should keep well out of reach of his heels and jaws."

"He is quiet enough when I am on his back," François laughed; "but I own that he is the terror of the stable-boys. This is Victor; he is not quite as handsome as Rollo, but he has speed and courage and good manners."

"He is a beautiful creature," Philip said enthusiastically. "I was very well satisfied with my purchase, but he will not show to advantage by the side of Victor."

"Ah, I see they have put him in the next stall," François said. "He is a fine animal too," he went on after examining the horse closely. "He comes from Gascony, I should say; he has signs of Spanish blood."

"Yes, from Gascony or Navarre. I was very fortunate in getting him," and he related how the animal had been left at La Rochelle.

"You got him for less than half his value, Philip. What are you going to call him?"

"I shall call him Robin; that was the name of my favourite horse at home. I see you have got some stout animals in the other stalls, though of course they are of a very different quality to your own."

"Yes; many of them are new purchases. We have taken on thirty men-at-arms; stout fellows, old soldiers all, whom my mother will send into the field if we come to blows. Besides these there will be some twenty of our tenants. We could have raised the whole number among them had we chosen; for if we called up the full strength of the estate, and put all bound to service in the field in war time, we could turn out fully three hundred; but of these well-nigh a third are Catholics, and could not in any way be relied on, nor would it be just to call upon them to fight against their co-religionists. Again, it would not do to call out all our Huguenot tenants, for this would leave their wives and families and homes and property, to say nothing of the chateau, at the mercy of the Catholics while they were away. I do not think that our Catholic tenants would interfere with them, still less with the chateau, for our family have ever been good masters, and my mother is loved by men of both parties. Still, bands might come from other districts or from the towns to pillage or slay were the estate left without fighting men. Therefore, we have taken these men-at-arms into our service, with twenty of our own tenants, all young men belonging to large families, while the rest will remain behind as a guard for the estate and chateau; and as in all they could muster some two hundred and fifty strong, and would be joined by the other Huguenots of the district, they would not likely be molested, unless one of the Catholic armies happened to come in this direction.

"Directly I start with the troop the younger sons of the tenants will be called in to form a garrison here. We have five-and-thirty names down, and there are twenty men capable of bearing arms among the household, many of whom have seen service. Jacques Parold, our seneschal, has been a valiant soldier in his time, and would make the best of them, and my mother would assuredly keep our flag flying till the last. I shall go away in comfort, for unless the Guises march this way there is little fear of trouble in our absence. We are fortunate in this province; the parties are pretty evenly divided, and have a mutual respect for each other. In districts where we are greatly outnumbered, it is hard for fighting men to march away with the possibility that on their return they will find their families murdered and their homes levelled.

"Now we will take a turn round the grounds; their beauty has been sadly destroyed. You see, before the troubles seven years ago broke out, there was a view from the windows on this side of the house over the park and shrubberies, but at that time my father thought it necessary to provide against sudden attacks, and therefore before he went away to the war he had this wall with its flanking towers erected. All the tenants came in and helped, and it was built in five weeks time. It has, as you see, made the place safe from a sudden attack, for on the other three sides the old defences remain unaltered. It was on this side only that my grandfather had the house modernized, believing that the days of civil war were at an end. You see, this new wall forms a large quadrangle. We call it the countess's garden, and my mother has done her best by planting it with shrubs and fast-growing trees to make up for the loss of the view she formerly had from the windows.

"Along one side you see there are storehouses, which are screened from view by that bank of turf; they are all full now of grain. There is a gate, as you see, opposite. In case of trouble cattle will be driven in there and the garden turned into a stock-yard, so that there is no fear of our being starved out."

"Fifty-five men are a small garrison for so large a place, François."

"Yes, but that is only against a sudden surprise. In case of alarm the Protestant tenants would all come in with their wives and families, and the best of their horses and cattle, and then there will be force enough to defend the place against anything short of a siege by an army. You see there is a moat runs all round; it is full now on three sides, and there is a little stream runs down from behind, which would fill the fourth side in a few hours. To-morrow we will take a ride through the park which lies beyond that wall."

Entering the house they passed through several stately apartments, and then entered a large hall completely hung with arms and armour.

"This is the grand hall, and you see it serves also the purpose of a *salle d'armes*. Here we have arms and armour for a hundred men, for although all the tenants are bound by the terms of their holding to appear when called upon fully armed and accoutred, each with so many men according to the size of his farm, there may well be deficiencies, especially as, until the religious troubles began, it was a great number of years since they had been called upon to take the field. For the last eight years, however, they have been trained and drilled; fifty at a time coming up once a week. That began two years before the last war, as my father always held that it was absurd to take a number of men wholly unaccustomed to the use of arms into the field. Agincourt taught that lesson to our nobles, though it has been forgotten by most of them. We have two officers accustomed to drill and marshal men, and these act as teachers here in the hall. The footmen practise with pike and sword. They are exercised with arquebus and cross-bow in the park, and the mounted men are taught to manœuvre and charge, so that in case of need we can show

PHILIP AND FRANÇOIS IN THE ARMOURY.

a good face against any body of troops of equal numbers. It is here I practise with my *maître d'armes*, and with Montpace and Bourdon, our two officers. Ah! here is Charles, my *maître d'armes*. Charles, this is my cousin Philip, who will also be a pupil of yours while he remains here. What do you say, Philip? Will we try a bout with blunted swords just now?"

"With pleasure," Philip said.

The art of fencing had not at that time reached the perfection it afterwards attained. The swords used were long and straight, and sharpened at both edges, and were used as much for cutting as thrusting. In single combat on foot, long daggers were generally held in the left hand, and were used for the purpose both of guarding and of striking at close quarters.

They put on thick quilted doublets and light helmets with visors.

"Do you use a dagger, Philip?"

"No, I have never seen one used in England. We are taught to guard with our swords as well as to strike with them."

"Monsieur has learned from English teachers?" the *maître d'armes* asked.

"I have had English teachers as well as French," Philip said. "We all learn the use of the sword in England, but my uncle, Monsieur Vaillant, has taken great pains in having me taught also by such French professors of arms as lived in Canterbury, or happened to pass through it; but I own that I prefer the English style of fighting. We generally stand upright to our work, equally poised on the two feet for advance or retreat, while you lean with the body far forward and the arm outstretched, which seems to me to cripple the movements."

"Yes, but it puts the body out of harm's way," François said.

"It is the arm's business to guard the body, François, and it is impossible to strike a downright blow when leaning so far forward."

"We strike but little now-a-days in single combat," the *maître d'armes* said. "The point is more effective."

"That is doubtless so, Maître Charles," Philip agreed; "but

I have not learned fencing for the sake of fighting duels, but to be able to take my part on a field of battle. The Spaniards are said to be masters of the straight sword, and yet they have been roughly used in the western seas by our sailors, who, methinks, always use the edge."

The two now took up their position facing each other. Their attitude was strikingly different. François stood on bent knees leaning far forward, while Philip stood erect with his knees but slightly bent, ready to spring either forwards or backwards, with his arm but half extended. For a time both fought cautiously. François had been well taught, having had the benefit whenever he was in Paris of the best masters there. He was extremely active, and as they warmed to their work Philip had difficulty in standing his ground against his impetuous rushes. Some minutes passed without either of them succeeding in touching the other. At length the *maître d'armes* called upon them to lower their swords.

"That is enough," he said, "you are equally matched. I congratulate you, Monsieur Philip. You have been well taught; and indeed there are not many youths of his age who could hold their own with my pupil. Take off your helmets, enough has been done for one day."

"*Peste*, Philip!" François said as he removed his helmet. "I was not wrong when I said that from your figure I was sure that you had learned fencing. Maître Charles interfered on my behalf, and to save me the mortification of defeat. I had nearly shot my bolt and you had scarcely begun. I own myself a convert. Your attitude is better than ours; that is, when the hand is skilful enough to defend the body. The fatigue of holding the arm extended as I do is much greater than it is as you stand, and in the long run you must get the better of anyone who is not sufficiently skilful to slay you before his arm becomes fatigued. What do you think, Maître Charles? My cousin is two years younger than I am, and yet his wrist and arm are stronger than mine, as I could feel every time he put aside my attacks."

"Is that so?" the *maître d'armes* said in surprise. "I had taken him for your senior. He will be a famous man-at-arms when he attains his full age. His defence is wonderfully strong, and although I do not admit that he is superior to you with the point, he would be a formidable opponent to any of our best swordsmen in a *mêlée*. If, as he says, he is more accustomed to use the edge than the point, I will myself try him to-morrow if he will permit me. I have always understood that the English are more used to strike than to thrust, and although in the duel the edge has little chance against the point, I own that it is altogether different in a *mêlée* on horseback, especially as the point cannot penetrate armour, while a stout blow, well delivered with a strong arm, can break it in. Are you skilled in the exercises of the ring, Monsieur Philip?"

"Not at all, I have had no practise whatever in them. Except in some of the great houses the tourney has gone quite out of fashion in England, and though I can ride a horse across country I know nothing whatever of knightly exercises. My father is but a small proprietor, and up to the time I left England I have been but a school-boy."

"If all your school-boys understand the use of their arms as you do," Maître Charles said courteously, "it is no wonder that the English are terrible fighters."

"I do not say that," Philip said smiling. "I have had the advantage of the best teaching, both English and French, to be had at Canterbury, and it would be a shame for me indeed if I had not learnt to defend myself."

A servant now entered and said that the countess desired their presence, and they at once went to the apartment where the sisters were talking.

"What do you think, mother?" François said. "This cousin of mine, whom I had intended to patronize, turns out to be already a better swordsman than I am."

"Not better, madame," Philip said hastily. "We were a fair match, neither having touched the other."

"Philip is too modest, mother," François laughed. "Maître Charles stopped us in time to save me from defeat. Why, he has a wrist like iron, this cousin of mine."

"We have done our best to have him well taught," Madame Vaillant said. "There were some good swordsmen among our Huguenot friends, and he has also had the best English teachers we could get for him. My husband always wished particularly that if he ever came over to visit our friends here he should not be deficient in such matters."

"I feel a little crestfallen," the countess said. "I have been rather proud of François' skill as a swordsman, and I own that it is a little mortifying to find that Philip, who is two years younger, is already his match. Still I am glad that it is so, for if they ride together into battle I should wish that Philip should do honour to our race. Now, Philip, I have been hearing all about your mother's life, as well as that of your uncle and aunt. Now let us hear about your own, which must needs differ widely from that to which François has been accustomed. Your aunt says that your English schools differ altogether from ours. With us our sons are generally brought up at home, and are instructed by the chaplain in Huguenot families or by the priest in Catholic families; or else they go to religious seminaries, where they are taught what is necessary of books and Latin, being under strict supervision, and learning all other matters such as the use of arms after leaving school, or when at home with their families."

Philip gave an account of his school life, and its rough games and sports.

"But is it possible, Philip," the countess said in tones of horror, "that you used to wrestle and to fight? Fight with your arms and fists against rough boys, the sons of all sorts of common people?"

"Certainly I did, aunt, and it did me a great deal of good, and no harm so far as I know. All these rough sports strengthen the frame and give quickness and vigour, just the same as exercises with the sword do. I should never have been so tall and strong as I am now, if, instead of going to an English school, I had been either, as you say, educated at home by a chaplain or sent to be taught and looked after by priests. My mother did not like it at first, but she came to see that it was good for me. Besides, there is not the same difference between classes in England as there is in France; there is more independence in the lower and middle classes, and less haughtiness and pride in the upper, and I think that it is better so."

"It is the English custom, Emilie," her sister said; "and I can assure you that my husband and I have got very English in some things. We do not love our country less, but we see that in many respects the English ways are better than ours; and we admire the independence of the people, every man respecting himself, though giving honour, but not lavishly, to those higher placed."

The countess shrugged her shoulders. "We will not argue, Marie. At any rate whatever the process, it has succeeded well with Philip."

The days passed quietly at the chateau. Before breakfast Philip spent an hour on horseback, learning to manage his horse by the pressure of knee or hand. This was the more easy, as both his horses had been thoroughly trained in the *ménage*, and under the instruction of Captain Montpace, who had been François' teacher, he made rapid progress.

"It is much easier to teach the man than the horse," his instructor said, "although a horse learns readily enough when its rider is a master of the art; but with horse and rider alike ignorant it is a long business to get them to work together as if they were one, which is what should be. As both your horses know their work, they obey your motions, however slight, and you will soon be able to pass muster on their backs; but it would take months of patient teaching for you so to acquire the art of horsemanship as to be able to train an animal yourself."

After the lesson was over François and Philip would tilt at rings and go through other exercises in the courtyard. Breakfast over they went hawking or hunting. Of the former sport Philip was entirely ignorant, and was surprised to learn how highly a knowledge of it was prized in France, and how necessary it was considered as part of the education of a gentleman. Upon the other hand his shooting with the bow and arrow astonished François; for the bow had never been a French weapon, and the cross-bow was fast giving way to the arquebus, but few gentlemen troubled themselves to learn the use of either one or the other. The pistol, however, was becoming a recognized portion of the outfit of a cavalier in the field, and following François' advice Philip practised with one steadily until he became a fair shot.

"They are cowardly weapons," François said, "but for all that they are useful in battle. When you are surrounded by three or four pikemen thrusting at you, it is a good thing to be able to disembarrass yourself of one or two of them. Besides, these German horsemen, of whom the Guises employ so many, all carry firearms, and the contest would be too uneven if we were armed only with the sword; though for my part I wish that all the governments of Europe would agree to do away with firearms of every description. They place the meanest footman upon the level of the bravest knight, and in the end will, it seems to me, reduce armies to the level of machines."

In the afternoons there were generally gatherings of Huguenot gentry, who came to discuss the situation, to exchange news, or to listen to the last rumours from Paris. No good had arisen from the Conference of Bayonne, and one by one the privileges of the Huguenots were being diminished. The uprising of the Protestants of Holland was watched with the greatest interest by the Huguenots of France. It was known that several of the most influential Huguenot nobles had met at Valery and at Chatillon, to discuss with the Prince of Condé and Admiral Coligny the question of again taking up arms in defence of their liberties. It was rumoured that the opinion of the majority was that the Huguenot standard should be again unfurled, and that this time there should be no laying down of their arms until freedom of worship was guaranteed to all; but that the admiral had used all his powers to persuade them that the time had not yet come, and that it was better to bear trials and persecutions for a time in order that the world might see they had not appealed to arms until driven to it by the failure of all other hope of redress of their grievances.

The elder men among the visitors at the chateau were of the admiral's opinion; the younger chafed at the delay. The position had indeed become intolerable. Protestant worship was absolutely forbidden, except in a few specified buildings near some of the large towns, and all Protestants save those dwelling in these localities were forced to meet secretly, and at the risk of their lives, for the purpose of worship. Those caught transgressing the law were thrown into prison, subjected to crushing fines, and even punished with torture and death. "Better a thousand times to die with swords in our hands in the open field than thus tamely to see our brethren ill-treated and persecuted!" was the cry of the young men, and Philip, who from daily hearing tales of persecution and cruelty had become more and more zealous in the Huguenot cause, fully shared their feeling.

In the presence of the elders, however, the more ardent spirits were silent. At all times grave and sober in manner and word, the knowledge that a desperate struggle could not long be deferred, and the ever-increasing encroachments of the Catholics, added to the gravity of their demeanour. Sometimes those present broke up into groups, talking in an undertone. Sometimes the gathering took the form of a general council. Occasionally some fugitive minister or a noble from some district where the persecution was particularly fierce would be present, and their narratives would be listened to with stern faces by the elders, and with passionate indignation by the younger men. In spite of the decrees the countess still retained her chaplain, and before the meetings broke up prayers were offered by him for their persecuted brethren, and for a speedy deliverance of those of the reformed religion from the cruel disabilities under which they laboured.

Services were held night and morning in the chateau. These were attended not only by all the residents, but by many of the farmers and their families. The countess had already received several warnings from the Catholic authorities of the province; but to these she paid no attention, and there were no forces available to enforce the decree in her case, as it would require nothing short of an army to overcome the opposition that might be expected, joined as she would be by the other Huguenot gentry of the district.

CHAPTER IV

AN EXPERIMENT

MARIE VAILLANT, after remaining six weeks at the chateau, returned to England, and Philip with a party of twelve men escorted her to La Rochelle. Her visit was cut short somewhat at the end by the imminence of the outbreak of hostilities, in which case she might have found a difficulty in traversing the country. Moreover, La Rochelle would probably be besieged soon after the war began; for being both an important town and port the Catholics would be anxious to obtain possession of it, and so cut off the Huguenots from escape to England, besides rendering it difficult for Elizabeth to send a force to their assistance.

"It has been a pleasant time," the countess said on the morning of her departure, "and your presence has taken me back five-and-twenty years, Marie. I hope that when these troubles are past you will again come over and spend a happier time with me. I was going to say that I will look well after Philip, but that I cannot do. He has cast his lot in with us and must share our perils. I am greatly pleased with him, and I am glad that François will have him as a companion in arms. François is somewhat impulsive and liable to be carried away by his ardour, and Philip, although the younger, is, it seems to me, the more thoughtful of the two. He is one I feel I can have confidence in. He is grave, yet merry; light-hearted in a way, and yet, I think, prudent and cautious. It seems strange, but I shall part with François with the more comfort in the thought that he has Philip with him. Don't come back more English than you are now, Marie, for truly you seem to me to have fallen in love with the ways of these islanders."

"I will try not to, Emilie; but I should not like the customs did it not seem to me that they are better than my own. In England Protestants and Catholics live side by side in friendship, and there is no persecution of anyone for his religion; the Catholics who have suffered during the present reign have done so not because they are Catholics, but because they plotted against the queen. Would that in France men would agree to worship, each in his own way, without rancour or animosity."

"Tell Lucie that I am very sorry she did not come over with you and Philip, and that it is only because you tell me how occupied she is that I am not furiously angry with her. Tell her, too," she went on earnestly, "that I feel she is one of us, still a Huguenot, a Frenchwoman, and one of our race, or she would never have allowed her only son to come over to risk his life in our cause. I consider her a heroine, Marie. It is all very well for me whose religion is endangered, whose friends are in peril, whose people are persecuted, to throw myself into the strife and to send François into the battle; but with her, working there with an invalid husband, and her heart, as it must be, wrapped up in her boy, it is splendid to let him come out here to fight side by side with us for the faith. Whose idea was it first?"

"My husband's. Gaspard regards Philip almost in the light of a son. He is a rich man now, as I told you, and Philip will become his heir. Though he has no desire that he should settle in France, he wished him to take his place in our family here, to show himself worthy of his race, to become a brave soldier, to win credit and honour, and to take his place perhaps some day in the front rank of the gentry of Kent."

"They were worldly motives, Marie, and our ministers would denounce them as sinful; but I cannot do so. I am a Huguenot, but I am a countess of France, a member of one noble family and married into another; and though, I believe, as staunch a Huguenot and as ready to lay down my life for our religion as any man or woman in France, yet I cannot give up all the traditions of my rank, and hold that fame and honour and reputation and courage are mere snares. But such were not Lucie's feelings in letting him go, I will be bound, nor yours."

"Mine partly," Marie said. "I am the wife now of a trader, though one honoured in his class, but have still a little of your feelings, Emilie, and remember that the blood of the De Moulins runs in Philip's veins, and hope that he will do credit to it. I don't think that Lucie has any such feelings. She is wrapped up in duty—first her duty to God, secondly her duty to her crippled husband, whom she adores; and I think she regarded the desire of Philip to come out to fight in the Huguenot ranks as a call that she ought not to oppose. I know she was heart-broken at parting with him, and yet she never showed it. Lucie is a noble character. Everyone who knows her loves her. I believe the very farm labourers would give their lives for her, and a more utterly unselfish creature never lived."

"Well, she must take a holiday and come over with you next time you come, Marie. I hope that these troubles may soon be over, though that is a thing one cannot foretell."

After seeing his aunt safely on board a ship at La Rochelle Philip prepared to return to the chateau. He and his aunt had stayed two nights at the house of Maître Bertram, and on his returning there the latter asked, "Have you yet found' a suitable servant, Monsieur Philip?"

"No; my cousin has been inquiring among the tenantry, but the young men are all bent on fighting, and indeed there are none of them who would make the sort of servant one wants in a campaign—a man who can not only groom horses and clean arms, but who knows something of war, can forage for provisions, cook, wait at table, and has intelligence. One wants an old soldier; one who has served in the same capacity if possible."

"I only asked because I have had a man pestering me to speak to you about him. He happened to see you ride off when you were here last, and apparently became impressed with the idea that you would be a good master. He is a cousin of one of my men, and heard I suppose from him that you were likely to return. He has been to me three or four times. I have told him again and again that he was not the sort of man I could recommend, but he persisted in begging me to let him see you himself."

"What sort of a fellow is he?"

"Well, to tell you the truth he is a sort of ne'er-do-well," the merchant laughed. "I grant that he has not had much chance. His father died when he was a child, and his mother soon married again. There is no doubt that he was badly treated at home, and when he was̄ twelve he ran away. He was taken back and beaten time after time, but in a few hours he was always off again, and at last they let him go his own way. There is nothing he hasn't turned his hand to. First he lived in the woods, I fancy, and they say he was the most arrant young poacher in the district, though he was so cunning that he was never caught. At last he had to give that up. Then he fished for a bit, but he couldn't stick to it. He has been always doing odd jobs, turning his hand to whatever turned up. He worked in a shipyard for a bit, then I took him as a sort of errand-boy and porter. He didn't stop long, and the next I heard of him he was servant at a priest's. He has been a dozen other things, and for the last three or four months he has been in the stables where your horse was standing. I fancy you saw him there. Some people think he is half a fool, but I don't agree with them; he is as sharp as a needle to my mind. But, as I say, he has never had a fair chance. A fellow like that without friends is sure to get roughly treated."

"Is he a young man of about one or two and twenty?" Philip asked. "I remember a fellow of about that age brought out the horse, and as he seemed to me a shrewd fellow, and had evidently taken great pains in grooming Robin, I gave him a crown. I thought he needed it, for his clothes were old and tattered, and he looked as if he hadn't had a hearty meal for a week. Well, Maître Bertram, can you tell me if among his other occupations he has ever been charged with theft?"

"No, I have never heard that brought against him."

"Why did he leave you?"

"It was from no complaint as to his honesty. Indeed he left of his own accord after a quarrel with one of the men, who was, as far as I could learn, in the wrong. I did not even hear that he had left until a week after, and it was too late then to go thoroughly into the matter. Boys are always troublesome, and as everyone had warned me that Pierre would turn out badly I gave the matter but little thought at the time. Of course you will not think of taking the luckless rascal as your servant."

"I don't know. I will have a talk with him anyhow. A fellow like that would certainly be handy, but whether he could be relied upon to behave discreetly and soberly and not to bring me into discredit is a different matter. Is he here now?"

"He is below. Shall I send him up here to you?"

"No, I will go down and see him in the courtyard. If he comes up here he would be perhaps awkward and unnatural, and would not speak so freely as he would in the open air."

The merchant shook his head. "If you take the vagabond, remember, Monsieur Philip, that it is altogether against my advice. I would never have spoken to you about him if I had imagined for a moment that you would think of taking him. A fellow who has never kept any employment for two months, how could he be fit for a post of confidence and be able to mix as your body-servant with the households of honourable families."

"But you said yourself, Maître Bertram, that he has never had a fair chance. Well, I will see him anyhow."

He descended into the courtyard, and could not help smiling as his eye fell upon a figure seated on the horse-block. He was looking out through the gateway, and did not at first see Philip. The expression of his face was dull and almost melancholy, but as Philip's eye fell on him his attention was attracted by some passing object in the street. His face lit up with amusement, his lips twitched and his eyes twinkled. A moment later and the transient humour passed, and the dull, listless expression again stole over his face.

"Pierre!" Philip said sharply. The young fellow started to his feet as if shot upwards by a spring, and as he turned and saw who had addressed him, took off his cap, and bowing stood twisting it round in his fingers. "Monsieur Bertram tells me you want to come with me as a servant, Pierre; but when I asked him about you he does not give you such a character as one would naturally require in a confidential servant. Is there anyone who will speak for you?"

"Not a soul," the young man said doggedly; "and yet, monsieur, I am not a bad fellow. What can a man do when he has not a friend in the world? He picks up a living as he can, but everybody looks at him with suspicion. There is no friend to take his part, and so people vent their ill-humours upon him, till the time comes when he revolts at the injustice and strikes back, and then he has to begin it all over again somewhere else. And yet, sir, I know that I could be faithful and true to anyone who would not treat me like a dog. You spoke kindly to me in the stable, and gave me a crown; no one had ever given me a crown before. But I cared less for that than for the way you spoke. Then I saw you start, and you spoke pleasantly to your men, and I said to myself, that is the master I would serve if he would let me. Try me, sir, and if you do not find me faithful, honest, and true to you, tell your men to string me up to a bough. I do not drink, and have been in so many services that, ragged as you see me, I can yet behave so as not to do discredit to you."

Philip hesitated. There was no mistaking the earnestness with which the youth spoke.

"Are you a Catholic or a Huguenot?" he asked.

"I know nothing of the difference between them," Pierre replied. "How should I? No one has ever troubled about me one way or the other. When my mother lived I went to Mass with her; since then I have gone nowhere. I have had no Sunday clothes. I know that the *bon Dieu* has taken care of me or I should have died of hunger long ago. The priest I was with used to tell me that the Huguenots were worse than heathen; but if that were so, why should they let themselves be thrown into prison, and even be put to death, rather than stay away from their churches. As for me, I know nothing about it. They say monsieur is a Huguenot, and if he were good enough to take me into his service, of course I should be a Huguenot."

"That is a poor reason, Pierre," Philip said smiling. "Still, you may find better reasons in time. However, you are not a Catholic, which is the principal thing at present. Well, I will try you, I think. Perhaps, as you say, you have never had a fair chance yet, and I will give you one. I believe what you say, that you will be faithful."

The young fellow's face lit up with pleasure.

"I will be faithful, sir. If I were otherwise I should deserve to be cut in pieces."

"As for wages," Philip said, "I will pay you what you deserve. We will settle that when we see how we get on together. Now follow me and I will get some suitable clothes for you."

There was no difficulty about this; clothes were not made to fit closely in those days, and Philip soon procured a couple of suits suitable for the serving-man of a gentleman of condition. One was a riding-suit, with high boots, doublet, and trunks of sober colour and of a strong tough material; a leather sword-belt and sword, and a low hat thickly lined and quilted and capable of resisting a heavy blow. The other suit was for wear in the house; it was of dark-green cloth of a much finer texture than the riding-suit, with cloth stockings of the same colour coming up above the knee, and then meeting the trunks or puffed breeches. A small cap with turned-up brim, furnished with a few of the tail feathers of a black-cock, completed the costume; a dagger being worn in the belt instead of the sword. Four woollen shirts, a pair of shoes, and a cloak were added to the purchases, which were placed in a valise to be carried behind the saddle.

"Is there any house where you can change your clothes, Pierre? Of course you could do so at Monsieur Bertram's, but some of the men I brought with me will be there, and it would be just as well that they did not see you in your present attire."

"I can change at the stables, sir, if you will trust me with the clothes."

"Certainly, I will trust you. If I trust you sufficiently to take you as my servant, I can surely trust you in a matter like this. Do you know of anyone who has a stout nag for sale?"

Pierre knew of several, and giving Philip an address the latter was not long in purchasing one, with saddle and bridle complete. He ordered this to be sent at once to the stables where Pierre had been employed, with directions that it was to be handed over to his servant.

It was one o'clock in the day when Madame Vaillant embarked, and it was late in the afternoon before Philip returned to Monsieur Bertram's house.

"What have you done about that vagabond Pierre?"

"I have hired him," Philip said.

"You don't say that you have taken him after what I have told you about him!" the merchant exclaimed.

"I have, indeed. He pleaded hard for a trial, and I am going to give him one. I believe that he will turn out a useful fellow. I am sure that he is shrewd, and he ought to be full of expedients. As to his appearance, good food and decent clothes will make him another man. I think he will turn out a merry fellow when he is well fed and happy; and I must say, Maître Bertram, that I am not fond of long faces. Lastly, I believe that he will be faithful."

"Well, well, well, I wash my hands of it altogether, Monsieur Philip. I am sorry I spoke to you about him, but I never for a moment thought you would take him. If harm comes of it don't blame me."

"I will hold you fully acquitted," Philip laughed. "I own that I have taken quite a fancy to him, and believe that he will turn out well."

An hour later one of the domestics came in with word that Monsieur Philip's servant was below, and wished to know if he had any commands for him.

"Tell him to come up," Philip said, and a minute later Pierre entered. He was dressed in his dark-green costume. He had had his hair cut, and presented an appearance so changed that Philip would hardly have known him.

"By my faith!" the merchant said, "you have indeed transformed him. He is not a bad-looking varlet, now that he has got rid of that tangled crop of hair."

Pierre bowed low at the compliment.

"Fine feathers make fine birds, Monsieur Bertram," replied

Pierre. "It is the first time I have had the opportunity of proving the truth of the proverb. I am greatly indebted to monsieur for recommending me to my master."

"It is not much recommendation you got from me, Pierre," the merchant said bluntly; "for a more troublesome young scamp I never had in my warehouse. Still, as I told Monsieur Philip, I think everything has been against you, and I do hope now that this English gentleman has given you a chance that you will take advantage of it."

"I mean to, sir," the young fellow said earnestly, and without a trace of the mocking smile with which he had first spoken. "If I do not give my master satisfaction it will not be for want of trying. I shall make mistakes at first—it will all be strange to me, but I feel sure that he will make allowances. I can at least promise that he will find me faithful and devoted."

"Has your horse arrived, Pierre?"

"Yes, sir. I saw him watered and fed before I came out. Is it your wish that I should go round to the stables where your horse and those of your troop are, and take charge of your horse at once?"

"No, Pierre; the men will look after him as usual. We will start at six in the morning. Be at the door on horseback at that hour."

Pierre bowed and withdrew.

"I do not feel so sure as I did that you have made a bad bargain, Monsieur Philip. As far as appearances go at any rate, he would pass muster. Except that his cheeks want filling out a bit, he is a nimble, active-looking young fellow, and with that little moustache of his and his hair cut short he is by no means ill-looking. I really should not have known him. I think at present he means what he says, though whether he will stick to it is another matter altogether."

"I think he will stick to it," Philip said quietly. "Putting aside what he says about being faithful to me, he is shrewd enough to see that it is a better chance than he is ever likely to have again of making a start in life. He has been leading a dog's life ever since he was a child, and to be well fed and well clothed and fairly treated will be a wonderful change for him. My only fear is that he may get into some scrape at the chateau. I believe that he is naturally full of fun, and fun is a thing that the Huguenots, with all their virtues, hardly appreciate."

"A good thrashing will tame him of that," the merchant said.

Philip laughed. "I don't think I shall be driven to try that. I don't say that servants are never thrashed in England, but I have not been brought up among the class who beat their servants. I think I shall be able to manage him without that. If I can't we must part. I suppose there is no doubt, Monsieur Bertram, how La Rochelle will go when the troubles begin?"

"I think not. All preparations are made on our part, and as soon as the news comes that Condé and the Admiral have thrown their flags to the wind, we shall seize the gates, turn out all who oppose us, and declare for the cause. I do not think it can be much longer delayed. I sent a trusty servant yesterday to fetch back my daughter, who, as I told you, has been staying with a sister of mine five or six leagues away. I want to have her here before the troubles break out. It will be no time for damsels to be wandering about the country when swords are once out of their scabbards."

The next morning the little troop started early from La Rochelle, Pierre riding gravely behind Philip. The latter presently called him up to his side.

"I suppose you know the country round here well?"

"Every foot of it. I don't think that there is a pond in which I have not laid my lines, not a streamlet of which I do not know every pool, not a wood that I have not slept in nor a hedge where I have not laid snares for rabbits. I could find my way about as well by night as by day; and you know, sir, that may be of use if you ever want to send a message into the town when the Guises have got their troops lying outside."

Philip looked sharply at him. "Oh, you think it likely that the Guises will soon be besieging La Rochelle?"

"Anyone who keeps his ears open can learn that," Pierre said quietly. "I haven't troubled myself about these matters. It made no difference to me whether the Huguenots or the Catholics were in the saddle; still, one doesn't keep one's ears closed, and people talk freely enough before me. 'Pierre does not concern himself with these things; the lad is half a fool; he pays no attention to what is being said;' so they would go on talking, and I would go on rubbing down a horse or eating my black bread with a bit of cheese or an onion, or whatever I might be about, and looking as if I did not even know they were there. But I gathered that the Catholics think that the Guises and Queen Catharine and Philip of Spain and the Pope are going to put an end to the Huguenots altogether. From those on the other side I learned that the Huguenots will take the first step in La Rochelle, and that one fine morning the Catholics are likely to find themselves bundled out of it. Then it doesn't need much sense to see that ere long we shall be having a Catholic army down here to retake the place, that is if the Huguenot lords are not strong enough to stop them on their way."

"And you think the Catholics are not on their guard at all?"

"Not they," Pierre said contemptuously. "They have been strengthening the walls and building fresh ones, thinking that an attack might come from without from the Huguenots, and all the time the people of that religion in the town have been laughing in their sleeves and pretending to protest against being obliged to help at the new works, but really paying and working willingly. Why, they even let the magistrates arrest and throw into prison a number of their party without saying a word, so that the priests and the commissioners should think they have got it entirely their own way. It has been fun watching it all, and I had made up my mind to take to the woods again directly it began. I had no part in the play, and did not wish to run any risk of getting a ball through my head, whether from a Catholic or a Huguenot arquebus. Now of course it is all different. Monsieur is a Huguenot, and therefore so am I. It is the Catholic bullets that will be shot at me, and as no one likes to be shot at I shall soon hate the Catholics cordially, and shall be ready to do them any ill-turn that you may desire."

"And you think that if necessary, Pierre, you could carry a message into the town, even though the Catholics were camped round it."

Pierre nodded. "I have never seen a siege, master, and don't know how close the soldiers might stand round a town; but I think that if a rabbit could get through I could, and if I could not get in by land I could manage somehow to get in by water."

"But such matters as this do not come within your service, Pierre. Your duties are to wait on me when not in the field, to stand behind my chair at meals, and to see that my horses are well attended to by the stable varlets. When we take the field you will not be wanted to fight, but will look after my things; will buy food and cook it, get dry clothes ready for me to put on if I come back soaked with rain, and keep an eye upon my horses. Two of the men-at-arms will have special charge of them; they will groom and feed them. But if they are away with me they cannot see after getting forage for them, and it will be for you to get hold of that, either by buying it from the villagers or employing a man to cut it. At any rate to see that there is food for them as well as for me when the day's work is over."

"I understand that, master; but there are times when a lad who can look like a fool but is not altogether one can carry messages and make himself very useful, if he does not place over much value on his life. When you want anything done, no matter what it is, you have only to tell me, and it will be done if it is possible."

In the afternoon of the second day after starting they approached the chateau. The old sergeant of the band, who with two of his men was riding a hundred yards ahead, checked his horse and rode back to Philip.

"There is something of importance doing, Monsieur Philip; the flag is flying over the chateau. I have not seen it hoisted before since my lord's death, and I can make out horsemen galloping to and from the gates."

"We will gallop on then," Philip said, and in ten minutes they arrived. François ran down the steps as Philip alighted in the courtyard.

"I am glad you have come, Philip. I had already given orders for a horseman to ride to meet you, and tell you to hurry on. The die is cast at last. There was a meeting yesterday at the Admiral's; a messenger came to my mother from my cousin, François de la Noüe. The Admiral and Condé had received news from a friend at court that there had been a secret meeting of the Royal Council, and that it had been settled that the Prince should be thrown into prison and Coligny executed. The Swiss troops were to be divided between Paris, Orleans, and Poitiers. The edict of toleration was to be annulled, and instant steps taken to suppress Huguenot worship by the sternest measures. In spite of this news the Admiral still urged patience; but his brother, D'Andelot, took the lead among the party of action, and pointed out that if they waited until they, the leaders, were all dragged away to prison, resistance by the Huguenots would be hopeless. Since the last war over three thousand Huguenots had been put to violent deaths. Was this number to be added to indefinitely? Were they to wait until their wives and children were in the hands of the executioners before they moved? His party were in the majority, and the Admiral reluctantly yielded. Then there was a discussion as to the steps to be taken. Some proposed the seizure of Orleans and other large towns, and that with these in their hands they should negotiate with the court for the dismissal of the Swiss troops, as neither toleration nor peace could be hoped for as long as this force was at the disposal of the Cardinal of Lorraine and his brothers.

"This council, however, was overruled. It was pointed out that at the beginning of the last war the Huguenots held fully a hundred towns, but nearly all were wrested from their hands before its termination. It was finally resolved that all shall be prepared for striking a heavy blow, and that the rising shall be arranged to take place throughout France on the 29th of September. That an army shall take the field, disperse the Swiss, seize if possible the Cardinal of Lorraine, and at any rate petition the king for a redress of grievances, for a removal of the Cardinal from his councils, and for sending all foreign troops out of the kingdom. We have, you see, a fortnight to prepare. We have just sent out messengers to all our Huguenot friends, warning them that the day is fixed, that their preparations are to be made quietly, and that we will notify them when the hour arrives. All are exhorted to maintain an absolute silence upon the subject, while seeing that their tenants and retainers are in all respects ready to take the field."

"Why have you hoisted your flag, François? That will only excite attention."

"It is my birthday, Philip, and the flag is supposed to be raised in my honour. This will serve as an excuse for the assemblage of our friends, and the gathering of the tenants. It has been arranged, as you know, that I, and of course you, are to ride with De la Noüe, who is a most gallant gentleman, and that our contingent is to form part of his command. I am heartily glad this long suspense is over, and that at last we are going to meet the treachery of the court by force. Too long have we remained passive, while thousands of our friends have in defiance of the edicts been dragged to prison and put to death. Fortunately the court is, as it was before the last war, besotted with the belief that we are absolutely powerless, and we have every hope of taking them by surprise."

"I also am glad that war has been determined upon," Philip said. "Since I have arrived here I have heard nothing but tales of persecution and cruelty. I quite agree with you that the time has come when the Huguenots must either fight for their rights, abandon the country altogether and go into exile, as so many have already done, or renounce their religion."

"I see you have a new servant, Philip. He is an active, likely-looking lad, but rather young. He can know nothing of campaigning."

"I believe he is a very handy fellow, with plenty of sense and shrewdness; and if he can do the work, I would rather have a man of that age than an older one. It is different with you. You are François, Count de Laville, and your servant whatever his age would hold you in respect; I am younger and of far less consequence, and an old servant might want to take me under his tuition. Moreover, if there is hard work to be done for me I would rather have a young fellow like this doing it than an older man."

"You are always making out that you are a boy, Philip. You don't look it, and you are going to play a man's part."

"I mean to play it as far as I can, François; but that does not really make me a day older."

"Well, mind, not a word to a soul as to the day fixed on."

For the next fortnight the scene at the chateau was a busy one. Huguenot gentlemen came and went. The fifty men-at-arms who were to accompany François were inspected, and their arms and armour served out to them. The tenantry came up in small parties, and were also provided with weapons, offensive and defensive, from the armoury, so that they might be in readiness to assemble for the defence of the chateau at the shortest notice. All were kept in ignorance as to what was really going on; but it was felt that a crisis was approaching, and there was an expression of grim satisfaction on the stern faces of the men that showed they rejoiced at the prospect of a termination to the long passive suffering which they had borne at the hands of the persecutors of their faith. Hitherto they themselves had suffered but little, for the Huguenots were strong in the south of Poitou, while in Niort, the nearest town to the chateau, the Huguenots, if not in an absolute majority, were far too strong to be molested by the opposite party. Nevertheless here, and in all other towns, public worship was suspended, and it was only in the chateaux and castles of the nobles that the Huguenots could gather to worship without fear of interruption or outrage. There was considerable debate as to whether François' troop should march to join the Admiral at Chatillon-sur-Loing, or should proceed to the south-east, where parties were nearly equally balanced; but the former course was decided upon. The march itself would be more perilous, but as Condé, the Admiral, and his brother D'Andelot would be with the force gathered there, it was the most important point; and moreover François de la Noüe would be there.

So well was the secret of the intended movement kept, that the French court, which was at Meaux, had no idea of the danger that threatened, and when a report of the intentions of the Huguenots came from the Netherlands, it was received with incredulity. A spy was, however, sent to Chatillon to report upon what the Admiral was doing, and he returned with the news that he was at home, and was busily occupied in superintending his vintage.

On the evening of the 26th the troop, fifty strong, mustered in the courtyard of the chateau. All were armed with breast and back pieces and steel caps, and carried lances as well as swords. In addition to this troop were Philip's four men-at-arms, and four picked men, who were to form François' body-guard, one of them carrying his banner. He took as his body-servant a man who had served his father in that capacity. He and Pierre wore lighter armour than the others, and carried no lances. François and Philip were both in complete armour, Philip donning for the first time that given to him by his uncle.

Neither of them carried lances, but were armed with swords, light battle-axes, and pistols. Before mounting service was held; the pastor offered up prayers for the blessing of God upon their arms, and for his protection over each and all of them in the field. The countess herself made them a stirring address, exhorting them to remember that they fought for the right to worship God unmolested, and for the lives of those dear to them. Then she tenderly embraced her son and Philip, the trumpets sounded to horse, and the party rode out from the gates of the chateau. As soon as they were away the two young leaders took off their helmets and handed them to their attendants, who rode behind them. Next to these came their eight body-guards, who were followed by the captain and his troop.

"It may be that this armour will be useful on the day of battle," Philip said, "but at present it seems to me, François, that I would much rather be without it."

"I quite agree with you, Philip. If we had only to fight with gentlemen, armed with swords, I would gladly go into battle unprotected; but against men with lances, one needs a defence. However, I do not care so much now that I have got rid of the helmet, which, in truth, is a heavy burden."

"Methinks, François, that armour will ere long be aban-doned, now that arquebuses and cannon are coming more and more into use. Against them they give no protection, and it were better, methinks, to have lightness and freedom of action, than to have the trouble of wearing all this iron stuff merely as a protection against lances.   You have been trained to wear armour, and therefore feel less inconvenience; but I have never had as much as a breast-plate on before, and I feel at present as if I had almost lost the use of my arms.   I think that at any rate I shall speedily get rid of these arm-pieces; the body armour I don't so much mind, now that I am fairly in the saddle.   The leg-pieces are not as bad as those on the arms; I was scarcely able to walk in them; still now that I am mounted I do not feel them much.   But if I am to be of any use in a *mêlée* I must have my arms free, and trust to my sword to protect them."

"I believe that some have already given them up, Philip; and if you have your sleeves well wadded and quilted, I think you might if you like give up the armour.   The men-at-arms are not so protected, and it is only when you meet a noble in full armour that you would be at a disadvantage."

"I don't think it would be a disadvantage, for I could strike twice with my arms free to once with them so confined."

"There is one thing, you will soon become accustomed to the armour."

"Not very soon, I fancy, François.   You know, you have been practising in it almost since you were a child, and yet you admit that you feel a great difference.   Still, I daresay as the novelty wears off I shall get accustomed to it to some extent."

CHAPTER V

TAKING THE FIELD

A GUIDE thoroughly acquainted with the country rode ahead of the party, carrying a lantern fixed at the back of his saddle. They had, after leaving the chateau, begun to mount the lofty range of hills behind. The road crossing these was a mere track, and they were glad when they began to descend on the other side. They crossed the Clain river some ten miles above Poitiers, a few miles farther forded the Vienne, crossed the Gartempe at a bridge at the village of Montmorillon, and an hour later halted in a wood, just as daylight was breaking, having ridden nearly fifty miles since leaving the chateau.

So far they had kept to the south of the direct course in order to cross the rivers near their sources.

Every man carried provisions for himself and his horse, and as soon as they had partaken of a hearty meal the armour was unstrapped, and all threw themselves down for a long sleep; sentries being first placed, with orders to seize any peasants who might enter the wood to gather fuel. With the exception of the sentries, who were changed every hour, the rest slept until late in the afternoon, then the horses were again fed and groomed, and another meal was eaten. At sunset the armour was buckled on again, and they started. They crossed the Creuse at the bridge of Argenton about midnight, and riding through La Chatre halted before morning in a wood two miles from St. Amand. Here the day was passed as the previous one had been.

"Tell me, François," Philip said, as they were waiting for the sun to go down, "something about your cousin De la Noüe. As we are to ride with him, it is as well to know something about him. How old is he?"

"He is thirty-six, and there is no braver gentleman in France. As you know, he is of a Breton family, one of the most illustrious of the province. He is connected with the great houses of Chateau-Briant and Matignon. As a boy he was famous for the vigour and strength that he showed in warlike exercises, but was in other respects, I have heard, of an indolent disposition, and showed no taste for reading or books of any kind. As usual among the sons of noble families he went up to the court of Henry II. as a page, and when there became seized with an ardour for study, especially that of ancient and modern writers who treated on military subjects. As soon as he reached manhood he joined the army in Piedmont, under Marshal de Brissac, that being the best military school of the time.

"On his return he showed the singular and affectionate kindness of his nature. His mother, unfortunately, while he was away, had become infected with the spirit of gambling, and the king, who had noted the talent and kind disposition of the young page, thought to do him a service by preventing his mother squandering the estates in play. He therefore took the management of her affairs entirely out of her hands, appointing a royal officer to look after them. Now most young men would have rejoiced at becoming masters of their estates, but the first thing that François did on his return was to go to the king, and solicit as a personal favour that his mother should be reinstated in the management of her estates. This was granted, but a short time afterwards she died. De la Noüe retired from court, and settled in Brittany upon his estates, which were extensive.

"Shortly afterwards D'Andelot, Coligny's brother, who was about to espouse Mademoiselle De Rieux, the richest heiress in Brittany, paid a visit there. He had lately embraced our faith and was bent upon bringing over others to it, and he brought down with him to Brittany a famous preacher named Cormel. His preaching in the chateau attracted large numbers of people, and although Brittany is perhaps the most Catholic province in France, he made many converts. Among these was De la Noüe, then twenty-seven years old. Recognizing his talent and influence, D'Andelot had made special efforts to induce him to join the ranks of the Huguenots, and succeeded. My cousin, who previous to that had, I believe, no special religious views, became a firm Huguenot. As you might expect with such a man, he is in no way a fanatic, and does not hold the extreme views that we have learned from the preachers of Geneva. He is a staunch Huguenot; but he is gentle, courtly, and polished, and has, I believe, the regard of men of both parties. He is a personal friend of the Guises, and was appointed by them as one of the group of nobles who accompanied Marie Stuart to Scotland.

"When the war broke out in 1562, after the massacre of Vassy, he joined the standard of Condé. He fought at Dreux, and distinguished himself by assisting the Admiral to draw off our beaten army in good order. The assassination of François de Guise, as you know, put an end to that war. De la Noüe bitterly regretted the death of Guise, and after peace was made retired to his estates in Brittany, where he has lived quietly for the last four years. I have seen him several times, because he has other estates in Poitou, within a day's ride of us. I have never seen a man I admire so much. He is all for peace, though he is a distinguished soldier. While deeply religious, he has yet the manners of a noble of the court party. He has no pride, and he is loved by the poor as well as by the rich. He would have done anything to have avoided war; but you will see that, now the war has begun, he will be one of our foremost leaders. I can tell you, Philip, I consider myself fortunate indeed that I am going to ride in the train of so brave and accomplished a gentleman."

During the day they learned from a peasant of a ford crossing the Cher, two or three miles below St. Amand. Entering a village near the crossing-place, they found a peasant who was willing for a reward to guide them across the country to Briare, on the Loire—their first guide had returned from their first halting-place,—and the peasant being placed on a horse behind a man-at-arms, took the lead. Their pace was much slower than it had been the night before, and it was almost daybreak when they passed the bridge at Briare, having ridden over forty miles. They rode two or three miles into the mountains after crossing the Loire, and then halted.

"We must give the horses twenty-four hours here," François said. "I don't think it is above twenty miles on to Chatillon-sur-Loing; but it is all through the hills, and it is of no use arriving there with the horses so knocked up as to be useless for service. We have done three tremendous marches, and anyhow we shall be there long before the majority of the parties from the west and south can arrive. The Admiral and Condé will no doubt be able to gather sufficient strength from Champagne and the north of Burgundy for his purpose of taking the court by surprise. I am afraid there is but little chance of their succeeding. It is hardly possible that so many parties of Huguenots can have been crossing the country in all directions to the Admiral's without an alarm being given. Meaux is some sixty miles from Chatillon, and if the court get the news only three or four hours before Condé arrives there, they will be able to get to Paris before he can cut them off."

In fact, even while they were speaking the court was in safety. The Huguenots of Champagne had their rendezvous at Rosoy, a little more than twenty miles from Meaux, and they began to arrive there in the afternoon of the 28th. The Prince of Condé, who was awaiting them, feeling sure that the news of the movement must in a few hours at any rate be known at Meaux, marched for Lagny on the Marne, established himself there late in the evening and seized the bridge. The news, however, had as he feared already reached the court, and messages had been despatched in all haste to order up six thousand Swiss troops, who were stationed at Chateau-Thierry, thirty miles higher up the Marne.

During the hours that elapsed before their arrival, the court was in a state of abject alarm; but at one o'clock the Swiss arrived, and two hours later the court set out under their protection for Paris. The Prince of Condé, who had with him but some four hundred gentlemen, for the most part armed only with swords, met the force as it passed by Lagny. He engaged in a slight skirmish with it, but being unable with his lightly-armed followers to effect anything against the solid body of the Swiss mountaineers armed with their long pikes, he fell back to await reinforcements, and the court reached Paris in safety.

A messenger had arrived at Chatillon with the news when François and Philip rode in. The castle gate stood open. Numbers of Huguenot gentlemen were standing in excited groups discussing the news.

"There is my cousin De la Notie!" François exclaimed as he alighted from his horse. "This is good fortune. I was wondering what we should do if we did not find him here," and he made his way to where a singularly handsome gentleman was talking with several others.

"Ah, François, is that you? Well arrived indeed! Gentlemen, this is my cousin and namesake, François de Laville. He has ridden across France to join us. Is that your troop, François, entering the gate now? Ah, yes, I see your banner. By my faith it is the best accoutred body we have seen yet, they make a brave show with their armour and lances. The countess has indeed shown her good-will right worthily, and it is no small credit to you that you should have brought them across from the other side of Poitou, and yet have arrived here before many who live within a few leagues of the castle. And who is this young gentleman with you?"

"It is my cousin, Philip Fletcher, son of my mother's sister Lucie. I spoke to you of his coming to us when you were at Laville three months since. He has come over in order that he may venture his life on behalf of our religion and family."

"I am glad to welcome you, young sir. We are, you see, connections, I being Philip's first cousin on his father's side, and you on that of his mother. Your spirit in coming over here shows that you inherit the bravery of your mother's race, and I doubt not that we shall find that the mixture with the sturdy stock of England will have added to its qualities. Would that your queen would but take her proper place as head of a league of the Protestants of Europe, our cause would then be well-nigh won without the need of striking a blow."

"Is it true, cousin, that the court has escaped to Paris?"

"Yes. I would that Condé had had but a few hours longer before they took the alarm, another day and he would have had such a gathering as it would have puzzled the Swiss to have got through. His forces were double yesterday, and eight hundred have ridden forth from here this morning to join him. I myself, though I made all speed, arrived but two hours since, and shall with all who come in this evening ride forward to-morrow. The Admiral, and his brother the Cardinal of Chatillon, will go with us. D'Andelot is already with Condé. Now as your troop is to ride with mine, I will see that they are disposed for the night together, and that their wants are attended to. My men have picketed their horses just outside the castle moat; for, as you see, we are crowded here with gentlemen and their personal followers, and it would be impossible to make room for all. I will take your officer to the seneschal, who will see that your men are provided with bread, meat, and wine. Ah, Captain Montpace, you are in command of the troop, I see. I thought the countess would send so experienced a soldier with them, and I am proud to have such a well-appointed troop behind me. None so well armed and orderly have yet arrived. My own at present are forty strong, and have, like you, made their way across France from Poitou.

"I could not bring my Bretons," he said turning to François. "The Huguenots there are but a handful among the Catholics. Happily on my estates they are good friends together, but I could not call away men from their homes at a time like this. Now, Captain Montpace, I will show you where your men are to bivouac next to my own. Then if you will come with me to the seneschal, rations shall be served out to them. Are your horses fit for another journey?"

"They will be by to-morrow morning, Count. They have only come from this side of Briare this morning, but though the journey is not long the road is heavy. They had twenty-four hours' rest before that, which they needed sorely, having travelled from Laville in three days."

"Draw a good supply of forage for them from the magazines," De la Noüe said. "See that the saddle-bags are well filled in the morning. There is another heavy day's work before them, and then they can take a good rest."

François and Philip accompanied the troop, and waited until they saw that they were supplied with provisions and forage, and with straw for lying down on, then they re-entered the castle. De la Noüe presented them to many of his friends, and then took them into the Admiral. He quite fulfilled the anticipations that Philip had formed of him. He was of tall figure, with a grave but kindly face. He was dressed entirely in black, with puffed trunks, doublet to match, and a large turned-down collar. As was usual, he wore over his shoulders a loose jacket with a very high collar, the empty sleeves hanging down on either side. When riding, the arms were thrust into these. He wore a low soft cap with a narrow brim all round. The expression of his face, with its short-pointed beard, moustache, and closely-trimmed whiskers, was melancholy. The greatest captain of his age, he was more reluctant than any of his followers to enter upon civil war, and the fact that he felt that it was absolutely necessary to save Protestantism from being extinguished in blood, in no way reconciled him to it.

He received François and his cousin kindly. " I am glad," he said to the former, " to see the representative of the Lavilles here. Your father was a dear friend of mine, and fell fighting bravely by my side. I should have been glad to have had you riding among my friends, but it is better still for you to be with your cousin De la Noüe, who is far more suitable as a leader and guide for youth than I am. You can follow no better example. I am glad also," he said turning to Philip, " to have another representative of the old family of the De Moulins here, and to find that though transplanted to England it still retains its affection for France. I trust that ere long I may have many of your countrymen fighting by my side. We have the same interests, and if the Protestant nations would unite, the demand for the right of all men, Catholic and Protestant, to worship according to their consciences could no longer be denied. I regret that your queen does not permit free and open worship to her Catholic subjects, since her not doing so affords some sort of excuse to Catholic kings and princes. Still I know that this law is not put rigidly into force, and that the Catholics do in fact exercise the rights of their religion without hindrance or persecution; and above all that there is no violent ill-will between the people of the two religions. Would it were so here. Were it not that you are going to ride with my good friend here, I would have said a few words to you, praying you to remember that you are fighting not for worldly credit and honour, but for a holy cause, and it behoves you to bear yourselves gravely and seriously; but no such advice is needed to those who come under his influence."

Leaving the Count de la Noüe in conversation with the Admiral, François and Philip made their way to the hall, where the tables were laid, so that all who came, at whatever hour, could at once obtain food. Their own servants, who were established in the castle, waited upon them.

"I think that lackey of yours will turn out a very useful fellow, Philip," François said as they left the hall. "He is quick and willing, and he turned out our dinner yesterday in good fashion. It was certainly far better cooked than it had been by Charles the day before."

"I fancy Pierre has done a good deal of cooking in the open air," Philip said, "and we shall find that he is capable of turning out toothsome dishes from very scanty materials."

"I am glad to hear it, for though I am ready to eat horse-flesh if necessary, I see not why because we happen to be at war one should have to spoil one's teeth by gnawing at meat as hard as leather. Soldiers are generally bad cooks, they are in too much haste to get their food at the end of a long day's work to waste much time with the cooking. Here comes La Noüe again."

"Will you order your troop to be again in the saddle at five o'clock in the morning, De Laville," the Count said. "I start with a party of two hundred at that hour. There will be my own men and yours, the rest will be gentlemen and their personal retainers."

"I would that it had been three hours later," François said as the Count left them and moved away, giving similar orders to the other gentlemen. "I own I hate moving before it is light. There is nothing ruffles the temper so much as getting up in the dark, fumbling with your buckles and straps, and finding everyone else just as surly and cross as you feel yourself. It was considered a necessary part of my training that I should turn out and arm myself at all times of the night. It was the part of my exercises that I hated the most."

Philip laughed. "It will not make much difference here, François. I don't like getting out of a warm bed myself on a dark winter's morning, but as there will be certainly no undressing to-night, and we shall merely have to get up and shake the straw off us, it will not matter much. By half-past five it will be beginning to get light. At any rate we should not mind it to-morrow, as it will be really our first day of military service."

Up to a late hour fresh arrivals continued to pour in, and the cooks and servants of the castle were kept hard at work administering to the wants of the hungry and tired men. There was no regular set meal, each man feeding as he was disposed. After it became dark all the gentlemen of family gathered in the upper part of the great hall, and there sat talking by the light of torches until nine, then the Admiral with a few of the nobles who had been in consultation with him joined them, and a quarter of an hour later a pastor entered and prayers were read. Then a number of retainers came in with trusses of straw, which were shaken down thickly beside the walls, and as soon as this was done, all present prepared to lie down.

"The trumpet will sound, gentlemen," François de la Noüe said in a loud voice, "at half-past four, but this will only concern those who, as it has already been arranged, will ride with me—the rest will set out with the Admiral at seven. I pray each of you who go with me to bid his servant cut off a goodly portion of bread and meat to take along with him, and to place a flask or two of wine in his saddle-bags, for our ride will be a long one, and we are not likely to be able to obtain refreshment on our way."

"I should have thought," François said, as he lay down on the straw by Philip's side, "that we should have passed through plenty of places where we could obtain food. Whether we go direct to Paris, or by the road by Lagny, we pass through Nemours and Mélun."

"These places may not open their gates to us, François, and in that case probably we should go through Montereau and Rosoy, and it may be considered that those who have already gone through to join Condé may have pretty well stripped both places of provisions."

The trumpet sounded at half-past four. The torches were at once relighted by the servants, and the gentlemen belonging to La Noüe's party rose, and their servants assisted them to buckle on their armour. They gave them instructions as to taking some food with them, and prepared for their journey by an attack on some cold joints that had been placed on a table at the lower end of the hall. There was a scene of bustle and confusion in the courtyard as the horses were brought up by the retainers. The Admiral himself was there to see the party off, and as they mounted each issued out and joined the men drawn up outside. Before starting, the minister according to Huguenot custom held a short service, and then with a salute to the Admiral, La Noüe took his place at their head and rode away.

With him went some twenty or thirty gentlemen, behind whom rode their body-servants. After these followed some fifty men-at-arms and the troops of La Noüe and Laville. As soon as they were off La Noüe reined in his horse so as to ride in the midst of his friends, and chatted gaily with them as they went along. An hour and a half's brisk riding took them to Montargis. Instead of keeping straight on, as most of those present expected, the two men who were riding a short distance in advance of the column turned sharp off to the left in the middle of the town.

"I am going to give you a surprise, gentlemen," De la Noüe said with a smile. "I will tell you what it is when we are once outside the place."

"I suppose," one of the gentlemen from the province, who was riding next to Philip, said, "we are going to strike the main road from Orleans north; to ride through Etampes, and take post between Versailles and Paris on the south side of the river, while the Prince and his following beleaguer the place on the north. It is a bold plan thus to divide our forces, but I suppose the Admiral's party will follow us, and by taking post on the south side of the river we shall straiten Paris for provisions."

"Gentlemen," the Count said, when they had issued from the streets of Montargis, "I can now tell you the mission which the Admiral has done me the honour to confide to me. It was thought best to keep the matter an absolute secret until we were thus fairly on our way, because, although we hope and believe that there is not a man at Chatillon who is not to be trusted, there may possibly be a spy of the Guises there, and it would have been wrong to run the risk of betrayal. Well, my friends, our object is the capture of Orleans."

An exclamation of surprise broke from many of his hearers.

"It seems a bold enterprise to undertake with but little over two hundred men," La Noüe went on with a smile; "but we have friends there. D'Andelot has been for the last ten days in communication with one of them. We may of course expect to meet with a stout resistance, but with the advantage of a surprise and with so many gallant gentlemen with me, I have no shadow of fear as to the result. I need not point out to you how important its possession will be to us. It will keep open a road to the south, will afford a rallying-place for all our friends in this part of France, and the news of its capture will give immense encouragement to our co-religionists throughout the country. Besides it will counterbalance the failure to seize the court, and will serve as an example to others to attempt to obtain possession of strong places. We shall ride at an easy pace to-day, for the distance is long and the country hilly. We could not hope to arrive there until too late to finish our work before dark. Moreover, most of our horses have already had very hard work during the past few days. We have started early in order that we may have a halt of four hours in the middle of the day. We are to be met to-night by our friend, the Master of Grelot, five miles this side of the city; he will tell us what arrangements have been made for facilitating our entrance."

"This is a glorious undertaking, Philip, is it not?" François said. "Until now I have been thinking how unfortunate we were in being too late to ride with Condé. Now I see that what I thought was a loss has turned out a gain."

"You do not think Condé will be able to do anything against Paris?" Philip asked.

"Certainly not at present. What can some fifteen hundred horsemen and as many infantry (and he will have no more force than that for another three or four days) do against Paris with its walls and its armed population, and the Guises and their friends and retainers, to say nothing of the six thousand Swiss? If our leaders thought they were going to fight at once they would hardly have sent two hundred good troops off in another direction. I expect we shall have plenty of time to get through this and other expeditions and then to join the Prince in front of Paris before any serious fighting takes place."

"Do you know how far it is across the hills to Orleans?" Philip asked the gentleman next to him on the other side.

"It is over fifty miles, but how much more I do not know. I am a native of the province, but I have never travelled along this road, which can be but little used. East of Montargis the traffic goes by the great road through Mélun to Paris, while the traffic of Orleans, of course, goes north through Etampes."

They rode on until noon, and then dismounted by a stream, watered and fed the horses, partook of a meal from the contents of their saddle-bags, and then rested for four hours to recruit the strength of their horses. The soldiers mostly stretched themselves on the sward and slept. A few of the gentlemen did the same, but most of them sat chatting in groups, discussing the enterprise upon which they were engaged. François and Philip went among their men with Captain Montpace, inspected the horses, examined their shoes, saw that fresh nails were put in where required, chatting with the men as they did so.

"I felt sure we should not be long before we were engaged on some stirring business," the Captain said. "The Count de la Noüe is not one to let the grass grow under his feet. I saw much of him in the last campaign, and the count, your father, had a very high opinion of his military abilities. At first he was looked upon somewhat doubtfully in our camp, seeing that he did not keep a long face, but was ready with a jest and a laugh with high and low, and that he did not affect the soberness of costume favoured by our party; but that soon passed off when it was seen how zealous he was in the cause; how ready to share in any dangerous business, while he set an example to all by the cheerfulness with which he bore fatigue and hardship. Next to the Admiral himself and his brother D'Andelot there was no officer more highly thought of by the troops. This is certainly a bold enterprise that he has undertaken now, if it be true what I have heard since we halted that we are going to make a dash at Orleans. It is a big city for two hundred men to capture, even though no doubt we have numbers of friends within the walls."

"All the more glory and credit to us, Montpace," François said gaily. "Why, the news that Orleans is captured will send a thrill through France, and will everywhere encourage our friends to rise against our oppressors. We are sure to take them by surprise, for they will believe that all the Huguenots in this part of France are hastening to join the Prince before Paris."

At four o'clock the party got in motion again, and an hour after dark entered a little village among the hills about five miles north of the town. De la Noüe at once placed a cordon of sentries, with orders that neither man, woman, nor child was to be allowed to leave it. Orders were issued to the startled peasants that all were to keep within their doors at the peril of their lives. The horses were picketed in the street, and the soldiers stowed in barns; trusses of straw were strewn round a fire for La Noüe and the gentlemen who followed him. At eight o'clock two videttes thrown forward some distance along the road rode in with a horseman. It was the Master of Grelot, who, as he rode up to the fire, was heartily greeted by the Count.

"I am glad to find you here, Count," he said; "I knew you to be a man of your word, but in warfare things often occur to upset the best calculations."

"Is everything going on well at Orleans?" De la Noüe asked.

"Everything. I have made all my arrangements. A party of five-and-twenty men I can depend on will to-morrow morning at seven o'clock gather near the gate this side of the town.

They will come up in twos and threes, and just as the guard are occupied in unbarring the gate they will fall upon them. The guard is fifteen strong, and as they will be taken by surprise they will be able to offer but a faint resistance. Of course you with your troop will be lying in readiness near. As soon as they have taken possession of the gateway the party will issue out and wave a white flag as a signal to you that all is clear, and you will be in before the news that the gateway has been seized can spread. After that you will know what to do. In addition to the men who are to carry out the enterprise you will shortly be joined by many others. Word has been sent round to our partisans that they may speedily expect deliverance, and bidding them be prepared whenever they are called upon to take up their arms and join those who come to free them.

"A large number of the town-folk are secretly either wholly with us or well disposed towards us, and although some will doubtless take up arms on the other side, I think that with the advantage of the surprise and with such assistance as our party can give you, there is every chance of bringing the enterprise to a successful issue. One of our friends, who has a residence within a bow-shot of the gates, has arranged with me that your troop, arriving there before daylight, shall at once enter his grounds, where they will be concealed from the sight of any country people going towards the city.

"From the upper windows the signal can be seen, and if you are mounted and ready you can be there in three or four minutes, and it will take longer than that before the alarm can spread, and the Catholics muster strongly enough to recapture the gate."

"Admirably arranged," the Count said warmly. "With a plan so well laid our scheme can hardly fail of success. If we only do our part as well as you have done yours, Orleans is as good as won. Now, gentlemen, I advise you to toss off one more goblet of wine, and then to wrap yourselves up in your cloaks for a few hours' sleep. We must be in the saddle soon after four, so as to be off the road by five."

At that hour the troop led by the Master of Grelot turned in at the gate of the chateau. The owner was awaiting them, and gave them a cordial welcome. The men were ordered to dismount and stand by their horses, while the leaders followed their host into the house, where a repast had been laid out for them, while some servitors took out baskets of bread and flagons of wine to the troopers.

At half-past six groups of countrymen were seen making their way along the road towards the gate, and a quarter of an hour later the troop mounted and formed up in readiness to issue out as soon as the signal was given, their host placing himself at an upper window whence he could obtain a view of the city gate. It was just seven when he called out "The gate is opening!" and immediately afterwards, "They have begun the work. The country people outside are running away in a panic. Ah! there is the white flag." Two servitors at the gate of the chateau threw it open, and headed by La Noüe and the gentlemen of the party they issued out and galloped down the road at full speed. As they approached the gate some men ran out waving their caps and swords.

"Well done!" La Noüe exclaimed as he rode up. "Now, scatter and call out all our friends to aid us in the capture."

The troop had already been divided into four parties, each led by gentlemen familiar with the town. François and Philip, with the men from Laville, formed the party led by the Count himself. The news of the tumult at the gate had spread, and just as they reached the market-place a body of horsemen equal in strength to their own rode towards them.

"For God and the religion!" La Noüe shouted as he led the charge. Ignorant of the strength of their assailants, and having mounted in haste at the first alarm, the opposing band hesitated, and before they could set their horses into a gallop the Huguenots were upon them.

The impetus of the charge was irresistible. Men and horses rolled over, while those in the rear turned and rode away, and the combat was over before scarce a blow had been struck. A party of infantry hastening up were next encountered; these offered a more stubborn resistance, but threw down their arms and surrendered when another of the Huguenot parties rode into the square. At the sound of the conflict the upper windows of the houses were opened, and the citizens looked out in alarm at the struggle. But the Catholics having neither orders nor plan dared not venture out, while the Huguenots mustered rapidly with arms in their hands, and rendered valuable assistance to the horsemen in attacking and putting to flight the parties of Catholic horse and foot as they came hurriedly up.

In an hour all resistance had ceased and Orleans was taken. The Count at once issued a proclamation to the citizens assuring all peaceable persons of protection, and guaranteeing to the citizens immunity from all interference with personal property and the right of full exercise of their religion. The charge of the gates was given over to the Huguenot citizens, parties of horse were told off to patrol the streets to see that order was preserved, and to arrest any using threats or violence to the citizens, and in a very few hours the town resumed its usual appearance. Now that all fear of persecution was at an end, large numbers of the citizens who had hitherto concealed their leanings towards the new religion openly avowed them, and La Noüe saw with satisfaction that the town could be safely left to the keeping of the Huguenot adherents with the assistance only of a few men to act as leaders. These he selected from the gentlemen of the province who had come with him, and as soon as these had entered upon their duties he felt free to turn his attention elsewhere.

Two days were spent in appointing a council of the leading citizens, the Huguenots of course being in the majority. To them was intrusted the management of the affairs of the town and the maintenance of order. The young nobleman appointed as governor was to have entire charge of military matters; all Huguenots capable of bearing arms were to be formed up in companies, each of which was to appoint its own officers. They were to practise military exercises, to have charge of the gates and walls, and to be prepared to defend them in case a hostile force should lay siege to the city. Three of the nobles were appointed to see to the victualling of the town; and all citizens were called upon to contribute a sum according to their means for this purpose. A few old soldiers were left to drill the new levies, to see that the walls were placed in a thorough condition of defence, and above all to aid the leaders in suppressing any attempt. at the ill-treatment of Catholics, or the desecration of their churches by the Huguenot portion of the population. When all arrangements were made for the peace and safety of the town, De la Noüe despatched most of the gentlemen with him and their followers to join the Prince of Condé before Paris, retaining only his Cousin François, Philip, the troop from Laville, and his own band of forty men-at-arms.

CHAPTER VI

THE BATTLE OF ST. DENIS

FRANÇOIS DE LAVILLE and Philip had fought by the side of La Noüe in the engagement in the streets of Orleans, but had seen little of the Count afterwards, his time being fully employed in completing the various arrangements to ensure the safety of the town. They had been lodged in the house of one of the Huguenot citizens, and had spent their time walking about the town or in the society of some of the younger gentlemen of their party.

"Are you both ready for service again?" the Count de la Noüe, who had sent for them to come to his lodgings, asked on the evening of the third day after the capture of Orleans.

"Quite ready," François replied. "The horses have all recovered from their fatigue, and are in condition for a fresh start. Are we bound for Paris, may I ask?"

"No, François, we are going on a recruiting tour: partly because we want men, but more to encourage our people by the sight of an armed party, and to show the Catholics that they had best stay their hands and leave us alone for the present. I take a hundred men with me, including your troop and my own, which I hope largely to increase. Sometimes we shall keep in a body, sometimes break up into two or three parties. Always we shall move rapidly, so as to appear where least expected, and so spread uneasiness as to where we may next appear. In the south we are, as I hear, holding our own. I shall therefore go first to Brittany, and if all is quiet, there raise another fifty men. We shall travel through Touraine and

Anjou as we go, and then sweep round by Normandy and La Perche, and so up to Paris. So you see we shall put a good many miles of ground under our feet before we join the Prince. In that way not only shall we swell our numbers and encourage our friends, but we shall deter many of the Catholic gentry from sending their retainers to join the army of the Guises."

"It will be a pleasant ride, cousin," François said, "and I hope that we shall have an opportunity of doing some good work before we reach Paris, and especially that we shall not arrive there too late to join in the coming battle."

"I do not think that there is much fear of that," the Count replied; "the Prince has not sufficient strength to attack Paris. And for my part, I think that it would have been far better, when it was found that his plan of seizing the court had failed, to have drawn off at once. He can do nothing against Paris, and his presence before it will only incite the inhabitants against us and increase their animosity. It would have been better to have applied the force in reducing several strong towns where, as at Orleans, the bulk of the inhabitants are favourable to us. In this way we should weaken the enemy, strengthen ourselves, and provide places of refuge for our people in case of need. However, it is too late for such regrets; the Prince is there, and we must take him what succour we can. I was pleased with you both in the fights upon the day we entered. You both behaved like brave gentlemen and good swordsmen. I expected no less from you, François; but I was surprised to find your English cousin so skilled with his weapon."

"He is a better swordsman than I am," François said; "which is a shame to me, since he is two years my junior."

"Is he indeed!" the Count said in surprise. "I had taken him to be at least your equal in years. Let me think, you are but eighteen and some months?"

"But a month over eighteen," François said, "and Philip has but just passed sixteen."

"You will make a doughty warrior when you attain your full strength, Philip. I saw you put aside a thrust from an officer in the *mêlée*, and strike him from his horse with a backhanded cut with your sword, dealt with a vigour that left nothing to be desired."

"I know that I am too fond of using the edge, sir," Philip said modestly; "my English masters taught me to do so, and although my French instructors at home were always impressing upon me that the point was more deadly than the edge, I cannot break myself altogether from the habit."

"There is no need to do so," the Count said. "Of late the point has come into fashion among us, and doubtless it has advantages, but often a downright blow will fetch a man from his saddle when you would in vain try to find with the point a joint in his armour. But you must have been well taught indeed if you are a better swordsman than my cousin, whose powers I have tried at Laville, and found him to be an excellent swordsman for his age."

"I have had many masters," Philip said. "Both my French and English teachers were good swordsmen, and it was seldom a Frenchman who had been in the wars passed through Canterbury that my uncle did not engage him to give me a few lessons. Thus, being myself very anxious to become a good swordsman, and being fond of exercises, I naturally picked up a great many tricks with the sword."

"You could not have spent your time better if you had an intention of coming over to take part in our troubles here. Your grandfather, De Moulins, was said to be one of the best swordsmen in France, and you may have inherited some of his skill. I own that I felt rather uneasy at the charge of two such young cockerels, though I could not refuse when the countess, my aunt, begged me to let you ride with me; but in future I shall feel easy about you, seeing that you can both take your own parts stoutly. Well, order your men to be ready and mounted in the market-place at half-past five. The west gate will be opened for us to ride forth at six."

Philip had every reason to be satisfied with the conduct of his new servant. In the town, as at Laville, Pierre behaved circumspectly and quietly, assuming a grave countenance in accordance with his surroundings; keeping his arms and armour brightly polished, and waiting at table as orderly as if he had been used to nothing else all his life.

"I am glad to hear it, sir," Pierre said, when Philip informed him that they would start on the following morning. "I love not towns, and here, where there is nought to do but to polish your armour and stand behind your chair at dinner, the time goes mighty heavily."

"You will have no cause to grumble on that account, Pierre, I fancy, for your ride will be a long one. I do not expect we shall often have a roof over our heads."

"All the better, sir, so long as the ride finishes before the cold weather sets in. Fond as I am of sleeping with the stars over me, I own that when the snow is on the ground I prefer a roof over my head."

At six o'clock the party started; only two other gentlemen rode with it, both of whom were, like the Count, from Brittany. The little group chatted gaily as they rode along. Unless they happened to encounter parties of Catholics going north to join the royal army, there was, so far as they knew, no chance of their meeting any body of the enemy on their westward ride. The towns of Vendome, Le Mans, and Laval were all strongly Catholic and devoted to the Guises. These must be skirted. Rennes in Brittany must also be avoided, for all these towns were strongly garrisoned, and could turn out a force far too strong for La Noüe to cope with.

Upon the march Pierre was not only an invaluable servant but the life of the troop, he being full of fun and frolic, and making even the gravest soldier smile at his sallies. When they halted he was indefatigable in seeing after Philip's comforts: he cut boughs of the trees best suited for the purpose of making a couch, and surprised his master and François by his ingenuity in turning out excellent dishes from the scantiest materials. He would steal away in the night to procure fowls and eggs from neighbouring farmhouses, and although Philip's orders were that he was to pay the full price for everything he required, Philip found when he gave an account a fortnight later of how he had spent the money he had given him, that there was no mention of any payment for these articles. When he rated Pierre for this the latter replied:

"I did not pay for them, sir. Not in order to save you money, but for the sake of the farmers and their families. It would have been worse than cruelty to have aroused them from sleep. The loss of a fowl or two and of a dozen eggs were nothing to them; if they missed them at all they would say that a fox had been there, and they would think no more of it. If, on the other hand, I had waked them up in the middle of the night to pay for these trifles they would have been scared out of their life, thinking when I knocked that some band of robbers was at the door. In their anger at being thus disturbed they would have been capable of shooting me, and it is well-nigh certain that at any rate they would have refused to sell their chickens and eggs at that time of the night. So you see, sir, I acted for the best for all parties. Two chickens out of scores was a loss not worth thinking of, while the women escaped the panic and terror that my waking them up would have caused them. When I can pay I will assuredly do so, since that is your desire; but I am sure you will see that under such circumstances it would be a crime to wake people from their sleep for the sake of a few sous."

Philip laughed.

"Besides, sir," Pierre went on, "these people were either Huguenots or Catholics. If they were Huguenots they would be right glad to minister to those who are fighting on their behalf; if they were Catholics they would rob and murder us without mercy. Therefore they may think themselves fortunate indeed to escape at so trifling a cost from the punishment they deserve."

"That is all very well, Pierre; but the orders are strict against plundering, and if the Admiral were to catch you you would get a sound thrashing with a stirrup-leather."

"I have risked worse than that, sir, many times in my life, and if I am caught I will give them leave to use the strap. But you will see, Monsieur Philip, that if the war goes on these niceties will soon become out of fashion. At present the Huguenot lords and gentlemen have money in their pockets to pay for what they want, but after a time money will become scarce. They will see that the armies of the king live on plunder as armies generally do, and when cash runs short they will have to shut their eyes and let the men provide themselves as best they can."

"I hope the war won't last long enough for that, Pierre. But at any rate we have money in our pockets at present, and can pay for what we require; though I do not pretend that it is a serious matter to take a hen out of a coop, especially when you can't get it otherwise, without, as you say, alarming a whole family. However, remember my orders are that everything we want is to be paid for."

"I understand, sir, and you will see that the next time we reckon up accounts every item shall be charged for, so that there will be nothing on your conscience."

Philip laughed again. "I shall be content if that is the case, Pierre, and I hope that your conscience will be as clear as mine will be."

On the third of November, just a month after leaving Orleans, De la Noüe with his troop augmented to three hundred joined the Prince of Condé before Paris. During the interval he had traversed the west of France by the route he had marked out for himself, had raised fifty more men among the Huguenots of Brittany, and had been joined on the route by many gentlemen with parties of their retainers. Several bodies of Catholics had been met and dispersed. Two or three small towns where the Huguenots had been ill-treated and massacred were entered, the ringleaders in the persecutions had been hung, and the authorities had been compelled to pay a heavy fine, under threat of the whole town being committed to the flames.

Everywhere he passed La Noüe had caused proclamations to be scattered far and wide to the effect that any ill-treatment of Huguenots would be followed by his return, and by the heaviest punishment being inflicted upon all who molested them. And so, having given great encouragement to the Huguenots and scattered terror among their persecutors, having ridden great distances and astonished the people of the western provinces by his energy and activity, La Noüe joined the Prince of Condé with three hundred men. He was heartily welcomed on his arrival at the Huguenot camp at St. Denis.

François de Laville and Philip Fletcher had thoroughly enjoyed the expedition. They had often been in the saddle from early morning till late at night, and had felt the benefit of having each two horses, as when the party halted for a day or two they were often sent out with half their troop to visit distant places to see friends, to bring into the camp magistrates and others who had been foremost in stirring up the people to attack the Huguenots, to enter small towns, throw open prisons and carry off the Huguenots confined there, and occasionally to hang the leaders of local massacres. In these cases they were always accompanied by one or other of the older leaders in command of the party.

Their spare chargers enabled them to be on horseback every day, while half the troop rested in turn. Sometimes their halts were made in small towns and villages, but more often they bivouacked in the open country; being thus, the Count considered, more watchful and less apt to be surprised. On their return from these expeditions Pierre always had a meal prepared for them. In addition to the rations of meat and bread, chicken and eggs, he often contrived to serve up other and daintier food. His old poaching habits were not forgotten. As soon as the camp was formed he would go out and set snares for hares, traps for birds, and lay lines in the nearest stream, while fish and game of some sort were generally added to the fare.

"Upon my word," the Count, who sometimes rode with them, said one evening, "this varlet of yours, Master Philip, is an invaluable fellow, and Condé himself cannot be better served than you are. I have half a mind to take him away from you, and to appoint him Provider-in-General to our camp. I warrant me he never learned thus to provide a table honestly; he must have all the tricks of a poacher at his fingers' end."

"I fancy when he was young he had to shift a good deal for himself, sir," Philip replied.

"I thought so," La Noüe laughed. "I marked him once or twice behind your chair at Orleans, and methought then that he looked too grave to be honest; and there was a twinkle in his eye that accorded badly with the gravity of his face and his sober attire. Well, there can be no doubt that in war a man who has a spice of the rogue in him makes the best of servants, provided he is but faithful to his master and respects his goods, if he does those of no one else. Your rogue is necessarily a man of resources, and one of that kind will on a campaign make his master comfortable where one with an over-scrupulous varlet will well-nigh starve. I had such a man when I was with Brissac in Northern Italy, but one day he went out and never returned. Whether a provost-marshal did me the ill service of hanging him, or whether he was shot by the peasants, I never knew, but I missed him sorely, and often went fasting to bed when I should have had a good supper had he been with me. It is lucky for you both that you haven't to depend upon that grim-visaged varlet of François'. I have no doubt that the countess thought she was doing well by my cousin when she appointed him to go with him, and I can believe that he would give his life for him, but for all that if you had to depend upon him for your meals you would fare badly indeed."

De la Noüe was much disappointed on joining the Prince at finding that the latter's force had not swollen to larger dimensions. He had with him, after the arrival of the force the Count had brought from the west, but two thousand horse. Of these a large proportion were gentlemen, attended only by a few personal retainers; a fifth only were provided with lances, and a large number had no defensive armour. Of foot soldiers he had about the same number as of horse, and of these about half were armed with arquebuses, the rest being pikemen. The force under the command of the Constable de Montmorency inside the walls of Paris was known to be enormously superior in strength, and the Huguenots were unable to understand why he did not come out to give them battle. They knew, however, that Count Aremberg was on his way from the Netherlands with seventeen hundred horse, sent by the Duke of Alva to the support of the Catholics, and they supposed that Montmorency was waiting for this reinforcement.

On the 9th of November news arrived that Aremberg was approaching, and D'Andelot, with five hundred horse and eight hundred of the best-trained arquebusiers, was despatched to seize Poissy, and so prevent Aremberg entering Paris. The next morning the Constable, learning that Condé had weakened his army by this detachment, marched out from

Paris. Seldom have two European armies met with a greater disparity of numbers, for while Condé had but fifteen hundred horse and twelve hundred foot, the Constable marched out with sixteen thousand infantry, of whom six thousand were Swiss, and three thousand horse. He had eighteen pieces of artillery, while Condé was without a single cannon. As soon as this force was seen pouring out from the gates of Paris the Huguenot trumpets blew to arms. All wore over their coats or armour a white scarf, the distinguishing badge of the Huguenots, and the horsemen were divided into three bodies. De la Noüe and his following formed part of that under the personal command of Condé.

"We longed to be here in time for this battle, Philip," François said, "but I think this is rather more than we bargained for. They must be nearly ten to one against us. There is one thing, although the Swiss are good soldiers, the rest of their infantry are for the most part Parisians, and though these gentry have proved themselves very valiant in the massacre of unarmed Huguenot men, women, and children, I have no belief in their valour when they have to meet men with swords in their hands. I would, however, that D'Andelot with his five hundred horse and eight hundred arquebusiers, all picked men, were here with us, even if Aremberg with his seventeen hundred horse were ranged under the Constable. As it is I can hardly believe that Condé and the Admiral will really lead us against that huge mass. I should think that they can but be going to manœuvre so as to fall back in good order and show a firm face to the enemy. Their footmen would then be of no use to them, and as I do not think their horse are more than twice our strength, we might turn upon them when we get them away from their infantry, and beyond the range of their cannon."

As soon, however, as the troops were fairly beyond the gates of St. Denis the leaders placed themselves at the head of the three columns, and with a few inspiring words led them forward. Coligny was on the right, La Rochefoucauld, Genlis, and other leaders on the left, and the column commanded by Condé himself in the centre. Condé, with a number of nobles and gentlemen, rode in front of the line.

Behind them came the men-at-arms with lances, while those armed only with swords and pistols followed. Coligny, on the right, was most advanced, and commenced the battle by charging furiously down upon the enemy's left. Facing Condé were the great mass of the Catholic infantry, but without a moment's hesitation the little band of but five hundred horse charged right down upon them. Fortunately for them it was the Parisians and not the Swiss upon whom their assault fell. The force and impetus of their rush was too much for the Parisians, who broke at the onset, threw away their arms, and fled in a disorderly mob towards the gates of Paris.

"Never mind those cowards," the Prince shouted, "there is nobler game;" and followed by his troop he rode at the Constable, who, with a thousand horse, had taken his post behind the infantry. Before this body of cavalry could advance to meet the Huguenots the latter were among them, and a desperate hand-to-hand *mêlée* took place. Gradually the Huguenots won their way into the mass, although the old Constable, fighting as stoutly as the youngest soldier, was setting a splendid example to his troops. Robert Stuart, a Scotch gentleman in Condé's train, fought his way up to him and demanded his surrender. The Constable's reply was a blow with the hilt of the sword which nearly struck Stuart from his horse, knocking out three of his teeth. A moment later the Constable was struck by a pistol-ball, but whether it was fired by Stuart himself or one of the gentlemen by his side was never known. The Constable fell, but the fight still raged.

The Royalists, recovered from the first shock, were now pressing their adversaries. Condé's horse was shot by a musket-ball, and in falling pinned him to the ground so that he was unable to extricate himself. De la Noüe, followed by François and Philip, who were fighting by his side, and other gentlemen, saw his peril, and rushing forward drove back Condé's assailants. Two gentlemen leaping from their horses extricated the Prince from his fallen steed, and, after hard fighting, placed him on a horse before one of them, and the troops, repulsing every attack made on them, fell slowly back to St. Denis. On the right Coligny had more than held his own against the enemy, but on the left the Huguenots, encountering Marshal de Montmorency, the eldest son of the Constable, and suffering heavily from the arquebus and artillery fire, had been repulsed, and the Catholics here had gained considerable advantages.

The flight of a large portion of the infantry, and the disorder caused in the cavalry by the charges of Condé and Coligny, prevented the Marshal from following up his advantage, and as the Huguenots fell back upon St. Denis the Royalists retired into Paris, where the wounded Constable had already been carried. Victory was claimed by both sides, but belonged to neither. Each party had lost about four hundred men, a matter of much greater consequence to the Huguenots than to the Catholics, the more so as a large proportion of the slain on their side were gentlemen of rank. Upon the other hand the loss of the Constable, who died next day, paralysed for a time the Catholic forces.

A staunch and even bigoted Catholic, and opposed to any terms of toleration being granted to the Huguenots, he was opposed to the ambition of the Guises, and was the head of the Royalist party as distinguished from that of Lorraine. Catharine, who was the moving spirit of the court, hesitated to give the power he possessed as Constable into hands that might use it against her, and persuaded the king to bestow the supreme command of the army upon his brother, Henri, Duke of Anjou. The divisions in the court caused by the death of the Constable, and the question of his successor, prevented any fresh movements of the army, and enabled the Prince of Condé, after being rejoined by D'Andelot's force, to retire unmolested three days after the battle, the advanced guard of the Royalists having been driven back into Paris by D'Andelot on his return, when in his disappointment at being absent from the battle he fell fiercely upon the enemy, and pursued them hotly to the gates, burning several windmills close under the walls.

On the evening of the battle De la Noüe had presented his cousin and Philip to the Prince, speaking in high terms of the bravery they displayed in the battle, and they had received Condé's thanks for the part they had taken in his rescue from the hands of the Catholics.   The Count himself had praised them highly, but had gently chided François for the rashness he had shown.

"It is well to be brave, François; but that is not enough. A man who is brave without being prudent, may with fortune escape as you have done from a battle without serious wounds, but he cannot hope for such fortune many times, and his life would be a very short one.   Several times to-day you were some lengths ahead of me in the *mêlée*, and once or twice I thought you lost, for I was too closely pressed myself to render you assistance.   It was the confusion alone that saved you. Your life is a valuable one.   You are the head of an old family, and have no right to throw your life away.   Nothing could have been more gallant than your behaviour, François, but you must learn to temper bravery by prudence.   Your cousin showed his English blood and breeding.   When we charged he was half a length behind me, and at that distance he remained through the fight, except when I was very hotly pressed, when he at once closed up beside me.   More than once I glanced round at him, and he was fighting with the coolness of a veteran.   It was he who called my attention to Condé's fall, which in the *mêlée* might have passed unnoticed by me until it was too late to save him.   He kept his pistols in his holsters throughout the fray, and it was only when they pressed us so hotly as we were carrying off the Prince that he used them, and, as I observed, with effect.   I doubt if there was a pistol save his undischarged at that time; they were a reserve that he maintained for the crisis of the fight.   Master Philip, I trust that you will have but small opportunity for winning distinction in this wretched struggle, but were it to last, which heaven forbid, I should say that you would make a name for yourself, as assuredly will my cousin François, if he were to temper his enthusiasm with coolness."

The evening before the Huguenots retired from St. Denis the Count sent for François and his cousin.

"As you will have heard," he said, "we retire to-morrow morning.   We have done all, and more than all, that could have been expected from such a force.   We have kept Paris shut up for ten weeks, and have maintained our position in

face of a force, commanded by the Constable of France, of
well-nigh tenfold our strength.   We are now going to march
east to effect a junction with a force under Duke Casimir.
He is to bring us over six thousand horse, three thousand
foot, and four cannon.   The march will be toilsome, but the
Admiral's skill will, I doubt not, enable us to elude the force
with which the enemy will try to bar our way.   The Admiral
is sending off the Sieur D'Arblay, whom you both know, to
the south of France in order that he may explain to our
friends there the reason for our movement to the east, for
otherwise the news that we have broken up from before Paris
may cause great discouragement.

"I have proposed to him that you should both accompany
him.   You have frequently ridden under his orders during our
expedition to the west, and he knows your qualities.   He has
gladly consented to receive you as his companions.   It will
be pleasant for him to have two gentlemen with him.   He
takes with him his own following of eight men; six of his
band fell in the battle.   The Admiral is of opinion that this
is somewhat too small a force for safety, but if you each take
the four men-at-arms who ride behind you it will double his
force.   Two of yours fell in the fight I believe, François."

"I have taken two others from the troop to fill their places."

"Your men all came out of it, Philip, did they not?"

"Yes, sir.   They were all wounded, but none of them seriously, and are all fit to ride."

"You will understand, François, that in separating you from
myself I am doing so for your sakes' alone.   It will be the
Admiral's policy to avoid fighting.   Winter is close upon us
and the work will be hard and toilsome, and doubtless ere we
effect a junction with the Germans very many will succumb
to cold and hardship.   You are not as yet inured to this
work, and I would rather not run the risk of your careers ending from such causes.   If I thought there was a prospect of
fighting I should keep you with me, but being as it is I think
it better you should accompany the Sieur D'Arblay.   The
mission is a dangerous one, and will demand activity, energy,
and courage, all of which you possess; but in the south you
will have neither cold nor famine to contend with, and far

greater opportunities maybe of gaining credit than you would in an army like this, where, as they have proved to the enemy, every man is brave. Another reason, I may own, is that in this case I consider your youth to be an advantage. We could hardly have sent one gentleman on such a mission alone, and with two of equal rank and age, each with eight followers, difficulties and dissensions might have arisen, while you would both be content to accept the orders of the Sieur D'Arblay without discussion, and to look up to him as the leader of your party."

Although they would rather have remained with the army, the lads at once thanked the Count and stated their willingness to accompany the Sieur D'Arblay, whom they both knew and liked, being, like De la Noüe, cheerful and of good spirits, not deeming it necessary to maintain at all times a stern and grave aspect, or a ruggedness of manner, as well as sombre garments. De la Noüe at once took them across to D'Arblay's tent.

"My cousin and his kinsman will gladly ride with you and place themselves under your orders, D'Arblay. I can warmly commend them to you. Though they are young I can guarantee that you will find them, if it comes to blows, as useful as most men ten years their senior, and on any mission that you may intrust to them I think that you can rely upon their discretion; but of that you will judge for yourself when you know somewhat more of them. They will take with them eight men-at-arms, all of whom will be stout fellows, so that with your own men you can traverse the country without fear of any party you are likely to fall in with."

"I shall be glad to have your cousin and his kinsman with me," D'Arblay said courteously. "Between you and I, De la Noüe, I would infinitely rather have two bright young fellows of spirit than one of our tough old warriors, who deem it sinful to smile, and have got a text handy for every occasion. It is not a very bright world for us at present, and I see not the use of making it sadder by always wearing a gloomy countenance."

The next morning the party started and rode south. Avoiding the places held by the Catholics, they visited many of the chateaux of Huguenot gentlemen, to whom D'Arblay communicated the instructions he had received from the Admiral as to the assemblage of troops and the necessity for raising such a force as would compel the Royalists to keep a considerable army in the south, and so lessen the number who would gather to oppose his march eastward.

After stopping for a short time in Navarre, and communicating with some of the principal leaders in that little kingdom they turned eastward. They were now passing through a part of the country where party spirit was extremely bitter, and were obliged to use some caution, as they were charged to communicate with men who were secretly well affected to the cause, but who, living within reach of the bigoted parliament of Toulouse, dared not openly avow their faith.

Toulouse had from the time the troubles first began distinguished itself for the ferocity with which it had persecuted the Huguenots, yielding obedience to the various royal edicts of toleration most reluctantly, and sometimes openly disobeying them. Thus for many miles round the city those of the Reformed faith lived in continual dread, conducting their worship with extreme secrecy when some pastor in disguise visited the neighbourhood, and outwardly conforming to the rites of the Catholic church. Many, however, only needed the approach of a Huguenot army to throw off the mask and take up arms, and it was with these that D'Arblay was specially charged to communicate. Great caution was needed in doing this, as the visit of a party of Huguenots would, if denounced, have called down upon them the vengeance of the parliament, who were animated not only by hatred of the Huguenots, but by the desire of enriching themselves by the confiscation of the estates and goods of those they persecuted.

The visits, consequently, were generally made after nightfall, the men-at-arms being left a mile or two away. D'Arblay found everywhere a fierce desire to join in the struggle, restrained only by the fear of the consequences to wives and families during absence. "Send an army capable of besieging and capturing Toulouse and there is not one of us who will not rise and give his blood for the cause, putting into the field every man he can raise and spending his last crown; but unless such a force approaches we dare not move. We know that we are strictly watched, and that on the smallest pretext we and our families would be dragged to prison. Tell the Admiral that our hearts and our prayers are with him, and that nothing in the world would please us so much as to be fighting under his banner; but until there is a hope of capturing Toulouse we dare not move."

Such was the answer at every castle, chateau, and farmhouse where they called. Many of the Huguenots contributed not only the money they had in their houses but their plate and jewels, for money was above all things needed to fulfil the engagements the Admiral had made with the German mercenaries who were on their march to join him. Sometimes Philip and François both accompanied their leader on his visits; sometimes they went separately, for they were always able to obtain from the leading men the names of neighbours who were favourable to the cause. In the way of money they succeeded beyond their expectations, for as the gentlemen in the district had not, like those where the parties were more equally divided, impoverished themselves by placing their retainers in the field, they were able to contribute comparatively large sums to the cause they had at heart.

CHAPTER VII

A RESCUE

D'ARBLAY and his two companions had been engaged for ten days in visiting the Huguenots within a circuit of four or five leagues round Toulouse when they learned that their movements had been reported to the authorities there. They had one day halted as usual in a wood, when the soldier on the look-out ran in and reported that a body of horsemen, some forty or fifty strong, were approaching at a gallop by the road from the city.

"They may not be after us," D'Arblay said, "but at any rate they shall not catch us napping."

Girths were hastily tightened, armour buckled on, and all took their places in their saddles. It was too late to retreat, for the wood was a small one, and the country around open. As the horsemen approached the wood they slackened speed and presently halted facing it.

"Some spy has tracked us here," D'Arblay said, "but it is one thing to track the game, another to capture it. Let us see what these gentlemen of Toulouse are going to do. I have no doubt that they know our number accurately enough, and if they divide, as I hope they will, we shall be able to give them a lesson."

This was evidently the intention of the Catholics. After a short pause an officer trotted off with half the troop, making a circuit to come down behind the wood and cut off all retreat. As they moved off the Huguenots could count that there were twenty-five men in each section.

"The odds are only great enough to be agreeable," D'Arblay laughed. "It is not as it was outside Paris, where they were ten to one against us. Counting our servants we muster twenty-two, while that party in front are only four stronger, for that gentleman with the long robe is probably an official of their parliament or a city councillor, and need not be counted. We will wait a couple of minutes longer until the other party is fairly out of sight, and then we will begin the dance."

A minute or two later he gave the word, and the little troop moved through the trees until nearly at the edge of the wood.

"Now, gentlemen, forward," D'Arblay said, "and God aid the right."

As in a compact body, headed by the three gentlemen, they burst suddenly from the wood, there was a shout of dismay, and then loud orders from the officer of the troop, halted a hundred and fifty yards away. The men were sitting carelessly on their horses; they had confidently anticipated taking the Huguenots alive, and thought of nothing less than that the latter should take the offensive. Scarcely had they got their horses into motion before the Huguenots were upon them. The conflict lasted but a minute. Half the Catholics were cut down, the rest turning their horses rode off at full speed. The Huguenots would have followed them, but D'Arblay shouted to them to halt.

"You have only done half your work yet," he said, "we have the other party to deal with."

Only one of his Huguenots had fallen, shot through the head by a pistol discharged by the officer, who had himself been a moment later run through by D'Arblay, at whom the shot had been aimed. Gathering his men together the Huguenot leader rode back, and when half-way through the wood they encountered the other party, whose officer had at once ridden to join the party he had left, when he heard the pistol-shot that told him they were engaged with the Huguenots. Although not expecting an attack from an enemy they deemed overmatched by their comrades, the troop, encouraged by their officer, met the Huguenots stoutly. The fight was for a short time obstinate. Broken up by the trees, it resolved itself into

a series of single combats. The Huguenot men-at-arms, however, were all tried soldiers, while their opponents were rather
accustomed to the slaughter of defenceless men and women
than to a combat with men-at-arms. Coolness and discipline
soon asserted themselves. François and Philip both held their
ground abreast of their leader, and Philip by cutting down the
lieutenant brought the combat to a close. His followers on
seeing their officer fall at once lost heart, and those who could
do so turned their horses and rode off. They were hotly pursued, and six were overtaken and cut down; eight had fallen
in the conflict in the wood.

"That has been a pretty sharp lesson," D'Arblay said, as
leaving the pursuit to his followers he reined in his horse at
the edge of the wood. "You both did right gallantly, young
sirs. It is no slight advantage in a *mêlée* of that kind to be
strong in officers. The fellows fought stoutly for a short time.
Had it not been for your despatching their officer, Monsieur
Fletcher, we should not have finished with them so quickly.
It was a right down blow, and heartily given, and fell just at
the joint of the gorget."

"I am sorry that I killed him," Philip replied. "He
seemed a brave gentleman, and was not very many years older
than I am myself."

"He drew it upon himself," D'Arblay said. "If he had not
come out to take us he would be alive now. Well, as soon as
our fellows return we will move round to Merlincourt on the
other side of the town. There are several of our friends there,
and it is the last place we have to visit. After this skirmish
we shall find the neighbourhood too hot for us. It is sure to
make a great noise, and at the first gleam of the sun on helm
or breast-plate some Catholic or other will hurry off to Toulouse with the news. In future we had best take some of the
men-at-arms with us when we pay our visits, or we may be
caught like rats in a trap."

Making a circuit of twenty miles they approached Merlincourt that evening, and establishing themselves as usual in a
wood, remained quiet there next day. After nightfall D'Arblay
rode off, taking with him François and five of his own men,
and leaving Philip in command of the rest. The gold and

jewels they had gathered had been divided into three portions, and the bags placed in the holsters of the saddles of the three lackeys, as these were less likely to be taken than their masters, and if one were captured a portion only of the contributions would be lost. D'Arblay had arranged that he would not return that night, but would sleep at the chateau of the gentleman he was going to visit.

"I will get him to send around to our other friends in the morning. The men will return when they see that all is clear. Send them back to meet us at the chateau to-morrow night."

The five men returned an hour after they set out and reported that all was quiet at Merlincourt, and that the Sieur D'Arblay. had sent a message to Philip to move a few miles farther away before morning, and to return to the wood soon after nightfall. Philip gave the men six hours to rest themselves and their horses, they then mounted and rode eight miles farther from Toulouse, halting before daybreak in a thick copse standing on high ground, commanding a view of a wide tract of country. Two of the troopers were sent off to buy provisions in a village half a mile away, two were placed on watch, some of the others lay down for another sleep, while Pierre redressed the wounds that five of the men had received in the fight. At twelve o'clock one of the look-outs reported that he could see away out on the plain a body of horsemen. Philip at once went to examine them for himself.

"There must be some two hundred of them I should say by the size of the clump," he remarked to the soldier.

"About that I should say, sir."

"I expect they are hunting for us," Philip said. "They must have heard from some villager that we were seen to ride round this way the day before yesterday, or they would hardly be hunting in this neighbourhood for us. It is well we moved in the night. I wish the Sieur D'Arblay and the Count de Laville were with us. No doubt they were hidden away as soon as the troop was seen, but one is never secure against treachery."

Philip was restless and uncomfortable all day, and walked about the wood impatiently longing for night to come. As soon as it was dark they mounted and rode back to the wood near Merlincourt.   The five men were at once sent off to the chateau where they had left their leaders.

"That is a pistol-shot!" Pierre exclaimed some twenty minutes after they had left.

"I did not hear it.   Are you sure, Pierre?"

"Quite sure, sir.   At least I will not swear that it was a pistol, it might have been an arquebus, but I will swear it was a shot."

"To your saddle, men," Philip said.   "A pistol-shot has been heard, and it may be that your comrades have fallen into an ambush.   Advance to the edge of the wood, and be ready to dash out to support them should they come."

But a quarter of an hour passed and there was no sound to break the stillness of the evening.

"Shall I go into the village and find out what has taken place, Monsieur Fletcher?   I will leave my iron cap and breast and back pieces here.   I shall not want to fight but to run, and a hare could not run in these iron pots."

"Do, Pierre.   We shall be ready to support you if you are chased."

"If I am chased by half a dozen men I may run here, sir; if by a strong force I shall strike across the country.   Trust me to double and throw them off the scent.   If I am not back here in an hour, it will be that I am taken or have had to trust to my heels, and you will find me in the last case to-morrow morning at the wood where we halted to-day.   If I do not come soon after daybreak, you will know that I am either captured or killed.   Do not delay for me longer, but act as seems best to you."

Pierre took off his armour and sped away in the darkness, going at a trot that would speedily take him to the village.

"Dismount and stand by your horses," Philip ordered. "We may want all their strength."

Half an hour later Pierre returned panting.

"I have bad news, sir.   I have prowled about the village, which is full of soldiers, and listened to their talk through open windows.   The Sieur D'Arblay, Monsieur François, and the owner of the chateau and his wife were seized and carried off to Toulouse this morning soon after daybreak.   By what I heard, one of the servants of the chateau was a spy set by the council of Toulouse to watch the doings of its owner, and as soon as Monsieur D'Arblay arrived there last night, he stole out and sent a messenger to Toulouse. At daybreak the chateau was surrounded and they were seized before they had time to offer resistance. The troop of horse we saw have all day been searching for us, and went back before nightfall to Merlincourt, thinking that we should be sure to be going there sometime or other to inquire after our captain. The five men you sent away were taken completely by surprise, and all were killed, though not without a tough fight. A strong party are lying in ambush with arquebuses, making sure that the rest of the troop will follow the five they surprised."

"You were not noticed, Pierre, or pursued?"

"No, sir; there were so many men about in the village that one more stranger attracted no attention."

"Then we can remain here safely for half an hour," Philip said.

The conversation had taken place a few paces from the troop. Philip now joined his men.

"The Sieur D'Arblay and Count François have been taken prisoners. Your comrades fell into an ambush, and have, I fear, all lost their lives. Dismount for half an hour, men, while I think over what is best to be done. Keep close to your horses, so as to be in readiness to mount instantly if necessary. One of you take my horse. Do you come with me, Pierre. This is a terrible business, lad," he went on as they walked away from the others. "We know what will be the fate of my cousin and Monsieur D'Arblay. They will be burnt or hung as heretics. The first thing is, how are we to get them out, and also if possible the gentleman and his wife who were taken with them."

"We have but ten of the men-at-arms left, sir, and four of them are so wounded that they would not count for much in a fight. There are the two other lackeys and myself; so we are but fourteen in all. If we had arrived in time we might have done something, but now they are firmly lodged in the prison at Toulouse I see not that we can accomplish anything."

Philip fell into silence for some minutes, then he said: "Many of the councillors and members of parliament live, I think, in villas outside the walls, if we seize a dozen of them, appear before the city and threaten to hang or shoot the whole of them if the four captives are not released, we might succeed in getting our friends into our hands, Pierre."

"That is so, sir. There really seems a hope for us in that way."

"Then we will lose no time. We will ride at once for Toulouse. When we get near the suburbs we will seize some countryman and force him to point out to us the houses of the principal councillors and the members of their parliament. These we will pounce upon and carry off, and at daybreak will appear with them before the walls. We will make one of them signify to their friends that if any armed party sallies out through the gates, or approaches us from behind, it will be the signal for the instant death of all of our captives. Now let us be off at once."

The party mounted without delay and rode towards Toulouse. This rich and powerful city was surrounded by handsome villas and chateaux, the abode of wealthy citizens and persons of distinction. At the first house at which they stopped Philip with Pierre and two of the men-at-arms dismounted and entered. It was the abode of a small farmer, who cultivated vegetables for the use of the townsfolk. He had retired to bed with his family, but upon being summoned came downstairs trembling, fearing that his late visitors were bandits.

"No harm will be done you if you obey our orders," Philip said, "but if not we shall make short work of you. I suppose you know the houses of most of the principal persons who live outside the walls?"

"Assuredly I do, my lord. There is the President of the Parliament and three or four of the principal councillors, and the Judge of the High Court and many others, all living within a short mile of this spot."

"Well, I require you to guide us to their houses. There will be no occasion for you to show yourself, nor will any one know that you have had aught to do with the matter. If you attempt to escape or to give the alarm, you will without scruple be shot; if on the other hand we are satisfied with your work, you will have a couple of crowns for your trouble."

The man seeing that he had no choice put a good face on it. "I am ready to do as your lordship commands," he said. "I have no reason for good-will towards any of these personages, who rule us harshly and regard us as if we were dirt under their feet. Shall we go first to the nearest of them?"

"No, we will first call on the President of the Parliament, and then the Judge of the High Court, then the councillors in the order of their rank. We will visit ten in all, and see that you choose the most important. Pierre, you will take charge of this man and ride in front of us. Keep your pistol in your hand, and shoot him through the head if he shows signs of trying to escape. You will remain with him when we enter the houses. Have you any rope, my man?"

"Yes, my lord, I have several long ropes with which I bind the vegetables on my cart when I go to market."

"That will do, bring them at once."

Pierre accompanied the man when he went to his shed. On his return with the ropes Philip told the men-at-arms to cut them into lengths of eight feet, and to make a running noose at one end of each. When this was done they again mounted and moved on.

"When we enter the houses," he said to the two other lackeys, "you will remain without with Pierre, and will take charge of the first four prisoners we bring out. Put the nooses round their necks and draw them tight enough to let the men feel that they are there. Fasten the other ends to your saddles, and warn them if they put up their hands to throw off the nooses you will spur your horses into a gallop. That threat will keep them quiet enough."

In a quarter of an hour they arrived at the gate of a large and handsome villa. Philip ordered his men to dismount and fasten up their horses.

"You will remain here in charge of the horses," he said to the lackeys, and then with the men-at-arms he went up to the house. Two of them were posted at the back entrance, two at the front, with orders to let no one issue out. Then with his dagger he opened the shutters of one of the windows, and followed by the other six men entered. The door was soon found, and opening it they found themselves in a hall where a hanging light was burning. Several servants were asleep on the floor. These started up with exclamations of alarm at seeing seven men with drawn swords.

"Silence!" Philip said sternly, "or this will be your last moment. Roger and Jules, do you take each one of these lackeys by the collar. That is right. Now put your pistols to their heads. Now, my men, lead us at once to your master's chamber. Eustace, light one of these torches on the wall at the lamp and bring it along with you. Henri, do you also come with us, the rest of you stay here and guard these lackeys. Make them sit down. If any of them move run him through without hesitation."

At this moment an angry voice was heard shouting above.

"What is all this disturbance about? If I hear another sound I will discharge you all in the morning."

Philip gave a loud and derisive laugh, which had the effect he had anticipated, for directly afterwards a man in a loose dressing-gown ran into the hall.

"What does this mean, you rascals?" he shouted angrily as he entered. Then he stopped petrified with astonishment.

"It means this," Philip said, levelling a pistol at him, "that if you move a step you are a dead man."

"You must be mad," the president gasped. "Do you know who I am?"

"Perfectly, sir. You are president of the infamous parliament of Toulouse. I am a Huguenot officer, and you are my prisoner. You need not look so indignant; better men than you have been dragged from their homes to prison and death by your orders. Now it is your turn to be a prisoner. I might, if I chose, set fire to this chateau and cut the throats of all in it, but we do not murder in the name of God, we leave that to you. Take this man away with you, Eustace. I give him into your charge; if he struggles or offers the least resistance stab him to the heart."

"You will at least give me time to dress, sir?" the president said.

"Not a moment," Philip replied. "The night is warm,

"IF YOU MOVE A STEP YOU ARE A DEAD MAN."

and you will do very well as you are. As for you," he went on turning to the servants, "you will remain quiet until morning, and if any of you dare to leave the house you will be slain without mercy. You can assure your mistress that she will not be long without the society of your master, for in all probability he will be returned safe and sound before midday to-morrow. One of you may fetch your master's cloak, since he seems to fear the night air."

The doors were opened and they issued out, Philip bidding the servants close and bar them behind them. When they reached the horses the prisoner was handed over to D'Arblay's lackey, who placed the noose round his neck and gave him warning as Philip had instructed him. Then they set off, Pierre with the guide again leading the way. Before morning they had ten prisoners in their hands. In one or two cases the servants had attempted opposition, but they were speedily overpowered, and the captures were all effected without loss of life. The party then moved away about a mile, and the prisoners were allowed to sit down. Several of them were elderly men, and Philip picked these out by the light of two torches they had brought from the last house, and ordered the ropes to be removed from their necks.

"I should regret, gentlemen," he said, "the indignity that I have been forced to place upon you had you been other than you are. It is well, however, that you should have felt, though in a very slight degree, something of the treatment that you have all been instrumental in inflicting upon blameless men and women, whose only fault was that they chose to worship God in their own way. You may thank your good fortune at having fallen into the hands of one who has had no dear friends murdered in the prisons of Toulouse. There are scores of men who would have strung you up without mercy, thinking it a righteous retribution for the pitiless cruelties of which the parliament of Toulouse has been guilty.

"Happily for you, though I regard you with loathing as pitiless persecutors, I have no personal wrongs to avenge. Your conscience will tell you that, fallen as you have into the hands of Huguenots, you could only expect death; but it is not for the purpose of punishment that you have been cap-

tured; you are taken as hostages.   My friends the Count de
Laville and the Sieur D'Arblay were yesterday carried prisoners into Toulouse, and with them Monseiur de Merouville,
whose only fault was that he had afforded them a night's shelter.   His innocent wife was also dragged away with him.
You sir," he said to one of the prisoners, "appear to me to
be the oldest of the party.   At daybreak you will be released,
and will bear to your colleagues in the city the news that these
nine persons are prisoners in my hands.   You will state that
if any body of men approaches this place from any quarter
these nine persons will at once be hung up to the branches
above us.   You will say that I hold them as hostages for the
four prisoners, and that I demand that these shall be sent out
here with their horses and the arms of my two friends and
under the escort of two unarmed troopers.   These gentlemen
here will, before you start, sign a document ordering the said
prisoners at once to be released, and will also sign a solemn
undertaking, which will be handed over to Monsieur de
Merouville, pledging themselves that should he and his wife
choose to return to their chateau no harm shall ever happen to
them, and no accusation of any sort in the future be brought
against them.

"I may add that should at any time this guarantee be broken,
I shall consider it my duty the moment I hear of the event to
return to this neighbourhood, and assuredly I will hang the
signatories of the guarantee over their own door-posts and will
burn their villas to the ground.   I know the value of oaths
sworn to Huguenots; but in this case I think they will be kept,
for I swear to you—and I am in the habit of keeping my oaths
—that if you break your undertaking I will not break mine."

As soon as it was daylight Pierre produced from his saddle-
bag an ink-horn, paper, and pens, and the ten prisoners
signed their name to an order for the release of the four captives.   They then wrote another document to be handed by
their representative to the governor, begging him to see that
the order was executed, informing him of the position they
were in, and that their lives would certainly be forfeited unless the prisoners were released without delay; they also earnestly begged him to send out orders to the armed forces who

were searching for the Huguenots, bidding them make no movement whatever until after mid-day.

The councillor was then mounted on a horse and escorted by two of the men-at-arms to within a quarter of a mile of the nearest gate of the city. The men were to return with his horse. The councillor was informed that ten o'clock was the limit given for the return of the prisoners, and that unless they had by that hour arrived it would be supposed that the order for their release would not be respected, and in that case the nine hostages would be hung forthwith, and that in the course of a night or two another batch would be carried off. Philip had little fear, however, that there would be any hesitation upon the part of those in the town in acting upon the order signed by so many important persons, for the death of the president and several of the leading members of the parliament would create such an outcry against the governor by their friends and relatives, that he would not venture to refuse the release of four prisoners of minor importance in order to save their lives.

After the messenger had departed Philip had the guarantee for the safety of Monsieur de Merouville and his wife drawn up and signed in duplicate.

"One of these documents," he said, "I shall give to Monsieur de Merouville, the other I shall keep myself, so that if this solemn guarantee is broken I shall have this as a justification for the execution of the perjured men who signed it."

The time passed slowly. Some of the prisoners walked anxiously and impatiently to and fro, looking continually towards the town; others sat in gloomy silence, too humiliated at their present position even to talk to one another. The soldiers on the contrary were in high spirits; they rejoiced at the prospect of the return of their two leaders, and they felt proud of having taken part in such an exploit as the capture of the chief men of the dreaded parliament of Toulouse. Four of them kept a vigilant guard over the prisoners, the rest ate their breakfast with great gusto and laughed and joked at the angry faces of some of their prisoners. It was just nine o'clock when a small group of horsemen were seen in the distance.

"I think there are six of them, sir," Eustace said.

"That is the right number, Eustace. The lady is doubtless riding behind her husband, two men are the escort, and the other is no doubt the councillor we released, who is now acting as guide to this spot. Bring my horse, Pierre," and mounting Philip rode off to meet the party. He was soon able to make out the figures of François and D'Arblay, and putting his horse to a gallop was speedily alongside of them.

"What miracle is this?" Monsieur D'Arblay asked after the first greeting was over. "At present we are all in a maze. We were in separate dungeons, and the prospect looked as hopeless as it could well do, when the doors opened and an officer followed by two soldiers bearing our armour and arms entered and told us to attire ourselves. What was meant we could not imagine. We supposed we were going to be led before some tribunal, but why they should arm us before taking us there was more than we could imagine. We met in the courtyard of the prison, and were stupefied at seeing our horses saddled and bridled there, and Monsieur de Merouville and his wife already mounted. Two unarmed troopers were also there, and this gentleman, who said sourly, 'Mount, sirs, I am going to lead you to your friends.' We looked at each other to see if we were dreaming, but you may imagine we were not long in leaping into our saddles. This gentleman has not been communicative. In fact by his manner I should say he is deeply disgusted at the singular mission with which he was charged, and on the ride here François, Monsieur de Merouville, and myself have exhausted ourselves in conjectures as to how this miracle has come about."

"Wait two or three minutes longer," Philip said with a smile. "When you get to yonder trees you will receive an explanation."

François and Monsieur D'Arblay gazed in surprise at the figures of nine men, all in scanty raiments, wrapped up in cloaks, and evidently guarded by the men-at-arms, who set up a joyous shout as they rode in. Monsieur de Merouville uttered an exclamation of astonishment as he recognized the dreaded personages collected together in such a plight.

"Monsieur de Merouville," Philip said, "I believe you

know these gentlemen by sight. Monsieur D'Arblay and François, you are not so fortunate as to be acquainted with them, and I have pleasure in introducing to you the President of the Parliament of Toulouse, the Judge of the High Court, and other councillors, all gentlemen of consideration. It has been my misfortune to have had to treat these gentlemen with scant courtesy, but the circumstances left me no choice. Monsieur de Merouville, here is a document, signed by these nine gentlemen, giving a solemn undertaking that you and Madame shall be in future permitted to reside in your chateau without the slightest let or hindrance, and that you shall suffer no molestation whatever, either on account of this affair or on the question of religion. I have a duplicate of this document, and have on my part given an undertaking that if its terms are broken I will at whatever inconvenience to myself return to this neighbourhood, hang these ten gentlemen if I can catch them, and at any rate burn their chateaux to the ground. Therefore, I think as you have their undertaking and mine you can without fear return home; but this, of course, I leave to yourself to decide. Gentlemen, you are now free to return to your homes, and I trust this lesson— that we on our part can strike if necessary—will have some effect in moderating your zeal for persecution."

Without a word the president and his companions walked away in a body. The troopers began to jeer and laugh, but Philip held up his hand for silence.

"There need be no extra scorn," he said, "these gentlemen have been sufficiently humiliated."

"And you really fetched all these good gentlemen from their beds," D'Arblay said, bursting into a fit of laughter. "Why, it was worth being taken prisoner were it only for the sake of seeing them. They looked like a number of old owls suddenly disturbed by daylight—some of them round-eyed with astonishment, some of them hissing menacingly. By my faith, Philip, it will go hard with you if you ever fall into the hands of those worthies. But a truce to jokes. We owe you our lives, Philip; of that there is not a shadow of doubt. Though I have no more fear than another of death in battle, I own that I have a dread of being tortured and burned. It was a bold stroke thus to carry off the men who have been the leaders of the persecution against us."

"There was nothing in the feat, if it can be called a feat," Philip said. "Of course directly we heard that you had been seized and carried into Toulouse, I cast about for the best means to save you. To attempt it by force would have been simple madness, and any other plan would have required time, powerful friends, and a knowledge of the city; and even then we should probably have failed to get you out of prison. This being so, it was evident that the best plan was to seize some of the citizens of importance, who might serve as hostages. There was no difficulty in finding out from a small cultivator who were the principal men living outside the walls, and their capture was as easy a business. Scarcely a blow was struck and no lives lost in capturing the whole of them."

"But some of the men are missing," D'Arblay said.

"Yes; five of your men, I am sorry to say. On getting back to the wood after dark I sent them, as you ordered, to fetch you from Monsieur de Merouville's; but of course you had been captured before that, and they fell into an ambush that was laid for them and were all killed."

"That is a bad business, Philip. Well, M. de Merouville, will you go with us or will you trust in this safeguard?"

"In the first place, you have not given me a moment's opportunity of thanking this gentleman, not only for having saved the lives of my wife and myself, but for the forethought and consideration with which he has, in the midst of his anxiety for you and Monsieur de Laville, shown for us who were entire strangers to him. Be assured, Monsieur Fletcher, that we are deeply grateful. I hope that some time in the future, should peace ever again be restored to France, we may be able to meet you again and express more warmly the obligations we feel towards you."

Madame de Merouville added a few words of gratitude, and then D'Arblay broke in with—

"De Merouville, you must settle at once whether to go with us or stay on the faith of this safeguard. We have no such protection, and if we linger here we shall be having half a dozen troops of horse after us. You may be sure they will be sent off as soon as the president and his friends reach the city, and if we were caught again we should be in an even worse plight than before. Do you talk it over with Madame, and while you are doing so François and I will drink a flask of wine, and eat anything we can find here, for they forgot to give us breakfast before they sent us off, and it is likely we shall not have another opportunity for some hours."

"What do you think, Monsieur Fletcher?" M. de Merouville said after speaking for a few minutes with his wife; "will they respect this pledge? If not we must go, but we are both past the age when we can take up life anew. My property would, of course, be confiscated, and we should be penniless among strangers."

"I think they will respect the pledge," Philip replied. "I assured them so solemnly that any breach of their promises would be followed by prompt vengeance upon themselves and their homes, that I feel sure they will not run the risk. Two or three among them might possibly do so, but the others would restrain them. I believe that you can safely return, and that, for a long time, at any rate, you will be unmolested. Still, if I might advise, I should say sell your property as soon as you can find a purchaser at any reasonable price, and then remove either to La Rochelle or cross the sea to England. You may be sure that there will be a deep and bitter hatred against you by those whose humiliation you have witnessed."

"Thank you, I will follow your advice, M. Fletcher, and I hope that I may ere long have the pleasure of seeing you, and of worthily expressing our deep sense of the debt of gratitude we owe you."

Five minutes later the troop mounted and rode away, while M. de Merouville, with his wife behind him, started for home.

"I hope, François," D'Arblay said as they galloped off from the wood, "that the next time I ride on an expedition your kinsman may again be with me, for he has wit and resources that render him a valuable companion indeed."

"I had great hopes, even when I was in prison, and things looked almost as bad as they could be," François said, "that Philip would do something to help us. I had much faith in his long-headedness, and so has the countess, my mother. She said to me when we started, 'You are older than Philip, François, but you will act wisely if in cases of difficulty you defer your opinions to his; his training has given him self-reliance and judgment, and he has been more in the habit of thinking for himself than you have,' and certainly he has fully justified her opinion. Where do you propose to ride next, D'Arblay?"

"For La Rochelle; I shall not feel safe until I am within the walls. Presidents of Parliament, judges of High Court, and dignified functionaries are not to be dragged from their beds with impunity. Happily it will take them an hour and a half to walk back to the town, or longer perhaps, for they will doubtless go first to their own homes. They will never show themselves in such sorry plight in the streets of the city where they are accustomed to lord it; so we may count on at least two hours before they can take any steps. After that they will move heaven and earth to capture us. They will send out troops of horse after us, and messengers to every city in the province calling upon the governors to take every means to seize us. We have collected a good sum of money, and carried out the greater portion of our mission. We shall only risk its loss, as well as the loss of our own lives, by going forward. The horses are fresh, and we will put as many miles between us and Toulouse as they can carry us before nightfall."

The return journey was accomplished without misadventure. They made no more halts than were required to rest their horses, and travelling principally at night they reached La Rochelle without having encountered any body of the enemy.

While they had been absent the army of Condé and the Admiral had marched into Lorraine, and eluding the forces that barred his march, effected a junction with the German men-at-arms who had been brought to their aid by the Duke Casimir, the second son of the Elector Palatine. However, the Germans refused to march a step farther unless they received the pay that had been agreed upon before they started. Condé's treasury was empty, and he had no means whatever of satisfying their demand. In vain Duke Casimir himself tried to persuade his soldiers to defer their claims and to trust their French co-religionists to satisfy their demands later on. They were unanimous in their refusal to march a step until they obtained their money.

The Admiral then addressed himself to his officers and soldiers. He pointed out to them that at the present moment everything depended upon their obtaining the assistance of the Germans, who were indeed only demanding their rights according to the agreement that had been made with them, and he implored them to come to the assistance of the Prince and himself at this crisis. So great was his influence among his soldiers that his appeal was promptly and generally acceded to, and officers and men alike stripped themselves of their chains, jewels, money, and valuables of all kinds, and so made up the sum required to satisfy the Germans.

As soon as this important affair had been settled, the united army turned its face again westward, with the intention of giving battle anew under the walls of Paris. It was, however, terribly deficient in artillery, powder, and stores of all kinds, and the military chest being empty, and the soldiers without pay, it was necessary on the march to exact contributions from the small Catholic towns and villages through which the army marched, and in spite of the orders of the Admiral a certain amount of pillage was carried on by the soldiers. Having recruited the strength of his troops by a short stay at Orleans, the Admiral moved towards Paris. Since the commencement of the war negotiations had been going on fitfully. When the court thought that the Huguenots were formidable they pushed on the negotiations in earnest. Whenever, upon the contrary, they believed that the royal forces would be able to crush those of the Admiral, the negotiations at once came to a stand-still.

During the Admiral's long march to the east they would grant no terms whatever that could possibly be accepted, but as soon as the junction was effected with Duke Casimir and his Germans, and the Huguenot army again turned its face to Paris, the court became eager to conclude peace. When the Prince of Condé's army arrived before Chartres the negotiators met, and the king professed a readiness to grant so many concessions that it seemed as if the objects of the Huguenots could be attained without further fighting, and the Cardinal of Chatillon and some Huguenot nobles went forward to have a personal conference with the royal commissioners at Lonjumeau.

After much discussion the points most insisted upon by the Huguenots were conceded and the articles of a treaty drawn up, copies of which were sent to Paris and Chartres. The Admiral and Condé both perceived that, in the absence of any guarantees for the observance of the conditions to which the other side bound themselves, the treaty would be of little avail, as it could be broken as soon as the army now menacing Paris was scattered. The feeling among the great portion of the nobles and their followers was, however, strongly in favour of the conditions being accepted. The nobles were becoming beggared by the continuance of the war, the expenses of which had, for the most part, to be paid from their private means. Their followers, indeed, received no pay, but they had to be fed, and their estates were lying untilled for want of hands. Their men were eager to return to their farms and families, and so strong and general was the desire for peace that the Admiral and Condé bowed to it.

They agreed to the terms, and pending their ratification raised the siege of Chartres. Already their force was dwindling rapidly; large numbers marched away to their homes without even asking for leave, and their leaders soon ceased to be in a position to make any demands for guarantees, and the peace of Lonjumeau was therefore signed. Its provisions gave very little more to the Huguenots than that of the preceding arrangement of the same kind, and the campaign left the parties in much the same position as they had occupied before the Huguenots took up arms.

CHAPTER VIII

THE THIRD HUGUENOT WAR

BEFORE the treaty of Lonjumeau had been signed many weeks, the Huguenots were sensible of the folly they had committed in throwing away all the advantages they had gained in the war by laying down their arms upon the terms of a treaty made by a perfidious woman, and a weak and unstable king, with advisers bent upon destroying the reformed religion. They had seen former edicts of toleration first modified and then revoked, and they had no reason even to hope that the new treaty, which had been wrung from the court by its fears, would be respected by it. The Huguenots were not surprised to find, therefore, that as soon as they had sent back their German auxiliaries and returned to their homes—the ink, indeed, was scarcely dry on the paper upon which the treaty was written—its conditions were virtually annulled.

From the pulpit of every Catholic church in France the treaty was denounced in the most violent language, and it was openly declared that there could be no peace with the Huguenots. These, as they returned home, were murdered in great numbers, and in many of the cities the mobs rose and massacred the defenceless Protestants. Heavy as had been the persecutions before the outbreak of the war, they were exceeded by those that followed it. Some of the governors of the provinces openly refused to carry out the conditions of the treaty. Charles issued a proclamation that the edict was not intended to include any of the districts that were appanages of his mother or of any of the royal or Bourbon princes. In the towns the soldiers were quartered upon the Huguenots, whom they robbed and ill-treated at their pleasure; and during the six months that this nominal peace lasted no less than ten thousand Huguenots were slaughtered in various parts of France.

"The Prince of Condé, the Admiral, his brothers, and our other leaders, may be skilful generals and brave men," the Countess de Laville said indignantly to François, when with the troop, reduced by war, fever, and hardship to one-third of its number, he had returned to the chateau, "but they cannot have had their senses about them when they permitted themselves to be cozened into laying down their arms without receiving a single guarantee that the terms of the treaty should be observed. Far better never to have taken up arms at all. The king has come to regard us as enemies; the Catholics hate us more than ever for our successful resistance. Instead of being in a better position than we were before, we shall be in a worse. We have given up all the towns we had captured, thrown away every advantage we had gained, and when we are again driven to take up arms we shall be in a worse position than before, for they no longer despise us, and will in future be on their guard. There will be no repeating the surprise of last September. I am disappointed above all in the Admiral, D'Andelot, La Rochefoucauld, and Genlis. Condé I have never trusted as one to be relied upon in an extremity. He is a royal prince, has been brought up in courts, and loves gaiety and ease; and although I say not that he is untrue to the Huguenot cause, yet he would gladly accommodate matters; and as we see even in this treaty, the great bulk of the Huguenots all over the country have been utterly deserted, their liberty of worship denied, and their very lives are at the mercy of the bigots. What do you think, Philip? Have you had enough of fighting for a party who wilfully throw away all that they have won by their sacrifices? Are you thinking of returning home, or will you wait for a while to see how matters go on?"

"I will, with your permission, wait," Philip said. "I lament this peace, which seems to me to leave us in a worse position than before the war; but I agree with you that it cannot last, and that ere long the Huguenots will be driven again to take up arms. François and I have become as brothers, and until the cause is either lost or won I would fain remain."

"That is well, Philip; I will be glad to have you with us, my nephew. La Noüe wrote to me a month since saying that both my son and you had borne yourselves very gallantly, that he was well pleased to have had you with him, and that he thought that if these wars of religion continued, which they might well do for a long time, as in Germany and Holland as well as in France the reformed religion is battling for freedom, you would both rise to eminence as soldiers. However, now that peace is made we must make the best of it. I should think it will not be broken until after the harvest and vintage, for until then all will be employed, and the Catholics as well as the Huguenots must repair their losses and gather funds before they can again take the field with their retainers. Therefore until then I think that there will be peace."

The summer passed quietly at Laville. The tales of massacre and outrage that came from all parts of France filled them with horror and indignation, but in their own neighbourhood all was quiet. Rochelle had refused to open her gates to the royal troops, and as in all that district the Huguenots were too numerous to be interfered with by their neighbours, the quiet was unbroken. Nevertheless it was certain that hostilities would not be long delayed. The Catholics, seeing the advantage that the perfect organization of the Huguenots had given them at the commencement of the war, had established leagues in almost every province. These were organized by the clergy and the party that looked upon the Guises as their leaders, and by the terms of their constitution were evidently determined to carry out the extirpation of the reformed religion with or without the royal authority, and were, indeed, bent upon forming a third party in the state, looking to Philip of Spain rather than to the King of France as their leader.

So frequent and daring were the outrages in Paris that Condé soon found that his life was not safe there, and retired to Noyers, a small town in Burgundy. Admiral Coligny, who had been saddened by the loss of his brave wife, who had died from a disease contracted in attending upon the sick and wounded soldiers at Orleans, had abandoned the chateau at Châtillon-sur-Loing, where he had kept up a princely hospitality, and retired to the castle of Tanlay, belonging to his brother D'Andelot, situated within a few miles of Noyers. D'Andelot himself had gone to Brittany, after writing a remonstrance to Catherine de Medici upon the ruin and desolation that the breaches of the treaty and the persecution of a section of the population were bringing upon France.

The Chancellor L'Hopital had in vain urged toleration. His adversaries in the royal council were too strong for him. The Cardinal of Lorraine had regained his old influence. The king appointed as his preachers four of the most violent advocates of persecution. The De Montmorencys for a time struggled successfully against the influence of the Cardinal of Lorraine, who sought supreme power under cover of Henry of Anjou's name. Three of the marshals of France, Montmorency, his brother Danville, and Vielleville, supported by Cardinal Bourbon, demanded of the council that D'Anjou should no longer hold the office of lieutenant-general. Catherine at times aided the Guises, at times the Montmorencys, playing off one party against the other, but chiefly inclining to the Guises, who gradually obtained such an ascendancy that the Chancellor L'Hopital in despair retired from the council, and thus removed the greatest obstacle to the schemes and ambition of the Cardinal of Lorraine.

At the commencement of August the king despatched to all parts of his dominions copies of an oath that was to be demanded from every Huguenot; it called upon them to swear never to take up arms save by the express command of the king, nor to assist with counsel, money, or food any who did so, and to join their fellow-citizens in the defence of their towns against those who disobeyed this mandate. The Huguenots unanimously declined to sign the oath.

With the removal of the chancellor from the council the party of Lorraine became triumphant, and it was determined to seize the whole of the Huguenot leaders, who were quietly residing upon their estates in distant parts of France. Gaspard de Tavannes was charged with the arrest of Condé and the Admiral; and fourteen companies of men-at-arms and as many of infantry were placed under his orders, and these were quietly and secretly marched to Noyers.

Fortunately Condé received warning just before the blow was going to be struck. He was joined at Noyers by the Admiral with his daughter and sons, and the wife and infant son of D'Andelot. Condé himself had with him his wife and children. They were joined by a few Huguenot noblemen from the neighbourhood, and these with the servants of the Prince and Admiral formed an escort of about a hundred and fifty horse. Escape seemed well-nigh hopeless. Tavannes' troops guarded most of the avenues of escape. There was no place of refuge save La Rochelle, several hundred miles away on the other side of France. Every city was in the hands of their foes, and their movements were encumbered with the presence of women and young children.

There was but one thing in their favour—their enemies naturally supposed that should they attempt to escape they would do so in the direction of Germany, where they would be warmly welcomed by the Protestant princes. Therefore it was upon that line that the greatest vigilance would be displayed by their enemies. Before starting Coligny sent off a very long and eloquent protest to the king, defending himself for the step that he was about to take, giving a history of the continuous breaches of the treaty, and of the sufferings that had been inflicted upon the Huguenots, and denouncing the Cardinal of Lorraine and his associates as the guilty causes of all the misfortunes that had fallen upon France.

It was on the 23d of August that the party set out from Noyers. Their march was prompt and rapid. Contrary to expectation they discovered an unguarded ford across the Loire, near the town of Laussonne. This ford was only passable when the river was unusually low, and had therefore escaped the vigilance of their foes. The weather had been for some time dry, and they were enabled with much difficulty to effect a crossing, a circumstance which was regarded by the Huguenots as a special act of Providence, the more so as heavy rain fell the moment they had crossed, and the river rose so rapidly that when, a few hours later, the cavalry of

Tavannes arrived in pursuit they were unable to effect a passage.

The party had many other dangers and difficulties to encounter, but by extreme caution and rapidity of movement they succeeded in baffling their foes and in making their way across France.

On the evening of the 16th of September a watchman on a tower of the chateau of Laville shouted to those in the courtyard that he perceived a considerable body of horsemen in the distance. A vigilant watch had been kept up for some time, for an army had for some weeks been collected with the ostensible motive of capturing Rochelle and compelling it to receive a royal garrison; and as on its approach parties would probably be sent out to capture and plunder the chateaux and castles of the Huguenot nobles, everything had been prepared for a siege. The alarm-bell was at once rung to warn the neighbourhood of approaching danger. The vacancies caused in the garrison during the war had been lately filled up, and the gates were now closed and the walls manned, the countess herself, accompanied by her son Philip, taking her place on the tower by the gateway.

The party halted three or four hundred yards from the gate, and then two gentlemen rode forward.

"The party look to me more like Huguenots than Catholics, mother," François had said. "I see no banners; but their dresses look sombre and dark, and I think that I can see women among them."

A minute later Philip exclaimed, "Surely, François, those gentlemen who are approaching are Condé and the Admiral?"

"Impossible!" the countess said; "they are in Burgundy, full three hundred miles away."

"Philip is right, mother," François said eagerly. "I recognize them now; they are, beyond doubt, the Prince and Admiral Coligny. Lower the drawbridge and open the gates," he called down to the warders.

The countess hastened down the stairs to the courtyard followed by François and Philip, and received her two unexpected visitors as they rode across the drawbridge.

"Madame," Condé said as he doffed his cap courteously,

"we are fugitives who come to ask for a night's shelter. I have my wife and children with me, and the Admiral has also his family. We have ridden across France from Noyers by devious roads and with many turnings and windings, have been hunted like rabid beasts, and are sorely in need of rest."

"You are welcome indeed, Prince," the countess said. "I esteem it a high honour to entertain such guests as yourself and Admiral Coligny. Pray enter at once; my son will ride out to welcome the princess and the rest of your party."

François at once leapt on to a horse and galloped off, and in a few minutes the party arrived. Their numbers had been considerably increased since they left Noyers, as they had been joined by many Huguenot gentlemen on the way, and they now numbered nearly four hundred men.

"We have grown like a snowball since we started," the Prince said, "and I am ashamed to invade your chateau with such an army."

"It is a great honour, Prince. We had heard a rumour that an attempt had been made to seize you and that you had disappeared no one knew whither, and men thought that you were directing your course towards Germany; but little did we dream of seeing you here in the west."

It was not until evening that the tale of the journey across France with its many hazards and adventures was told, for the countess was fully occupied in seeing to the comforts of her guests of higher degree, while François saw that the men-at-arms and others were bestowed as comfortably as might be. Then oxen and sheep were killed, casks of wine broached, forage issued for the horses; while messengers were sent off to the nearest farms for chickens and ducks, and with orders for the women to come up to assist the domestics at the chateau to meet this unexpected strain.

"It is good to sit down in peace and comfort again," Condé said, as, supper over, they strolled in the garden enjoying the cool air of the evening. "This is the first halt that we have made at any save small villages since we left Noyers. In the first place our object was concealment, and in the second, though many of our friends have invited us to their castles, we would not expose them to the risk of destruction for having shown us hospitality. Here, however, we have entered the stronghold of our faith, for from this place to La Rochelle the Huguenots can hold their own against their neighbours, and need fear nothing save the approach of a large army, in which case, countess, your plight could scarcely be worse for having sheltered us. The royal commissioners of the province must long have had your name down as the most stiff-necked of the Huguenots of this corner of Poitou, as one who defies the ordinances and maintains public worship in her chateau. Your son and nephew fought at St. Denis, and you sent a troop across France at the first signal to join me. The cup of your offences is so full that this last drop can make but little difference one way or the other."

"I should have felt it as a grievous slight had you passed near Laville without halting here," the countess said. "As for danger, for the last twenty years we have been living in danger, and indeed during the last year I have felt safer than ever; for now that La Rochelle has declared for us, there is a place of refuge for all of the reformed religion in the provinces round such as we have not before possessed. During the last few months I have sent most of my valuables in there for safety, and if the tide of war comes this way, and I am threatened by a force against which it would be hopeless to contend, I shall make my way thither. But against anything short of an army I shall hold the chateau. It forms a place of refuge to which, at the approach of danger, all of our religion for many miles round would flock in, and as long as there is a hope of successful resistance I would not abandon them to the tender mercies of Anjou's soldiers."

"I fear, countess," the Admiral said, "that our arrival at La Rochelle will bring trouble upon all the country round it. We had no choice between that and exile. Had we consulted our own peace and safety only we should have betaken ourselves to Germany; but had we done that it would have been a desertion of our brethren, who look to us for leading and guidance. Here at La Rochelle we shall be in communication with Navarre and Gascony, and doubt not that we shall ere very long be again at the head of an army with which we can take the field even more strongly than before; for after the breaches of the last treaty, and the fresh persecutions and murders throughout the land, the Huguenots everywhere must clearly perceive that there is no option between destruction and winning our rights at the point of the sword. Nevertheless, as the court will see that it is to their interest to strike at once before we have had time to organize an army, I think it certain that the whole Catholic forces will march without loss of time against La Rochelle. Our only hope is that, as on the last occasion, they will deceive themselves as to our strength. The evil advisers of the king, when persuading him to issue fresh ordinances against us, have assured him that with strong garrisons in all the great towns in France, and with his army of Swiss and Germans still on foot, we are altogether powerless, and are no longer to be feared in the slightest degree. We know that even now, while they deem us but a handful of fugitives, our brethren throughout France will be everywhere banding themselves in arms. Before we left Noyers we sent out a summons calling the Huguenots in all parts of France to take up arms again. Their organization is perfect in every district. Our brethren have appointed places where they are to assemble in case of need; and by this time I doubt not that, although there is no regular army yet in the field, there are scores of bands ready to march as soon as they receive orders.

"It is true that the Catholics are far better prepared than before. They have endeavoured by means of these leagues to organize themselves in our manner; but there is one vital difference. We know that we are fighting for our lives and our faith, and that those who hang back run the risk of massacre in their own homes. The Catholics have no such impulse. Our persecutions have been the work of the mobs in the towns excited by the priests, and these ruffians, though ardent when it is a question of slaying defenceless women and children, are contemptible in the field against our men. We saw how the Parisians fled like a flock of sheep at St. Denis. Thus, outnumbered as we are, methinks we shall take up arms far more quickly than our foes, and that, except from the troops of Anjou and the levies of the great Catholic nobles, we shall have little to fear. Even in the towns the massacres have ever been during what is called peace, and there was far less persecution during the last two wars than in the intervals between them."

The next morning the Prince and Admiral with their escort rode on towards La Rochelle, which they entered on the 18th September. The countess with a hundred of her retainers and tenants accompanied them on the first day's journey, and returned the next day to the chateau.

The news of the escape, and the reports that the Huguenots were arming, took the court by surprise, and a declaration was at once published by the king guaranteeing his royal protection to all adherents of the reformed faith who stayed at home, and promising a gracious hearing to their grievances. As soon, however, as the Catholic forces began to assemble in large numbers the mask of conciliation was thrown off, all edicts of toleration were repealed, and the king prohibited his subjects in all parts of his dominions of whatever rank from the exercise of all religious rites other than those of the Catholic faith, on pain of confiscation and death.

Nothing could have been more opportune for the Huguenot leaders than this decree. It convinced even the most reluctant that their only hope lay in resistance, and enabled Condé's agents at foreign courts to show that the King of France was bent upon exterminating the reformed faith, and that its adherents had been forced to take up arms in self-preservation. The fanatical populations of the towns rejoiced in the new decree. Leagues for the extermination of heresy were formed in Toulouse and other towns under the name of Crusades, and high masses were celebrated in the churches everywhere in honour of the great victory over heresy.

The countess had offered to send her son with fifty men-at-arms to swell the gathering at La Rochelle, but the Admiral declined the offer. Niort was but a day's march from the chateau, and although its population were of mixed religion, the Catholics might, under the influence of the present excitement, march against Laville. He thought it would be better, therefore, that the chateau should be maintained with all its fighting force as a centre to which the Huguenots of the neighbourhood might rally.

"I think," he said, "that you might for some time sustain a siege against all the forces that could be brought from Niort, and if you are attacked I will at once send a force from the city to your assistance. I have no doubt that the Queen of Navarre will join us, and that I shall be able to take the offensive very shortly."

Encouraged by the presence of the Admiral at La Rochelle, the whole of the Huguenots of the district prepared to take the field immediately. Laville was the natural centre, and two hundred and fifty men were ready to gather there directly an alarm was given.

Three days later a man arrived at the chateau from Niort soon after daybreak. He reported that on the previous day the populace had massacred thirty or forty Huguenots, and that all the rest they could lay hands on, amounting in number to nearly two hundred, had been dragged from their homes and thrown into prison. He said that in all the villages round, the priests were preaching the extermination of the Huguenots, and it was feared that at any moment those of the religion would be attacked there, especially as it was likely that the populace of the town would flock out and themselves undertake the work of massacre should the peasants, who had hitherto lived on friendly terms with the Huguenots, hang back from it.

"We must try to assist our brethren," the countess said when she heard the news. "François, take what force you can get together in an hour and ride over towards Niort. You will get there by mid-day. If these ruffians come out from the town do you give them a lesson, and ride round to the villages and bring off all of our religion there. Assure them that they shall have protection here until the troubles are over, or until matters so change that they can return safely to their homes. We cannot sit quietly and hear of murder so close at hand. I see no prospect of rescuing the unfortunates from the prison at Niort, and it would be madness with our small force to attack a walled city; but I leave you free to do what may seem best to you, warning you only against undertaking any desperate enterprise. Philip will of course ride with you."

"Shall we ring the alarm-bell, mother?"

"No; it is better not to disturb the tenantry unless on very grave occasion. Take the fifty men-at-arms, your own men, and Philip's. Sixty will be ample for dispersing disorderly mobs, while a hundred would be of no use to you against the armed forces of the town and the garrison of two hundred men."

In a quarter of an hour the troop started. All knew the errand on which they were bent, and the journey was performed at the highest speed of which the horses were capable.

"They can have a good long rest when they get there," François said to Philip, "and half an hour earlier or later may mean the saving or losing of fifty lives. The mob will have been feasting and exulting over the slaying of so many Huguenots until late last night, and will not be astir early this morning. Probably too they will, before they think of sallying out, attend the churches, where the priests will stir them up to fury before they lead them out on a crusade into the country. I would that we knew where they are likely to begin. There are a dozen villages round the town."

"What do you say to dividing our force, François? As we near the town, you with one party could ride round to the left, I with the other to the right, and searching each village as we go, could join forces again on the other side of the town. If Montpace had been with us, of course he would have taken the command of one of the parties. It is unfortunate that he is laid up with that wound he got at St. Denis."

"I am afraid he will never be fit for active service again, Philip. But I am not sorry that he is not here. He might have objected to our dividing the troop, and besides I am glad that you should command, putting aside everything else. We understand each other. You will, of course, cut down the ruffians from the towns without mercy if you find them engaged in massacre. If not, you will warn the Huguenots of the villages as you pass through to leave their homes at once and make for Laville, giving a sharp intimation to the village *maires* that if the Protestants are interfered with in any way, or hindered from taking their goods and setting out, we will on our return burn the village about their ears and hang up any who have interfered with our people."

"I should say, François, that we should take prisoners and hold as hostages any citizens of importance, or priests, whom we may find encouraging the townsfolk to massacre. I would take the village priests, and *maire* too, so as to carry out the same plan that acted so well at Toulouse. We could then summon Niort, and say that unless the Huguenots in prison are released, and they and all the Huguenots in the town allowed to come out and join us, we will in the first place burn and destroy all the Catholic villages round the town, and the pleasure-houses and gardens of the citizens, and that in the second place we will carry off the prisoners in our hands and hang them at once if we hear of a single Huguenot being further ill-treated."

"That would be a capital plan, Philip, if we could get hold of anyone of real importance. It is likely some of the principal citizens, and perhaps Catholic nobles of the neighbourhood, will be with those who sally out, so that they can claim credit and praise from the court party for their zeal in the cause. I wish our parties had been a little stronger, for after we have entered a village or two we shall have to look after the prisoners."

"I do not think it matters, François; a dozen stout men-at-arms like ours would drive a mob of these wretches before them. They will come out expecting to murder unresisting people, and the sight of our men-at-arms in their white scarves will set them off running like hares."

"Let it be understood," Philip continued, "that if when one of us gets round to the other side of the town he should not meet the other party, and can hear no tidings of it, he shall gallop on till he meets it; for it is just possible, although I think it unlikely, that one or other of us may meet with so strong a party of the enemy as to be forced to stand on the defensive until the other arrives."

"I think there is little chance of that, Philip; still it is as well that we should make that arrangement."

As they neared Niort they met several fugitives. From them they learned that, so far, the townspeople had not come out, but that the Catholics in the villages were boasting that an end would be made of the Huguenots that day, and that many of them were in consequence deserting their homes, and making their escape as secretly as they could across the country.   When within two miles of Niort, a column of smoke was seen to arise on the left of the town.

"They have begun the work!" François exclaimed.   "That is my side!" and he placed himself at the head of half the troop, giving them orders that they were to spare none whom they found engaged in massacring Huguenots, save priests and other persons acting as leaders.   These were to be taken as hostages for the safety of their brethren in the town.   "You need not be over-careful with them," he said.   "Throw a picket-rope round their necks and make them trot beside you. They came out for a little excitement, let them have enough of it."

As François rode off one way, Philip led his party the other.

"You have heard these orders," he said, "they will do for you also."

The first place they rode into they found the Catholic inhabitants in the streets, while the houses of the Huguenots were closed and the shutters barred.   The men fled as the troop dashed in.

"Pursue them," Philip cried, "and thrash them back with the flat of your swords, but wound no one."

Most of the men were soon brought back.   By this time the Huguenots had opened their doors, and with shouts of joy were welcoming their deliverers.

"Have they threatened you with harm?" Philip asked.

"Yes; there has been mass in the church this morning, and the priest has told them to prepare to join in the good work as soon as the townspeople arrive."

The priest had already been fetched from his house guarded by two troopers.   The *maire* was next pointed out and seized. Two horses were brought out, and the prisoners placed on them.

"Put a rope round each of their necks," Philip ordered. "Fasten it firmly."

Two troopers took the other ends.

"Now you will come along with us," Philip went on, "and if you try to escape so much the worse for you.   Now," he said to the villagers, "we shall return here shortly, and then woe betide you if our orders are not executed. Every house in the village shall be burned to the ground, every man we lay hold of shall be hung. You will at once place every horse and cart here at the disposal of your Huguenot brethren; you will assist them to put their household goods in them, and will at once start with them for Laville. Those who do so will be allowed to return unharmed with their animals and carts. Eustace, you will remain here with two men and see that this order is carried out. Shoot down without hesitation any man who murmurs. If there is any trouble whatever before our return, the priest and the *maire* shall dangle from the church tower."

The next two villages they entered the same scene was enacted. As they approached the fourth village they heard cries and screams.

"Lower your lances, my friends. Forward!" And at a gallop the little band dashed into the village.

It was full of people. Several bodies of men and women lay in the road. Pistol-shots rang out here and there, showing that some of the Huguenots were making a stout defence of their homes. Through and through the crowd the horsemen rode, those in front clearing their way with their lances, those behind thrusting and cutting with their swords. The Catholics were for the most part roughly armed. Some had pikes, some had swords, others axes, choppers, or clubs, but none now thought of defence. The arms that had been brought out for the work of murder were thrown away, and there was no thought save of flight. The doors of the Huguenot houses were thrown open, and the men issuing out fell upon those who were just before their assailants. Philip saw some horsemen and others collected round a cross in the centre of the village, and calling upon the men near him to follow, dashed forward and surrounded the party before they apprehended the meaning of this sudden tumult. Two or three of the men drew their swords as if to resist, but seeing that their friends were completely routed, they surrendered. The party consisted of three men, who were by their dresses persons of rank, four or five citizens, also on horseback, four priests, and a dozen acolytes with banners and censers.

"Tie their hands behind them," Philip ordered. "Not the boys; let them go."

"I protest against this indignity," one of the gentlemen said; "I am a nobleman."

"If you were a prince of the blood, sir, and I found you engaged in the massacre of innocent people, I would tie you up and set you swinging from the nearest tree without compunction."

Their arms were all tightly bound behind them.

"Would you touch a servant of the Lord?" the leading priest said.

"Your clothing is that of a servant of the Lord," Philip replied; "but as I find you engaged upon the work of the devil, I can only suppose that you have stolen the clothes. Four of you take these priests behind you," he said to his men; "tie them tightly with their backs to yours, that will leave you the use of your arms. Pierre, do you ride beside the other prisoners, and if you see any attempt at escape shoot them at once. Quick, my lads; there may be more of this work going on ahead."

He then gave similar instructions for the carriage of the Huguenot goods as he had at the preceding places. At the next village they were in time to prevent the work of massacre from commencing. A party of horsemen and some priests, followed by a mob, were just entering it as they rode up. The horsemen were overthrown by their onset, the mob sent flying back towards the town, the Huguenots charging almost up to the gates. The horsemen and priests were made prisoners as before, and when the rest of the band returned from their pursuit they again rode on. They had now made half a circuit of Niort, and presently saw François and his party galloping towards them.

"I had begun to be afraid that something had happened," François said as he rode up. "I waited a quarter of an hour and then rode on, as we agreed. Well, I see you have got a good batch of prisoners."

"We have lost no time," Philip said. "We have been through five villages. At one we were just in time, for they had begun the work of massacre before we got up; at another we met them as they arrived; but at the other three, although the villagers were prepared for the work, the townsmen had not arrived."

"There were only three villages on my side," François said. "At the first they had nearly finished their work before we arrived. That was where we saw the smoke rising. But we paid them for it handsomely, for we must have cut down more than a hundred of the scoundrels. At one of the others the Huguenots were defending themselves well, and there too we gave the townspeople a lesson. At the third all was quiet. We have taken six or eight burghers, as many gentlemen, and ten priests."

Philip told him the orders he had given for the Catholics to place their horses and carts at the disposal of their Huguenot fellow-villagers.

"I wish I had thought of it," François said. "But it is not too late; I will ride back with my party and see all our friends well on their way from the villages. I left four men at each tokeep the Catholics from interfering. If you will go back the way you came we will meet again on the main road on the other side of the town. I don't think there is any fear of their making a sortie. Our strength is sure to be greatly exaggerated, and the fugitives pouring in from each side of the town with their tales will spread a report that Condé himself, with a whole host of horsemen, is around them."

Philip found all going on well as he returned through the villages, the scare being so great that none thought of disobeying the orders, and in a couple of hours he rejoined François, having seen the whole of the Huguenot population of the villages well on their way.

"Now, Philip, we will go and summon the town. First of all, though, let us get a complete list of the names of our prisoners."

These were all written down, and then the two leaders with their eight men-at-arms rode towards the gates of Niort, a white flag being raised on one of the lances.

CHAPTER IX

AN IMPORTANT MISSION

WE have made an excellent haul," François said, as, while awaiting the answer to their signal, they looked down the list of names. "Among the gentlemen are several connected with some of the most important Catholic families of Poitou. The more shame to them for being engaged in so rascally a business; though when the court and the king, Lorraine and the Guises, set the example of perscution, one can scarcely blame the lesser gentry, who wish to ingratiate themselves with the authorities, for doing the same. Of the citizens we have got one of the magistrates, and four or five other prominent men, whom I know by reputation as having been among the foremost to stir up the people against the Huguenots. These fellows I could hang up with pleasure, and would do so were it not that we need them to exchange for our friends.

"Then we have got thirty priests. The names of two of them I know as popular preachers, who, after the last peace was made, denounced the king and his mother as Ahab and Jezebel for making terms with us. They, too, were it not for their sacred office, I could string up without having any weight upon my conscience. Ah! there is the white flag, let us ride forward."

The gates remained closed, and they rode up to within a hundred yards of them. In a few minutes several persons made their appearance on the wall over the gateway, and they then advanced to within twenty paces of the gate.

Then one from the wall said: "I am John De Luc, royal

commissioner of this town, this is the reverend bishop of the town, this is the *maire*, and these the magistrates; to whom am I speaking?"

"I am the Count François de Laville," François replied; "and I now represent the gentlemen who have come hither, with a large body of troops, to protect those of our faith from persecution and massacre. We arrived too late to save all, but not to punish, as the ruffians of your town have learned to their cost. Some two or three hundred of them came out to slay and have been slain. The following persons are in our hands," and he read the list of the prisoners. "I now give you notice that, unless within one hour of the present time, all those of the reformed faith whom you have thrown into prison, together with all others who wish to leave, are permitted to issue from this gate free and unharmed, and carrying with them what portion of their worldly goods they may wish to take, I will hang up the whole of the prisoners in my hands— gentlemen, citizens, and priests—to the trees of that wood a quarter of a mile away. Let it be understood that the terms are to be carried out to the letter. Proclamation must be made through your streets that all of the reformed faith are free to depart, taking with them their wives and families, and such valuables and goods as they may choose. I shall question those who come out, and if I find that any have been detained against their will, or if the news has not been so proclaimed that all can take advantage of it, I shall not release the prisoners. If these terms are not accepted, my officers will first hang the prisoners, then they will ravage the country round, and will then proceed to besiege the city, and when they capture it, take vengeance for the innocent blood that has been shed within its walls. You best know what is the strength of your garrison, and whether you can successfully resist an assault by the troops of the Admiral. I will give you ten minutes to deliberate. Unless by the end of that time you accept the conditions offered, it will go hard with those in our hands."

"Impious youth," the bishop, who was in full pontificals, said, "you would never dare to hang priests."

"As the gentlemen of your party have thought it no sin to put to death scores of our ministers, and as I found these most holy persons hounding on a mob to massacre, I shall certainly feel no compunction whatever in executing the orders of my leader, to hang them with the other malefactors," François replied; "and methinks that you will benefit these holy men more by advising those with you to agree to the conditions which I offer than by wasting your breath in controversy with me."

There was a hasty conversation between those on the wall, and it was not long before they came to an agreement. De Luc feared that he should incur the enmity of several powerful families if he left their relatives for execution. The citizens were equally anxious to save their fellows, and were, moreover, scared at the threat of the neighbourhood being laid waste and the town attacked by this unknown force that had appeared before it. They had heard vague rumours of the arrival of the Prince and Admiral with a large force at La Rochelle, but it might well be that he had turned aside on his journey at the news of the occurrences at Niort.

The bishop was equally anxious to rescue the priests, for he felt that he might be blamed for their death by his ecclesiastical superiors. Their consultation over, De Luc turned to the Count.

"Do you give me your solemn assurance and word as a noble of France that upon our performing our part of the condition the prisoners in your hands shall be restored unharmed?"

"I do," François replied. "I pledge my honour, that as soon as I find that the whole of those of our religion have left the town peaceably, the prisoners shall be permitted to return unharmed in any way."

"Then we accept the terms. All those of the reformed religion in the town, whether at present in prison or in their homes, who may desire to leave, will be permitted to pass. As soon as you retire the gate shall be opened."

François and his party fell back a quarter of a mile. In a short time people began to issue in twos and threes from the gate. Many bore heavy bundles on their backs, and were accompanied by women and children all similarly laden. A few had with them carts piled up with household goods. From the first who came François learned that the conditions had been carried out, the proclamation being made in every street at the sound of the trumpet that all who held the reformed religion were free to depart, and that they might take with them such goods as they could carry or take in carts.

At first it had been thought that this was but a trap to get the Huguenots to reveal themselves, but the reports of those who had returned discomfited to the town that there was a great Huguenot force outside, and that many people of consideration had been taken prisoners, gave them courage, and some of the leading citizens went round to every house where persons suspected of being Huguenots were living, to urge them to leave, telling them that a treaty had been made securing them their safety. Before the hour had passed more than five hundred men, women, and children had left the town. As all agreed that no impediment had been placed in their way, but that upon the contrary every person even suspected as having Huguenot leanings had been urged to go, François and Philip felt assured that at any rate all who wished to leave had had the opportunity of doing so. They waited ten minutes over the hour, and then seeing that no more came forth they ordered the prisoners to be unbound and allowed to depart for the city.

As the fugitives had come along they were told that the Prince of Condé with a strong force had entered La Rochelle, and were advised to make for that city, where they would find safety and welcome. Those, however, who preferred to go to Laville, were assured that they would be welcomed and cared for there until an opportunity arose for their being sent under escort to La Rochelle. The greater portion decided to make at once for the Huguenot city.

"I think, Philip, you had better take forty of the men to act as a rear-guard to these poor people till you are within sight of La Rochelle. The fellows whom we have let free will tell on their return to the town that we are but a small party, and it is possible they may send out parties in pursuit."

"I don't think it is likely; the townspeople have been too roughly handled to care about running any risks. They have no very large body of men-at-arms in the town. Still, if they do pursue, it will be by the road to La Rochelle, for that is the one they will think that most of the fugitives will take. Had we not better divide the troop equally, François?"

"No, I think not. They will imagine we shall all be going by that road, and that, moreover, some of the other gentlemen of our faith may be coming to meet us with their retainers. Twenty will be ample for me, do you take the rest."

Two hours later Philip saw a cloud of dust rising from the road in his rear. He hurried on with the fugitives in front of him until, half an hour later, they came to a bridge over a stream. This was only wide enough for four horsemen to cross abreast, and here he took up his station. In a few minutes a number of horsemen approached. They were riding without order or regularity, intent only on overtaking their prey. Seeing the disorder in which they came Philip advanced from the bridge, formed up his men in two lines, and then charged at full gallop. The men-at-arms tried to rein in their horses and form in order, but before they could do so the Huguenots burst down upon them. The horses of the Catholics, exhausted with the speed at which they had been ridden, were unable to withstand the shock, and they and their riders went down before it. A panic seized those in the rear, and turning quickly they fled in all directions, leaving some thirty of their number dead on the ground. Philip would not permit his followers to pursue.

"They outnumber us four times," he said, "and if we scatter they may turn and fall upon us. Our horses have done a long day's work, and deserve rest. We will halt here at the bridge. They are not likely to disturb us, but if they do we can make a stout resistance here. Do you ride on, Jacques, and tell the fugitives that they can press forward as far as they like, and then halt for the night. We will take care that they are not molested, and will ride on and overtake them in the morning."

The night passed quietly, and late the following evening the party were in sight of La Rochelle. Philip had intended to turn at this point, where all danger to the fugitives was over, and to start on his journey back. But the hour was late, and he would have found it difficult to obtain food and forage without pressing the horses. He therefore determined to pass the night at La Rochelle, as he could take the last news thence back to Laville.

The streets of the town presented a busy aspect; parties of Huguenot gentlemen and their retainers were constantly arriving, and fugitive villagers had come in from a wide extent of country.

Large numbers of men were working at the walls of the town; the harbour was full of small craft; lines of carts brought in provisions from the surrounding country, and large numbers of oxen, sheep, and goats were being driven in.

"As we shall start for Laville in the morning," Philip said to his men, "it is not worth while to trouble to get quarters; and, indeed, I should say from the appearance of the place that every house is already crowded from basement to roof. Therefore we will bivouac down by the shore, where I see there are many companies already bestowed."

As soon as they had picketed their horses a party were sent off to purchase provisions for the troop and forage for their horses, and when he had seen that the arrangements were complete, Philip told Pierre to follow him, and went up to the castle, where Condé and Coligny with their families were lodged.

He was greeted warmly by several of the gentlemen who had stopped at the chateau a few days before. The story of the fugitives from Niort had already spread through the town, and Philip was eagerly questioned about it. Just as he was about to tell the story, Condé and the Admiral came out from an inner room into the large ante-room where they were talking.

"Ah! here is the young Count's cousin, Monsieur Fletcher," the Admiral said; "now we shall hear about this affair of Niort, of which we have received half a dozen different versions in the last hour. Is the Count himself here?"

"No, sir; he returned to Laville, escorting the fugitives who went thither, while he sent me with the larger portion of the troop to protect the passage hither of the main body."

"But it was reported to me that the troop with which you entered was but forty strong. I hear you fought a battle on the way; did you lose many men there?"

"None, sir. Indeed I am glad to say, that beyond a few

trifling wounds the whole matter has been carried out without any loss to the party that rode from Laville."

"How strong were they altogether, monsieur?"

"Sixty, sir."

"Then where did you join the force that, as we hear, cut up the townspeople of Niort as they were massacring our people in the villages round, and afterwards obtained from the town the freedom of those who had been cast into prison, and permission for all Huguenots to leave the town?"

"There was no other force, sir; we had just the sixty men from Laville, commanded by my cousin François. When the news arrived of the doings at Niort there was no time to send round to gather our friends, so we mounted the men-at-arms at the chateau and rode with all speed, and were but just in time. Had we delayed another half hour to gather a larger force we should have been too late."

"Tell us all about it," the Prince said. "This seems to have been a gallant and well-managed affair, Admiral."

Philip related the whole circumstances of the affair; how the townspeople had been heavily punished and the chief men taken as hostages, and the peasants compelled to assist to convey the property of the Huguenots to Laville; also the subsequent negotiations and the escape of all the Huguenots from Niort, and how the troop under him had smartly repulsed, with the loss of over thirty men, the men-at-arms from the city.

"A gallant enterprise," the Prince said. "What think you, Admiral?"

"I think, indeed, that this young gentleman and his cousin, the young Count of Laville, have shown singular prudence and forethought, as well as courage. The matter could not have been better managed had it been planned by any of our oldest heads. That they should at the head of their little bodies of men-at-arms have dispersed the cowardly mob of Niort, is what we may believe that any brave gentleman would have done; but their device of taking the priests and the other leaders as hostages, their boldness in summoning the authorities of Niort under the threat of hanging the hostages and capturing the town, is indeed most excellent and commendable. I heard that the number of fugitives from Niort was nearly six hundred, and besides these there were, I suppose, those from the villages."

"About two hundred set out from the villages, sir."

"Eight hundred souls. You hear that, gentlemen; eight hundred souls have been rescued from torture and death by the bravery and prudence of these two young gentlemen, who are in years but youths. Let it be a lesson to us all of what can be done by men engaged in a good work, and placing their trust in God. There is not one of us but might have felt proud to have been the means of doing so great and good a work with so small a force, and to have saved eight hundred lives without the loss of a single one, to say nothing of the sharp lesson given to the city mobs that the work of massacre may sometimes recoil upon those who undertake it. Our good friend De la Noüe has more than once spoken very highly to the Prince and myself respecting the young Count and this young English gentleman, and they certainly have more than borne out his commendations."

"And more than that," the Prince put in, "I myself in no small degree owe my life to them; for when I was pinned down by my horse at St. Denis they were among the foremost of those who rushed to my rescue. Busy as I was I had time to mark well how stoutly and valiantly they fought. Moreover, Monsieur D'Arblay has spoken to me in the highest terms of both of them, but especially of Monsieur Fletcher, who, as he declared, saved his life and that of the Count de Laville by obtaining their release from the dungeons of Toulouse by some such device as that he has used at Niort. And now, gentlemen, supper is served. Let us go in at once; we must have already tried the patience of our good hosts, who are doing their best to entertain us right royally, and whom I hope to relieve of part of the burden in a very few days. Monsieur Fletcher, you shall sit between the Admiral and myself, for you have told us your story but briefly, and afterwards I would fain question you farther as to that affair at Toulouse."

The two nobles, indeed, inquired very minutely into all the incidents of the fight. By closely questioning him they learned that the idea of forcing the peasants to lend their horses and carts to convey the Huguenot villagers' goods to

Laville was his own, and occurred to him just as he was about to start from the first village he entered.

"The success of military operations," the Admiral said, "depends greatly upon details. It is one thing to lay out a general plan, another to think amid the bustle and excitement of action of the details, upon which success so largely depends; and your thought of making the men who were about to join in the slaughter of their fellow-villagers the means of conveying their goods and chattels to a place of safety is one that shows that your head is cool, and able to think and plan in moments when most men would be carried away by the excitement of the occasion. I am pleased with you, sir, and shall feel that if I have any matter on hand demanding discretion and prudence, as well as bravery, I can, in spite of your years, confidently intrust you with it. Are you thinking of returning to-morrow to Laville?"

"I was intending to do so, sir. It may be that the people of Niort may endeavour to revenge the stroke that we have dealt them, and the forty men with me are necessary for the defence of the chateau."

"I do not think there is any fear of an attack from Niort," the Admiral said. "They will know well enough that our people are flocking here from all parts, and will be thinking of defence rather than of attack, knowing that while we are almost within striking distance the royal army is not in a condition as yet to march from Paris. Where are you resting for the night?"

"My troops are down by the shore, sir. Seeing how full the town was I thought it was not worth while to look for quarters, and intended to sleep down there among them, in readiness for an early start."

"Then after supper I would that you go down to them and tell them not to be surprised if you do not join them till morning, then return hither for the night; it may be that we may want to speak to you again."

Late in the evening a page came to Philip, and saying that the Prince wished to speak with him, conducted him to a small apartment, where he found Condé and the Admiral.

"We have a mission with which we would intrust you, if you

are willing to undertake it," the Admiral said; "it is a dangerous one, and demands prudence and resource, as well as courage. It seems to the Prince and myself that you possess these qualities, and your youth may enable you to carry out the mission perhaps more easily than another would do. It is no less than to carry a letter from the Prince and myself to the Queen of Navarre. She is at present at Nérac. Agents of Catharine have been trying to persuade her to go with her son to Paris, but fortunately she discovered that there was a plot to seize her and the young Prince her son at the same time that we were to be entrapped in Burgundy. De Lossy, who was charged with the mission of seizing her at Tarbes, was fortunately taken ill, and she has made her way safely up to Nérac.

"All Guyenne swarms with her enemies. D'Escars and four thousand Catholics lie scattered along from Perigueux to Bordeaux, and other bands lie beween Perigueux and Tulle. If once past those dangers her course is barred at Angoulême, Cognac, and Saintes. I want her to know that I will meet her on the Charente. I do not say that I shall be able to take those three towns, but I will besiege them; and she will find me outside one of them if I cannot get inside. It is all important that she should know this, so that she may judge whither to direct her course, when once safely across the river Dronne and out of Guyenne.

"I dare not send a written despatch, for were it to fall into the hands of the Catholics they would at once strengthen the garrisons of the town on the Charente, and would keep so keen a watch in that direction that it would be impossible for the queen to pass. I will give you a ring, a gift from the queen herself, in token that you are my messenger, and that she can place every confidence in you. I will leave to you the choice of how you will proceed. You can take some of your men-at-arms with you, and try to make your way through with a sudden dash; but as the bridges and fords will be strongly watched, I think that it will be much wiser for you to go in disguise, either with or without a companion. Certainty is of more importance than speed. I found a communication here, sent by the queen before she started, to the authorities of the town, saying that she should try to make her way to them, and she knew that the Prince and myself would also come here if we found our personal safety menaced in Burgundy.

"She foresaw that her difficulties would be great, and requested that if we arrived here we would send her word as to our movements, in order that she might accommodate hers to them. I have chosen you for several reasons, one being, as I have told you, that I see you are quick at forming a judgment and cool in danger. The second is that you will not be known to any of the enemy whom you may meet on your way. Most of the Huguenots here come from the neighbouring provinces, and would almost certainly be recognized by Catholics from the same neighbourhood. Of course you understand that if suspicion should fall upon you of being a messenger from this place, you will have but a short shrift."

"I am quite ready to do my best, sir, to carry out your mission. Personally I would rather ride fast with half a dozen men-at-arms; but, doubtless, as you say, the other would be the surest way. I will take with me my servant, who is shrewd and full of resources, and, being a native of these parts, could pass as a countryman anywhere. My horses and my four men I will leave here until my return. The troop will of course start in the morning for Laville."

"We have another destination for them," the Prince said. "A messenger rode yesterday to Laville, to bid the young Count start the day after to-morrow with every man he can raise to join me before Niort, for which place I set out to-morrow at mid-day. Of course we had no idea that he had already come to blows with that city, but we resolved to make its capture our first enterprise, seeing that it blocks the principal road from Paris hither, and is indeed a natural outpost of La Rochelle. Niort taken, we shall push on and capture Parthenay, which still further blocks the road, and whose possession will keep a door open for our friends from Brittany, Normandy, and the north. When those places are secured and garrisoned, we can then set about clearing out the Catholics from the towns to the south."

"Very well, sir. Then I will give orders to them that they

are to accompany your force to-morrow, and join the Count before Niort."

"Here is a large map of the country you will have to traverse. You had best take it into the next room and study it carefully, especially the course and direction of the rivers and the points of crossing. It would be shorter, perhaps, if you could have gone by boat south to Arcachon and thence made your way to Nérac; but there are wide dunes to be crossed, and pine-forests to be travesed, where a stranger might well die of hunger and thirst; the people too are wild and savage, and look upon strangers with great suspicion, and would probably have no compunction in cutting your throat. Moreover, the Catholics have a flotilla at the mouth of the Gironde, and there would be difficulty and danger in passing.

"You will, of course, make all speed that you can. I shall presently see some of the council of the town, and if they tell me that a boat can take you down the coast as far as the Seudre, some ten miles north of the mouth of the Gironde, you will avoid the difficulty of crossing the Boutonne at St. Jean d'Angely, and the Charente at Saintes or Cognac. It would save you a quarter of your journey. I expect them shortly, so that by the time you have studied the map I shall be able to tell you more."

An hour later Philip was again summoned. To his surprise he found Maître Bertram with the Prince.

"Our good friend here tells me that he is already acquainted with you, Monsieur Fletcher. He will house you for to-night, and at daybreak put you on board a small coasting-vessel, which will carry you down to the mouth of the Seudre. He will also procure for you whatever disguises you may require for yourself and your attendant. He has relations with traders in many of the towns. Some of these are openly of our faith, others are time-servers, or are not yet sufficiently convinced to dare persecution and death for its sake. He will give you the names of some of these, and you may at a push be able to find shelter with them, obtain a guide, or receive other assistance. Here is the ring. Hide it carefully on the way, for were you searched a ring of this value would be considered a proof that you were ɔot what you

seemed. You quite understand my message. I pray the
queen to trust to no promises, but using all care to avoid
those who would stop her, to come north as speedily as possible before the toils close round her; and you will assure her
that she will find me on the Charente, and that I shall have
either taken Cognac or be occupied in besieging it."

"If I fail, sir, it shall be from no lack of prudence on my
part, and I hope to prove myself worthy of the high honour
that the Prince and yourself have done me in selecting me
for the mission."

"Farewell then," the Admiral said. "I trust that in ten
days' time I shall meet you at Cognac. I have arranged with
Maître Bertram, who will furnish you with the funds necessary for your expedition."

Philip bowed deeply to the two nobles, and retired with the
merchant. He had directed Pierre to remain among the
lackeys at the foot of the grand staircase, as he would be
required presently, and as he passed through he beckoned to
him to follow.

"You have seen my horses comfortably stabled, Pierre?"

"It was done an hour since, monsieur."

"And my four men understand that they are to remain here
in charge of them until I return?"

"Yes, sir. Their own horses are also bestowed here, and
mine."

"Very well. We sleep to-night at Maître Bertram's."

"I am right glad to hear it, sir; for truly this castle is full
from the top to the bottom, and I love not to sleep in a
crowd."

"You still have Pierre with you?" the merchant said.

"Yes; and he has turned out an excellent servant. It was
a fortunate day for me when I insisted on taking him in spite
of your warning. He is a merry varlet, and yet knows when
to joke and when to hold his peace. He is an excellent
forager,"—"Ah! that I warrant he is," Maître Bertram put
in,—"and can cook a dinner or a supper with any man in the
army. I would not part with him on any consideration."

"A fellow of that sort, Master Fletcher, is sure to turn out
either a rogue or a handy fellow. I am glad to hear that he

has proved the latter. Here we are at the house. At ordinary times we should all be abed and asleep at this hour, but the place is turned upside down since the Prince and the Admiral arrived; for every citizen has taken in as many men as his house will hold. I have four gentlemen and twenty of their retainers lodging here; but I will take you to my own den, where we can talk undisturbed, for there is much to say and to arrange as to this expedition of yours, in which there is more peril than I should like to encounter. However, that is your affair. You have undertaken it, and there is nought for me to do save to try and make it as successful as possible. You have already been studying the map, I hear, and know something of the route. I have a good map myself, and we will follow the way together upon it. It would be as well to see whether your rascal knows anything of the country. In some of his wanderings he may have gone south."

"I will question him," Philip said; and reopening the door of the room he told Pierre, whom he had bidden follow him upstairs, to enter. "I am going down into Gascony, Pierre; it matters not at present upon what venture. I am going to start to-morrow at daylight in a craft of Maître Bertram's, which will land me ten miles this side the mouth of the Gironde, by which, as you will see, I avoid having to cross the Charente, where the bridges are all in the hands of the Catholics. I am going in disguise, and I propose taking you with me."

"It is all one to me, sir. Where you go I am ready to follow you. I have been at Bordeaux, but no farther south. I don't know whether you think that three would be too many. Your men are all Gascons, and one or other of them might know the part of the country you wish to travel."

"I had not thought of it," Philip said; "but the idea is a good one. It would depend greatly upon our disguises."

"Do you travel as a man-at-arms, or as a countryman, or a pedlar, or maybe as a priest, sir?"

"Not as a priest, assuredly," Philip laughed. "I am too young for that."

"Too young to be in full orders, but not too young to be a

theological student: one going from a theological seminary at Bordeuax to be initiated at Perigueux, or further south to Agen."

Philip shook his head. "I should be found out by the first priest who questioned me."

"Then, sir, we might go with sacks of ware on our backs as travelling pedlars; or, on the other hand, we might be on our way to take service under the Catholic leaders. If so we might carry steel caps and swords, which methinks would suit you better than either a priest's cowl or a pedlar's pack. In that case there might well be three of us, or even four. Two of your men-at-arms would go as old soldiers, and you and I as young relations of theirs, anxious to turn our hands to soldiering. Once in Gascony their dialect would help us rarely, and our story should pass without difficulty; and even on the way it would not be without its use, for the story that they have been living near La Rochelle, but owing to the con-course of Huguenots could no longer stay there, and were therefore making south to see in the first place their friends at home and then to take service under some Catholic lord, would sound likely enough."

"I don't know that we can contrive a better scheme than that, Maître Bertram. What do you think?"

"It promises well," the trader agreed. "Do you know what part of Gascony these men come from, Pierre?"

"They come from near Dax."

"That matters little," Philip said, "seeing that it is only to the south of Guyenne that we are bound. Still, they will probably have traversed the province often, and in any case there should be no trouble in finding our way, seeing that Agen lies on the Garonne, and we shall only have to keep near the river all the way from the point where we are landed. Our great difficulty will be in crossing the Dordogne, the Dronne, and the Lot, all of which we •are likely to find guarded."

"If you can manage to cross the Garonne here, near Lan-gon," the merchant said, placing his finger on the map, "you would avoid the two last rivers, and by keeping west of Bazas you would be able to reach Nérac without difficulty. You have to cross somewhere, and it might be as easy there as at Agen."

"That is so," Philip agreed; "at any rate we will try there first. I don't know which of the men I had best take with me. They are all shrewd fellows, as Gascons generally are, so I don't know how to make my choice."

"I don't think there is much difference, sir," Pierre said. "I have seen enough of them to know at least that they are all honest fellows."

"I would let them decide the matter for themselves," Philip said. "Some might like to go, and some to stay behind. If I chose two the others might consider themselves slighted. Do you know where "they have bestowed themselves, Pierre?"

"Down in the stables with the horses, sir. I could pretty well put my hand on them in the dark."

"Well, go and fetch them hither, then. Say nothing about the business on which they are required."

In a quarter of an hour Pierre returned with the four men. Philip explained to them briefly that he wanted two of them to journey with him on a mission of some danger through Guyenne.

"I have sent for you all," he said, "in order that you might arrange among yourselves which two shall go; therefore do you settle the matter, and if you cannot agree then cast lots and leave it to fortune. Only, as you are two sets of brothers, these had best either go or stay together; therefore if you cast lots do it not singly, but two against two."

"We may as well do it at once, Monsieur Philip," Eustace said. "I know beforehand that we would all choose to follow you; therefore if you will put two papers into my steel cap, one with my name, and one with Jacques', Pierre shall draw. If he takes out the one with my name, then I and Henri will go with you; if he draws Jacques', then he and Roger shall go."

This was done, and Jacques and Roger won.

"You will have plenty to do while we are away," Philip said to Eustace. "There will be seven horses to look after, including my chargers."

"How long are you likely to be away, sir?"

"I may return in ten days, I may be away three weeks. Should any evil chance befall us you will take the horses over to Laville, and hand them over to my cousin, who will, I am sure, gladly take you and Henri into his service. As we leave here at daybreak, you, Jacques, and your brother Roger had better wrap yourselves up in your cloaks and lie down in the hall below. I would that we could in the morning procure clothes for you, older and more worn than those you have on. You are going as men who have formerly served, but have since been living in a village tilling the land, just as you were when you first joined me."

"Then we have the very clothes ready to hand," Jacques said. "When we joined you we left ours with a friend in the town to hold for us. There is no saying how long military service may last, and as our clothes were serviceable we laid them by. We can go round and get them the first thing in the morning, leaving these we wear in his care until we return."

"That will do well; but you must be up early, for it is important we should make our start as soon as possible."

"I also have my old clothes held in keeping for me by one who worked in the stable with me," Pierre said. "A man who is going to the war can always find others ready to take charge of whatever he may leave behind, knowing full well that the chances are that he will never return to claim them."

"That simplifies matters," Maître Bertram said. "There remains only your dress, Monsieur Philip; and I shall have no difficulty in getting from my own knaves a doublet, cloak, and other things to suit you. I have plenty of steel caps and swords in my warehouse."

"You had best leave your breast-pieces here," Philip said to the men; "the number of those who carry them is small, and it will be enough to have steel caps and swords. We are going to walk fast and far, and the less weight we carry the better."

PHILIP AND HIS FOLLOWERS EMBARKING.

CHAPTER X

THE QUEEN OF NAVARRE

THE sun had just risen, when Maître Bertram, accompanied by four men in the attire of peasants, went down to the port. Two of them wore steel caps, and had the appearance of discharged soldiers, the other two looked like fresh country-men, and wore the low caps in use by the peasantry on their heads, carrying steel caps slung by cords from their shoulder; all four had swords stuck into their leathern belts. Similar groups might have been seen in hundreds all over France, making their way to join the forces of the contending parties. The craft upon which the trader led them was a small one of four or five tons burden, manned by three men and a boy.

"You understand, Johan, if you meet with no interruption you will land your passengers at the mouth of the Seudre; but if you should come across any of the craft that have been hovering about the coast, and find that they are too fast for you, put them ashore wherever they may direct. If you are too hotly chased to escape after landing them, you had best also disembark and make your way back by land as best you can, leaving them to do what they will with the boat. As like as not they would cut your throats did they take you, and if not, would want to know whom you had landed and other matters. I do not want to lose the craft, which has done me good service in her time, and is a handy little coaster, but I would rather lose it than that you should fall into the hands of the Bordeaux boats and get into trouble. The fact that you made for shore to land passengers would be sufficient to show

163

that those passengers were of some importance.   Now good
luck to you, Master Philip; I trust to see you back here again
before long."

They kept straight out from La Rochelle to the Isle of
Oléron, and held along close to its shore, lest boats coming
out from the Charente might overhaul them.   From the
southern end of the island it was only a run of some eight
miles into the mouth of the Seudre.   A brisk wind had blown,
and they made the forty miles voyage in seven hours.   They
could see several white sails far to the south as they ran in,
but had met with nothing to disquiet them on the way.
They were rowed ashore in the little boat the craft carried,
and landed among some sand-hills, among which they at once
struck off and walked briskly for a mile inland, so as to avoid
any questionings from persons they might meet as to where
they had come from.   Jacques and his brother carried bags
slung over their shoulders, and in these was a store of food with
which the merchant had provided them, and two or three flasks
of good wine, so that they might make a day's journey at least
without having to stop to purchase food.

It was two o'clock when they landed, and they had therefore
some five hours of daylight, and before this had faded they
had passed Royan, situated on the Gironde.   They did not
approach the town, but keeping behind it came down upon
the road running along the shore three miles beyond it, and
walked along it until about ten o'clock, by which time all were
thoroughly tired with their unaccustomed exercise.   Leaving
the road, they found a sheltered spot among the sand-hills, ate
a hearty meal, and then lay down to sleep.   They were afoot
again at daylight.   The country was sparsely populated.   They
passed through a few small villages, but no place of any
importance, until, late in the afternoon, they approached
Blaye, after a long day's tramp.   As they thought that here
they might learn something of the movements of the large
body of Catholic troops Philip had heard of as guarding the
passages of the Dordogne, they determined to enter the town.
They passed through the gates half an hour before they were
closed, and entered a small cabaret.   Here, calling for some
bread and common wine, they sat down in a corner, and lis-

tened to the talk of the men who were drinking there. It was all about the movements of troops, and the scraps of news that had come in from all quarters.

"I don't know who they can be all arming against," one said. "The Queen of Navarre has no troops, and even if a few hundreds of Huguenots joined her, what could she do? As to Condé and the Admiral, they have been hunted all over France ever since they left Noyers. They say they hadn't fifty men with them. It seems to me they are making a great fuss about nothing."

"I have just heard a report," a man who had two or three minutes before entered the room, said, "to the effect that they arrived four days since at La Rochelle, with some five or six hundred men who joined them on the way."

An exclamation of surprise broke from his hearers.

"Then we shall have trouble," one exclaimed. "La Rochelle is a hard nut to crack in itself, and if the Prince and the Admiral have got in the Huguenots from all the country round will rally there, and may give a good deal of trouble after all. What can the Catholic lords have been about that they managed to let them slip through their hands in that way? They must have seen for some time that they were making for the one place where they would be safe, unless indeed they were making down for Navarre. That would account for the way in which all the bridges and fords across the rivers are being watched."

"I expect they are watching both ways," another said. "These Huguenots always seem to know what is going on, and it is likely enough, that while our people all thought that Condé was making for Germany, there was not a Huguenot throughout France who did not know he was coming west to La Rochelle, and if so, they will be moving in all directions to join him there, and that is why D'Escars has got such a force at all the bridges. I heard from a man who came in yesterday that the Lot is watched just as sharply from the Garonne through Cahors right on to Espalion, and he had heard that at Agen and along the Aveyron the troops hold the bridges and fords as if they expected an enemy. No doubt, as soon as they hear that Condé and his party are in La

Rochelle they will close round them and catch them in a trap. That will be as good as any other way, and save much trouble. It is a long chase to catch a pack of wolves scattered all over the country, but one can make short work of them all when you get them penned up in an inclosure."

Philip cast a warning glance at his companions, for he felt so inclined to retort himself that he feared they might give way to a similar impulse. Jacques and his brother, however, were munching their bread stolidly, while Pierre was looking at the speaker with a face so full of admiring assent to his remark that Philip had to struggle hard to repress a laugh.

"It must be owned," another of the group said, "that these wolves bite hard. I was in Paris last year with the Count de Caussac. Well, we laughed when we saw the three parties of white wolves ride out from St. Denis; but I tell you there was no laughing when they got among us. We were in the Constable's troop, and though, as far as I know, we were all pretty stout men-at-arms, and were four to one against them at least, we had little to boast of when the fight was over. At any rate, I got a mark of the wolves' teeth, which has put a stop to my hunting, as you see," and he held out his arm. "I left my right hand on the field of battle. It was in the fight round Condé. A young Huguenot—for he was smooth-faced, and but a youth—shred it off with a sweeping back-handed blow as if it had been a twig. So there is no more wolf-hunting for me; but even if I had my right hand back again I should not care for any more such rough sport as that."

Philip congratulated himself that he was sitting with his back to the speaker, for he remembered the incident well, and it was his arm that had struck the blow. His visor had been up, but as his face was shaded by the helmet and cheek-pieces, and the man could have obtained but a passing glance at him, he felt sure on reflection that he would not be recognized.

"Ah! well, we shall do better this time," the first speaker said. "We are better prepared than we were then, and except La Rochelle and four or five small towns, every place in France is in our hands. I expect the next news will be that the Prince and Coligny and the others have taken ship for England. Then when that pestilent Queen of Navarre and her boy are in our hands the whole thing will be over, and the last edict will be carried out, and each Huguenot will have the choice between the mass and the gallows. Well, I will have one more stoup of wine, and then I will be off, for we march at day-break."

"How many ride out with you?" the man who had lost his hand asked.

"A hundred. The town has voted the funds, and we march to join D'Escars to-morrow. I believe we are not going to Perigueux, but are to be stationed somewhere on the lower Dordogne to prevent any of the Huguenots from the south making their way towards La Rochelle."

The frequenters of the cabaret presently dropped off. Jacques, who acted as spokesman, had on entering asked the landlord if they could sleep there, and he said there was plenty of good hay in the loft over the stable. As his duties were now over, he came across to them.

"Which way are you going, lads?" he asked. "Are you bound like the others to join one of the lords on the Dor-dogne?"

"No," Jacques said, "we are bound for Agen. We come from near there."

"I thought your tongue had a smack of Gascon in it."

"Yes, we come from across the border. We are tired of hard work in the vineyards, and are going to take up with our own trade, for my comrade here and I served under De Brissac in Italy; we would rather enlist under our own lord than under a stranger."

"Yes, that I can understand," the landlord said; "but you will find it no easy work travelling at present, when every bridge and ford across the rivers is watched by armed men, and all who pass are questioned sharply as to their business."

"Well, if they won't let us pass," Jacques said carelessly, "we must join some leader here; though I should like to have had a few days at home first."

"Your best plan would have been to have gone by boat to Bordeaux. There has been a strong wind from the west for the last three days, and it would save you many a mile of weary tramping."

"That it would," Jacques said; "but could one get a passage?"

"There will be no difficulty about that.   There is not a day passes, now that the wind is fair, that three or four boats do not go off to Bordeaux with produce from the farms and vineyards.   Of course you wouldn't get up without paying; but I suppose you are not without something in your pockets. There is a cousin of mine, a farmer, who is starting in the morning, and has chartered a boat to carry his produce.   If I say a word to him I have no doubt he would give the four of you a passage for a crown."

"What do you say, comrades?" Jacques said.   "It would save us some thirty or forty miles walking, and perhaps some expense for ferrys, to say nought of trouble with the troops, who are apt enough moreover to search the pockets of those who pass."

"I think it would be a good plan," his brother replied; and the other two also assented.

"Very well then," the landlord said; "my cousin will be here in the morning, for he is going to leave two or three barrels of last year's vintage with me.   By the way, I daresay he will be easy with you as to the passage-money, if you agree to help him carry up his barrels to the magasins of the merchant he deals with, and aid him with his other goods.   It will save him from having to employ men there, and those porters of Bordeaux know how to charge pretty high for their services.   I will make you up a basket for your journey.   Shall I say a bottle of wine each and some bread, and a couple of dozen eggs, which I will get boiled hard for you?"

"That will do well, landlord," Jacques said, "and we thank you for having put us in the way of saving our legs to-morrow. What time do you think your cousin will be in?"

"He will have his carts at the gates by the time they open them.   He is not one to waste time; besides, every minute is of importance; for with this wind he may well hope to arrive in Bordeaux in time to get his cargo discharged by nightfall."

"That was a lucky stroke indeed," Philip said when they had gained the loft, and the landlord, having hung up a lantern, had left them alone.   "Half our difficulties will be over when we get to Bordeaux. I had began to fear, from what we heard of the watch they are keeping at the bridges, that we should have found it a very difficult matter crossing the rivers. Once out of Bordeaux the Ciron is the only stream we shall have to cross, and that is but a small river, and is not likely to be watched, for no one making his way from the south to La Rochelle would keep to the west of the Garonne."

They were downstairs by six, had a meal of bread and spiced wine, and soon after seven there was a rumble of carts outside, and two of them stopped at the cabaret. They were laden principally with barrels of wine; but in one the farmer's wife was sitting surrounded by baskets of eggs, fowls, and ducks, and several casks of butter. Three of the casks of wine were taken down and carried into the house. The landlord had a chat apart with his cousin, who then came forward to where they were sitting at a table.

"My cousin tells me you want to go to Bordeaux, and are willing to help load my boat, and to carry the barrels to the warehouse at Bordeaux in return for a passage. Well, I agree to the bargain; the warehouse is not very far from the wharf, but the men there charge an extortionate price."

"We will do your work," Jacques said.

"But how am to I know that when you land you will not slip away without fulfilling your share of the bargain?" the farmer asked. "You look honest fellows, but soldiers are not gentry to be always depended upon. I mean no offence, but business is business, you know."

Jacques put his hand in his pocket. "Here is a crown," he said. "I will hand it over to you as earnest; if we do not do your work, you can keep that to pay the hire of the men to carry your barrels."

"That is fair enough," the farmer said, pocketing the coin. "Now let us go without delay."

The landlord had already been paid for the supper of the night before, the lodging, and the contents of the basket, and without more words they set out with the cart to the river side. Here the boat was in waiting, and they at once set to work with the drivers of the two carts to transfer their contents to it. As they were as anxious as the farmer that no time should be lost, they worked hard, and in a quarter of an hour all was on board. They took their places in the bow, the farmer, his wife, and the two boatmen being separated from them by the pile of barrels. The sail was at once hoisted, and as the west wind was still blowing strongly Blaye was soon left behind.

"This is better than walking by a long way," Philip said. "We are out of practice, and my feet are tender from the tramp from the coast. It would have taken us two days to get to Bordeaux even if we had no trouble in crossing the Dordogne, and every hour is of importance. I hope we may get out of the city before the gates close, then we shall be able to push on all night."

They passed several islands on their way, and after four hours' run saw the walls and spires of Bourg, where the Dordogne unites with the Garonne to form the great estuary known as the Gironde. At three o'clock they were alongside the wharves of Bordeaux. They stowed away their steel caps and swords, and at once prepared to carry up the barrels.

"Do you make an excuse to move off, master," Pierre said; "we three will soon get these barrels into the store, and it is no fitting work for you."

"Honest work is fitting work, Pierre; and methinks that my shoulders are stronger than yours. I have had my sail, and I am going to pay for it by my share of the work."

The store was nearer than Philip had expected to find it. A wide road ran along by the river bank, and upon the other side of this was a line of low warehouses, all occupied by the wine merchants, who purchased the produce of their vineyards from the growers, and, after keeping it until it matured, supplied France and foreign countries with it. Several ships lay by the wharves. Some were bound for England, others for Holland; some were freighted for the northern ports of France, and some of smaller size for Paris itself. Several men came up to offer their services as soon as the boat was alongside; and these, when they saw that the owner of the wines had brought men with them who would transport the wine to the warehouses, indulged in some rough jeers before moving away. In the first place Philip and his companions, aided by the boatmen, carried the cargo ashore, while the farmer crossed the road to the merchant with whom he dealt. His store was not more than fifty yards from the place of landing, and as soon as he returned the work began. In an hour and a half the whole of the barrels were carried over. The farmer's wife had seen to the carriage of her portion of the cargo to the inn her husband frequented on these occasions. It was close to the market-place, and there she would, as soon as the market opened in the morning, dispose of them, and by nine o'clock they would be on board again. When the last barrel was carried into the store, the farmer handed Jacques the crown he had taken as pledge for the performance of the bargain.

"You are smart fellows," he said, "and nimble. The same number of these towns-fellows would have taken double the time that you have done, and I must have had six at least to have got the wine safely stored before nightfall."

"We are well contented with our bargain," Jacques said; "it is better to work hard for two hours than to walk for two days. So good-day to you, master, for we shall get on our way at once, and do not want to spend our money in the wine-shops here."

Possessing themselves of their steel caps and swords again, they made their way through the busy town to the south gates, through which a stream of peasants with carts, horses, and donkeys was passing out, having disposed of the produce they had brought in.

"Where are you bound to, you two with steel caps?" the officer at the gate asked.

Jacques and his brother paused, while Philip and Pierre, who had stowed their caps in the bundles they carried, went on without stopping, as it had previously been agreed that in case of one or more of his followers being stopped, Philip should continue his way, as it was urgent that he should not suffer anything to delay him in the delivery of his message. He waited, however, a quarter of a mile from the gates, and the two men then rejoined him.

"We had no difficulty, sir," Jacques said. "We said that we once had served and were going to do so again, having grown sick working in the vineyards, and that we had come up from Blaye with a cargo of wine and had taken our discharge, and were now bound for Agen to see our families before joining the force that the Viscount de Rouillac, under whom our father held a farm, would no doubt be putting in the field. That was sufficient, and he let us go on without further question, except that he said that we should have done better by going up to Saintes or Cognac and taking service with the force there, instead of making this long journey up to Agen."

They walked steadily on until, when it was nearly midnight, they arrived at a small village on the banks of the Ciron. As the inhabitants would have been in bed hours before, they made up their minds not to attempt to find a shelter there, but to cross by the bridge and sleep in the first clump of trees they came to. As they approached the bridge, however, they saw a fire burning in the centre of the road. Two men were sitting beside it, and several others lay round.

"Soldiers!" Philip said.   "It would not do to try to cross at this time of night. We will retire beyond the village and wait until morning."

They turned off into a vineyard as soon as they were outside the village and lay down among the vines that had some weeks before been cleared of their grapes.

"How far does this river run before it becomes fordable, Jacques?"

"I do not know, sir. There are hills run along in a line with the Garonne some ten or twelve miles back, and I should say that when we get there we shall certanly find points at which we might cross this stream."

"That would waste nearly a day, and time is too precious for that. We will go straight on in the morning. Our story has been good enough thus far, there is no reason why it should not carry us through."

Accordingly, as soon as the sun was up they entered the village and went into a cabaret and called for wine and bread.

"You are travelling early," the landlord said.

"Yes, we have a long tramp before us, so we thought we had better perform part of it before breakfast."

"These are busy times; folks are passing through one way

or the other all day. It is not for us innkeepers to grumble, but peace and quiet are all we want about here; these constant wars and troubles are our ruin. The growers are all afraid to send their wine to market, for many of these armed bands are no better than brigands, and think much more of robbing and plundering than they do of fighting. I suppose by your looks you are going to take service with some lord or other?"

Jacques repeated the usual tale.

"Well, well, every man to his liking," the landlord said; "but for my part I can't think what Frenchmen want to fly at each others' throats for. We have got thirty soldiers quartered in the village now, though what they are doing here is more than I can imagine. We shall be glad when they are gone, for they are a rough lot, and their leader gives himself as many airs as if he had conquered the place. I believe they belong to a force that is lying at Bazas, some five leagues away. One would think that the Queen of Navarre had got a big Huguenot army together and was marching north."

"I should not think she could raise an army," Philip said carelessly; "and if she is wise she will stop quietly down in Béarn."

"There is a rumour here," the landlord said, "that she is at Nérac, with only a small party of gentlemen, and that she is on her way to Paris to assure the king that she has no part in these troubles. I don't know whether that has anything to do with the troops, who, as I hear, are swarming all over the country. They say that there are fifteen hundred men at Agen."

"I am afraid we shall have trouble at this bridge," Philip said, as the landlord left them; "they seem to be a rough lot, and this truculent lieutenant may not be satisfied with a story that his betters would accept without question. We will ask our host if there is any place where the river can be forded without going too far up. We can all swim, and as the river is no great width we can make a shift to get across even if the ford is a bad one."

The landlord presently returned. Jacques put the question: "By your account of those fellows at the bridge, we might have trouble with them?"

"As like as not," the landlord said; "they worry and vex all who come past, insult quiet people, and have seized several who have happened to have no papers of domicile about them and sent them off to Bazas. They killed a man who resented their rough usage two days ago. There has been a talk in the village of sending a complaint of their conduct to the officer at Bazas; but perhaps he might do nothing, and if he didn't it would only make it the worse for us here."

"We don't want troubles," Jacques said, "and therefore if we could pass the river without having to make too wide a detour we would do so. Do you know of any fords?"

"Yes, there are two or three places where it can be crossed when the water is low, and as there has been no rain for some weeks past you will be able to cross now easily enough. There is one four miles higher up. You will see a clump of willow-trees on this side of the river, and there is a pile of stones some five feet high on the other. You enter the river close by the trees and then keep straight for the pile of stones, which is some fifty yards higher up, for the ford crosses the river at an angle."

"Well, we will take that way then," Jacques said; "it is better to lose an hour than to have trouble here."

An hour later the party arrived at the ford and crossed it without difficulty, the water being little above their waists. Some miles farther they saw ahead of them the towers of Bazas, and struck off from the road they were traversing to pass to the east of it. They presently came upon a wide road.

"This must be the road to Nérac," Philip said. "There are neither rivers nor places of any size to be passed now, the only danger is from bodies of horse watching the road."

"And if I mistake not, sir, there is one of them approaching now," Pierre said, pointing ahead. As he spoke the heads and shoulders of a body of horsemen were seen as they rode up from a dip the road made into a hollow, half a mile away. Philip glanced round. The country was flat, and it was too late to think of concealment.

"We will go quietly on," he said. "We must hope they will not interfere with us."

The troop consisted of some twenty men, two gentlemen

riding at their head, and as they came up they checked their horses.

"Whither come you, and where are you bound, my men?"

"We come from Bordeaux, sir, and we are bound for Agen," Jacques replied. "My comrade and I served under De Brissac when we were mere lads, and we have a fancy to try the old trade again; and our young cousins also want to try their metal."

"You are a Gascon, by your tongue?"

"That is so," Jacques said; "and it is for that reason we are going south. We would rather fight in a company of our own people than with strangers."

"Whom have you been serving at Bordeaux? I am from the city, and know most of those in and round it."

"We have not been working there, sir. We come fro m near Blaye, and made the journey thence to Bordeaux by a boat with our master, Jacques Blazin, who was bringing to Bordeaux a cargo of his wines."

"Why waste time, Raoul?" the other gentleman said impatiently. "What matter if they came from Bordeaux or Blaye, these are not of those whom we are here to arrest. Anyhow they are not Huguenot lords, but look what they say they are; but whether men-at-arms or peasants they concern us not. Maybe while we are questioning them a party of those we are in search of may be traversing some other road. Let us be riding forward."

He roughly pricked his horse with his spur, and the troop rode on.

"I think you are wrong to be so impatient, Louis," the one who had acted as interrogator said. "Anyone could see with half an eye that those two fellows were, as they said, old men-at-arms. There is a straightness and a stiffness about men who have been under the hands of the drill-sergeant there is no mistaking, and I could swear that fellow is a Gascon as he said. But I am not so sure as to one of the young fellows with them. I was about to question him when you broke in. He did not look to me like a young peasant, and I should not be at all surprised if he is some Huguenot gentleman making his way to Nérac with three of his followers."

"Well, if it was so, Raoul, he will not swell the queen's army to any dangerous extent. I am glad that you didn't ask him any questions, for if he declared himself a Huguenot, and to do them justice the Huguenots will never deny their faith, I suppose it would have been our duty to have fallen upon them and slaughtered them; and though I am willing enough to draw when numbers are nearly equal and it is a fair fight, I will take no part in the slaughter of men when we are twenty to one against them. Three or four men more or less at Nérac will make no difference. The Queen of Navarre has but some fifty men in all, and whenever the orders come to seize her and her son, it may be done easily enough whether she has fifty or a hundred with her. War is all well enough, Raoul, but the slaughtering of solitary men is not an occupation that suits me. I am a good Catholic, I hope, but I abhor these massacres of defenceless people only because they want to worship in their own way. I look to the pope as the head of my religion on earth, but why should I treat as a mortal enemy a man who does not recognize the pope's authority?"

"That is dangerous doctrine, Louis."

"Yes, but why should it be? You and I were both at the colloquy at Poissy, and we saw that the Cardinal of Lorraine and all the bishops failed totally to answer the arguments of the Huguenot minister Beza. The matter was utterly beyond me, and had Beza argued ten times as strongly as he did it would in no way have shaken my faith; but I contend that if Lorraine himself and the bishops could not show this man to be wrong, there can be nothing in these people's interpretation of Scripture that can be so terrible as to deserve death. If they become dangerous to the state, I am ready to fight against them as against any other enemies of France, but I can see nothing that can excuse the persecutions and massacres. And if these men be enemies of France, of which as yet no proof has been shown, it is because they have been driven to it by persecution."

"Louis, my cousin," the other said, "it is dangerous, indeed, in these days to form an opinion. You must remember our greatest statesman, L'Hopital, has fallen into some disgrace, and has been deprived of rank and dignity, because he has been an advocate of toleration."

"I know that, Raoul; but I also know there are numbers of our nobles and gentlemen, who, although staunch Catholics, are sickened at seeing the king acting as the tool of Philip of Spain and the pope, and who shudder as I do at beholding France stained with blood from end to end simply because people choose to worship God in their own way. You must remember that these people are not the ignorant scum of our towns, but that among them are a large number of our best and wisest heads. I shall fight no less staunchly when fighting has to be done because I am convinced that it is all wrong. If they are in arms against the king, I must be in arms for him; but I hope none the less that when arms are laid down there will be a cessation of persecution, at anyrate a cessation of massacre. It is bringing disgrace on us in the eyes of all Europe, and I trust that there may be a league made among us to withstand the Guises, and to insist that there shall be in France no repetition of the atrocities by which Philip of Spain and the Duke of Alva are trying to stamp out the reformed religion in the Netherlands."

"Well, I hope at anyrate, Louis," his cousin said impatiently, "that you will keep these opinions to yourself, for assuredly they will bring you into disgrace, and may even cost you your possessions and your head if they are uttered in the presence of any friend of the Guises."

CHAPTER XI

JEANNE OF NAVARRE

"IT is lucky," Philip said to Jacques as they proceeded on their way after the troop had ridden on, "that he did not think of asking us if we were Huguenots."

"I was expecting it myself, sir," Jacques said; "and I was just turning it over in my conscience how I could answer."

"There could be but one answer, Jacques, though no doubt it would have cost us our lives."

"I should not deny my faith, even to save my life, sir, if the question were put to me, Are you a Huguenot? But I think that when four lives are at stake it is lawful to take any opening there may be to get out of it."

"But how would there have been an opening, Jacques?"

"Well, sir, you see, if he had asked, 'Are you Huguenots?' I think I could have said 'No' with a clear conscience, seeing that you are an Englishman; your religion may be like ours but you are not a Huguenot, and although Pierre does not seem to me to have quite made up his mind as to what he is, assuredly I should not call him a Huguenot. So you see, sir, that as only two out of the four are Huguenots, there would have been no lie to my saying 'no' to that question. But if he had said 'Are you Catholics?' I must have answered 'No,' seeing that none of us go to mass."

"It is a nice question," Philip said; "but seeing that the Catholics never keep their oaths and their promises to what they call heretics, I think that one would be justified, not in telling a lie, for nothing can justify that, but in availing one's self of a loophole such as one would scorn to use to others. I should be sorry to have the question asked me, though seeing I am not myself a Huguenot, although I am fighting with them, I think that I could reply 'no,' especially as it is not a question of my own life only, but one involving the whole cause of the Huguenots. If I were in your place I don't know that I should do so; but as you say that you could do it without your conscience pricking you, I certainly should not put pressure upon you to say yes. However, I hope you may never be asked the question, and that we shall meet with no more interruptions until we get to Nérac. There can be little doubt that at present the Catholics have received no orders to seize the queen and her son at Nérac, although they have orders to prevent her at all costs from going forward to Paris except under escort, and are keeping a sharp look-out to prevent her from being joined by parties of Huguenots who would render her force formidable. I should hope that by this time we are past the last of their bands. Those we met just now doubtless belonged to the force gathered in Bazas, and it is in the direction of the north rather than the west that the Catholics are most vigilant. If she succeeds in making her way through them, it will be well-nigh a miracle. Now that we are well past Bazas we will leave the road and make our way across the fields, for it is upon the roads that any watch there may be will be set."

It was a long day's journey, and at eight o'clock in the evening they lay down in a wood ten miles from Nérac, having walked fully fifty miles since crossing the river Ciron.

"I am very glad, Monsieur Philip, that we were not here four hours earlier."

"Why, Pierre?"

"Because, sir, in that case you would have insisted on pushing on to Nérac so as to enter it before the gate is closed, and in that case I doubt whether with the best will I could have got that far, and I am sure that Jacques and Roger could not have done so."

"No, indeed," Jacques said, "I have done my last inch. For the last four hours I felt as if walking upon hot irons, so sore are my feet; and indeed I could not have travelled at all if I had not taken your advice and gone barefoot."

They had bought some wine and bread in a little village through which they had passed, and as soon as they had finished their supper they lay down to sleep. They were up next morning long before daybreak, and were at the gates of Nérac before they opened. A group of countrymen were gathered there, and as soon as the drawbridge was lowered they entered the town with them. They observed that there were sentries all round the walls, and that a keen watch was kept. As Philip was aware, the majority of the inhabitants there were Huguenots, and the governor was a nobleman of Béarn; and it was doubtless for this reason that the Queen of Navarre had halted here, as Nérac was a strong town, and not to be taken without a regular siege.

They had no difficulty in ascertaining where the queen was lodged. Early as it was, several Huguenot gentlemen, armed to the teeth, were gathered round the door. Philip, leaving his companions behind him, went up to the group, and addressing one of them said:

"I am the bearer of a message for the queen; it is important. May I pray you, sir, to cause this ring to be conveyed to her. It is a token that she will recognize."

The gentleman glanced at the ring.

"She may well do that," he said, "seeing that it bears her own cognizance. The queen is already up, and I will cause it to be sent in to her at once."

Two minutes later another gentleman came out.

"Her majesty will at once see the messenger who has brought the ring," he said, and Philip at once followed him into the house. He was conducted to a room, where a lady was sitting, whom he recognized by the descriptions he had read of her as the Queen of Navarre. Beside her stood a lad of fifteen.

"You come from the Admiral?" she said. "Have you despatches for me?"

"I have a paper sewn up in my boot, your majesty, but it was read over to me several times in case either water or wear should render it illegible."

"He has reached La Rochelle safely, as I heard three days since," the queen said, "with but a small following?"

"He and the Prince had over five hundred with them when they rode in, your majesty, and parties were arriving hourly to swell his force. On the day I left he was going out to attack Niort, and that captured he was going to move south. That was the message I was charged to deliver. You will find him either in Cognac or in front of that town."

"That is good news, indeed," the queen said, "for I should have had to make a wide detour to pass round the Charente, all the towns and bridges being held by our enemies. It will be difficult enough to cross the intervening rivers. Indeed as the news that I had started hence would arrive long before I did myself, it would be hopeless-to elude their vigilance, and I should have had to make a long bend to the east, and might well have been cut off before I could reach him. And who are you, sir, that the Admiral should think fit to intrust so important a message to you?"

"I am English born, madam, and my name is Philip Fletcher. My mother was French, being the daughter of the Count de Moulins, and she sent me over to reside with her sister the Countess of Laville, in order that I might fight for the cause of the religion by the side of my cousin François. I rode with him through the last campaign in the train of ·François de la Noüe, and having had the good fortune to attract the notice of the Prince of Condé and the Admiral, they selected me to bear this message to you, thinking that, being but a lad, I should better escape suspicion and question than a French gentleman would do, especially as he would risk being recognized, while my face would be altogether unknown. Now, if your majesty will permit me, I will open the lining of my shoe. You will find, however, that the despatch contains but a few words. At first the Admiral thought only to give me a message, but he afterwards wrote what he had said, in order that should any evil befall me by the way, one of the three men who accompanied me should take my shoe and bring it to your majesty."

By this time he had slit open the lining of his shoe with his knife, and handed the little piece of paper to the queen. It contained only the words,

"*All goes well. Am hoping to see you. You will find me in or near Cognac.*"

There was no signature.

"You have done good service to the cause, Monsieur Fletcher," the queen said. "How did you manage to pass south, for I hear that every bridge and ford is guarded by the Catholics?"

Philip gave a brief account of his journey.

"You have acted prudently and well, young sir, and fully justified the Admiral's confidence in your prudence. What are your orders now?"

"They are simply to accompany your majesty on your way north, if it be your pleasure to permit me to ride in your train."

"I shall do that right willingly, sir, and it will be a pleasure for my son to hear from your lips a full account of your journey hither, and something of your native land, in which it may be that he will be some day compelled to take refuge."

"You shall ride by my side, Monsieur Philip," the young Prince said. "You look as if you could laugh and joke. These Huguenot lords are brave and faithful, but they have ever serious faces."

"Hush, Henri! it is not fitting to speak so. They are brave and good men."

"They may be that, mother, but they weary me dreadfully; and I am sure it would be much more cheerful having this English gentleman as my companion."

The young Prince was tall for his age, active and sinewy. His mother had brought him up as if he had been a peasant boy. As a child he had run about barefoot, and as he grew had spent much of his time among the mountains, sometimes with shepherds, sometimes engaged in the chase. Jeanne herself had a horror of the corruption of the French court, and strove to make her son hardy and robust, with simple tastes and appetites, and preferring exercise, hard work, and hunter's food to the life of the town. He had practised constantly in arms, and his mother regretted nothing so much as the fact that, next to the king and his brothers, he stood in succession to the French throne, and would have been far happier that he should rule some day over the simple and hardy people of Navarre.

"The first thing to do, Monsieur Fletcher," the queen said, "is to obtain more suitable garments for yourself and your followers. This my chamberlain shall see about without delay. I will then present you to the gentlemen who accompany me. They are but a small party, but we have received promises from many others, who will join us on our way. I may tell you it is already arranged that I shall set forward this evening. Monsieur D'Escars has, I hear, some four thousand gentlemen under arms; but these are widely scattered, and I hope to have a sufficient force to overcome them at any point we may make for. Some friends have secretly collected two or three boats near Tonneins, where there is but a small part of the Catholics assembled. Once past the Garonne we shall feel safe for a time."

"Would it please you that I should ride on first to Tonneins, your majesty, and ascertain if the garrison there are not alert, and have no suspicion that you are about to cross so close to them? Being a stranger here I could pass unsuspected, while were any of the gentlemen with you seen near Tonneins it would create suspicion that you yourself were about to cross in the neighbourhood."

"I thank you for that offer," the queen said, "and will speak to you about it later on."

As Philip had been furnished with money he did not trouble the queen's chamberlain, but at once purchased clothes for himself and his three followers, together with breast and back piece for Jacques and Roger. On his return to the queen after an hour's absence, he was informed that Prince Henri had made inquiries for him, and was shown into a room where the young Prince was sitting down to his breakfast, the queen being engaged in business with some of her councillors.

"That is right, Monsieur Fletcher; I have been waiting breakfast for you for half an hour. Come, sit you down with me. I warrant you have been too busy since you arrived at Nérac to think of a meal."

"I don't think, Prince," Philip began, "that it would be seemly that I—"

"Nonsense," the Prince interrupted, "we are not at the court of France, thank goodness, and we have no ceremony at

Béarn.   Besides, a simple gentleman may dine with the king any day.   So sit down without any more delay, and let me hear all your adventures."

Philip still hesitated, and the Prince said:

"I told my mother that I was going to have you to breakfast with me, and I believe she was well satisfied that I should for a time be out of her way."

This removed any doubt from Philip's mind, and he at once sat down with the Prince and ate a hearty meal, after which he chatted with him for an hour, telling him about the journey from La Rochelle, the rescue of the Huguenots near Niort, and some of the adventures in the last war.

"And you were with my cousin Condé and the Admiral in the battle of St. Denis.   What luck you have had, Monsieur Fletcher; I hope the day will come when I too shall take a part in war and be a great leader like the Admiral, but I would rather that it was against Spaniards or others than against Frenchmen."

The door opened and the queen entered.   Philip rose hastily, but she motioned him to be seated.   "No ceremony, I beg of you, Master Philip.   I am glad to find you here with my son. I have spoken to some of my friends of your offer to go to Tonneins, but they think not well of it.   It is a small place, and a stranger would be sure to be questioned, but it was agreed that if you would ride through Agen you might do us great service.   Five leagues from Tonneins, Fontarailles, the seneschal of Armagnac, will be waiting for me in the morning with a troop of horse and a regiment of infantry.   If the governor of Agen has news of his coming he may send out a force to attack him, or should he not feel strong enough for that, he may at least think that I am intending to join the seneschal, and in that case he may send out troops to bar the roads leading thither from the river.   As many will be passing through Agen on their way to join D'Escars, the passage of a gentleman and two men-at-arms will excite no attention, and if you put up for a short time at an inn you may be able to gather whether there has been any movement of the troops, or whether there is any talk of the departure of any this evening. Should all be quiet you can join me on the road, or ride direct to the village of Villeneuve d'Agenois, where the seneschal will arrive some time to-night. If you should hear of any movements of troops ride down on the other side of the river till within two miles of Tonneins, then, if you place your men at intervals of three or four hundred yards apart, you will be sure to see us cross, and can give us warning of danger, and such indications as you may gather as to the points where the troops are likely to be posted. We shall cross about midnight."

"I will gladly undertake the mission," Philip said. "I will go out and procure some horses at once."

"That is unnecessary," the queen said; "we have brought several spare horses with us, and I have already ordered four to be saddled for you. You have no armour, I see."

"I would rather ride without it, your majesty, especially on such a mission as the present; besides, if in full armour I might well be accosted and asked to whose party I belong, while riding in as I am unarmed, save for my sword, I should have the air of a gentleman of the neighbourhood, who had merely ridden in on business or to learn the latest news."

The queen smiled approvingly.

"You see, Henri, this gentleman, although about to undertake a dangerous business, does not proceed rashly or hastily, but thinks coolly as to the most prudent course to pursue. You will understand, Monsieur Fletcher, that several of the gentlemen with me have volunteered for this duty, and that we have accepted your offer solely because they could scarcely enter Agen without meeting some who know them, while you, being a stranger, do not run this risk."

"Moreover, madam, I have another advantage. Were any of them questioned, and asked directly, Are you a Huguenot? they could not but answer yes; whereas were that question put to me I could reply no, seeing that I am an English Protestant, and in no way, save in my sympathies, a Huguenot."

"That is an advantage, certainly; but it may be the question will be put, Are you a Catholic?"

"In that case, your majesty, I could only reply 'no;' but methinks the other question is the most likely one."

"I wish I were going to ride with Monsieur Fletcher, mother."

"That is impossible, Henri, for scarce a Gascon gentleman but has been down at one time or other to Béarn. Do not be anxious for adventures; they will come in time, my son, and plenty of them. Would that you could pass your life without one; but in these troubled times, and with France divided against itself, that is too much to hope. Should you by any chance, Monsieur Fletcher, fail to rejoin us at Villeneuve d'Agenois, you may overtake us farther on. But run no risk to do so. You know whither we are bound, and I trust that when we arrive there we may find you before us. I myself will retain the ring that you brought me, and will return it to the Admiral, but wear this in remembrance of one in whose service you risked your life," and she handed him a diamond ring, which he knew enough of gems to be aware was of considerable value.

"And take this dagger," the Prince said, taking a small and beautifully tempered weapon from his belt. "It is but a bodkin, but it is of famous steel. It was sent me by Philip of Spain at a time when he was trying to cajole my mother, and is of the best workmanship of Toledo."

Philip expressed his thanks for the gifts in suitable words, and then taking leave of the queen and Prince went down to the courtyard. Here he found Pierre and the two men-at-arms standing at the head of three powerful horses, while one of the queen's retainers held a very handsome animal in readiness for himself.

"Her majesty begs you to accept these horses, sir, as a slight token of her good-will." In five minutes the party had issued from Nérac, Pierre as usual keeping close behind Philip, and the two men-at-arms riding a few lengths behind.

"This is truly a change for the better, Monsieur Philip," Pierre said; "we entered Nérac as tillers of the soil, we ride out in knightly fashion."

"Yes, Pierre, it is good to be on the back of a fine horse again, and this one I am riding is worthy of a place beside Victor and Robin."

"Yes, he is as good as either of them, sir; I am not sure that he is not better. We, too, are well content with the Queen of Navarre's generosity, for her steward gave us, before we started, each a purse of twenty crowns, which has been a wonderful salve to our sore feet. I trust there will be no more occasion to use them for a time."

"I hope not. It was a long journey, but it was fortunate that we pushed on as we did, for had we been twelve hours later we should not have found the queen at Nérac."

"And why does not your honour stay to ride with her?" Pierre asked.

"I hope to join her again to-night. We are going through Agen, where I hope to gather such news of the movements of the Catholic troops as may be of use to her."

Agen was about fifteen miles distance from Nérac, and as there was no occasion for haste, and Philip did not wish the horses to have the appearance of being ridden fast, they took three hours in traversing the distance. When they neared the town he said to Pierre, "I shall not take you with me. If there should be trouble—though I do not see how this can well come about—four men could do no more than one. There-fore, Pierre, do you follow me no nearer than is sufficient to keep me in sight, the other two will follow you at an equal distance, together or separately. Should any accident befall me you are on no account to ride up or to meddle in the busi-ness. I have told you what my instructions are, and it will be your duty to carry them out if I am taken. You will put up your horse, and mingling with the soldiers and townspeople find out if there is any movement in the wind, or whether any troops have already gone forward. Jacques and Roger will do the same, and you will meet and exchange news. If you find that anything has been done, or is going to be done, towards putting more guards on the river, or despatching a force that might interfere with the passage of the queen from Tonneins to Villeneuve d'Agenois, Roger and Jacques will ride to the point where I told you the crossing is to be made, and will warn the queen of the danger. I leave you free to ride with them, or to stay in the town till you learn what has happened to me. If you should find that there is no movement of troops, you and the others will be free either to ride to Pontier or to make your way back to Cognac, and to join my cousin and give him news of what has happened to me. If I am only held as a prisoner the Admiral will doubtless exchange a Catholic gentleman for me; he is sure to take many prisoners at the capture of the towns."

He then called the two men-at-arms up, and repeated the instructions relating to them.

· "But may we not strike in should you get into trouble, master? Roger and I would far rather share whatever may befall you."

"No, Jacques, it would be worse in every way; force could be of no avail, and it would lessen my chance of escape were you beside me. Single-handed I might get through and trust to the speed of my horse, if taken I might plan some mode of escape. In either case it would hamper me were you there. Above all it is important that my mission should be fulfilled, therefore my commands on that head are strict. I do not apprehend trouble in any way; but if it should occur you will at once turn your horses down the first street you come to, so that you may in no way be connected with me. Pierre will of course turn first. You will follow him, see where he stables his horse, then go on to some other cabaret, and having put up your horses go back to the place where he has stopped, wait till he joins you outside, then arrange for the hour at which you are to meet again, and then go off in different directions to gather the news of which we are in search. Take no further thought about me at all; give your whole minds to the safety of the queen. Upon that depends greatly the issue of this war. Were she and her son to fall into the hands of the Catholics, it would be a fatal blow to the cause."

So saying, he rode on again at the head of the party. When within a quarter of a mile of the town he again called Pierre up to him.

"Pierre, do you take this ring and dagger. Should I be taken I shall assuredly be searched to see whether I am the bearer of despatches. I should grieve to lose these gifts as much as I should to fall into the hands of the Catholics. Keep them for me until you learn that there is no chance of my ever returning to claim them, and then give them to my cousin, and beg him in my name to return the ring to the Queen of Navarre, and the dagger to the young Prince."

"I like not all these provisions," Pierre said to himself. "Hitherto the master has never, since I first knew him, given any commands to me as to what was to be done in case he were captured or killed. It seems to me that the danger here is as nothing to that he has often run before, and yet he must have some sort of foreboding of evil. If I were not a Huguenot, I would vow a score of pounds of candles to be burnt at the shrine of the Holy Virgin if the master gets safe out of yonder town."

Philip rode on across the bridge and entered the gates without question. Up to this time his followers had kept close behind him, but now, in accordance with his instructions, they dropped behind. He continued his way to the principal square, rode up to an inn, entered the courtyard, and gave his horse to the stableman.

"Give it a feed," he said, "and put it in the stable. I shall not require it until the afternoon."

Then he went into the public room, called for food and wine, and sat down. The tables were well nigh full, for there were many strangers in the town. After a first glance at the newcomer none paid him any attention. Pierre and the two men had, in accordance with his instructions, passed the inn they had seen him enter, and put up at other places. There was a loud buzz of conversation, and Philip listened attentively to that between four gentlemen who had just sat down at the next table to him. Three of them had come in together, and the fourth joined them just as Philip's meal was brought to him.

"Well, have you heard any news at the governor's, Maignan?" one of them asked the last comer.

"Bad news. Condé and the Admiral are not letting the grass grow under their feet. They have captured not only Niort, as we heard yesterday, but Parthenay."

"*Peste!* that is bad news indeed. What a blunder it was to let them slip through their fingers, when they might have seized them with two or three hundred men in Burgundy."

"It seems to me that they are making just the same mistake here," another put in. "As Jeanne of Navarre is wellnigh as dangerous as the Admiral himself, why don't they seize her and her cub and carry them to Paris?"

"Because they hope that she will go willingly of her own accord, St. Amand. La Motte-Fenelon has been negotiating with her for the last fortnight on behalf of the court. It is clearly far better that she should go there of her own will than that she should be taken there a prisoner. Her doing so would seem a desertion of the Huguenot cause, and would be a tremendous blow to them. On the other hand, if she were taken there as a prisoner, it would drive many a Huguenot to take up arms who is now content to rest quiet. And moreover, the Protestant princes of Germany and Elizabeth of England would protest; for whatever the court may say of the Admiral, they can hardly affirm that Jeanne of Navarre is thinking of making war against Charles for any other reason than the defence of her faith. Besides, she can do no harm at Nérac, and we can always lay hands on her when we like. At anyrate there is no fear of her getting farther north, the rivers are too well guarded for that."

"I don't know," another said, "after the way in which Condé and the Admiral, though hampered with women and children, made their way across France, I should never be surprised at anything. You see there is not a place where she has not friends; these pestilent Huguenots are everywhere. She will get warning of danger, and guides across the country —peasants who know every by-road through the fields and every shallow in the rivers. It would be far better to make sure of her and her son by seizing them at Nérac."

"Besides," St. Amand said, "there are reports of movements of Huguenots all over Guyenne; and I heard a rumour last night that the Seneschal of Armagnac has got a considerable gathering together. These Huguenots seem to spring out of the ground. Six weeks ago no one believed that there was a corner of France where they could gather a hundred men together, and now they are everywhere in arms."

"I think," Maignan said, "that you need not be uneasy about the Queen of Navarre. I am not at liberty to say what I have heard, but I fancy that before many hours she will be on her way to Paris, willingly or unwillingly. As for the seneschal, he and the others will be hunted down as soon as this matter is settled. A day or two sooner or later will make no difference there, and until the queen is taken the troops will have to stay in their present stations. My only fear is that, seeing she can have no hope of making her way north, she will slip away back to Navarre again. Once there, she could not be taken without a deal of trouble. Whatever is to be done must be done promptly. Without direct orders from the court no step can be taken in so important a matter. But the orders may arrive any hour; and I think you will see that there will be no loss of time in executing them."

"And Nérac could not stand a long siege even if it were strongly garrisoned, and the handful of men she has got with her could not defend the walls for an hour. I hope she may not take the alarm too soon; for as you say, once back in Navarre it would be difficult indeed to take her. It is no joke hunting a bear among the mountains; and as her people are devoted to her, she could play hide-and-seek among the valleys and hills for weeks—ay, or months—before she could be laid hold of. It is well for our cause, Maignan, that she is not a man. She would be as formidable a foe as the Admiral himself. Huguenot as she is, one can't help respecting her. Her husband was a poor creature beside her; he was ready to swallow any bait offered him; while even if it would seat her son on the throne of France, she would not stir a hand's-breadth from what she thinks right."

Philip finished his meal and then went out into the square. The news was satisfactory. No order had yet arrived for the seizure of the queen; and though one was evidently looked for to arrive in the course of a few hours, it would then be too late to take any steps until nightfall at the earliest, and by nine o'clock the queen would have left Nérac. No movement was intended at present against the seneschal, nor did the idea that the queen might attempt to join him seem to be entertained. It was possible, however, that such a suspicion might have occurred to the governor, and that some troops might secretly be sent off later. He must try to learn something more.

Confident that he could not be suspected of being aught but what he appeared, a Catholic gentleman—for his garments were of much brighter hue than those affected by the Huguenots,—he strolled quietly along, pausing and looking into shops when he happened to pass near groups of soldiers or gentlemen talking together. So he spent two or three hours. No word had reached his ear indicating that any of the speakers were anticipating a sudden call to horse. He saw that Pierre was following him, keeping at some distance away, and pausing whenever he paused. He saw no signs of the other two men, and doubted not that they were, as he had ordered, spending their time in wine-shops frequented by the soldiers, and listening to their talk.

Feeling convinced that no orders had been given for the assembly of any body of troops, he sat down for a time at a small table in front of one of the principal wine-shops, and called for a bottle of the best wine, thinking that the fact that he was alone would be less noticeable so than if he continued to walk the streets. Presently a party of four or five gentlemen sat down at a table a short distance off. He did not particularly notice them at first, but presently glancing that way saw one of them looking hard at him; and a thrill of dismay ran through him as he recognized the gentleman addressed as Raoul, the leader of the party that had stopped him near Bazas. He had, however, presence of mind enough to look indifferently at him, and then to continue sipping his wine.

The possibility that this gentleman with his troop should have come to Agen had never entered his mind; and though the encounter was a most unfortunate one, he trusted that the complete change in his appearance would be sufficient to prevent recognition, although it was evident by the gaze fixed on him that the gentleman had an idea that his face was familiar. To move now would heighten suspicion if any existed, and he therefore sat quiet, watching the people who passed in front of him, and revolving in his mind the best course to be taken should Raoul address him. The latter had just spoken to his cousin, who was sitting next to him.

"Do you know that young gentleman, Louis?" he asked. "I seem to know his face well, and yet he does not know me, for he just now glanced at me without recognizing me. You know most of the gentry in this neighbourhood, do you know him?"

"No, I cannot say that I do, Raoul; though I too seem to have a recollection of his face. It is a sort of face one remembers too. I should think his family must belong to the north, for you do not often see men of that complexion about here. He looks very young, not above nineteen or twenty; but there is a look of earnestness and resolution about his face that would point to his being some years older."

Dismissing the matter from his mind Raoul joined in the conversation round him. Presently he grasped his cousin's arm.

"I know where we saw the face now, Louis; he was one of the four fellows we stopped two days since near Bazas."

"Impossible, Raoul! Those men were peasants, though two of them had served for a time in the army; the others—" and he stopped.

"You see it yourself, Louis. One of the others was a dark active man, the other was but a lad—a tall, well-built young fellow with fair complexion and gray eyes. I thought of it afterwards, and wondered where he got that skin and hair from. I put it down that it was a trace of English blood, of which there is a good deal still left in Guyenne and some of the other provinces they held long ago."

"I certainly see the likeness now you mention it, Raoul, but it can hardly be the same. This is a gentleman; he is certainly that, whoever he may be. How could a gentleman be masquerading about as a peasant?"

"That is what I am going to find out, Louis. He may have been a Huguenot making his way down to join the Queen of Navarre at Nérac; he may be one of her train there, who had gone out in disguise to reconnoitre the country and see what forces of ours were in the neighbourhood, and where posted. That may be his mission here, but this time he has chosen to come in his proper attire."

"That can hardly be his attire if he is one of Jeanne of Navarre's followers. He may have got a suit for the purpose, but assuredly the colours are too gay for a Huguenot in her train. For my part, I see nothing suspicious about

his appearance.   There, he is paying his reckoning and
going."

"And I am going after him," Raoul said rising.   "There
is something strange about the affair, and there may be some
plot.   Do you come with me, Louis.   Monsieur D'Estanges,
I have a little matter of business on hand, will you come with
me?"

CHAPTER XII

AN ESCAPE FROM PRISON

GLANCING half round as he turned away from the wine-shop, Philip saw Raoul and two of his companions rising. He walked off in a leisurely manner, and a few paces farther turned down a side street. He heard steps following him, and then a voice said:

"Hold, young sir; I would have a word with you." Philip turned with an expression of angry surprise.

"Are you addressing me, sir? I would have you know that I am not accustomed to be spoken to in that fashion, and that I bear an insult from no one."

Raoul laughed. "Are you equally particular, sir, when you are going about in peasant's clothes?"

"I am not good at riddles, sir," Philip said haughtily, "and can only suppose that your object is to pick a quarrel with me; though I am not conscious of having given you offence. However, that matters little. I suppose you are one of those gallants who air their bravery when they think they can do so with impunity. On the present occasion you may perchance find that you are mistaken. I am a stranger here, and know of no place where this matter can be settled, nor am I provided with a second; but I am quite content to place myself in the hands of one of these gentlemen, if they will act for me."

"I am sure, Raoul, there is some mistake," Louis began, putting his hand on his cousin's shoulder. But the other shook it off angrily. He was of a passionate and overbearing temper, and Philip's coolness, and the manner in which he had turned the tables upon him and challenged him to a duel, inflamed him to the utmost.

"Hands off, Louis," he said. "Do you think that I, Raoul de Fontaine, am to be crowed over by this youth? He has challenged me to fight, and fight he shall."

"You provoked him," Louis said firmly. "You gave him provocation such as no gentleman of honour could suffer. It was not for this that I came out with you, but because you said that you wished to unravel what may be a plot."

"I will cut it, which will be easier than unravelling it," Raoul replied. "It is shorter and easier work to finish the matter with a sword-thrust than to provide for his being swung at the end of a rope."

"We had best waste no time in empty braggadocio," Philip said coldly, "but proceed at once to some quiet spot where this matter can be settled undisturbed."

"I think the young gentleman is right," M. D'Estanges, a gentleman of the court, said gravely. "The matter has gone too far for anything else now, and I am bound to say that your adversary, of whose name I am ignorant, has borne himself in a manner to merit my esteem, and that as your cousin will of course act for you, I shall be happy to place my services at his disposal."

"Let us get beyond the gates," Raoul said abruptly, turning on his heel and retracing his steps up the lane to the main street.

"I thank you, sir, for offering to stand by one of whose very name you are ignorant," Philip said, as, accompanied by Monsieur D'Estanges, he followed the others. "It is, however, right that you should know it. It is Philip Fletcher; on my father's side I am English, on my mother's I am of noble French blood, being cousin to François de Laville, whose mother and mine were daughters of the Count de Moulins."

"Two distinguished families of Poitou," M. D'Estanges said courteously. "It needed not that to tell me that you were of good blood. I regret much that this encounter is going to take place. Monsieur Raoul de Fontaine was in the wrong in so rudely hailing you, and I cannot blame you for taking it up sharply; although, seeing your age and his, and that he is a good swordsman, it might have been more prudent to have overlooked his manner. Unless, indeed," and he smiled, "Monsieur Raoul was right, and that you are engaged on some weighty matter here, and preferred to run the risk of getting yourself killed rather than have it inquired into. The Countess of Laville and her son are both staunch Huguenots, and you may well be on business here that you would not care to have investigated. You have not asked my name, sir; it is Charles D'Estanges. I am a cousin of the Duc de Guise, and am naturally of the court party; but I can esteem a brave enemy, and regret to see one engaged in an encounter in which he must needs be overmatched."

"I am a fair swordsman, sir," Philip said, "though my arm may lack somewhat of the strength it will have a few years later. But had it been otherwise I should have still taken the course I have. I do not say your conjecture is a correct one, but at anyrate I would prefer the most unequal fight to being seized and questioned. One can but be killed once, and it were better that it should be by a thrust in the open air than a long imprisonment, ending perhaps with death at the stake."

Monsieur D'Estanges said no more. In spite of his relationship with the Guises he, like many other French Catholic nobles, disapproved of the persecutions of the Huguenots, and especially of the massacres perpetrated by the lower orders in the towns, men for whom he had the profoundest contempt. He felt sorry for his companion, whose youth and fearless demeanour moved him in his favour, and who, he doubted not, had come to Agen to confer with some of the Huguenots, who were to be found in every town.

Issuing from the gates, they went for a quarter of a mile along the road, and then Raoul led the way into a small wood. Here, without a word being spoken, Raoul and Philip threw aside their cloaks and doublets.

"Gentlemen," M. D'Estanges said, "surely this quarrel might be arranged without fighting. Monsieur de Fontaine addressed my principal, doubtless under a misapprehension, with some roughness, which was not unnaturally resented. If Monsieur de Fontaine will express his regret, which he certainly could do without loss of dignity, for the manner in which he spoke, my principal would, I am sure, gladly accept his apology."

"That is my opinion also," Louis de Fontaine said, "and I have already expressed it to my cousin."

"And I have already said that I will do nothing of the sort," Raoul said. "I am fighting not only in my own quarrel, but in that of the king, being well assured in my mind that this young man, whether he be, as he now appears, a gentleman of birth, or whether, as I saw him last, a peasant-boy, is engaged in some plot hostile to his majesty."

"Then there is nothing more to be said," Monsieur D'Estanges said gravely; "but before you begin I may tell you, Monsieur de Fontaine, that this gentleman belongs to a family no less noble than your own. He has confided to me his name and position, which I think it as well not to divulge. Now, Louis, we may as well stand aside. We have done our best to stop this quarrel, and to prevent what I cannot but consider a most unequal contest from taking place."

The last words were galling in the extreme to Raoul de Fontaine. Monsieur D'Estanges stood high at court, was a gentleman of unblemished reputation, and often appealed to on questions of honour, and this declaration that he considered the combat to be an unequal one was the more irritating since he was himself conscious of the fact. However, he could not recoil now, but with an angry expression of face drew his sword and stood on guard. Philip was no less ready. The easy attitude he assumed, with his weight for the most part on his left leg, differed so widely from the forward attitude then in fashion among French duellists, that Monsieur D'Estanges, convinced that he knew nothing of sword-play, shrugged his shoulders pityingly. The moment, however, that the swords grated against each other, and Philip put aside with a sharp turn of the wrist a lunge with which his opponent intended at once to finish the combat, the expression of his face changed.

"The lad did not speak boastfully when he said he was a fair swordsman," he muttered to himself. "He does not fight in our fashion, but at least he knows what he is about."

For some minutes the fight continued, Raoul's temper rising higher and higher as he found every attack baffled by a foe he had despised, and who refused to fall back even an inch, however hotly he pressed him. He had at first intended either to wound or disarm him, but he soon fought to kill. At last there was a fierce rally, ending by Philip parrying a home-thrust and returning it with lightning swiftness, running Raoul de Fontaine through the body with such force that the hilt of his sword struck against his chest, and he sank lifeless to the ground.

"By our Lady, young gentleman," M. D'Estanges exclaimed, "but you have done well! You said that you were a fair swordsman; truly you are of the highest class. Raoul's temper has led him into many a duel, and he has always wounded or killed his man. Who could have thought that he would receive his death-blow at the hands of a youth? But whom have we here? *Peste!* this is awkward." As he spoke, Count Darbois, the governor of Agen, with a body of troopers, rode up. He had ridden to within a mile or two of Nérac, and questioning persons from the town learned that everything was quiet there, and that no fresh body of Huguenots had arrived. He was on his way back when, hearing the clash of swords, he had ridden into the wood to inquire into its meaning.

"What is this?" he exclaimed. "Why, what is this, Monsieur de Fontaine? Your cousin, Count Raoul, dead!"

Louis, who was leaning over his cousin, looked up.

"Alas! I fear that it is so, Monsieur le Comte. My poor cousin has fallen in a duel."

"What a misfortune, and at such a moment! Is it not scandalous that at a time like this, when every gentleman's sword is needed in defence of our king and faith, they should indulge in private quarrels? And is it you, Monsieur D'Estanges, who has done his majesty this bad service?" for by this time Philip had resumed his doublet and cloak.

"No. I only stood as second to his opponent, who has behaved fairly and honourably in the matter, as I am sure Count Louis will testify."

"Your word is quite sufficient, Monsieur D'Estanges. And who is this gentleman who has thus slain one who had no mean reputation as a swordsman?"

"A young gentleman passing through Agen. The quarrel arose through a *rencontre* in the street. Count Raoul was, as was his nature, hasty, and put himself in the wrong. The gentleman resented his language, and a meeting was at once arranged. Count Louis and myself were with Raoul, and as his opponent was alone, and it was not desirable to draw others into the matter, I offered to act as his second, and he accepted it at once. We came here. Count Louis and I made a final effort to persuade Raoul to apologize for his language. He refused to do so and they fought, and you see the consequence."

"But who is this stranger?" the governor asked again.

"Count Raoul did not feel it necessary to ask, Count; and I think, as he waived the point, and the affair is now terminated, it would be well that his opponent should be permitted to withdraw without questions."

"That is all very well for you, Monsieur D'Estanges, as a party in a private quarrel, but as governor of Agen it is my duty to satisfy myself as to who this stranger who has killed an officer of the king may be."

He turned his horse, and for the first time obtained a view of Philip, who, seeing the impossibility of escape, had been standing quietly by.

"Why, it is but a youth!" he exclaimed. "You say he slew Count Raoul in fair fight, Monsieur D'Estanges?"

"In as fair a fight as ever I saw, Monsieur le Comte."

"Who are you, sir?" the governor asked Philip.

"I am a stranger travelling through Agen on private business," Philip said quietly.

"But what is your name and family, sir?"

"I am English," Philip replied. "My name is Philip Fletcher."

"A Huguenot, I will be bound?" the governor said angrily.

"Not at all, Count. I am of the religion of my nation—a Protestant."

"It is the same thing," the governor said. "It is clear that, for whatever purpose you may be in Agen, you are here for no good. This is a serious matter, Monsieur D'Estanges."

"As I have said, I know nothing of this gentleman, Count.

I saw him for the first time a little over half an hour ago, and on every account I wish that I had not seen him. He has killed my friend Raoul, deprived his majesty of a staunch adherent, and has got himself into trouble. But for all that, I am assured by his conduct and bearing in this business that he is an honourable gentleman, and I intreat you, as a personal favour, Count, that you allow him to go free."

"I would do much to oblige you, Monsieur D'Estanges, but he is an Englishman, and a Protestant by his own confession, and therefore can only be here to aid the men who have risen in rebellion, and to conspire with the king's enemies. He will be placed in close charge, and when the present pressing affairs have been put out of hand, I doubt not we shall find means of learning a good deal more about this mysterious person, who claims to be English but who yet speaks our language like a Frenchman."

"As to that matter, I can satisfy you at once," Philip said. "My mother was a French lady, a daughter of the Count de Moulins of Poitou."

"A Huguenot family, if I mistake not," the governor said coldly. "Well, we have other things to think of now. Captain Carton, place two troopers one on each side of this person. I authorize you to cut him down if he tries to escape. Let four others dismount and carry the body of the Count de Fontaine into the city. You will, of course, take the command of his troop, Count Louis, seeing that, if I mistake not, you are his nearest relative and the heir to his possessions."

As Philip was led through the streets he caught sight of Pierre, who made no sign of recognition as he passed. He was taken to the castle, and confined in a room in a turret looking down upon the river. The window was closely barred, but otherwise the room though small was not uncomfortable. It contained a chair, a table, and a couch. When the door was barred and bolted behind him, Philip walked to the window and stood looking out at the river.

The prospect seemed dark; the governor was unfavourably disposed towards him now, and when the news came on the morrow that the Queen of Navarre had slipped through his fingers his exasperation would no doubt be vented on him.

What was now but a mere suspicion would then become almost a certainty, and it would, as a matter of course, be assumed that he was there on matters connected with her flight. That he was a Protestant was alone sufficient to condemn him to death, but his connection with the queen's flight would, beyond all question, seal his fate. Pierre, he felt sure, would do all that he could for him; but that could amount to almost nothing. Even if he had the means of filing through or removing the bars, it would need a long stout rope to enable him to descend to the water's edge, a hundred feet below him; and that he could obtain possession of either file or rope seemed to him as absolutely impossible.

"Nevertheless," he said to himself, "I will let Pierre know where I am confined. I do not see that it can do any good. But he is a fellow of resource; I have great faith in him, and though I can see no possible plan of escape, he, being without, may try something. I have no doubt that his first endeavour will be to find out where I am confined. I warrant he will know my cap if he sees it. He has an eye like a hawk, and if he sees anything outside one of the windows he will suspect at once that it is a signal, and when he once looks closely at it he will make out its orange tint and these three long cock's feathers."

So saying he thrust one of his arms through the bars with the cap, which he allowed to hang down against the wall below. There he stood for two hours, closely examining every boat that came along. At last he saw one rowed by two men with a third sitting in the stern, and had no difficulty in making out, as it came closer, that this was Pierre, who was gazing at the castle. Presently he saw him suddenly clap his hands and speak to the rowers. These did not look up but continued to row on in the same leisurely way as before, nor did Pierre again glance at the castle. Satisfied that his signal had been observed, Philip withdrew it but continued to watch the boat. It went half a mile higher up, then turned and floated quietly down the stream again. When he had seen it pass the bridge he threw himself down on the couch.

"There is nothing more for me to do," he said; "the matter is in Pierre's hands now."

PHILIP IN PRISON.

He listened for a time to the tramp of a sentry backwards and forwards outside his door and then fell off to sleep, from which he did not awake until he heard the bars withdrawn and the key turned in the lock. Then a man accompanied by two soldiers entered, and placed a chicken, a bottle of wine, and a loaf of bread on the table. "Monsieur D'Estanges sends this with his compliments," he said; and then Philip was again left alone.

Two hours after it became dark he thought he heard a confused sound as of the trampling of a number of horsemen in the courtyard of the castle. He went to the door and placing his ear against it was convinced that he was not mistaken.

"That looks as if an expedition were about to start somewhere," he said; "if they are bound for Nérac they will arrive there too late, for the queen will by this time be setting out. They cannot intend to scale the walls to-night, and the gates will have been shut long ago; they are probably going into ambush somewhere near so as to ride in in the morning. I wish I could be certain they are bound in that direction. There was certainly no idea of an expedition this morning, but it is possible that the messenger with the order for the arrest of the queen and prince may have arrived this afternoon, and the governor is losing no time. I trust it is so, and not that news has come from some spy at Nérac that she will leave the place to-night. If it is so this party may be setting out to strengthen the guards on the river, or to occupy the roads by which she would travel were her purpose to join the seneschal. I trust that Pierre and the others are on the alert and not wasting their time in thinking about me, and that if this troop make along the river they will ride to warn the queen in time. Hearing nothing she will assume that the road is clear, and that she can go on fearlessly. It is enough to drive one mad being cooped up here when the whole success of the cause is at stake."

The character of the sentry's walk had changed. He had been relieved some four hours before, and his walk at times ceased as if he were leaning against the wall to rest himself, while at times he gave an impatient stamp with his feet.

"I expect they have forgotten to relieve him," Philip said to himself; "if a strong body has gone out that might very well be."

Another half-hour passed, and then he heard steps ascending the stone staircase and the sentry exclaimed angrily, "Sapristie, comrade, I began to think I was going to be kept all night at my post, and that every one had ridden out with that party that started half an hour ago. Now, then; the orders are, '*Permit no one to approach, refuse even to allow officers to visit the prisoner without a special order of the governor.*' That is all. Now I am off for a tankard of spiced wine, which I think I have earned well, for it is a good hour after my time of relief."

Then Philip heard his footsteps descending the stairs, while the man who had relieved him walked briskly up and down in front of the door. In a minute or two he stopped, then Philip turned with a start from the window at which he was standing, as he heard through the keyhole a loud whisper, "Monsieur Philip, are you asleep? It is I!"

"Why, Pierre!" he exclaimed, running to the door and putting his mouth to the keyhole; "how did you come here?"

"I will tell you that later, master, the thing is now to get you out; the bolts here are easy enough to draw, but this lock puzzles me. I have brought up two thin saws and an auger, and thought to cut round it, but there is a plate of iron outside."

"And there is one inside too, Pierre. How about the hinges, Pierre?"

"There is no doing anything with them, master, the iron-work goes right across the door. There is nothing for it but to cut right round the iron plate."

"That won't take very long if the saws are good, Pierre."

Philip heard a rasping sound, and in a short time the auger passed through the woodwork. Two other holes adjoining the first were soon made, and then the end of a saw was pushed through.

"If you can make a hole large enough at the bottom of the plate, Pierre, and pass me the other saw through, I can work that way to meet you."

"It would take too long to make, sir. I have plenty of oil,

and it won't take me long to saw round the plate. I only brought the second saw in case the first should break. But this oak is pretty nearly as hard as iron."

It took over an hour's work before the cut was complete. When it was nearly finished Pierre said, "Be ready to seize the piece that is cut out as soon as I am through with it, master, otherwise it may fall down as the door opens and make a clatter that will be heard all over the castle."

As the last piece was sawn through Philip pressed the door, and as it opened seized the portion cut out, drew it backward, and laid it gently on the stone floor, then he rose and grasped Pierre's hand.

"My brave Pierre, you have accomplished what I thought was an impossibility. Now, what is the next thing to be done?"

"The next thing is to unwind this rope from my body. It is lucky I am so lean that it did not make me look bulky. It is not very thick, but it is new and strong, and there are knots every two feet. Roger is waiting for us below in a boat."

"Where is Jacques?"

"Jacques has ridden off. He learned before sunset that orders had been issued for the troops to assemble; he and Roger had taken the four horses beyond the walls an hour after you were arrested, and had left them at a farmer's a mile away. So he arranged with me that he should follow the troop on foot, which he could do, as there are footmen as well as horse in the party that has gone out. Then as soon as he discovered which way they were going he would slip off and make for the farmhouse and mount. If they were bound for Nérac he will wait for us at the point on the other side of the river. If they follow the river down, he will ride at full speed, make a circuit, and warn the queen of the danger. He will have plenty of time to do that, as the column will have to move at the pace of the infantry."

"That is a load off my mind, Pierre." While they were speaking they had unwound the rope, fastened one end to the battlement and lowered the other down.

"I will go first, master; I am the lightest, and will steady the rope for you from below."

In two or three minutes Philip felt that the rope was no longer tight, and at once swung himself over and lowered himself down. The water washed the foot of the wall, and he stepped directly into the boat, which Roger was keeping in its place with a pole while Pierre held the rope. An exclamation of thankfulness broke from the two men as his feet touched the gunwale of the boat, and then without a word Roger began to pole the boat along against the tide, keeping close to the foot of the wall. Once fairly beyond the castle the pole was laid in and the two men took the oars, and the boat shot across the river. Then they rowed up under the opposite bank, until a voice from above them said:

"Is all well—is Monsieur Philip with you?"

"All is well, Jacques," Philip exclaimed delighted, for the fact that his follower was there showed that the troops had gone in the direction that did not threaten the safety of the queen. They leapt ashore and pushed the boat off to allow it to float down with the stream.

It was a mile to the spot where the horses had been left. On the way Philip heard how his escape had been effected.

"I saw you go out from the town, monsieur, and could not for the life of me make out what was going to happen. I did not know the gentleman you were walking with, but I recognized the two in front of you as the officers of the troop that had questioned us near Bazas. One of them was talking angrily to the other. As it seemed to me that you were going willingly and not as a prisoner, and especially as you were going out of the town, I thought that it was my business to wait until you returned. I saw half an hour later some horsemen coming up the street, and some one said that it was the governor, who had been out with a party. It gave me a bad turn when I saw you walking as a prisoner in the middle of them. I saw you glance at me but of course made no sign, and I followed until you entered the castle. When I was walking away I saw a crowd. Pushing forward I found they were surrounding four soldiers who were carrying a body on their shoulders, and made out at once it was the officer who had been talking so angrily to his companion. Then I understood what had puzzled me before, and what you had gone outside the walls for; the rest was easy to guess. The governor had come along, you had been questioned, and had been arrested as a Huguenot. It was evident that no time was to be lost, and that if you were to be got out it must be done quickly.

"I hurried away to the cabaret where Jacques and Roger were drinking. We talked the matter over, and agreed that the first thing was to get the four horses out of the town. So I went to the inn where you had put up, said I was your servant, paid the reckoning, and took away the horse. Then I got my own and joined the other two, who were mounted and ready. They each took a horse and rode off, settling to leave them at some farmhouse a short distance away, explaining there that the town was so full they could find no room for them. Directly they had started I set off to have a look round the castle. The great thing was to know where they had lodged you. If it was in a cell looking outward, I thought that, knowing I should be searching for you, you would make a signal. If I could see nothing I determined to accost some servant coming out from the castle, to make acquaintance with him, and over a bottle of wine to find out in what part of the castle you were lodged.

"On the land side I could see nothing, and then went back and waited till Jacques and Roger returned. Then we took a boat, and as you know rowed up, and I soon made out your cap outside the wall. Then as we rowed back we arranged matters. Jacques was to carry out your former orders: find out about the movement of troops, and warn the queen if danger threatened. Roger was to be at the foot of the wall with a boat as soon as it became dark; I was to undertake to get you out. The first thing to do was to get a rope. This I carried to a quiet place on the wall, knotted it and put it round me under my doublet; then there was nothing to do but to wait. I went several times to hear if Jacques had any news, and was glad when he told me that most of the troops were ordered to be under arms at eight o'clock. This would make matters simpler for me, for with numbers of people going in and coming out of the castle it would be easy to slip in unnoticed.

"As soon as it was dark Jacques and I went down a lane, and he gave me his steel cap and breast-piece and took my cap in exchange. Then I went up towards the castle. The gates were open, and I was told that they would not be closed until midnight as so many were coming out and going in, and there was no hostile force anywhere in these parts. Presently numbers of gentlemen began to arrive with their retainers, and I soon went in with a party of footmen. The courtyard was full of men, and I was not long before I found the staircase leading up to the top of the wall on the river side. I went boldly up, and half-way found a door partly open. Looking in I saw that it was evidently used by some gentlemen who had gone down in haste to join the party below, so I shut the door and waited. I heard the troops start, and guessed from the quiet that followed that the greater portion of the garrison had left. I felt pretty sure that there would be a sentry at your door, and waited until the time I thought he would be expecting a relief; then I went up. He was in a mighty hurry to get down, and did not stop to see who I was, or to ask any questions; which was well for him, for I had my knife in my hand, and should have stabbed him before he could utter a cry. Everything went off well, and you know the rest, sir."

"You managed wonderfully, Pierre. I thought over every plan by which you might aid me to escape, but I never thought of anything so simple as this. Nor, indeed, did I see any possible way of your freeing me. How are we going to get our horses? The farmer will think that we are a party of thieves."

"They are in an open shed," Jacques said. "I told the farmer that our reason for bringing them out of the town was that you might have to start with orders any time in the night, and that it would be troublesome getting them out from town stables and having the gates opened for them to pass out, while on foot you could issue from the postern without trouble. I paid him for the corn when I left them."

The horses, indeed, were got out without any stir in the house indicating that its occupants were awakened.

"Give me your sword, Pierre," Philip said as he mounted.

"I trust that we shall meet with no enemies on the road; still we may do so, and I should not like to be unarmed. You have your arquebus."

This had been brought in the boat by Roger, and on landing Pierre had exchanged the steel cap and breast-piece for his own cap. The road to Villeneuve D'Agenois was a cross-country one, and would be impossible to follow in the dark. Consequently, after keeping on the main road for half an hour, they turned off a road to the right, rode until they came to a wood, and there alighted.

"Shall I light a fire, sir?" Pierre asked.

"It is not worth while, Pierre; it must be getting on for midnight now, and we must be in the saddle again at day-break. By this time they have no doubt found that I have escaped. The first time they send up a man to relieve you the open door will be noticed. They will certainly make no search to-night, and to-morrow they will have something else to think about; for doubtless some spy at Nérac will, as soon as the gates are open, take the news to the governor's party that the queen has left."

Two hours' brisk ride in the morning took them within sight of Villeneuve D'Agenois. Riding across the bridge over the river Lot he entered the town. The street was full of troops, and three gentlemen standing at the door of an inn looked with suspicion on the gay colouring of Philip's costume, and as he alighted they stepped forward to accost him.

"May I ask who you are, sir?" one said advancing; "and what is your business here?"

"Certainly you may," Philip said, as he dismounted. "My name is Philip Fletcher. I am here at the order of her majesty the Queen of Navarre, who, I trust, has arrived here safely."

"The queen arrived here three hours since, Monsieur Fletcher; and I may say that she did you the honour to inquire at once if a gentleman of your name had arrived."

"I should have met her at the river near Tonneins; but the governor of Agen laid an embargo on me, yet thanks to these three faithful fellows I got safely out of his clutches."

"We shall march in an hour, Monsieur Fletcher, and as

soon as the queen is up I will see that she is acquainted with your coming.   Allow me to introduce myself first, Gaston de Rebers.   Breakfast is ready in this cottage, and we were about to sit down when we saw you riding up. · I shall be glad if you will share it with us.   These are my comrades, Messieurs Duvivier, Harcourt, and Parolles."   He then called a sergeant.

"Sergeant, see that Monsieur Fletcher's servant and men-at-arms have a good meal."

"I think they must want it," Philip said.   "They have been so busy in my service that I doubt if they have eaten since breakfast yesterday.   I myself supped well, thanks to the courtesy of Monsieur D'Estanges, who was good enough to send up an excellent capon and a bottle of wine to my cell."

"You know Monsieur D'Estanges?" Gaston de Rebers asked courteously.   "He is a gentleman of high repute, and though connected with the Guises he is said to be opposed to them in their crusade against us."

"I had only the honour of meeting him yesterday," Philip said, as they sat down to table; "but he behaved like a true gentleman, and did me the honour of being my second in an unfortunate affair into which I was forced."

"Who was your opponent, may I ask, sir?"

"Count Raoul de Fontaine."

"A doughty swordsman! Gaston de Rebers exclaimed; "but·one of our bitterest opponents in this province.   You are fortunate indeed to have escaped without a serious wound, for he has been engaged in many duels, and but few of his opponents have escaped with their lives."

"He will neither persecute you nor fight more duels," Philip said quietly; "for I had the misfortune to kill him."

The others looked at him with astonishment.

"Do I understand rightly, Monsieur Fletcher, that you have slain Raoul de Fontaine in a duel?"

"That is the case," Philip replied.   "Monsieur D'Estanges, as I have said, acted as my second, Count Louis de Fontaine acted for his cousin."

"You will pardon my having asked you the question again," De Rebers said; "but really it seemed well-nigh impossible that a gentleman, who, as I take it, can yet be scarcely of age, should have slain Raoul de Fontaine."

"I lack four years yet of being of age," Philip said; "for it will be another month before I am seventeen. But I have had good teachers, both English and French, and our games and exercises at school. naturally bring us forward in point of strength and stature in comparison with your countrymen of the same age. Still, doubtless, it was as much due to good fortune as to skill that I gained my success. I assuredly had no desire to kill him; the less so because, to a certain extent, the duel was of my making. There was, as it seemed to me, no choice between fighting him and being denounced by him as a spy. Therefore when he accosted me roughly, I took the matter up hotly, and there was nothing for it but an encounter. As I have said, I meant only to wound him, but his skill and his impetuosity were so great that I was forced in self-defence to run him through. After all I gained nothing by the duel, for the governor with a troop of horse came up just as it concluded, and as I could give no satisfactory account of myself, I was hauled off a prisoner to the castle."

"And how did you escape thence?" Gaston asked.

Philip gave an account of the manner in which his servant had rescued him.

"*Parbleu!* you are fortunate in your servant. I would that so shrewd a knave—. But there, the trumpets are sounding. I will take you at once to the queen, who is doubtless ready to mount."

CHAPTER XIII

AT LAVILLE

THE queen was standing at the door of the house where she had lain down for a few hours' rest after her arrival; the Prince was standing beside her.

"Here is our English friend, mother," he exclaimed, running forward to meet Philip. "Welcome, Monsieur Fletcher. When we found that you were not here on our arrival last night we feared that some evil had befallen you."

"Monsieur Fletcher is well able to take care of himself, Prince; he has been having adventures enough," Gaston de Rebers said.

"You must tell me about them as we ride," the Prince said. "I love adventures, M. Fletcher."

They had now reached the queen. "I am glad to see you, Monsieur Fletcher. Of course it was in one way a relief to us when we crossed the river and did not find you there, for I was sure you would have been there to give us warning had there been danger on the way; but I thought you might come in any case, and when we found that you had not arrived here before us I was afraid that something might have befallen you."

"I have had some slight troubles, your majesty, and to my great regret I was unable to meet you at the passage of the river. I should have been here long before daylight, but we were unable to find the road in the dark, and had to wait until we could inquire the way."

"Monsieur Fletcher is pleased to say that he has had some slight troubles, madame," Gaston said; "but as the troubles included the slaying in a duel of Raoul de Fontaine, one of the bitterest enemies of our faith, and moreover a noted duellist, and an escape from the castle of Agen, where he was confined as a suspected Huguenot and spy, the term slight does not very aptly describe them."

"What!" a tall soldierly old man standing next to the queen exclaimed. "Do you mean to say, De Rebers, that Monsieur Fletcher has killed Raoul de Fontaine in a duel? If so, I congratulate your majesty. He was a bitter persecutor of the Huguenots, and one of the hottest-headed and most troublesome nobles in the province. Moreover, he can put a hundred and fifty men into the field; and although his cousin Louis, who is his heir, is also Catholic; he is a man of very different kind, and is honoured by Huguenot and Catholic alike. But how this gentleman could have killed so notable a swordsman is more than I can understand; he looks, if you will pardon my saying so, a mere youth."

"He rode beside François de la Noüe in the battle of St. Denis, seneschal," the queen said; "and as he was chosen by my cousin Condé and Admiral Coligny for the difficult and dangerous enterprise of carrying a communication to me, it is clear that whatever his years he is well fitted to act a man's part."

"That is so," the seneschal said heartily. "I shall be glad to talk to you again, sir; but at present, madame, it is time to mount. The troops are mustering, and we have a long ride before us. If you will lead the way with the infantry at once, Monsieur de Rebers, we will follow as soon as we are mounted. We must go your pace, but as soon as we start I will send a party to ride a mile ahead of you, and see that the roads are clear."

At starting the queen rode with the Prince and the seneschal at the head of the mounted party, some two hundred and fifty strong, and behind followed the noblemen and gentlemen who had come with her, and those who had accompanied the seneschal.

Philip, who knew no one, rode near the rear of this train, behind which followed the armed retainers. In a short time a gentleman rode back through the party. "Monsieur

Fletcher," he said when he reached Philip, "the Prince has asked me to say that it is his wish that you shall ride forward and accompany him."

Philip turned into the field, and rode to the head of the party. The Prince, who was looking round, at once reined in his horse and took his place beside him.

"Now, Monsieur Philip, you must tell me all about it. I am tired of hearing consultations about roads and Catholic forces. I want to hear a full account of your adventures, just as you told me the tale of your journey to Nérac."

During the course of the day several parties of gentlemen joined the little force. So well organized were the Huguenots, that during the last two or three days the news had passed from mouth to mouth throughout the province for all to assemble, if possible, at points indicated to them; and all knew the day on which the seneschal would march north from Villeneuve. Yet so well was the secret kept, that the Catholics remained in total ignorance of the movement. Consequently at every village there were accessions of force awaiting the seneschal, and parties of from ten to a hundred rode up and joined them on the march. After marching twenty miles they halted at the foot of a chain of hills, their numbers having been increased during the day to over twelve hundred men. The queen and her son found rough accommodation in a small village, the rest bivouacked round it.

At midnight three hundred cavalry and two hundred footmen started across the hills, so as to come down upon Bergerac and seize the bridge across the Dordogne; then at daylight the rest of the force marched. On reaching the river they found that the bridge had been seized without resistance. Three hundred gentlemen and their retainers, of the province of Perigord, had assembled within half a mile of the other side of the bridge, and had joined the party as they came down. A Catholic force of two hundred men in the town had been taken by surprise and captured, for the most part in their beds.

The queen had issued most stringent orders that there was to be no unnecessary bloodshed, and the Catholic soldiers, having been stripped of their arms and armour, which were divided among those of the Huguenots who were ill-provided,

were allowed to depart unharmed the next morning, some fifteen gentlemen being retained as prisoners. Three hundred
more Huguenots rode into Bergerac in the course of the day.
The footmen marched forward in the afternoon, and were
directed to stop at a village twelve miles on. As the next
day's journey would be a long one, the start was again made
early, and late in the afternoon the little army, which had been
joined by two hundred more in the course of the day, arrived
within sight of Périgueux. Five hundred horsemen had ridden
forward two hours before to secure the bridge.

The seneschal had, after occupying Bergerac, placed horsemen on all the roads leading north to prevent the news from
spreading, and Périgueux, a large and important town, was
utterly unprepared for the advent of an enemy. A few of the
troops took up arms and made a hasty resistance, but were
speedily dispersed; the greater portion fled at the first alarm
to the castle, where D'Escars himself was staying. He had
only two days before sent off a despatch to the court declaring
that he had taken his measures so well that not a Huguenot in
the province would take up arms. His force was still superior
to that of the horsemen, but his troops were disorganized, and
many in their flight had left their arms behind them, and he
was therefore obliged to remain inactive in the citadel; and
his mortification and fury were complete when the seneschal's
main body marched through the town and halted for the night
a league beyond it.

The next day they crossed the Dronne at Brantôme, and
then turned to the west. The way was now open to them, and
with two thousand men the seneschal felt capable of coping
with any force that could be got together to attack them. A
halt was made for a day to rest the men and horses, and four
days later, after crossing the Perigord hills, and keeping ten
miles south of Angoulême, they came within sight of Cognac.
Messages had already been sent on to announce their coming,
and five miles from the town they were met by the Prince of
Condé and the Admiral.

"Your first message lifted a load from our minds, madame,"
the Admiral said; "the last news I received of you was that
you were still at Nérac, and as an intercepted despatch

informed us that orders had been sent from the court for your immediate arrest, we were in great uneasiness about you."

"We left Nérac just in time," the queen said; "for, as we have learned, the governor of Agen with a strong force left that city to effect our capture àt the very hour that we started on our flight."

"Did you know where you would find us, madame? We sent off a message by trusty hands, but whether the gentleman reached you we know not."

"Indeed he did, and has since rendered us good service; and Henri here has taken so great a fancy to him that since we left Villeneuve he has always ridden by his side."

After Condé had presented the gentlemen who had ridden out with him to the queen, and the seneschal in turn had introduced the most important nobles and gentlemen to the prince and Admiral, they proceeded on their way.

"Have you taken Cognac, cousin?" the queen asked Condé.

"No, madame; the place still holds out. We have captured St. Jean d'Angély, but Cognac is obstinate, and we have no cannon with which to batter its walls."

As soon, however, as the queen arrived at the camp a summons was sent in in her name, and, influenced by this and by the sight of the reinforcements she had brought with her, Cognac at once surrendered. As soon as Philip rode into camp he was greeted joyously by his cousin François.

"We did not think when we parted outside Niort that we were going to be separated so long," he said, after they had shaken hands heartily. "I was astonished indeed, when two days later I met the Admiral outside the walls of the town again, to hear that you had gone off to make your way through to Nérac. I want to hear all your adventures. We have not had much fighting; Niort made but a poor resistance, and Parthenay surrendered without striking a blow; then I went with the party that occupied Fontenay. The Catholics fought stoutly there, but we were too strong for them. Those three places have given La Rochelle three bulwarks to the north. Then we started again from La Rochelle and marched to St. Jean d'Angély, which we carried by storm. Then we came on here, and I believe we shall have a try at Saintes or Angou-

lême.   When we have captured them we shall have a complete
cordon of strong places round La Rochelle.   We expect La
Noüe down from Brittany every hour, with a force he has
raised there and in Normandy; and we have heard that a
large force has gathered in Languedoc, and is advancing to
join us; and all is going so well that I fancy if Monsieur
d'Anjou does not come to us before long we shall set out in
search of him.   So much for our doings; now sit down comfortably in my tent and tell me all about your journey.   I see
you have brought Pierre and your two men back with you."

"You would be nearer the truth if you said that Pierre and
the two men had brought me back," Philip laughed; "for if
it had not been for them I should probably have lost my head
the day after the queen left Nérac."

"That is a good beginning to the story, Philip; but tell me
the whole in proper order as it happened."

Philip told his story at length, and his cousin was greatly
pleased at the manner in which he had got through his various
dangers and difficulties.

The queen remained but a few hours with the army after
Cognac had opened its gates.   After a long conference with
the Prince of Condé, the Admiral, and the other leaders, she
left under a strong escort for La Rochelle, leaving the young
prince with the army, of which he was given the nominal
command, as his near connection with the royal family, and
the fact that he was there as the representative of his mother,
strengthened the Huguenot cause, which could no longer be
described by the agents of the French court with foreign powers
as a mere rising of slight importance, the work only of Condé,
Coligny, and a few other ambitious and turbulent nobles.

"I asked my mother to appoint you as one of the gentlemen
who are to ride with me, Monsieur Fletcher," the young prince
said to Philip when he saw him on the day after the queen's
departure; "but she and the Admiral both said no.   It is not
because they do not like you, you know; and the Admiral said
that he could very well trust me with you.   But when my
mother told him that I had ridden with you for the last four
days, he said that it would cause jealousy, when there were so
many young French nobles and gentlemen in the camp, if I

were to choose you in preference to them as my companion, you being only French on your mother's side and having an English name.   I begged them to let me tell you this, for I would rather ride with you than with any of them; and I should not like you to think that I did not care to have you with me any more.   I think it hard.   They call me the commander of this army, and I can't have my own way even in a little thing like this.   Some day, Monsieur Fletcher, I shall be able to do as I please, and then I hope to have you near me."

"I am greatly obliged to your Highness," Philip said; "but I am sure the counsel that has been given you is right, and that it is far better for you to be in the company of French gentlemen.   I have come over here solely to do what little I can to aid my mother's relations, and those oppressed for their faith; and though I am flattered by your wish that I should be near you, I would rather be taking an active share in the work that has to be done."

"Yes, the Admiral said that.   He said that while many a youth would be most gratified at being selected to be my companion, he was sure that you would far rather ride with your cousin M. De Naville, and that it would be a pity to keep one who bids fair to be a great soldier acting the part of nurse to me.   It was not quite civil of the Admiral, for I don't want a nurse of that kind, and would a thousand times rather ride as an esquire to you and take share in your adventures.   But the Admiral is always plain-spoken; still as I know well that he is good and wise, and the greatest soldier in France, I do not mind what he says."

Angoulême and Saintes were both captured without much difficulty, and then moving south from Angoulême the army captured Pons and Blaye, and thus possessed themselves of a complete semicircle of towns round La Rochelle.   A short time afterwards they were joined by a strong force of Huguenots from Languedoc and Provence.   These had marched north without meeting with any enemy strong enough to give them battle, and when they joined the force under the Admiral they raised its strength to a total of three thousand cavalry and twenty thousand infantry.   By this time the royal army of the

Prince d'Anjou, having united with that raised by the Guises, had advanced to Poitiers. The season was now far advanced; indeed winter had already set in. Both armies were anxious to fight; but the royalist leaders, bearing in mind the desperate valour that the Huguenots had displayed at St. Denis, were unwilling to give battle unless in a position that afforded them every advantage for the movements of their cavalry, in which they were greatly superior in strength to the Huguenots.

The Admiral was equally determined not to throw away the advantage he possessed in his large force of infantry; and after being in sight of each other for some time, and several skirmishes having taken place, both armies fell back into winter quarters—the severity of the weather being too great to keep the soldiers without tents or other shelter in the field.

During these operations Philip and his cousin had again ridden with François de la Noüe, who had rejoined the army after a most perilous march, in which he and the small body of troops he had brought from Brittany had succeeded in making their way through the hostile country, and in crossing the fords of the intervening rivers after hard fighting and considerable loss.

As soon as the intense cold had driven both armies to the shelter of the towns, the count said to François: "You and Philip had better march at once with your troop to Laville. It will cost far less to maintain them at the chateau than elsewhere; indeed the men can for the most part return to their farms. But you must be watchful, François, now that a portion of Anjou's army is lying at Poitiers. They may, should the weather break, make raids into our country; and as Laville is the nearest point to Poitiers held for us, they might well make a dash at it."

The countess welcomed them back heartily, but expressed great disappointment that the season should have passed without the armies meeting.

"It was the same last time, it was the delay that ruined us. With the best will in the world there are few who can afford to keep their retainers in the field for month after month, and the men themselves are longing to be back to their farms and families. We shall have to keep a keen look-out through the winter. Fortunately our harvest here is a good one and the granaries are all full, so that we shall be able to keep the men-at-arms on through the winter without much expense. I feel more anxious about the tenants than about ourselves."

"Yes, mother, there is no doubt there is considerable risk of the enemy trying to beat us up; and we must arrange for signals, so that our people may have time to fall back here. Philip and I will think it over. We ought to be able to contrive some scheme between us."

"Do so, François. I feel safe against surprise here; but I never retire to rest without wondering whether the night will pass without the tenants' farms and stacks being set ablaze, and they and their families slaughtered on their own hearth-stones."

"I suppose, François," Philip said to him as they stood at the look-out next morning, "there is not much doubt which way they would cross the hills coming from Poitiers. They would be almost sure to come by that road that we travelled by when we went to Chatillon. It comes down over the hills two miles to the west. There it is, you see; you just catch sight of it as it crosses that shoulder. Your land does not go as far as that, does it?"

"No, it only extends a mile in that direction and four miles in the other, and five miles out into the plain."

"Are there many Huguenots on the other side of the hill?"

"Yes, there are some; but, as you know, our strength is in the other direction. What are you thinking of?"

"I was thinking that we might make an arrangement with someone in a village some seven or eight miles beyond the hills, to keep a boy on watch night and day, so that directly a body of Catholic troops were seen coming along he should start at full speed to some place a quarter of a mile away, and there set light to a beacon piled in readiness.

"We on our part would have a watch set on the top of this hill behind us, at a spot where the hill on which the beacon was placed would be visible. Then at night the fire and by day the smoke would serve as a warning. Our watchman would at once fire an arquebus and light another beacon, which would be the signal for all within reach to come here as quickly as possible. At each farmhouse a look-out must, of course, be kept night and day. I should advise the tenants to send up as much of their corn and hay as possible at once, and that the cattle should be driven up close to the chateau at night."

"I think that would be a very good plan, Philip. I am sure that among our men-at-arms must be some who have acquaintances and friends on the other side of the hill. It will be best that they should make the arrangements for the firing of the signal beacon. We might even station one of them in a village there, under the pretence that he had been knocked up with the cold and hardship and was desirous of staying quietly with his friends. He would watch at night and could sleep by day, as his friends would waken him at once if any troops passed along."

The same afternoon one of the men-at-arms prepared to start for a village eight miles beyond the hill.

"There is no rising ground near it," he said to François, "that could well be seen from the top of the hill here; but about half a mile away from the village there is an old tower. It is in ruins, and has been so ever since I can remember. I have often climbed to its top when I was a boy. At this time of year there is no chance of anyone visiting the place. I could collect wood and pile it ready for a fire without any risk whatever. I can point out the exact direction of the tower from the top of the hill, so that the watchers would know where to keep their attention fixed."

"Well, you had better go up with us at once then, so that I shall be able to instruct the men who will keep watch. We will build a hut up there for them and keep three men on guard, so that they will watch four hours apiece day and night."

The distance was too great to make out the tower; but as the soldier knew its exact position, he drove two stakes into the ground three feet apart.

"Now," he said, "a man looking along the line of the tops of these stakes will be looking as near as may be at the tower."

The tenants were all visited, and were warned to keep a member of their family always on the watch for fire or smoke from the little hut at the top of the hill. As soon as the signal was seen night or day, they were to make their way to the chateau, driving their horses and most valuable stock before them, and taking such goods as they could remove.

"You had better let two horses remain with their harness on night and day, and have a cart in readiness close to your house. Then, when the signal is given, the women will only have to bundle their goods and children into the cart, while the men get their arms and prepare to drive in their cattle.

"The Catholics will show no mercy to any of the faith they may find, while as to the chateau it can make a stout resistance, and you may be sure that it will not be long before help arrives from Niort or La Rochelle."

Arrangements were also made with the Huguenot gentry in the neighbourhood that they should keep a look-out for the signal, and on observing it light other beacons, so that the news could be spread rapidly over that part of the country. As soon as the fires were seen the women and children were to take to the hills, the cattle to be driven off by the boys, and the men to arm themselves and mount.

"Of course," the countess said, at a council where all these arrangements were made, "we must be guided by the number sent against us. If by uniting your bands together you think you can raise the siege, we will sally out as soon as you attack and join you, but do not attack unless you think that our united forces can defeat them. If we could defeat them we should save your chateaux and farms from fire and ruin. If you find they are too strong to attack, you might harass parties sent out to plunder, and so save your houses, while you despatch men to ask for help from the Admiral. If, however, they are so strong in cavalry that you could not keep the field against them, I should say it were best that you should ride away and join any party advancing to our assistance."

A month passed quietly. Every day a soldier carrying wine and provisions rode to the hut that had been built on the crest of the hill three miles away. Eight o'clock one evening towards the end of January the alarm-bell rang from the look-out tower. Philip and his cousin ran up.

"There is the beacon alight at the hut, count," the look-out said.

"Light this bonfire then, Jules, and keep the alarm-bell going. To horse, men!" he cried looking over the parapet. "Bring out our horses with your own."

The men had been previously told off in twos and threes to the various farmhouses to aid in driving in the cattle, and as soon as they were mounted each party dashed off to its destination. From the watch-tower four or five fires could be seen blazing in the distance, showing that the look-outs had everywhere been vigilant, and that the news had already been carried far and wide. François and Philip rode up to the hut on the hill.

"There is no mistake, I hope?" François said as, a quarter of a mile before they reached it, they met the three men-at-arms coming down.

"No, count, it was exactly in a line with the two stakes, and I should think about the distance away that you told us the tower was. It has died down now."

The beacon-fire near the hut had been placed fifty yards below the crest of the hill, so that its flame should not be seen from the other side. This had been at Philip's suggestion. "If it is put where they can see it," he said, "they will feel sure that it is in answer to that fire behind them, and will ride at full speed so as to get here before the news spreads. If they see no answering fire, they may suppose that the first was but an accident. They may even halt at the village, and send off some men to see what has caused the fire, or if they ride straight through they will be at some little distance before Simon has got to the fire and lighted it, and may not care to waste time sending back. At any rate it is better that they should see no flame up here."

They had often talked the matter over, and had agreed that even if the column was composed only of cavalry, it would be from an hour and a half to two hours before it arrived at the chateau, as.it would doubtless have performed a long journey, while if there were infantry with them they would take double that time. Directly an alarm had been given two of the youngest and most active of the men-at-arms had set off to take post at the point where the road crossed the hill. Their orders were to lie still till all had passed, and then to make their way back along the hill at full speed to inform the garrison of the strength and composition of the attacking force.

When they returned to the chateau people were already pouring in from the neighbouring farms; the women staggering under heavy burdens, and the men driving their cattle before them or leading strings of horses. The seneschal and the retainers were at work trying to keep some sort of order, directing the men to drive the cattle into the countess's garden, and the women to put down their belongings in the courtyard where they would be out of the way; while the countess saw that her maids spread rushes thickly along by the walls of the rooms that were to be given up to the use of the women and children. Cressets had been lighted in the courtyard, but the bonfire was now extinguished so that the enemy on reaching the top of the hill should see nothing to lead them to suppose that their coming was known. The alarm-bell had ceased sending its loud summons into the air; but there was still a variety of noises that were almost deafening, the lowing of cattle disturbed and angered at the unaccustomed movement, mingled with the shouts of men, the barking of dogs, and the crying of frightened children.

"I will aid the seneschal in getting things into order down here, François," Philip said, "while you see to the defence of the walls, posting the men, and getting everything in readiness to give them a reception. I will look after the postern doors, and see that the planks across the moats are removed and the bolts and bars in place."

François nodded, and bidding the men-at-arms, who had already returned, stable their horses and follow him, he proceeded to the walls.

"This is enough to make one weep," Pierre said as the oxen poured into the courtyard, and then through the archway that led to the countess's garden.

"What is enough, Pierre? to see all these poor women and children who are likely to behold their homesteads in flames before many hours?"

"Well, I did not mean that, master, though I don't say that is not sad enough in its way; but that is the fortune of war, as it were. I meant the countess's garden being destroyed.

The beasts will trample down all the shrubs, and in a week it will be no better than a farmyard."

Philip laughed. "That is of very little consequence, Pierre. A week's work with plenty of hands will set that right again. Still, no doubt it will vex the countess, who is very fond of her garden."

"A week!" Pierre said. "Why, sir, it will take years and years before those yew hedges grow again."

"Ah well, Pierre, if the countess keeps a roof over her head she may be well content in these stormy times. You had better go and see if she and her maids have got those chambers ready for the women. If they have, get them all in as quickly as you can. These beasts come into the courtyard with such a rush that some of the people will be trampled upon if we do not get them out of the way."

"Most of them have gone into the hall, sir. The countess gave orders that all were to go in as they came, but I suppose the servants have been too busy to tell the late-comers. I will get the rest in at once."

As soon as the farmers and their men had driven the animals into the garden they went up to the walls, all having brought their arms in with them. The boys were left below to look after the cattle.

"Nothing can be done to-night," Philip said to some of the men. "The cattle will come to no harm, and as the boys cannot keep them from breaking down the shrubs they had best leave them alone; or they will run the risk of getting hurt. The boys will do more good by taking charge of the more valuable horses as they come in, and fastening them up to the rings round the wall here. The cart horses must go in with the cattle."

Several gentlemen with their wives and families came in among the fugitives. Their houses were not in a condition to withstand a siege, and it had long been settled that they should come into the chateau if danger threatened. The ladies were taken to the countess's apartments, while the gentlemen went to aid François in the defence.

An hour and a half after the lads returned to the castle, the men-at-arms who had been sent to watch the road came in.

They reported that the column approaching consisted of about three hundred mounted men and fifteen hundred infantry. Roger had all this time been standing by the side of his saddled horse.   Philip hurried to him as soon as the men came in.

"Three hundred horsemen and fifteen hundred foot!   Ride at full speed to La Rochelle.   Tell the Admiral the numbers, and request him in the name of the countess to come to her assistance.   Beg him to use all speed, for no doubt they will attack hotly, knowing that aid will soon be forthcoming to us."

Roger leapt to his saddle and galloped out through the gate. A man had been placed there to mark off the names of all who entered, from the list that had been furnished him.   Philip took it and saw that a cross had been placed against every name.   He therefore went up to the top of the wall.

"The tenants are all in, François?"

"Very well, then, I will have the drawbridge raised and the gates closed; I am glad indeed that we have had time given us for them all to enter.   My mother would have been very grieved if harm had come to any of them.   I have everything in readiness here.   I have posted men at every window and loophole where the house rises from the side of the moat; all the rest are on the walls.   I will take command here by the gate and along the wall.   Do you take charge of the defence of the house itself.   However, you may as well stay here with me until we have had our first talk with them.   Pass the word along the walls for perfect silence."

In another half-hour they heard a dull sound.   Presently it became louder, and they could distinguish, above the trampling of horses, the clash of steel.   It came nearer and nearer until within two or three hundred yards of the chateau, then it ceased.   Presently a figure could be made out creeping quietly forward until it reached the edge of the moat.   It paused a moment and then retired.

"He has been sent to find out whether the drawbridge is down," François whispered to Philip.   "We shall see what they will do now."   There was a pause for ten minutes, then a heavy mass of men could be seen approaching.

"Doubtless they will have planks with them to push across the moat," Philip said.

"We will let them come within twenty yards," François replied, "then I think we shall astonish them."

Believing that all in the chateau were asleep, and that even the precaution of keeping a watchman on the walls had been neglected, the assailants advanced eagerly. Suddenly the silence on the walls was broken by a voice shouting, "Give fire!" and then from along the whole face of the battlement a deadly fire from arquebuses was poured into them. A moment later half a dozen fire-balls were flung into the column, and a rain of cross-bolts followed.

Shouts of astonishment, rage, and pain broke from the mass, and breaking up they recoiled in confusion, while the shouts of the officers urging them forward could be heard. The heavy fire from the walls was, however, too much for men who had expected no resistance, but had moved forward believing that they had but to sack and plunder, and in two or three minutes from the first shot being fired all who were able to do so had retired, though a number of dark figures dotting the ground showed how deadly had been the fire of the besieged.

"They will do nothing more to-night, I fancy," one of the Huguenot gentleman standing by the two friends remarked. "They expected to take you entirely by surprise. Now that they have failed in doing so they will wait until morning to reconnoitre and decide on the best points of attack. Besides, no doubt they have marched far, and are in need of rest before renewing the assault."

"Well, gentlemen," François said, "it would be needless for you all to remain here, and when they once begin in earnest there will be but slight opportunity of rest until relief reaches us, therefore I beg you to go below. You will find a table laid in the hall and two chambers roughly prepared for you, and you can get a few hours' sleep. I myself with my own men will keep watch. Should they muster for another attack my horn will summon you again to the wall. Philip, will you go down and see that these gentlemen have all that they require? You can dismiss all save our own men from guard on the other side of the house.   The tenants and their men will all sleep in the hall."

Philip went down and presided at the long table.   The gentlemen were seated near him, while below them the tenants and other followers took their places.   There was enough cold meat, game, and pies for all, and when they had finished, the defenders of the wall came down half at a time for a meal. When the gentlemen had retired to their apartments, and the farmers and their men had thrown themselves down upon the rushes strewn on each side of the hall, Philip went up to join François.

"Any sign of them, François?"

"None at all.   I expect they are thoroughly tired out, and are lying down just as they halted.   There is no fear that we shall hear any more of them to-night."

CHAPTER XIV

THE ASSAULT ON THE CHATEAU

THE night passed quietly. Just as the sun rose a trumpet sounded, calling for a truce, and two knights in armour rode forward, followed by an esquire carrying a white flag. They halted thirty or forty yards from the gate; and the countess herself came up on to the wall, when the knight raised his vizor.

"Countess Amelie de Laville, I summon you in the name of his majesty the king to surrender. I have with me an ample force to overcome all resistance, but his gracious majesty in his clemency has empowered me to offer to all within the walls their lives, save only that you and your son shall accompany me to Paris, there to be dealt with according to the law, under the accusation of having taken up arms against his most sacred majesty."

"Methinks, sir," the countess said in a loud clear voice, "that it would have been better had you delayed until this morning instead of attempting like a band of midnight thieves to break into my chateau. I fancy we should have heard but little of his majesty's clemency had you succeeded in your attempt. I am in arms, not against the king, but against his evil counsellors, the men who persuade him to break his pledged word, and to treat his unoffending subjects as if they were the worst of malefactors. Assuredly their royal highnesses the Princes of Condé and Navarre have no thought of opposing his majesty, but desire above all things that he should be able to act without pressure from Lorraine or Guise,

from pope or King of Spain, and when they lay down their
arms I shall be glad to do so.   Did I know that the king himself of his own mind had sent you here to summons me, I
would willingly accompany you to Paris to clear myself from
any charges brought against me; but as your base attempt
without summons or demand to break into my chateau last
night shows that you can have no authority from his majesty
to enter here, I refuse to open my gates, and shall defend
this place until the last against all who may attack it."

The knights rode away.   They had, after the rough reception on their arrival, perceived that the countess was determined to defend the chateau, and had only summoned her to
surrender as a matter of form.

"I would we had never entered upon this expedition, De
Brissac.   They told us that the house was but poorly fortified,
and we thought we should assuredly carry it last night by surprise, and that by taking this obstinate dame prisoner, burning her chateau, and sweeping all the country round, we
should give a much-needed lesson to the Huguenots of the
district.   One could not have expected to find the place
crowded with men, and everyone ready with lighted matches
and drawn cross-bows to receive us.   I believe now that that
fire we saw two or three miles in our rear as we came along
was a signal; but even if it were, one would not have given
them credit for gathering so promptly to withstand us.   As
for the place itself, it is, as we heard, of no great strength.
'Tis but a modern house, inclosed on three sides with a wall
some twenty feet high, and surrounded by a moat of the same
width.   With our force we should carry it in half an hour.
We know that the garrison consists of only fifty men besides a
score or so of grooms and servants."

"So we heard; but I am mistaken if there were not more
than double that number engaged on the wall.   Still, as you
say, there will be no great difficulty in carrying the place.
The ladders will be ready in a couple of hours, and De Beauvoir will bring in from the farmhouses plenty of planks and
beams for throwing bridges across the moat.   It is two hours
since he set out with the horsemen, so as to catch the Huguenot farmers asleep."

As they returned to the spot where the men were engaged in cooking their breakfast, while some were occupied in con‑structing ladders from young trees that had been felled for the purpose, a gentleman rode in.

"What is your news, De Villette?"

"The news is bad. De Beauvoir asked me to ride in to tell you that we find the farmhouses completely deserted, and the whole of the cattle and horses have disappeared, as well as the inhabitants. Save for some pigs and poultry we have not seen a living thing."

"*Sapristie!* The Huguenot dogs must have slept with one eye open. Either they heard the firing last night and at once made off, or they must have learned we were coming and must have gathered in the chateau. Their measures must have been indeed well planned and carried out for them all to have got the alarm in time to gather here before our arrival. I hope that is what they have done, for we reckoned upon carrying off at least a thousand head of cattle for the use of the army. It was for that as much as to capture the countess and strike a blow at this hive of Huguenots that the expedi‑tion was arranged. However, if they are all in there it will save us the trouble of driving them in."

"In that case though, De Brissac, the fifty men will have been reinforced by as many more at least."

"Ay, maybe by a hundred and fifty with the farmers and all their hands; but what are a hundred and fifty rustics and fifty men-at-arms against our force?"

De Brissac had guessed pretty accurately the number of fighting men that could be mustered among the tenants of the countess. The training that they had undergone had, how‑ever, made them more formidable opponents than he sup‑posed, and each man was animated by hatred of their perse‑cutors and a stern determination to fight until the last in defence of their lives and freedom of worship. They had been mustered at the first dawn of day in the courtyard, their arms inspected, and all deficiencies made up from the armoury. Fifty men were placed under Philip's orders for the defence of that portion of the house that rose directly from the edge of the moat. The lower windows were small and strongly barred, and there was little fear of an entrance being forced. The postern gate here had during the night been strengthened with stones, and articles of heavy furniture piled against it. A few men were placed at the lower windows, the main body on the first floor, where the casements were large, and the rest distributed at the upper windows to vex the enemy by their fire as they approached.

Philip appointed Eustace to take the command of the men at the lower windows, and Roger of those on the upper floor, he with Jacques posting himself on the first floor, against which the enemy would attempt to fix their ladders. Great fires were lighted in all the rooms, and cauldrons of water placed over them, and boys with pails stood by these in readiness to bring boiling water to the windows when required.

The walls round the courtyard and garden were not of sufficient thickness for fires to be lighted along the narrow path on which the defenders were posted, but fires were lighted in the courtyard, and boiling water prepared there in readiness to carry up when the assault began. The Huguenot gentlemen were placed in command at the various points along the wall most likely to be assailed.

Had the besiegers been provided with cannon the defence could not have lasted long, for the walls would not have resisted battering by shot, but cannon in those times were rare, and were too clumsy and heavy to accompany an expedition requiring to move with speed. For a time the men-at-arms alone garrisoned the wall, the farmers and their men being occupied in pumping water from the wells and carrying it to the cattle, of which some eight hundred had been driven in. The granaries were opened, and a plentiful supply of food placed in large troughs. At ten o'clock a trumpet called all the defenders to their posts. The enemy were drawn up in order and moved towards the house in six columns, two taking their way towards the rear to attack the house on that side, while the others advanced toward different points on the wall.

Ladders and long planks were carried at the head of each column. As they approached the assailants halted, and the arquebusiers came forward and took their post in line to cover

by their fire the advance of the storming parties. As soon
as these advanced a heavy fire was opened by the besieged
with cross-bow and arquebus.   The parapet was high, and
while they exposed only their heads to fire, and were altogether sheltered while loading, the assailants were completely
exposed.   Orders were given that the defenders should entirely
disregard the fire of the matchlock men, and should direct
their aim upon the storming parties.   These suffered heavily,
but, urged forward by their officers, they gained the edge of
the moat, pushed the planks across, and placed the ladders;
but as fast as these were put into position they were hurled
down again by the defenders, who, with long forked sticks,
thrust them out from the wall and hurled them backwards,
sometimes allowing them to remain until a line of men had
climbed up, and then pouring a pail of boiling water over the
wall upon them.

The farmers vied with the men-at-arms in the steadiness of
the defence, being furious at the sight of columns of smoke
which rose in many directions, showing that the cavalry of the
besiegers were occupied in destroying their homesteads.
Sometimes, when four or five ladders were planted together,
the assailants managed to climb up to the level of the parapet, but only to be thrust backward with pikes, and cut down
with swords and axes.   For two hours the assault continued,
and then De Brissac, seeing how heavy was the loss, and how
vain the efforts to scale the wall at any point, ordered the
trumpeters to sound the retreat, when the besiegers drew off,
galled by the fire of the defenders until they were out of
range.   The attempts of the two columns which had attacked
the house itself were attended with no greater success than
those of their fellows, their efforts to gain a footing in any of
the rooms on the first floor having been defeated with heavy
loss.

The leaders of the assailants held a consultation after their
troops had drawn off.

"It is of no use," De Brissac said, "to repeat the attack
on the walls, they are too stoutly defended.   It is out of the
question for us to think of returning to Poitiers.   We undertook to capture the place, to harry the farms, to destroy all

the Huguenots, and to return driving in all the cattle for the use of the army. Of all this we have only so far burned the farmhouses, and we have lost something like a couple of hundred men. This time we must try by fire. The men must gather bundles of firewood, and must attack in three columns, the principal against the great gate, the others against the two posterns, the one at the back of the house itself, the other nearest the angle where the wall joins it. If we had time to construct machines for battering the walls it would be an easy business, but that is out of the question. In a couple of days at the latest we shall have them coming out like a swarm of hornets from La Rochelle. It is not likely, when they had all their measures so well prepared, that they omitted to send off word at once to Coligny, and by to-morrow at noon we may have Condé and the Admiral upon us. Therefore we must make an end of this by nightfall. Have you any better plans to suggest, gentlemen?"

There was no reply. Several of those present had been wounded more or less severely, and some terribly bruised by being hurled back from the ladders as they led the troops to the assault. Five or six of the young nobles who had joined what they regarded as an expedition likely to meet with but slight resistance had been killed, and all regretted that they had embarked upon an affair that could bring them but small credit, while they were unprovided with the necessary means for attacking a place so stoutly defended. De Brissac at once issued orders, and strong parties of soldiers scattered and proceeded to cut down fences and bushes and to form large faggots. Their movements were observed by the men placed on the summit of the tower, and no doubt was entertained of the intentions of the enemy.

"What do you think we had better do, Philip?" François asked as they stood together at the top of the tower watching the Catholics at work. "We may shoot a number of them, but if they are determined they will certainly be able to lay their faggots, and in that case we shall be open to attack at three points, and likely enough they will at the same time renew their attack on the walls."

"That is the most dangerous part of it," Philip said. "We

ought to have no difficulty in holding the three entrances. The posterns are narrow, and forty men at each should be able to keep back a host, and this would leave you a hundred and twenty to hold the main gates; but if we have to man the walls too the matter would be serious. If we had time we might pull down one of the outbuildings and build a thick wall behind the gates, but in an hour they will be attacking us again." He stood thinking for a minute or two, and then exclaimed: "I have it, François.   Let us at once kill a number of the cattle and pile their carcasses up two deep against the gates. They may burn them down if they like then, but they can do nothing against that pile of flesh; the weight of the carcasses will keep them in a solid mass. At any rate, we might do that at the two posterns; the great gates are perhaps too wide and lofty, but if we formed a barricade inside them of say three bodies high a hundred men ought to be able to defend it, and that will leave a hundred for the walls and house."

"That is a capital idea, Philip. We will not lose a moment in carrying it out."

Two of the principal tenants were called up and told to see to the slaughtering instantly of sufficient cattle to pile two deep against the posterns. Calling a number of men together, these at once set about the business.

"We will see to the other barricade ourselves, Philip.   That is where the fighting will be."

The entrance behind the gateway was some twenty-five feet in width and as much in depth before it entered the courtyard. The bullocks were brought up to the spot and slaughtered there. The first line were about to be dragged into place when Philip suggested that they should be skinned.

"What on earth do you want to skin them for, Philip?" François asked.

"When they are arranged in a row I would throw the skins over them again, inside out.   The weight of the next row will keep the skins in their places, and it will be impossible for anyone to obtain a footing on that slippery surface, especially if we pour some blood over it."

François at once saw the point of the suggestion.   "Excellent, Philip.   I wish my brain was as full of ideas as yours is."

The same course was pursued with the other two tiers of carcasses, the hides of the upper row being firmly pegged into the flesh to prevent their being pulled off. The breastwork was about five feet high, and was absolutely unclimbable.

"It could not be better," François said. "A solid work would not be half so difficult to get over. Twenty men here could keep a host at bay."

Another tier of unskinned carcasses was laid down behind the breastwork for the defenders to stand on, and earth was piled over it to afford a footing. They had but just completed their preparations when the trumpet from above sounded the signal that the enemy were approaching. All took the posts that they had before occupied. The enemy approached as they had expected in three bodies, each preceded by a detachment that carried in front of them great faggots which served as a protection against the missiles of the besieged. Among them were men carrying sacks.

"What can they have there?" Philip asked one of the Huguenot gentlemen.

"I should say it was earth," he replied.

"Earth!" Philip repeated, puzzled. "What can they want that for?"

"I should think it is to cover the planks thickly before they lay down the faggots, otherwise the planks would burn and perhaps fall bodily in the water before the fire had done its work on the doors."

"No doubt that is it," Philip agreed. "I did not think of that before."

As soon as the heads of the columns approached within a hundred yards the men with arquebuses opened fire, and those with cross-bows speedily followed suit. Four hundred men with arquebuses at once ran forward until within a short distance of the moat, and opened so heavy a fire against the defenders of the wall and house that these were compelled to stoop down under shelter. Some of them would have still gone on firing from the windows, but Philip ordered them to draw back.

"It is of no use throwing away life," he said. "We cannot hope to prevent them planting their faggots and firing them."

He himself went up into a small turret partly overhanging the wall, and through a loophole watched the men at work. The contents of the sacks were emptied out upon the planks, the latter having been first soaked with water drawn from the moat by a pail one of the men carried. The earth was levelled a foot deep, and then a score of buckets of water emptied over it. Then the faggots were piled against the door. A torch was applied to them; and as soon as this was done the assailants fell back, the defenders plying them with shot and cross-bolts as soon as they did so.

Philip now paid a hasty visit to the walls. Here the assailants had suffered heavily before they had planted their faggots, the defenders being better able to return their fire than were those at the windows. In both cases, however, they had succeeded in laying and firing the faggots, although much hindered at the work by pails of boiling water emptied upon them. Some ten of the defenders had been shot through the head as they stood up to fire. Attempts were made, by pouring water down upon the faggots, to extinguish the flames, but the time taken in conveying the water up from the courtyard enabled the fire to get such hold that the attempt was abandoned.

"It is just as well," François said. "If we could extinguish the fire we should lose the benefit of the surprise we have prepared for them."

In a quarter of an hour light flames began to flicker up at the edges of the great gates.

"Do you stay here with me, Philip," François said. "Our own band will take post here; they are more accustomed to hand-to-hand fighting. The tenants will guard the wall. Montpace will be in command there. Beg De Riblemont to take command at the back of the house. Tell him to send for aid to us if he is pressed. I would put your own three men down at the postern there. I feel sure they can never move that double row of bullocks; but it is as well to make certain, and those three could hold the narrow postern till help reaches them. Place a boy with them to send off for aid if necessary. Bourdou is stationed behind the other postern with three men. It will be half an hour before the gates are down yet."

The two together made a tour of the defences. All was in readiness. The men after their first success felt confident that they should beat off their assailants; and even the women, gathered round the great fires in the house and courtyard, with pails in readiness to carry boiling water to the threatened points, showed no signs of anxiety, the younger ones laughing and chatting together as if engaged in ordinary work. The countess went round with her maids carrying flagons and cups, and gave a draught of wine to each of the defenders. The minister accompanied her. As yet there were no wounded needing their care, for all who had been hit had been struck in the head, and death had in each case been instantaneous.

At last the great gates fell with a crash, and a shout of exultation arose from the Catholics, answered by the Huguenots on the wall by one of defiance. In half an hour the assailants again formed up. The strongest column advanced towards the great gate, others against the posterns; and four separate bodies, with planks and ladders, moved forward to bridge the moat and to attack at other points. The defenders on the walls and at the windows were soon at work, and the assailants suffered heavily from the fire as they advanced. The fifty men-at-arms behind the barricade remained quiet and silent, a dozen of them with arquebuses lining the barricade. With loud shouts the Catholics came on, deeming the chateau as good as won. The arquebusiers poured their fire into them as they crossed the moat, and then fell back behind their comrades, who were armed with pike and sword. As they passed through the still smoking gateway the assailants saw the barricade in front of them, but this did not appear formidable, and, led by a number of gentlemen in complete armour, they rushed forward.

For a moment those in front recoiled as they reached the wall of slippery hides; then, pressed forward from behind, they made desperate attempts to climb it. It would have been as easy to try to mount a wall of ice; their hands and feet alike failed to obtain a hold, and from above the defenders with pike and sword thrust and cut at them; while the arquebusiers, as fast as possible, discharged their pieces into the crowd, loaded each time with three or four balls.

For half an hour the efforts to force the barricade continued. So many had fallen that the wall was now no higher than their waist, but even this could not be surmounted in face of the double line of pikemen; and at last the assailants fell back, baffled. At the two posterns they had failed to make any impression upon the carcasses that blocked their way. In vain they strove, by striking the curved points of their halberts into the carcasses, to drag them from their place; but the pressure of the weight above, and of the interior line of carcasses that were piled on the legs of the outside tiers, prevented the enemy from moving them in the slightest degree. While so engaged, those at work were exposed to the boiling water poured from above, and the soldiers standing behind in readiness to advance when the entrance was won were also exposed to the fire of the defenders.

The assaults on the walls and at the windows were far less obstinate than those in the previous attack, as they were intended only as diversions to the main assaults on the posterns and gate; and when the assailants at these points fell back, the storming parties also retreated. They had lost in all nearly four hundred men in the second attack, of whom more than a hundred and fifty had fallen in the assault upon the barricade. The instant they retreated François and Philip led out their men, cleared the earth from the planks, and threw these into the water. They were not a moment too soon, for just as they completed their task the Catholic cavalry thundered down to the edge of the moat, regardless of the fire from the walls, which emptied many saddles. Finding themselves unable to cross, they turned and galloped off after the infantry.

"We were just in time, Philip," François said. "If they had crossed the moat it would have gone hard with us, for, with that bank of bodies lying against the breastwork, they might have been able to leap it. At any rate, their long lances would have driven us back, and some would have dismounted and climbed over. As it is, I think we have done with them. After two such repulses as they have had, and losing pretty nearly half their infantry, they will never get the men to try another attack."

An hour later, indeed, the whole Catholic force, horse and foot, were seen to march away by the road along which they had come. As soon as they did so a trumpet summoned the defenders from the walls and house; the women and children also poured out into the courtyard; and the minister taking his place by the side of the countess on the steps of the chateau, a solemn service of thanksgiving to God, for their preservation from the danger that had threatened them, was held. It was now five o'clock and the short winter day was nearly over. Many of the tenants would have started off to their farms, but François begged them to remain until next morning.

"The smoke told you what to expect," he said. "You will find nothing but the ruins of your houses, and in this weather it would be madness to take your wives and families out. In the morning you can go and view your homes. If there are still any sheds standing that you can turn into houses for the time, you can come back for your wives and families; if not, they must remain here till you can get up shelter for them. In this bitter cold weather you could not think of rebuilding your houses regularly, nor would it be any use to do so until we get to the end of these troubles. But you can fell and saw wood, and erect cottages that will suffice for present use and serve as sheds when better times return. The first thing to do is to attend to those who have fallen. The dead must be removed and buried, but there must be many wounded, and these must be brought in and attended to. There is an empty granary that we will convert into a hospital."

"Before we do anything else, François, we must fish the planks from the moat, to serve until a fresh drawbridge is constructed. Eustace, do you get two heavy beams thrust over and lay the planks across them; then with Roger, mount, cross the moat as soon as it is bridged, and follow the road after the Catholics. They may not have gone far, and might halt and return to attack us when we shall be off our guard. Follow them about five miles; then, if they are still marching, you had both better come back to us. If they halt before that, do you remain and watch them, and send Roger back with the news."

A hundred and thirty wounded men were brought in, some wounded by shot or crossbow bolt, some terribly scalded, others with broken limbs from being hurled backwards with the ladders. The countess with her maids and many of the women attended to them as they were brought in, and applied salves and bandages to the wounds. Among the mass that had fallen inside the gate seven gentlemen who still lived were discovered. These were brought into the chateau and placed in a room together. The task was carried on by torch-light and occupied some hours. Towards midnight the trampling of a large body of horse was heard. Arms were hastily snatched up and steel caps thrust on, and pike in hand they thronged to defend the entrance. ˉ François ran to the battlements.

"Who comes there?" he shouted. "Halt and declare yourselves or we fire."

The horsemen halted, and a voice cried, "Is that you, François?"

"Yes, it is I, De la Noüe," François shouted back joyously.

"Is all well? Where are the enemy?" was asked in the Admiral's well-known voice.

"All is well, sir; they retreated just before nightfall, leaving seven hundred of their infantry wounded or dead behind them."

A shout of satisfaction rose from the horsemen.

"Take torches across the bridge," François ordered; "it is the Admiral come to our rescue."

A minute later the head of the column crossed the temporary bridge. François had run down and received them in the gateway.

"What is this?" the Admiral asked; "have they burnt your drawbridge and gate?"

"Yes, sir."

"How was it, then, they did not succeed in capturing the place? Ah, I see, you formed a barricade here." Two or three of the carcasses had been dragged aside to permit the men carrying the wounded to enter.

"Why, what is it, François—skins of freshly-slain oxen?"

"Yes, sir, and the barricade is formed of their bodies. We

had neither time nor materials at hand, and my cousin suggested bringing the oxen up and slaughtering them here. In that way we soon made a barricade. But we should have had hard work in holding it against such numbers had he not also suggested our skinning them and letting the hides hang as you see with the raw sides outwards. Then we smeared them thickly with blood, and though the Catholics strove their hardest not one of them managed to get a footing on the top."

"A rare thought indeed," the Admiral said warmly. "De la Noüe, these cousins of yours are truly apt scholars in war; the oldest soldier could not have thought of a better device. And you say you killed seven hundred of them, Laville?"

"That is the number, sir, counting in a hundred and thirty wounded who are now lying in a granary here."

"They must have fought stoutly. But what was your strength?"

"We had fifty men-at-arms, sir, five or six Huguenot gentlemen with their retainers, and a hundred and fifty men from our own estate, all of whom fought as doughtily as old soldiers could have done. The enemy thought to take us by surprise yesterday evening, but we were ready for them, and our discharge killed over fifty. Then they drew off and left us until this morning. They made two great attacks, the first by throwing planks across the moat and placing ladders at three places, the second by trying again to storm with ladders, while other bands tried to force their way in at this gateway and at the two posterns. Of course they have burned all the farms to the ground, but the cattle were all safely driven in here before they arrived. Now, if you will enter, sir, we will endeavour to provide for your wants. No one is yet in bed, we have been too busy carrying out the dead and collecting the wounded to think of sleep."

The countess was at the steps of the chateau to receive the Admiral as he dismounted.

"Accept my heartiest thanks for the speed with which you have come to our aid, Admiral, we did not expect you before to-morrow morning at the earliest."

"It has been a long ride truly," the Admiral said. "Your messenger arrived at daybreak, having walked the last five miles, for his horse had foundered. I flew to horse the moment I received the news, and with four hundred horsemen, for the most part Huguenot gentlemen, we started at once. We halted for three hours in the middle of the day to rest our horses, and again for an hour just after nightfall. We feared that we should find your chateau in flames, for although your messenger said that your son thought you could hold out against all attacks for two days, it seemed to us that so strong a force as was beleaguering you would carry the place by storm in a few hours. I have to congratulate you on the gallant defence that you have made."

"I have had nothing to do with it," the countess replied; "but, indeed, all have fought well. Now, if you will follow me in I will do my best to entertain you and the brave gentlemen who have ridden so far to my rescue, but I fear the accommodation will be of the roughest."

The horses were ranged in rows in the courtyard, haltered to ropes stretched across it, and an ample supply of food was given to each; some of the oxen that had done such good service were cut up and were soon roasting over great fires; while the women spread straw thickly in the largest apartments for the new-comers to sleep on.

"Where are the Catholics?" the Admiral asked.

"They have halted at a village some seven miles away," François said. "We sent two mounted men after them to make sure that they had gone well away and did not intend to try to take us by surprise in the night. They returned some hours since with the news."

"What do you say, De la Noüe," the Admiral exclaimed, "shall we beat them up to-night? They will not be expecting us, and after their march here and their day's fighting they will sleep soundly."

"I should like nothing better, Admiral; but in truth I doubt whether our horses could carry us, they have already made a twenty-league journey."

"We have at least two hundred horses here, Admiral," François said; "we have those of my own troop and fully a hundred and fifty that were driven in by the tenants. My own troop will of course be ready to go, and you could shift your saddles on to the other horses. There is not one of our men who would not gladly march with you, for although we have beaten the Catholics well the tenants do not forget that they are homeless, and will, I am sure, gladly follow up the blow."

"Then so it shall be," the Admiral said; "a hundred and fifty of the gentlemen who came with me shall ride with your troop, the rest of us will march with your tenants. I think we are capable of doing that even after our ride, gentlemen?"

There was a chorus of assent from those standing round, and De la Noüe added, "After supper, Admiral?"

"Certainly after supper," Coligny assented with a smile. "Another hour will make no difference. You may be sure they will not be moving before daylight. If we start from here at three, we shall be in ample time."

Philip at once went out and ordered the attendants and men-at-arms to lie down for two hours, as the Admiral was going to lead them to attack the Catholics at their halting-place, news which was received with grim satisfaction. In the meantime François gave a detailed account of the events of the siege, and the Admiral insisted upon going at once to inspect by torchlight the novel manner in which the two posterns had been blocked up.

"Nothing could have been better, De Laville," he said. "Your English cousin is indeed full of resources. Better material than this for blocking up a narrow gateway could hardly be contrived. Fire, as it was proved, was of no avail against it, for it would be impossible to dislodge the carcasses by main force, and even if they had cannon, the balls would not have penetrated this thickness of flesh, which must have been torn to pieces before it yielded. The idea of covering the carcasses at the gates with their own raw hides was an equally happy one. Upon my word, De la Noüe, I do not think that if you or I had been in command here we could have done better than these two young fellows."

At three o'clock all was ready for a start. De la Noüe took the command of the two hundred horsemen. The Admiral declined to ride, and placed himself at the head of the column of infantry, which was three hundred strong, thirty of the original defenders having been either killed or disabled, and twenty being left as a guard at the chateau.

The surprise of the Catholics was complete. Three hundred were killed, two hundred, including their commander, De Brissac, and thirty other gentlemen, were made prisoners, the remaining six hundred escaped in the darkness, their arms, armour, and the whole of the horses falling into the hands of the victors, who halted at the village until morning.

"Well, De Brissac," the Count de la Noüe said as they started on their return, "the times have changed since you and I fought under your father in Italy, and we little thought then that some day we should be fighting on opposite sides."

"Still less that I should be your prisoner, De la Noüe," the other laughed. "Well, we have made a nice business of this. We thought to surprise De Laville's chateau without having to strike a blow, and that we were going to return to Poitiers with at least a thousand head of cattle. We were horribly beaten at the chateau, have now been surprised ourselves, and you are carrying off our horses, to say nothing of ourselves. We marched out with eighteen hundred men horse and foot, and I don't think more than five or six hundred at the outside have got away and that in the scantiest apparel. Anjou will be furious when he hears the news. When I am exchanged I expect I shall be ordered to my estates. Had De Laville some older heads to assist him?"

"No, he and that young cousin of his riding next to him acted entirely by themselves, and the cousin, who is an English lad, is the one who invented that barricade of bullocks that stopped you."

"That was a rare device," De Brissac said. "I fought my way to it once, but there was no possibility of climbing it. It is rather mortifying to my pride to have been so completely beaten by the device of a lad like that. He ought to make a great soldier some day, De la Noüe."

CHAPTER XV

THE BATTLE OF JARNAC

WHILE the two armies were lying inactive through the winter the agents of both were endeavouring to interest other European powers in the struggle. The pope and Philip of Spain assisted the Guises, while the Duc de Deux-Ponts was preparing to lead an army to the assistance of the Huguenots from the Protestant states of Germany. The Cardinal Chatillon was in England eloquently supporting the letters of the Queen of Navarre to Elizabeth, asking for aid and munitions of war, men, and money—the latter being required especially to fulfil the engagements made with the German mercenaries. Elizabeth listened favourably to these requests, while with her usual duplicity she gave the most solemn assurances to the court of France that, so far from assisting the Huguenots, she held in horror those who raised the standard of rebellion against their sovereigns. She lent, however, £7000 to the King of Navarre, taking ample security in the way of jewels for the sum, and ordered Admiral Winter to embark six cannons, three hundred barrels of powder, and four thousand balls, and carry them to La Rochelle.

The admiral, well aware of the crooked policy of the queen and her readiness to sacrifice any of her subjects in order to justify herself, absolutely refused to sail until he received an order signed by the queen herself. His caution was justified, for upon the French ambassador remonstrating with her upon supplying the king's enemies, she declared that the assistance was wholly involuntary, for that Admiral Winter had entered the port of La Rochelle simply to purchase wine and other merchandise for some ships that he was convoying. The governor, however, had urged him so strongly to sell to him some guns and ammunition, that he, seeing that his ships were commanded by the guns of the forts, felt himself obliged to comply with the request.

The court of France professed to be satisfied with this statement, although perfectly aware of its absolute untruth, but they did not wish while engaged in the struggle with the Huguenots to be involved in open war with England. As soon as spring commenced both armies again prepared to take the field. The position of the Huguenots was by no means so strong as it had been when winter set in. Considerable numbers had died from disease, while large bodies had returned to their homes, the nobles and citizens being alike unable to continue any longer in the field owing to the exhaustion of their resources.

Upon the other hand, although the army of Anjou had suffered equally from disease it had not been diminished by desertion, as the troops were paid out of the royal treasury. Two thousand two hundred German horsemen, a portion of the large force sent by the Catholic princes of Germany, had joined him, and the Count de Tende had brought 3000 soldiers from the south of France. Other nobles came in as the winter broke with bodies of their retainers. The southern Huguenot leaders, known as the Viscounts, remained in Guyenne to protect the Protestant districts. The plan of Condé and the Admiral was to effect a junction with them, and then to march and meet the army of the Duc de Deux-Ponts. They therefore left Niort, which had for some time been their headquarters, and marched south towards Cognac, while the Duc d'Anjou moved in the same direction.

Both armies reached the river Charente at the same time but upon opposite sides. The Royalists seized the town of Chateau Neuf, half-way between Jarnac and Cognac, and set to work to repair the bridge which had been broken down by the Huguenots. Their main army marched down to Cognac and made a pretence of attacking the town. The Huguenots were spread over a long line, and the Admiral, seeing the danger of being attacked while so scattered, sent to Condé, who commanded the most advanced part of the army opposite Chateau Neuf, begging him to retire.   Condé, however, with his usual rashness declined to fall back, exclaiming that a Bourbon never fled from a foe.

The troop of François de Laville was with a large body of horse commanded by the the Count de la Noüe.   Life had passed quietly at the chateau after the repulse of the attack, for the occupation of Niort by a large force under the Admiral secured Laville from any risk of a repetition of the attack. The garrison and the whole of the tenantry, after they had erected huts for their families, devoted themselves to the work of strengthening the defences.   Flanking towers were erected at the angles of the walls.   The moat was doubled in width, and a work erected beyond it to guard the approach across the drawbridge.   The windows on the unprotected side were all partially closed with brickwork, leaving only loop-holes through which the defenders could fire.   The battle-ments of the wall were raised two feet and pierced with loop-holes, so that the defenders would no longer be obliged to raise their heads above its shelter to fire, and the narrow path was widened by the erection of a platform, so as to give more room for the men to use their weapons.   A garrison composed of fifty of the younger men on the farms took the place of the troop when it rode away.

Anjou had prepared several bridges, and suddenly crossed the river on the night of the 12th of March, the movement being so well managed that even the Huguenot divisions in the neighbourhood were unaware until morning of what was taking place.   As soon as the Admiral was informed that the enemy had crossed in great force, messengers were sent off in all directions to order the scattered divisions to concentrate. The operation was a slow one.   Discipline was lax, and many of the commanders instead of occupying the positions assigned to them had taken up others where better accommodation could be obtained, and much time was lost before the orders reached them.   Even then their movements were slow, and it was afternoon before those in the neighbourhood were assembled, and the Admiral prepared to fall back towards the main body of the army which lay near the position occupied by Condé. But before this could be done the whole Royalist army were upon him. He had taken part at Bassac, a little village with an abbey, with but De la Noüe's cavalry and a small number of infantry with him, and though the latter fought desperately they could not check the advance of the enemy.

"This is worse than St. Denis, François," De la Noüe said, as he prepared to charge a vastly superior body of the enemy's cavalry advancing against the village. "However, it must be done, for unless Anjou's advance is checked the battle will be lost before Condé can arrive. You and your cousin had best put yourself at the head of your own troop."

On reaching his men François gave the order. "Now, my men, is the time to show that you have profited by your drill. Keep in a solid body. Do not break up and engage in single conflicts, for if you do we must be overpowered by numbers. Ride boot to boot. Keep your eyes fixed on our plumes, and when we turn do you turn also and follow us closely."

When De la Noüe's trumpet sounded the charge, the band of horsemen burst down upon the Catholic cavalry, broke their ranks and pierced far into them. François and Philip were but a horse's length ahead of their men, and the pressure of the enemy soon drove them back into their ranks. Keeping in a close and compact body they fought their way on until François perceived that they were separated from the rest of the force. Then he put the horn that he wore slung over his shoulder to his lips and gave the command to wheel round. It was obeyed, and the line, which was four deep, fought their way round until facing the rear, and then putting spurs to their horses they overthrew all opposition and cleft their way out through the enemy, and then galloped back to Bassac. The village was lost, and the defenders were falling back in disorder upon D'Andelot, who with his division was just arriving to their assistance.

For a moment the fugitive horse and foot broke up his ranks. But he rallied his men, and advancing, drove the Catholics out of the village and retook the abbey. But as a whole army was opposed to him the success was but brief. After a desperate struggle the village was again lost, and the

Huguenots fell back, contesting every foot of the ground, along a raised causeway. The enemy were, however, fast outflanking them, and they were on the point of destruction when Condé arrived with three hundred knights with whom he had ridden forward, leaving the infantry to follow, as soon as Coligny's message for help had reached him. He himself was in no condition for battle. His arm had been broken by a cannon shot, and just as he reached the scene of battle his hip was fractured by the kick of a horse ridden by his brother-in-law, La Rochefoucault; nevertheless he did not hesitate, but calling on his little band to follow him, rode full at a body of eight hundred of the Catholic cavalry.

For a time the struggle was a desperate one. The Huguenots performed prodigies of valour, but the Royalists were reinforced, and the devoted band melted away. One Huguenot nobleman named La Vergne fought surrounded by twenty-five of his kinsmen whom he brought into the field. He himself and fifteen of his followers fell in a circle. Most of the others were taken prisoners. At last Condé's horse was killed under him and fell, pinning him to the ground. Condé raised his visor and surrendered to two knights to whom he was known. They raised him from the ground respectfully, but as they did so Montesquiou, captain of Anjou's guards, rode up, and drawing a pistol, shot Condé in the back, killing him almost instantaneously. Several other Huguenot nobles were killed in cold blood after they had surrendered.

But Condé's magnificent charge had not been without effect, for it enabled the Admiral to draw off from the field without further loss. The accounts of the number of killed and wounded differ, but numerically it was very small. The Huguenot infantry were not engaged at all, with the exception of a small body of the regiment of Plupiart. But of their cavalry nearly four hundred were killed or taken prisoners, and of these a hundred and forty were nobles and gentlemen, the flower of the Huguenot nobility. Among the prisoners were La Noüe, Soubise, La Loüe, and many others of distinction.

Coligny's retreat was not interfered with. The satisfaction of the Catholics at the death of Condé was so great that they were contented to rest upon their success. There were great rejoicings throughout France and the Catholic countries of Europe over the exaggerated accounts issued by Anjou of his victory, and it was generally considered that the Huguenot cause was lost. However, out of a hundred and twenty-eight troops of cavalry only fifteen had been engaged, and only six out of two hundred companies of infantry.

The army retired to Cognac, where the brave Queen of Navarre at once hurried on hearing the intelligence, and herself addressed the army, reminding them that though the Prince of Condé was dead the good cause was still alive, and that God would provide fresh instruments for carrying on His work. She then hurried away to La Rochelle to make provision for the needs of the army. The young Prince Henri was, at Condé's death, nominally placed in command of the army as general-in-chief, and he was joined by his cousin, the young Prince of Condé, a lad of about his own age.

D'Anjou, one of the most despicable of the princes of France, was so intoxicated by the success that he had gained that for a time he made no effort to follow up his advantage. He disgraced himself by having the body of Condé stripped and carried on a donkey to Jarnac, and there exposed for four days by the house where he lodged, while he occupied himself in writing vainglorious despatches to all the Catholic kings and princes. At last he moved forward to the siege of Cognac. Seven thousand infantry, for the most part new levies, had been placed here by Coligny, and these received the royal army with great determination. Not only were the assaults upon the walls repulsed with heavy loss, but the garrison made many sallies, and after wasting a month before the town, Anjou, despairing of its capture, drew off the army, which had suffered heavier losses here than it had done in the battle of Jarnac. He then besieged St. Jean d'Angely, where the garrison commanded by Count Montgomery also repulsed all attacks. Angoulême was attacked with an equal want of success, but Mucidan, a town to the southwest of Perigueux, was captured. The attack upon it, however, cost the life of De Brissac, one of his best officers—a loss which Anjou avenged by the murder in cold blood of the garrison, which surrendered on condition that life and property should be spared.

As a set-off to the success of the Huguenots, they suffered a heavy blow in the death of the gallant D'Andelot, the Admiral's brother—an officer of the highest ability, who had, before the outbreak of the troubles, occupied the rank of colonel-general of the French infantry. His death was attributed by both parties to poison, believed to have been administered by an emissary of Catherine de Medici. The fact, however, was not clearly established, and possibly he fell a victim to arduous and unceasing toil and exertion.

Both François de Laville and Philip Fletcher had been severely wounded in the battle of Jarnac, and some twenty of their troop had fallen in the fight. They were able, however, to sit their horses until they reached Cognac. The Admiral visited them as soon as he arrived there. He had noticed the little band as it emerged unbroken from the charge, and at once ranged itself up to aid him in retreating from the village of Bassac, until Condé's charge enabled him to draw off. He praised the cousins highly for their conduct, and as soon as they were able to be about again he bestowed on both the honour of knighthood, and then sent them to La Rochelle to remain there until perfectly cured. The vacancies in the troop were filled up by young men from the estate, who responded to the summons of the countess for men to take the place of those who had fallen, in her son's command.

The young Prince of Navarre had, while at Cognac, paid frequent visits to Philip, for whom he had taken a great liking, and he again begged Coligny to appoint him as one of the knights told off as his special body-guard. The Admiral, however, repeated the arguments he had before used.

"He is very young, prince, though he has borne himself so well, and it would create much jealousy among our young nobles were I to choose a foreigner for so honourable a post."

"But my councillors are all staid men, Admiral, and I want someone I can talk to without ceremony."

"There are plenty of young Frenchmen, prince. If you must choose one why not take the Count de Laville? You were saying but yesterday that you liked him."

"Yes, he is something like his cousin; I think being

together has given him Philip's manner.　If I cannot have Philip I should like to have him."

"He would doubtless feel it a great honour, prince, while I doubt, were I to offer the post to the young Englishman, if he would accept it.　He has not come here to seek honour, but to fight for our faith.　I had a conversation with him one day, and found that it was with that simple purpose he came here, and however honourable the post, I am sure he would prefer one that gave him full opportunity for taking an active part.　With De Laville it is different.　He is a French noble, and maybe some day you will be king of France.　He is of a brave and adventurous spirit, but methinks that the young Englishman has a greater genius for war.　His cousin, although older, I·observe generally appeals to him for his opinion, and has frankly and nobly given him the chief credit in the affairs in which he has been engaged."

The Admiral was not mistaken.　François, when asked if he would like to be appointed as one of the gentlemen about the prince's person, at once embraced the offer, which, as he saw, afforded him great openings for advancement in the future. His only regret was that it would separate him from Philip. When he said as much to his cousin, on informing him of the unexpected honour that had befallen him, Philip replied at once, "Do not think of that, François.　I shall of course be sorry, but I shall see you often, and you would be wrong to refuse such an offer.　The King of France has no children. His two brothers are unmarried.　Anjou is, from all accounts, reckless and dissolute, and Alençon is sickly.　They alone stand between Henri of Navarre and the throne of France, and should he succeed to it his intimates will gain honours, rank, and possessions.　There is not a young noble but would feel honoured by being selected for the post.　As for fighting, no one can say how long these troubles may last, and I am greatly mistaken if those round Henri of Navarre, when he reaches manhood, will not have their full share of it."

Therefore, when the two newly-made young knights went to La Rochelle for quiet and sea-air, it was with the understanding that as soon as their strength was thoroughly recovered François should resign the command of the troop to Philip, and would himself ride with the Prince of Navarre and his cousin Condé. François had at once written to his mother with the news of his appointment, and a few days after they reached La Rochelle received an answer expressing her gratification.

"I rejoice," she said, "not only because it is a post of high honour, but because it will take you somewhat out of the heat of the fray. I have not hesitated to let you risk your life in the cause; but you are my only son, and were you slain I should be alone in the world, and the title would go to one of your cousins, for whom I care nothing, and it will be a comfort for me to know in the future you will not be running such fearful risks."

At La Rochelle they took up their abode at Maître Bertram's, and were most kindly received by him and his daughter.

"It is but two years since you landed here with madame, your mother, Monsieur Fletcher. You were but a stripling then, though you gave wonderful promise of size and strength. Now you are a man, and have won the honour of knighthood, and methinks that in thew and sinew there are not many in our army who would overmatch you."

"Oh, yes, there are, Maître Bertram," Philip laughed. "I have a big frame like my father's, I will admit, and to look at it may be as you say, but I shall want many another year over my head before my strength matches my size. I am but just eighteen, and men do not come to their full strength till they are five-and-twenty."

"You are strong enough for anything now," the merchant said, "and I should not like to stand a downright blow from you in the best suit of armour ever forged. I was glad to see that rascal Pierre come back with you. He is a merry fellow, though I fear that he causes idleness among my servants for all the grave looks he puts on as he waits on you at dinner. Is he valiant?"

"He has had no great opportunity of showing valour," Philip replied, "but he is cool, and not easily ruffled, and he fought stoutly in the defence of the Count de Laville's chateau; but of course it is not his business to ride behind me in battle."

Philip had corresponded regularly with his parents, and had received letters in reply from them, and also from his uncle and aunt, though these of course came irregularly, as ships happened to be sailing for La Rochelle. His father wrote but briefly, but his letters expressed satisfaction.

"I am right glad," he said, "to think that a Fletcher is again cracking the skulls of Frenchmen—I mean, of course, of Catholic Frenchmen—for I regard the Huguenots, being of our religion, as half English. I don't say take care of yourself, my lad—it is not the way of Englishmen to do that on the battlefield—but it would be a grievous day for us all here if we heard that aught had befallen you."

The letters of his mother and aunt were of a different character, and dwelt strongly upon the sacred cause upon which he was engaged, and both rejoiced greatly over the number of Huguenots he and François had rescued round Niort. His uncle's letters were more worldly.

"Your aunt's letters to my wife," he said, "speak very warmly in praise of you. She said you have distinguished yourself highly, that you have attracted the attention of the Prince of Condé and the Admiral, have rendered service to the Queen of Navarre and her son, and have received tokens of their esteem; also that you stand high in the regard of the Count de la Noüe, who is in all respects a most accomplished gentleman, and that he has told her that he hopes before long you will receive the honour of knighthood. Worldly honours, Philip, are not to be despised, especially when they are won by worthy service, although I know that my wife and your mother think but lightly of them, and that it is the fashion of those of our faith to treat them with contempt. Such is not my opinion. I am gratified to think that the money I have made in trade will descend to one of whom I can be proud, and who in this country may occupy the position that his ancestors on his mother's side did in my own, and to me it will be a matter of extreme gratification if I hear that you have won your spurs, especially at the hand of so great a leader and so worthy a one as Admiral Coligny. I promise you that there shall be feasting among the poor of Canterbury on the day when the news comes. Of late you have drawn but slightly upon me, for, as you say, you have few expenses save the pay of your five men when staying at Laville; but do not stint money should there be an occasion."

Upon rejoining the camp Philip found the time hang somewhat heavily upon his hands. François was necessarily much with the prince. Captain Montpace looked after the troop, and the Count de la Noüe was in captivity. A few days after he rejoined, however, one of the Admiral's pages came to his tent and requested him to call upon Coligny.

"The camp will break up to-morrow, Chevalier Fletcher," the latter said. "We are going down to join the Viscounts, and then march to effect a junction with the Duc de Deux-Ponts, who we hear has now fairly set out on his forward march. I wish to send a despatch to him, and I know no one to whom I could better intrust it than yourself. It is a mission of honour, but of danger. However, you have already exhibited such tact and discretion as well as bravery, that I believe if anyone can reach the duke through the two royal armies that are trying to intercept him you can do so. Will you undertake the mission?"

"I am greatly honoured by your intrusting me with it, sir, and will assuredly do my best."

"I do not propose that you should travel in disguise," the Admiral said, "for disguise means slow motion, and there is need for despatch. Therefore, I should say, take a small body of well-mounted men with you, and ride as speedily as you can. How many to take I leave to your discretion. The despatches will be ready for you by ten o'clock to-night."

"I shall be ready to start at that hour, sir," and Philip returned to his tent. After sitting thinking for a few minutes he called to Pierre, who was sitting outside.

"Pierre, I want your advice. I am about to start on a journey to the east of France. I do not go this time in disguise, but ride straight through. What think you? how many men shall I take with me—one or fifty?"

"Not fifty certainly," Pierre said promptly. "There is mighty trouble in feeding fifty men; besides, you may have to pass as a Royalist, and who can answer for the discretion of so many? Besides, if we have to turn and double, there is no hiding fifty men. If you ride through the smallest village at midnight the noise would wake the inhabitants, and when the enemy came up they would get news of your passage. I do not see that you can do better than take Eustace and Roger and myself. Henri will not be fit to ride for weeks yet, and although Jacques is recovering from the loss of his bridle-arm you settled that he was to go to Laville, where the countess would take him into her service. Jarnac lessened your force by half, but I think that two will be as good as four on a journey like this. Such a party can pass unnoticed. It is but a gentleman with two retainers behind him from a neighbouring chateau."

"That is what I concluded myself, Pierre, but I thought I would ask your opinion about it, for you have shown yourself a shrewd fellow. All your horses are in good condition, and it is well that I exchanged those you rode before for some of the best of the three hundred we captured from the assailants of the chateau. Of course, you will ride one of my horses, changing the saddle every day as your weight is so much less than mine. I shall not take armour with me, the extra weight tells heavily on a long journey; and besides, a knight in full armour would attract more attention than one riding as it would seem for pleasure. Let Eustace and Roger pick the two best horses."

"When do we start, sir?"

"We must be saddled and ready to start by ten to-night. See that a bottle of wine, a cold fowl, and a portion of bread for each are brought along with us. We shall have a long night's ride. We will carry no valises, they add to the weight and look like travelling. Let each man make a small canvas bag and place in it a change of linen. It can be rolled up in the cloak and strapped behind the saddle. A dozen charges for each pistol will be more than we shall be likely to require. Tell them to take no more. They must take their breastpieces and steel caps, of course. They can leave the backpieces behind them. I will go round to the hospital and say good-bye to Henri and Jacques, they will feel being left behind sorely."

After visiting his wounded followers he went to the house

occupied by the Prince of Navarre, where François also was lodged.

"So I hear you are off again, Philip," the latter said, as his cousin entered the salon where two or three of the prince's companions were sitting. "I should feel envious of you were it not that we also are on the point of starting."

"How did you know I was going off, François?"

"The prince told me half an hour since. He heard it from the Admiral. He told me he wished he was going with you instead of with the army. He is always thirsting after adventure. He bade me bring you in to him if you came. I said you would be sure to do so. It was useless my going out to look for you, as I could not tell what you might have to do before starting."

The young prince threw aside the book he was reading when they entered.

"Ah, monsieur the Englishman," he said, "so you are off again like a veritable knight-errant of romance in search of fresh adventure."

"No, sir, my search will be to avoid adventure."

"Ah, well, you are sure to find some whether or not. *Sapristie*, but it is annoying to be born a prince."

"It has its advantages also, sir," Philip said smiling.

The prince laughed merrily.

"So I suppose, but for my part I have not discovered them as yet. I must hope for the future, but it appears to me now that it can never be pleasant. One is obliged to do this, that, and the other because one is a prince. One always has to have one's head full of politics, to listen gravely to stupidities, to put up with tiresome people, and never to have one's own way in anything. However, I suppose my turn will come, but at present I would rather be hunting the wild goats in Navarre than pretending to be general-in-chief of an army, when everyone knows that I am not even as free to go my own way as a common soldier. I shall look to see you again, Chevalier Philip, and shall expect you to have some more good stories to tell me."

Having handed him his despatches, the Admiral pointed out to him the position, as far as he knew by recent report, of the forces under the Dukes of Aumale and Nemours.

"Possibly there will be other enemies," the Admiral said, "for our friends in Paris have sent me word that the Spanish ambassador has at the king's request written to beg the Duke of Alva, and Mansfeld, governor of Luxembourg, to send troops to aid in barring the way to the Duc de Deux-Ponts. I hope Alva has his hands full with his own troubles in the Netherlands, and although Spain is always lavish of promises it gives but little real aid to the king. Then again, on the road you may meet with bands of German mercenaries sent by the Catholic princes to join the royal forces. As you see, the despatches are written small, and at your first halt it will be well if you sew them in the lining of your boot, they will escape observation there however closely you may be searched, for they are but of little bulk, and I have written them on the softest paper I could obtain, so that it will not crackle to the touch.

"I leave it to yourself to choose the route, but I think that you could not do better than take that one you before followed when you and Laville joined me at Chatillon, thence keep well south through Lorraine. The royal forces are at Metz. I can give you no farther instructions, for I cannot say how rapidly Deux-Ponts may move, or what route he may be obliged to take to avoid the royal forces. And now farewell, lad. Remember that it is an important service you are rendering to our cause and that much depends on your reaching Deux-Ponts, for the despatches tell him the route by which I intend to move, indicate that which he had best follow in order that he may effect a junction, and give him many details as to roads, fords, and bridges that may be of vital importance to him."

Philip rode forty miles that night, and put up just as daylight was breaking at the village of Auverge. There they rested for six hours and then rode on to Laville, where he was received with great joy by his aunt, for whom he bore a letter from François. After halting here for a few hours they continued their journey. So far they had been riding through a friendly country, but had now to travel with due precautions, journeying fast, and yet taking care that the horses should not be overworked, as sudden occasion might arise for speed or endurance, and as the journey was some eight hundred miles long it behoved him to carefully husband the strength of the animals.

After riding another fifteen miles they stopped for the night at a village, as Philip intended to journey by day, for his arrival at inns early in the morning would excite comment. The three men had been carefully instructed in the story they were to tell at the inns where they halted. Their master was M. de Vibourg, whose estate lay near the place at which they halted on the preceding night, and who was going for a short visit to friends at the next town at which they would arrive. If questioned as to his politics, they were to say that he held aloof from the matter, for he considered that undue violence was exercised towards the Huguenots, who, he believed, if permitted to worship in their own way, would be good and harmless citizens.

So day by day they journeyed along, avoiding all large towns and riding quietly through small ones where their appearance attracted no attention whatever. On the fourth day, when as usual they had halted to dine and give their horses a couple of hours' rest, Philip heard the trampling of horses outside the inn. Going to the window he saw two gentlemen with eight armed retainers dismounting at the door. The gentlemen wore the Royalist colours. At the same moment Pierre came into the room.

" I have told Eustace and Roger to finish their meal quickly and then to get the horses saddled, to mount and take ours quietly to the end of the village and wait for us there, sir, so that if there should be trouble we have but to leap through the casement and make a short run of it."

"That is very well done, Pierre," Philip said, reseating himself at the table, while Pierre took his place behind his chair as if waiting upon him. The door opened and the two gentlemen entered. They did not as usual remove their hats, but seated themselves at a table and began talking noisily. Presently one made a remark in a low tone to the other, who turned round in his chair and stared offensively at Philip. The latter continued his meal without paying any attention to him.

"PHILIP STRUCK HIM FULL IN THE FACE."

"And who may you be, young sir?" the man said, rising and walking across the room.

"I am not in the habit of answering questions addressed to me by strangers," Philip said quietly.

"*Parbleu*, custom or no custom, you have to answer them now. This is not a time when men can go about unquestioned. You do not wear the Royalist colours, and I demand to know who you are."

"I would wear the Royalist colours if I were on the way to join the Royalist army," Philip replied calmly; "as at present I am not doing so, but am simply travelling as a private gentleman, I see no occasion for putting on badges."

"You have not answered my question. Who are you?"

"I do not intend to answer the question; my name is a matter which concerns myself only."

"You insolent young knave," the man said angrily, "I will crop your ears for you."

Philip rose from the table, and the other was for a moment surprised at the height and proportions of one whom he had taken for a mere lad.

"I desire to have no words with you," Philip said; "eat your dinner in peace and let me eat mine, for if it comes to cutting off ears you may find that you had better have left the matter alone."

The gentleman put his hand to the hilt of his sword and was in the act of drawing it when Philip, making a step forward, struck him full in the face with all his strength, knocking him backwards to the ground. His companion leapt from his seat drawing a pistol from his belt as he did so, when Pierre sent a plate skimming across the room with great force. It struck the man in the mouth, cutting his lips and knocking out some of his front teeth. The pistol exploded harmlessly in the air, while the sudden shock and pain staggered and silenced him, and before he could recover sufficiently to draw his sword or to shout, Philip and Pierre leaped through the open casement and ran down the street.

CHAPTER XVI

"THAT was a good shot, Pierre," Philip said as they ran, "and has probably saved my life."

"I am accustomed to throw straight, sir; my dinner has frequently depended on my knocking down a bird with a stone, and it was not often that I had to go without it. They are making a rare hubbub back at the inn."

Loud shouts were heard behind them.

"We have plenty of time," Philip said as he moderated the pace at which they had started. "The men will be confused at first, knowing nothing of what it all means. Then they will have to get the horses out of the stables."

"And then they will have trouble," Pierre added.

"What trouble, Pierre?"

"I gave a hint to Eustace," Pierre said with a laugh, "that it would be just as well before he mounted to cut off all the bridles at the rings. A nice way they will be in when they go to mount!"

"Did you cut their bridles for them, Eustace?" he asked as they came up to the others.

"Ay, and their stirrup-leathers too, Pierre."

"Good, indeed!" Philip exclaimed. "Without bridles or stirrup-leathers they can scarce make a start, and it will take them some minutes to patch them up. We will ride hard for a bit, that will put us far enough ahead to be able to take any by-road and throw them off our traces. I have no fear of their catching us by straight riding. The masters' horses may be as good as ours, but those of the men can hardly be so; still, they might come up to us wherever we halted for the night."

They looked back when they were some two miles from the village, and along the long straight road could make out some figures that they doubted not were horsemen just starting in pursuit.

"They waited to mend their leathers," Pierre remarked.

"They were right there," Philip said; "for a man can fight but poorly without bridle or stirrups. The horses will not have been fed, so we have an advantage there. I do not think we need trouble ourselves much more about them."

"There is one thing, sir, they won't mind foundering their horses, and we have to be careful of ours."

"That is so, Pierre; and besides, at the first place they come to they may send others on in pursuit with fresh horses. No, we must throw them off our track as soon as we can. There is a wood a mile or so ahead; we will leave the road there."

They were riding on the margin of turf bordering the road on either side so as to avoid the dust that lay thick and white upon it, and they held on at an easy canter till they reached the trees. Then, at Philip's order, they scattered and went at a walk, so as to avoid leaving marks that could be seen at once by anyone following them. A couple of hundred yards farther they came upon a stream running through a wood; it was but a few inches deep.

"This will do for us," Philip said. "Now follow me in single file, and see that your horses step always in the water."

He led them across the road and on for half a mile; then they left the stream and soon afterwards emerged from the wood and struck across the country.

"I should think they will have had pretty well enough of it by the time they get to the wood," Philip said, "and at any rate will lose a lot of time there. They will trace our tracks to the edge of the stream, and will naturally suppose that we will follow it up as we struck it on the other side of the road. It is like enough they will be half an hour searching before they find where we left the stream, and will know well enough then it will be hopeless trying to catch us."

"They saw we had good horses," Eustace said, "for as we

led them out one of them made the remark that they were as good-looking a lot of horses as you would often see together. No doubt at first their leaders were so furious that they thought of nothing but mending the leathers and getting off; but when they get a check in the wood it is probable that someone will venture to tell them how well we are mounted, and that pursuit will be hopeless."

"Nevertheless I think they will pursue, Monsieur Philip," Pierre said. "They did not look like men who would swallow an injury and think no more of it. As long as there remains a single chance of discovering you they will not give up pursuit. Of course they have no reason for suspicion that you are anything but what you seem to be, a gentleman of the neighbourhood, and will consider that at one or other of the towns or villages ahead of us they are sure to hear of our passing through, and perhaps to learn who you are and where you reside. Doubtless they asked at the inn before starting whether you were known; and as soon as they find they are not likely to catch us by hard riding, they will make straight forward, dividing into several parties at the next place they come to, and scattering in order to obtain news of us."

"Which they will not get," Philip said, "as we will take good care to avoid passing through villages. For to-night we will sleep in the woods, as the weather is warm and pleasant."

After riding another fifteen miles they halted in a wood. They always carried some food and wine with them, as circumstances might at any time arise that would render it imprudent for them to put up at an inn, and each also carried a feed of corn for his horse. Leaving Pierre to unsaddle and rub down his horse, Philip walked to the farther edge of the wood to view the country beyond. They were, he knew, not far from La Châtre, and he was not surprised to see the town, lying in a valley, to which the ground sloped down from the wood. It was about a mile and a half distant. Nearer the wood, but half a mile to the west, the towers of a fortified chateau rose from a clump of trees. The country was rich and well cultivated, and everything had an aspect of peace and comfort.

"What a hideous thing it is," Philip said to himself, "that

in so fair a country people cannot live in peace together, and should fly at each other's throats simply because they cannot agree that each shall worship God after his own fashion! It might be Canterbury, with the hills rising round it and the little river, save that it lacks the cathedral rising over it; and yet I doubt not there are many there who live in daily peril of their lives, for there is not a town in France that has not its share of Huguenots, and they can never tell when the storm of popular fury may burst upon them."

The shades of evening were beginning to fall when he rejoined his companions. They had already rubbed down their horses and replaced the saddles, and the animals were contentedly eating their corn.

"They look well," Philip said as he walked from one to the other.

"Yes, sir, they are none the worse for their travel so far, and could carry us on a hard race for our lives. Shall we light a fire?"

"I do not think it is worth while, Eustace. The evening is warm, and we shall be off at daybreak. Someone passing through the wood might see the flames and carry the news down to La Châtre, which is but a mile and a half away; and it is quite possible that those fellows we had to do with to-day may be there if they are travelling the same way that we are, and may consider it likely we shall halt there for the night. At any rate, as we do not need the fire, we will run no risks."

They ate their supper, and an hour later wrapped themselves in their cloaks and lay down. Philip was just dropping off to sleep when Pierre touched him. He sat up with a start.

"There are some people in the wood," Pierre said.

Philip was wide awake now, and the sound of singing at no great distance came to his ears.

"It is a Huguenot hymn," he exclaimed. "There must be a meeting in the wood. No doubt it is some of the people from the town who have come out to hold a secret meeting here. I will go and see it. Come with me, Pierre. We will go very quietly, for it would scare them terribly did they hear anyone approaching."

Making their way noiselessly through the wood they came,

after walking about three hundred yards, to the edge of an open space among the trees, where they halted. In the centre they could see in the moonlight a body of some seventy or eighty people gathered. Standing upon the trunk of a fallen tree was a minister who was addressing them.

"My brethren," he was saying when they could catch his words, "this is the last time we shall meet here. We know that suspicions have already arisen that we are holding meetings, and that we do so at the peril of our lives. The search for me has been hot for some days; and though I am willing enough to give my life in the cause of our Lord, I would not bring destruction upon you at the present moment. Were the prospects hopeless I should say, let us continue together here to the last; but the sky is clearing, and it may be that ere long freedom of worship may be proclaimed throughout France. Therefore, it is better that for a time we should abstain from gathering ourselves together. Even now the persecutors may be on our track."

"Pierre," Philip whispered, "do you go over in that direction until you come to the edge of the wood. If you see any signs of men moving about, run quickly to the others and bring the horses up here."

"I had better go back there first, had I not, Monsieur Philip? and bring the men and horses along with me to the edge of the wood, for I might lose a quarter of an hour in searching for them."

"That would be the best plan, Pierre. Should you hear a sudden noise here, hurry in this direction, and I will come to meet you. It may well be that, guessing the Huguenots would place someone on watch towards the town, the Catholics may, if they come, approach from the other side. Should you see anyone coming, give a loud shout at once. It will act as a warning to these people, and enable them to scatter and fly before their foes arrive."

For an hour the preacher continued to address his hearers, exhorting them to stand firm in the faith, and to await with patience the coming of better days.

They were not more than twenty paces away from the spot where Philip was standing, and in the moonlight he could clearly see the faces of the assembly, for the preacher was standing with his back to him. From their dress he judged that most of them belonged to the poorer classes, though three or four were evidently *bourgeois* of the well-to-do class. Seated on the trunk on which the preacher was standing, and looking up at him so that her profile was clearly visible to Philip, sat a young girl whose face struck Philip as of singular beauty. The hood of the cloak in which she was wrapped had fallen back from her head, and her hair looked golden in the moonlight. She was listening with rapt attention. The moonlight glistened on a brooch which held the cloak together at her throat. A young woman stood by her, and a man, in steel cap and with a sword at his side, stood a pace behind her. Philip judged that she belonged to a rank considerably above that of the rest of the gathering. When the address had concluded the preacher began a hymn in which all joined. Just as they began Philip heard the crack of a stick among the trees. It was not on the side from which Pierre would be coming. He listened attentively, but the singing was so loud that he could hear nothing, except that once a clash such as would be made by a scabbard or piece of armour striking against a bough came to his ears. Suddenly he heard a shout.

"That is Pierre!" he exclaimed to himself, and ran forward into the circle. There was a cry of alarm, and the singing suddenly stopped.

"I am a friend," he exclaimed. "I have come to warn you of danger. There are men coming in this direction from the town."

"My brethren, we will separate," the minister said calmly. "But first I will pronounce the benediction." This he did solemnly, and then said: "Now let all make through the wood, and, issuing from the other side, return by a circuit to the town. Mademoiselle Claire, I will accompany you to the chateau."

At this moment Philip heard horses approaching.

"This way, Pierre," he shouted, and ran to meet them. Fifty yards away he came upon them, and leapt into his saddle. "See to your weapons, lads," he said; "I believe there are others in the wood already."

He was within twenty yards of the clearing when he heard a sudden shout of "Down with the Huguenot dogs! Kill! kill!" He dashed forward, followed by his men. A mob of armed men, headed by two or three horsemen, had burst from the opposite side of the glade, and were rushing upon the Huguenots, who had just broken up into small groups. They stood as if paralysed at this sudden attack. No cry or scream broke from the women; most of these threw themselves upon their knees; a few of the men followed their example, and prepared to die unresistingly. Some sprang away among the trees, and above the din the preacher's voice was heard commencing a Huguenot hymn beginning, "*The gates of heaven are opened*," in which, without a moment's hesitation, those who remained around him joined.

In a moment, with savage shouts and yells, their assailants were upon them, smiting and thrusting. With a shout Philip spurred forward from the other side. He saw at once that against such numbers he and his three followers could do nothing, but his rage at this massacre of innocent people—a scene common enough in France, but which he now for the first time witnessed—half-maddened him. One of the horsemen, whom he recognized at once as the man Pierre had knocked down with the plate, rode at the girl Philip had been watching, and who was standing with upturned face joining in the hymn. The man attending her drew his sword, and placed himself in the way of the horsemen, but the latter cut him down, and raised the sword to strike full at the girl, when Philip shot him through the head. Instantly another horseman, with a shout of recognition, rode at him. Philip thrust his still smoking pistol in his holster, and drew his sword.

"This is more than I hoped for," his assailant said as he dealt a sweeping blow at him.

"Do not congratulate yourself too soon," Philip replied as he guarded the blow, and, lunging in return, the point glided off his adversary's armour. He parried again, and then with a back-handed sweep he struck his opponent on the neck with his whole force. Coming out to take part in a Huguenot hunt, in which he expected no opposition, the knight had left his helmet behind him, and fell from his horse with his head half-severed from his body. In the meantime the two men-at-arms and Pierre had driven back the mob of townsmen, who, however, having massacred most of the unresisting Huguenots, were surging up round them.

"Give me your hand, mademoiselle, and put your foot on mine," Philip exclaimed to the girl, who was still standing close to him. "Pierre," he shouted, as, bewildered by the uproar, the girl instinctively obeyed the order, "take this woman up behind you." Pierre made his horse plunge and so freed himself from those attacking him, then reining round he rode to Philip's side, and helped the companion of the young lady to the croup of his saddle, Philip dashing forward to free his two followers from their numerous assailants.

"To the left, Eustace;" and cutting their way through the crowd the three horsemen freed themselves, and, as they dashed off, were joined by Pierre.

"We must work back by the way we came, Monsieur Philip," Pierre said; "there is another body coming up in front to cut off fugitives, and that was why I shouted to you."

In a minute or two they were out of the wood. Men were seen running across the fields, but these they easily avoided.

"Now turn again and make straight for La Châtre," Philip said, "we can cross the bridge and ride through the place without danger. Those who would have interfered with us are all behind us."

As he had expected, the place was perfectly quiet. The better class of the *bourgeois* were all asleep, either ignorant or disapproving of the action of the mob. As soon as they were through the town Philip checked the speed of his horse.

"Mademoiselle," he said, "I am as yet in ignorance of your name. I am the Chevalier Philip Fletcher, an English gentleman fighting, for the cause of the reformed religion, under Admiral Coligny. I am on my way east with important despatches, and I was bivouacking with my three followers in the wood when I was attracted by the singing. Judging from the words of the minister that there was danger of an attack I put one of my men on the watch, while I myself remained in the wood by your meeting-place. Unfortunately the sound of the last hymn you sang drowned the noise made by the party that assailed you. However, happily we were in time to save you and your servant, and our sudden appearance doubtless enabled many to escape who would otherwise have been massacred."

The girl had burst into a fit of sobbing as soon as the danger was over, but she had now recovered.

"My name is Claire de Valecourt, monsieur," she said. "My father is with the Admiral. He will be deeply grateful to you for saving my life."

"I have the honour of knowing the Count de Valecourt, mademoiselle, and am glad indeed that I have been able to be of service to his daughter. The count is one of the gentlemen who act as guardians to the Prince of Navarre, whom I have also the honour of knowing. And now, what are your wishes? It is not too late even now, should you desire it, for me to take you back to the chateau."

"I should be defenceless there, sir," she said. "There are but a score of men-at-arms, and though formerly a place of some strength, it could not be defended now. See, sir, it is too late already."

Philip looked round and saw a bright light suddenly rising from the clump of trees on which the chateau stood. He gave an exclamation of anger.

"It cannot be helped," she said quietly; "it is but a small place. It was part of my mother's dower. Our estates, you know, are in Provence. My father thought I should be safer here than remaining there alone while he was away. We have always been on good terms with the townspeople here, and they did not interfere with those of our religion during the last war, so we thought that it would be the same now; but of late some people have been here stirring up the townsmen, and some travelling friars preached in the market-place not long since, upbraiding the people with their slackness in not rooting us out altogether.

"A month ago one of the persecuted ministers came to the chateau at night, and has been concealed there since. Seeing that there will be no minister here for some time, word was sent round secretly to those of our religion in the town, and twice a week we have had meetings in the wood. Many of the servants of the chateau are Catholics, and of the men-at-arms the majority are not of our faith, therefore I used to steal out quietly with my attendant. We heard two days ago that a rumour of the meetings had got about, and to-night's was to have been the last of them."

"And now, mademoiselle, what are your wishes? Have you any friends with whom I could place you until you could rejoin your father?"

"None near here, monsieur; I have always lived in the south."

"I should not have taken you for a lady of Provence," Philip said. "Your hair is fair, and you have rather the appearance of one of my own countrywomen than of one born in the south of France."

"I am partly of northern blood," she said. "My mother was the daughter of Sir Allan Ramsay, a Scottish gentleman who took service in France, being driven from home by the feuds that prevailed there. I knew but little about her, for she died when I was a child, and my father, who loved her greatly, seldom speaks to me of her."

Philip rode for some time in silence.

"I feel that I am a terrible burden on your hands, monsieur," she said quietly at last; "but I will do anything that you think best. If you set us down we will try and find refuge in some peasant's hut, or we can dress ourselves as countrywomen and try to make our way westward to La Rochelle."

"That is not to be thought of," he replied gravely. "Were it not that my despatches may not be delayed without great danger to our cause the matter would be of no inconvenience, but we must ride fast and far. As to leaving you to shift for yourselves, it is impossible; but if we could find a Huguenot family with whom I could place you it would be different. But, unfortunately, we are all strangers to the country."

"I can ride well," the girl said, "and, if horses could be procured, would with my maid try to reach La Rochelle, travelling by night, and hiding in the woods by day. We could carry food with us, so as not to have to enter any place to purchase it."

Philip shook his head.

"We will halt at yonder clump of trees," he said; "it is not yet midnight, and then we can talk the matter over further."

As soon as they halted he unrolled his cloak.

"Do you, mademoiselle, and your attendant lie down here. We shall be but a short distance away, and two of us will keep watch, therefore you can sleep without fear of surprise."

"This is an unfortunate business, Pierre," he said after the latter had fastened the horses to the trees.

"I can understand that, monsieur. I have been talking to the maid, and it seems that they have no friends in these parts."

"That is just it, Pierre. One thing is certain, they cannot ride on with us. We must journey as fast as possible, and delicate women could not support the fatigue, even were it seemly that a young lady of good family should be galloping all over France with a young man like myself."

"I should not trouble about that, monsieur. At ordinary times, doubtless, it would cause a scandal, but in days like these, when in all parts of France there are women and children hiding from the persecution or fleeing for their lives, one cannot stand upon niceties; but doubtless, as you say, they would hinder our speed and add to our dangers."

"I see but two plans, Pierre. The one is that they should journey to La Rochelle in charge of yourself and Eustace. We have now twice crossed the country without difficulty, and as there would be no need of especial speed you could journey quietly, choosing quiet and lonely places for your halts, such as farmhouses, or groups of two or three cottages where there is a tiny inn."

"What is your other plan, sir?"

"The other plan is that you should start forward at once so as to enter St. Amboise early. Stable your horse at an inn, and order rooms, saying that you are expecting your master and a party, who are on their way to join the army. You might also order a meal to be cooked. Then you could enter into conversation with stablemen and others, and find out whether there are any castles in the neighbourhood held for us by Huguenot lords or by their wives in their absence. If not, if there are any Huguenot villages. In fact, try and discover some place where we may leave the young lady in safety. You can have three hours to make your inquiry.

"At the end of that time, whether successful or not, say that you are going out to meet your master and lead him to the inn. Give the host a crown as an earnest of your return and on account of the meal you have ordered, and then ride to meet us. We shall start from here at daybreak. If you succeed in hearing of some place where, as it seems, she can be bestowed in safety, we will take her there at once. If not, you and Eustace must start back with them, travelling slowly. The horses will carry double easily enough. Do not forget to get a cold capon or two, some good wine, and a supply of white bread while you are waiting in the town."

"Which horse shall I take, sir?"

"You had best take Robin; he is the faster of the two, though not quite so strong as Victor."

"I understand, monsieur, and will carry out your orders. If there be a place within twenty miles, or within forty if lying on the right road, where the young lady can be left in safety, rely upon it I will hear of it, for there is nought I would not do rather than turn back at the outset of our journey, while you have to journey on with only Roger, who is a stout man-at-arms enough, but would be of little use if you should find yourself in difficulties, for his head is somewhat thick and his wits slow."

Robin had already finished his scanty ration of food, and when Pierre tightened the girths before mounting looked round in mild surprise at finding himself called upon to start for the second time after he had thought that his work was done.

"You shall have a good feed at St. Amboise," Pierre said, patting its neck, "and beyond that there will be no occasion, I hope, for such another day's work."

After seeing Pierre start Philip threw himself down for two hours' sleep, and then went to relieve Eustace, who was keeping watch at the edge of a clump of trees. As soon as it was broad daylight he went across to where Claire de Valecourt was lying down by the side of her maid, with a cloak thrown over them. She sat up at once as his step approached.

"I am afraid you have not had much sleep, mademoiselle."

"No, indeed," she said, "I have scarce closed my eyes. It will be long before I shall sleep quietly. That terrible scene of last night will be before my eyes for a long time. Do you think that the minister escaped, Monsieur Fletcher?"

"I fear that he did not. I saw him cut down by the fellow I shot just before he turned to ride at you."

"How many do you think escaped?"

"A score perhaps, or it may be more. Some fled at once, others I noticed make off as we rode forward."

"Did not one of your men ride off last night soon after we lay down?"

"Yes, I sent off my servant." And he told her the mission upon which Pierre had been despatched.

"That is a good plan," she said. "I would much rather hide anywhere than that you should go forward on your long journey with but half your little force. Does it not seem strange, monsieur, that while but a few hours ago I had never so much as heard your name, now I owe my life to you, and feel that I have to trust to you in everything? I am quite surprised now I look at you; I scarce saw your face last night, and only noticed as I sat in front of you that you seemed very big and strong; and as you talked of what I must do, just as if you had been my father, I have been thinking of you as a grave man like him; now I see you are quite young, and that you don't look grave at all."

Philip laughed.

"I am young, and not very grave, mademoiselle; I am not at all fit to be the protector of a young lady like yourself."

"There I am sure you are wronging yourself, Monsieur Fletcher. The Admiral would never have sent you so far with important despatches had he not full confidence that you were wise as well as brave. And you said you were a chevalier too. My cousin Antoine looks ever so much older than you do, and he has not been knighted yet. I know young gentlemen are not made knights unless they have done something particularly brave."

Philip smiled.

"I did not do anything particularly brave, mademoiselle, but what I did do happened to attract the Admiral's attention. Now here are the remains of a cold capon, some bread, and wine. You and your attendant had better eat something while we are saddling the horses and preparing for a start."

Four hours later they halted three miles from St. Amboise, taking refuge in a wood near the road where they could see Pierre as he returned. Half an hour later he rode up. Philip went down the road to meet him.

"Well, Pierre, what success?"

"I have heard of a place where I think Mademoiselle de Valecourt would be safe for the present. It is the chateau of Monsieur de Landres. It lies some five-and-twenty miles away, and is in the forest, at a distance from any town or large village. It is a small place, but is strong. M. de Landres is with the army in the west, but he has only taken a few of his men with him, and forty they say have been left to guard the tower. As most of the Catholics round here have obeyed the king's summons, and are either with the royal army in the west or with the two dukes at Metz, there seems no chance of any attack being made upon Landres."

"That will do excellently, Pierre. No doubt the lady will be happy to receive Mademoiselle de Valecourt, whose father is a well-known nobleman and at present in the same army as the lady's husband. At any rate we will try that to begin with."

They started without delay, and riding briskly reached Landres in four hours, having had a good deal of difficulty in finding the way. As soon as they issued from the forests into a cleared space, half a mile across, in the the centre of which stood the fortalice, a horn was heard to sound and the drawbridge was at once raised. Philip saw with satisfaction that Pierre had not been misinformed. The castle was an old one and had not been modernized, and with its solid-looking walls and flanking towers was capable of standing a siege. Halting the others when half-way across to the tower, he rode on alone.   As he approached a lady appeared on the battlements over the gate, while the parapet was occupied with armed men with spears and cross-bows.   Philip removed his cap.

"Madame," he said, "I am a soldier belonging to the army of the Prince of Navarre, and am riding on the business of Admiral Coligny.   On my way hither I had the good fortune to save a Huguenot congregation, and the daughter of the Count de Valecourt, from massacre by the people of La Châtre. My business is urgent, and I am unable to turn back to conduct her to her father, who is with the army of the prince; hearing that you are of the reformed religion, I have ventured to crave your protection for the young lady until I can return to fetch her, or can notify to her father where he may send for her."

"The lady is welcome," Madame de Landres said; "in such times as these it is the duty of all of our religion to assist each other, and the daughter of the Count de Valecourt, whom I know by reputation, will be specially welcomed."

Bowing to the lady Philip rode back to his party.

"The matter is settled, mademoiselle; the chatelaine will be glad to receive you."

By the time they reached the castle the drawbridge had been lowered, and Madame de Landres stood at the gate ready to receive her guest.   As Philip, leaping off, lifted the girl to the ground, the lady embraced her kindly.

"I am truly glad to be able to offer you a shelter for a time. You are young indeed to be abroad without a natural protector, for, as I gather, this gentleman, whose name I have not yet learned, rescued you by chance from an attack by the Catholics."

"God sent him to my succour as by a miracle," Claire said simply.   "The Chevalier Fletcher is known to my father. Had he arrived but one minute later I should be one among seventy or eighty who are now lying dead in a wood near La Châtre.   My father had a chateau close by, but it was fired after the massacre."

"And now, mademoiselle, with your permission and that of Madame de Landres we will ride on at once.   We must do another thirty miles before sunset."

PIERRE LISTENS AT THE OPEN WINDOW OF THE INN.

Madame de Landres, however, insisted on Philip and his men stopping to partake of a meal before they rode on, and although they had breakfasted heartily four hours before upon the provisions Pierre had brought back with him from Amboise, their ride had given them an appetite, and Philip did not refuse the invitation. Madame de Landres expressed much satisfaction on hearing that the Huguenot army was likely to pass somewhere near the neighbourhood of the chateau on its way to effect a junction with the Duc de Deux-Ponts, and promised to send one of her retainers with a message to the count that his daughter was in her keeping. The meal was a short one, and Philip after a halt of half an hour mounted and rode on again.

"My father will thank you when you meet him, Monsieur Fletcher; as for me I cannot tell you what I feel, but I shall pray for you always, and that God who sent you to my aid will watch over you in all dangers," Claire de Valecourt had said as she bade him good-bye.

They halted that night at a small village, and as Philip was eating his supper Pierre came in.

"I think, monsieur, that it would be well for us to move on for a few miles farther."

"Why, Pierre? We have done a long day's journey, and the horses had but a short rest last night."

"I should like to rest just as well as the horses," Pierre said, "but I doubt if we should rest well here. I thought when we drew bridle that the landlord eyed us curiously, and that the men who sauntered up regarded us with more attention than they would ordinary travellers. So I told Eustace and Roger as they led the horses to the stable to keep the saddles on for the present, and I slipped away round to the back of the house and got my ear close to the open window of the kitchen. I got there just as the landlord came in saying: 'These are the people, wife, that we were told of three hours ago. There are the same number of men, though they have no women with them as I was told might be the case. Their leader is a fine-looking young fellow, and I am sorry for him, but that I can't help. I was told that if they came here I was to send off a messenger at once to Nevers, and that if I failed to do so my

house should be burnt over my head, and I should be hung
from the tree opposite as a traitor to the king. Who he is I
don't know, but there can be no doubt he is a Huguenot, and
that he has killed two nobles. I daresay they deserved it if
they were, as the men said, engaged in what they call the good
work of slaying Huguenots, which is a kind of work with which
I do not hold. But that is no business of mine; I am not
going to risk my life in the matter. Besides, if I don't send
off it will make no difference, for they told half-a-dozen men
before they started that they would give a gold crown to the
first who brought them news of the party, and it is like enough
someone has slipped off already to earn the money. So I
must make myself safe by sending off Jacques at once. The
men said that their lords had powerful friends at Nevers, and
I am not going to embroil myself with them for the sake of a
stranger.'

"'We have nothing to do with the Huguenots one way or
other,' the woman said; 'there are no Huguenots in this village, and it is nothing to us what they do in other parts. Send
off Jacques if you like, and perhaps it will be best, but I don't
want any fighting or bloodshed here.'

"I slipped away then," continued Pierre, "as I thought the
landlord would be coming out to look for this Jacques; if it
had not been for what he said about the reward offered, and
the likelihood that others would already have started with the
news, I should have watched for the man and followed him
when he started; I don't think he would have carried his
message far. As it was I thought it best to let you know at
once, so that we could slip out of this trap in time."

CHAPTER XVII

THE BATTLE OF MONCONTOUR

WHEN Pierre left him in order to look after the horses, Philip continued his meal. There could be no hurry, for Nevers was twelve miles away, and it would be four hours at least before a party could arrive. The landlady herself brought in the next course. After placing the dish upon the table she stood looking earnestly at him for a minute and then said: "You spoke of stopping here to-night, sir; the accommodation is very poor, and if you will take my advice you will ride farther. There have been some men along here this afternoon inquiring for a party like yours, and offering a reward to any who would carry the news to them should you pass through. Methinks their intentions were not friendly."

"I thank you very much for your counsel," Philip said, "and will take it. I know that there are some who would gladly hinder me in my journey, and if there is, as you say, a risk of there coming here for me, it were as well that I rode farther, although I would gladly have given my horses a night's rest. I thank you warmly for having warned me."

"Do not let my husband know that I have spoken to you," she said; "he is an honest man but timid, and in these days 'tis safest not to meddle with what does not concern one."

Philip waited for two hours, and then told Pierre to saddle the horses and tell the landlord that he wished to speak to him.

"I have changed my mind, landlord," he said, "and shall ride forward. The horses will have rested now, and can very well do another fifteen miles, so let me have your reckoning.

You can charge for my bed-room, as doubtless it has been put in order for me."

Philip saw that the landlord looked pleased though he said nothing, and in a few minutes the horses were brought round, the bill paid, and they started. They struck off from the road three or four miles farther, and halted in a wood which they reached after half an hour's riding. The grain bags had been filled up again at the inn, but as the horses had eaten their fill these were not opened; and after loosening the girths and arranging the order in which they should keep watch the party threw themselves on the ground. Two hours after their arrival Eustace, who was on watch, heard the distant sounds of a body of horsemen galloping along the main road in the direction of the village they had left.

In the morning at daybreak they started again, directing their way to the south-west and following the course of the Loire, which they crossed at Estrée, and so entered Burgundy. Crossing the great line of hills they came down on the Saone, which they crossed at a ferry fifteen miles below Dijon.   They here obtained news of the position of the Duc de Deux-Ponts, and finally rode into his camp near Vesoul.   They had been fortunate in avoiding all questioning, it being generally assumed, from their travelling without baggage, that they belonged to the neighbourhood.

Riding into the camp they were not long in discovering an officer who spoke French, and upon Philip saying that he was the bearer of despatches for the Duc from Admiral Coligny he was at once conducted to his pavilion. He had, when the camp was in sight and all dangers at an end, taken his despatches from his boots, and these he at once presented to the duke, who came to the door of his tent on hearing that a gentleman had arrived with letters from Coligny himself.

"I am glad to get some news direct at last," the Duc said, "for I have heard so many rumours since I crossed the frontier that I know not whether the Admiral is a fugitive or at the head of a great army.   Which is nearest the truth?"

"The latter assuredly, sir.   The Admiral is at the head of as large a body of men as that with which he offered battle to the Duc d'Anjou when winter first set in."

"Come in, monsieur, and sit down while I read the despatches. How many days have you taken in traversing France?"

"It is the tenth day since I left La Rochelle, sir."

"And have you ridden the same horses the whole way?"

"Yes, sir."

"Then they must be good beasts, for you must have done over forty miles a day."

"We carried no baggage, sir, and, as you see, no armour, and we have husbanded our horses' strength to the best of our power."

The duke sat down and read the papers of which Philip was the bearer.

"The Admiral speaks very highly of you, sir, both as regards discretion and bravery, and mentions that he knighted you himself for your conduct in the battle of Jarnac. He need not have said so much, for the fact that he chose you to carry these despatches is the highest proof of his confidence. And now tell me all particulars of your journey, and what news you have gathered on your way as to the movement and positions of the forces of the royal dukes. This will supplement the Admiral's despatches."

Philip gave a full report of his route, of the state of the roads, the number of cattle in the country through which he had passed, the accounts he had heard of the forces assembled in the cities, and the preparations that had been made to guard the passages across the rivers of Burgundy.

"I will travel by the route that the Admiral indicates, so far as I can do so undisturbed by the armies of the two French dukes. I have with me some good guides, as many French gentlemen joined me not long since with the Prince of Orange. I had already decided, by their advice, upon following nearly the route commended by the Admiral. I trust that you, sir, will ride among my friends, to whom I will introduce you this evening at supper."

The Duc's army amounted to some fifteen thousand men, of whom seven thousand five hundred were horsemen from the states of Lower Germany, and six thousand infantry from Upper Germany, the remaining fifteen hundred being French and Flemish gentlemen, who had joined him with the Prince of Orange.   The armies under the French dukes were together considerably superior in force to that of Deux-Ponts, but singly they were not strong enough to attack him, and the mutual jealousies of their commanders prevented their acting in concert.   Consequently the German force moved across Comté, and on to Autun in the west of Burgundy, without meeting with any opposition.   Then they marched rapidly down.   The bridges upon the Loire were all held, but one of the French officers who knew the country discovered a ford by which a portion of the army crossed.   The main body, laid siege to the town of La Charité, and compelled it to surrender, thus gaining a bridge by which they crossed the Loire.

As the enemy were now in great force in front of them they turned to the south-west, several messengers being sent off to appoint a fresh meeting-place with Coligny; and skirting the hills of Bourbonais, Auvergne, and Limousin, they at last arrived within a day's march of Limoges, the journey of five hundred miles through a hostile country being one of the most remarkable in military history.   That evening Admiral Coligny and his staff rode into camp, having arrived with his army at Limoges.   The Duc had been for some time suffering from fever, and had for the last week been carried in a litter, being unable to sit his horse.   He was, when the Admiral arrived, unconscious, and died the next morning, being succeeded in his command by the Count of Mansfeldt.   Next day the two armies joined with great demonstrations of joy.

The Duc d'Anjou had been closely watching the army of Coligny, his army being somewhat superior in force to that of the allies, who now numbered some twenty-five thousand, for the duke had been recently reinforced by five thousand papal troops, and twelve hundred Florentines.   A part of his force under General Strozzi was at La Roche Abeille.   They were attacked by the Huguenots.   Four hundred Royalists were killed and many taken prisoners, among them their general. There was for a time a pause.   The court entered into fresh negotiations with the Admiral, being anxious to delay his operations, as many of the nobles who were with the Duc d'Anjou, wearied by the burdens imposed upon them, insisted upon returning for a time to their homes.

The Huguenots were above all things anxious for peace, and allowed themselves to be detained for nearly a month by these negotiations. On the march down after the capture of La Charité, the German force had passed within a few miles of the Chateau de Landres, and Philip rode over to see whether Claire was still there. She received him with the frank pleasure of a girl.

"We have heard very little of what is going on outside, Monsieur Fletcher," Madame de Landres said, after the first greetings were over, "though the air has been full of rumours. Again and again reports were brought in that the duke's army had been entirely destroyed by the Royalist forces. Then after a day or two we heard of it as still advancing, but in danger hourly of being destroyed. Then came the news that every town commanding a bridge across the Loire was being put in a state of defence, and strong bodies of troops thrown into them, and we heard that as soon as the Germans reached the river, and farther advance was impossible, they would be attacked by the armies of Nemours and Aumale. But by this time we had become so accustomed to these tales that we were not much alarmed. We were, however, surprised when we heard that a strong body of the Germans had forded the river, and had blockaded La Charité on this side while it had been besieged on the other. I hear that a strong garrison has been left there."

"Yes, madame, the place is of great importance, as it gives us a means of crossing the Loire at any time. We find, too, that a large part of the population are Huguenot, and the place will certainly be held against any attack the Royalists may make against us."

"The news will be received with joy, indeed, by all of our religion in this part of France. Hitherto we have had no place of refuge whatever. There was but the choice of dying in our own houses or villages, or taking refuge in the woods until hunted down. It will be to us what La Rochelle is to the Huguenots of the west. Besides, the garrison there will make the Catholics very chary of attacking us. Moreover, having now this passage across the Loire it is likely that our party will largely use it on their marches, and would be able to punish heavily any places at which there had been massacres. It is by this way, too, the Germans are sure to return, therefore I feel that for a time my young charge will be perfectly safe here. I sent off a messenger to our army on the day you left us, but have had no reply, and know not whether he reached it in safety. At any rate you cannot be very long before your force joins the Admiral, and as we felt quite sure that you would come to see us as you passed, we have our letters ready to my husband and the Count de Valecourt. You will, I am sure, deliver them as soon as you join the Admiral."

"That I will assuredly do, madame. I expect that we shall meet him near Limoges, that is the direction in which we are now marching."

The Count de Valecourt was one of the gentlemen who rode into the Duc de Deux-Ponts' camp with the Admiral, and as soon as they dismounted, and Coligny entered the tent of the dying general, Philip made his way to his side.

"Ah! Monsieur Fletcher, I am glad to see you again. You accomplished, then, your journey in safety. The Prince of Navarre often spoke of you and wondered how you were faring."

"I did very well, sir, but I have not thrust myself upon you at the moment of your arrival to speak of my own journey, but to deliver you a letter which I have the honour of being the bearer from your daughter."

The count stepped backwards a pace with a cry of astonishment and pleasure. "From my daughter! Is it possible, sir? How long is it since you saw her?"

"It is nigh three weeks back, sir."

"The Lord be praised!" the count said solemnly, taking off his cap and looking upwards. "He has shown me many mercies, but this is the greatest. For the last two months I have mourned her as dead. News was brought to me by one of my retainers that she was with a congregation who were attacked by the people of La Châtre, and that all had been massacred. My chateau near there was attacked and burnt, and those of the men who were Huguenots slain, save the one who brought me the news."

"You will see, sir, that your daughter escaped," Philip said, handing him the letter. "She is now in the safe custody of Madame de Landres."

The count tore open the letter, and he had read but a few lines when he uttered an exclamation of surprise, and turning towards Philip, who had moved a few paces away, ran to him and threw his arms round his neck.

"It is you who have, with God's blessing, rescued my daughter from death," he exclaimed. "She is my only child. Ah, monsieur, what joy have you brought to me, what thankfulness do I feel, how deeply am I indebted to you! I had thought that there remained to me but to do my duty to God and His cause, and then if I lived to see the end of the war, to live out my days a childless old man. Now I seem to live again. Claire is alive; I have still something to love and care for. I will first run through the rest of the letter, and then you shall tell me in full all the story. But which is your tent? Pray take me there. I would be alone a little while to thank God for this great mercy."

Half an hour later the count reappeared at the entrance of the tent. Pierre had wine and refreshments ready, and placing them on a box that served as a table retired, leaving his master and the count together.

"Now, tell me all about it," the count said; "Claire's description is a very vague one, and she bids me get all the details from you. She only knows that a man on horseback rode at her with uplifted sword. She commended her soul to God, and stood expecting the blow, when there was a pistol-shot close to her and the man fell from his horse. Then another dashed forward, while you on horseback threw yourself between her and him. There was a terrible clashing of swords, and then he too fell. Then you lifted her on to your horse, and for a short time there was a whirl of conflict. Then you rode off with three men, behind one of whom her maid Annette was sitting. That is all she knows of it except what you told her yourself."

"That is nearly all there is to know, count. The fray lasted but two minutes in all, and my being upon the spot was due to no forethought of mine, but was of the nature of a pure accident."

"Nay, sir, you should not say that; you were led there by the hand of God. But tell me how you came to be in the wood, and pray omit nothing."

Philip related the whole story, from the time of the incident at the inn to the time when he handed over Claire to the care of Madame de Landres.

"It was well done, sir," the count said, laying his hand affectionately on his shoulder when he concluded. "The young prince said you would have a story to tell him when you came back, but I little dreamt that it would be one in which I had such interest. Well, Claire cannot do better than remain where she is for the present, until at any rate I can remove her to La Rochelle, which is the only place where she can be said to be absolutely safe; but so long as we hold La Charité there is, as you say, but slight fear of any fresh trouble there. From all other parts of France we hear the same tales of cruel massacre and executions by fire and sword."

François de Laville was not with Coligny's army, as he was with the Prince of Navarre, who had remained near La Rochelle, but he was very pleased to find the Count de la Noüe, who had just rejoined the army, having been exchanged for a Royalist officer of rank who had fallen into the hands of the Huguenots.

"You have been doing great things while I have been lying in prison, Philip," the count said warmly. "I hear that the Admiral has made you and my cousin knights, and more than that, I heard half an hour since from De Valecourt that while carrying despatches to the Germans you had time to do a little knight-errant's work, and had the good fortune to save his daughter from being massacred by the Catholics. By my faith, chevalier, there is no saying what you will come to if you go on thus."

"I don't want to come to anything, count," Philip said laughing. "I came over here to fight for the Huguenot cause, and with no thought of gaining anything for myself. I am, of course, greatly pleased to receive the honour of knighthood, and that at the hands of so great and noble a general as Admiral Coligny. I have been singularly fortunate, but I owe my good fortune in no small degree to you, for I could have had no better introduction than to ride in your train."

"You deserve all the credit you have obtained, Philip. You have grasped every opportunity that was presented to you, and have always acquitted yourself well. A young man does not gain the esteem and approval of a Coligny, the gratitude of a Valecourt, and the liking of all who know him, including the Queen of Navarre and her son, unless by unusual merit. I am proud of you as a connection, though distant, of my own, and I sincerely trust you will, at the end of this sad business, return home to your friends none the worse for the perils you have gone through."

At the end of a month the negotiations were broken off, for the court had no real intention of granting any concessions. The Huguenots again commenced hostilities. Two or three strong fortresses were captured, and a force despatched south under Count Montgomery, who joined the army of the Viscounts, expelled the Royalists from Béarn, and restored it to the Queen of Navarre. There was a considerable division among the Huguenot leaders as to the best course to be taken. The Admiral was in favour of marching north and besieging Saumur, which would give them a free passage across the lower Loire to the north of France, as the possession of La Charité kept open for them a road to the west; but the majority of the leaders were in favour of besieging Poitiers, one of the richest and most important cities in France.

Unfortunately their opinion prevailed, and they marched against Poitiers, of which the Count de Lude was the governor. Before they arrived there Henry, Duke of Guise, with his brother the Duke of Mayenne, and other officers, threw themselves into the town. A desperate defence was made, and every assault by the Huguenots was repulsed with great loss. A dam was thrown across a small river by the besieged, and its swollen waters inundated the Huguenot camp, and their losses at the breaches were greatly augmented by the ravages of disease. After the siege had lasted for seven weeks the Duc d'Anjou laid siege to Chatelherault, which the Huguenots had lately captured, and Coligny raised the siege, which had cost him two thousand men, and marched to its assistance.

The disaster at Poitiers was balanced to a certain extent by a similar repulse which a force of seven thousand Catholics had sustained at La Charité, which for four weeks successfully repelled every assault, the assailants being obliged at last to draw off from the place.   In Paris and other places the murders of Huguenots were of constant occurrence, and at Orleans two hundred and eighty who had been thrown into prison were massacred in a single day.   The Parliament of Paris rendered itself infamous by trying the Admiral in his absence for treason, hanging him in effigy, and offering a reward of fifty thousand gold crowns to anyone who should murder him.

But a serious battle was now on the eve of being fought. The Duc d'Anjou had been largely reinforced, and his army amounted to nine thousand cavalry and eighteen thousand infantry, while Coligny's army had been weakened by his losses at Poitiers, and by the retirement of many of the nobles whose resources could no longer bear the expense of keeping their retainers in the field.   He had now only some eleven thousand foot and six thousand horse.   He was therefore anxious to avoid a battle until joined by Montgomery, with the six thousand troops he had with him at Béarn.   His troops from the south, however, were impatient at the long inaction and anxious to return home, while the Germans threatened to desert unless they were either paid or led against the enemy.   La Noüe, who commanded the advance-guard, had captured the town of Moncontour, and the Admiral, advancing in that direction, and ignorant that the enemy were in the neighbourhood, moved towards the town.

When on the march the rear was attacked by a heavy body of the enemy.   De Mouy, who commanded there, held them at bay until the rest of the Huguenot army gained the other side of a marsh through which they were passing, and entered the town in safety.   The Admiral would now have retreated, seeing that the whole force of the enemy were in front of him, but the Germans again mutinied, and the delay before they could be pacified enabled the French army to make a detour and overtake the Huguenots soon after they left Moncontour. The Admiral, who commanded the left wing of the army,

Count Louis of Nassau commanding the right, first met them, and his cavalry charged that of the Catholics, which was commanded by the German Rhinegrave. The latter rode well in advance of his men, while Coligny was equally in front of the Protestants. The two leaders therefore met. The conflict was a short one. Coligny was severely wounded in the face and the Rhinegrave was killed.

While the cavalry on both sides fought desperately for victory, the infantry was speedily engaged. The combat between the Huguenot foot and the Swiss infantry in the Royalist ranks was long and doubtful. The Duc d'Anjou displayed great courage in the fight, while on the other side the Princes of Navarre and Condé, who had that morning joined the army from Parthenay, fought bravely in the front of the Huguenots. The Catholic line began to give way, in spite of their superiority in numbers, when Marshal Cossé advanced with fresh troops into the battle, and the Huguenots in turn were driven back. The German cavalry of the Huguenots, in spite of the valour of their leader Louis of Nassau, were seized with a panic and fled from the field, shattering on their way the ranks of the German infantry.

Before the latter could recover their order the Swiss infantry poured in among them. Many threw down their arms and shouted for quarter, while others defended themselves until the last; but neither submission nor defence availed, and out of the four thousand German infantry but two hundred escaped. Three thousand of the Huguenot infantry were cut off by Anjou's cavalry; a thousand were killed, and the rest spared at the Duc's command. In all two thousand Huguenot infantry and three hundred knights perished on the field, besides the German infantry, while on the Catholic side the loss was but a little over five hundred men.

La Noüe was again among those taken prisoner. Before the battle began he had requested Philip to join his cousin, who had come up with the princes, and to attach himself to their body-guard during the battle. They kept close to the princes during the fight, riding far enough back for them to be seen by the Huguenots, and closing round when the enemy poured down upon them. When the German horsemen fled and the infantry were enveloped by the Catholics, they led Henri and Condé from the field, charging right through a body of Catholic horse who had swept round to the rear, and carrying them off to Parthenay.

Here they found the Admiral, who had been borne off the field grievously wounded. For a moment the lion-hearted general had felt despondency at the crushing defeat, being sorely wounded and weakened by loss of blood, but as he was carried off the field his litter came alongside one in which L'Estrange, a Huguenot gentleman, also sorely wounded, was being borne. Doubtless the Admiral's face expressed the deep depression of his spirit, and L'Estrange, holding out his hand to him, said, "Yet is God very gentle." The words were an echo of those which formed the mainspring of the Admiral's life. His face lit up, and he exclaimed, "Thanks, comrade; truly God is merciful, and we will trust him always." He was much pleased when the two young princes, both un-hurt, rejoined him. He issued orders to his officers to rally their troops as they came in, to evacuate Parthenay, and march at once to Niort.

The gallant De Mouy was appointed to command the city, and three or four days were spent there in rallying the remains of the army. Scarce had they reached Niort when the Queen of Navarre arrived from La Rochelle, whence she had has-tened as soon as she had heard the news of the defeat. The presence of this heroic woman speedily dispelled the despon-dency among the Huguenots. Going about among them, and addressing the groups of officers and soldiers, she communi-cated to them her own fire and enthusiasm. Nothing was lost yet, she said; tne Germans had failed them, but their own valour had been conspicuous, and with the blessing of God matters would soon be restored. Already the delay of the Catholics in following up their victory had given them time to rally, and they were now in a position to give battle again.

Leaving a strong garrison at Niort Coligny moved with a portion of his army to Saintes, while the southern troops from Dauphiné and Provence marched to Angoulême. These troops were always difficult to retain long in the field, as they were anxious for the safety of their friends at home. They now clamoured for permission to depart, urging that the news of the defeat of Moncontour would be the signal for fresh persecutions and massacres in the south. Finally they marched away without Coligny's permission, and atfer some fighting reached Dauphiné in safety.

In the meantime Niort had been attacked. De Mouy defended the place stoutly, and sallied out and repulsed the enemy. His bravery, however, was fatal to him. A Catholic named Maurevel, tempted by the fifty thousand crowns that had been offered for the assassination of Coligny, had entered the Protestant camp, pretending that he had been badly treated by the Guises. No opportunity for carrying out his design against the Admiral presented itself, and he remained at Niort with De Mouy, who, believing his protestations of attachment for the cause, had treated him with great friendship. As the Huguenots were returning after their successful sortie he was riding in the rear with De Mouy, and, seizing his opportunity, he drew a pistol and shot the Huguenot leader, mortally wounding him. He then galloped off and rejoined the Catholics, and was rewarded for the treacherous murder by receiving from the king the order of St. Michael, and a money reward from the city of Paris.

The garrison of Niort, disheartened at the death of their leader, surrendered shortly after. Several other strong places fell, and all the conquests the Protestants had made were wrested from their hands. The battle of Moncontour was fought on October 3d, on the 14th the southern troops marched away, and four days later Coligny with the remains of the army started from Saintes. He had with him but six thousand men, of whom three thousand were cavalry. His plan was an extremely bold one. In the first place he wished to obtain money to pay the German horsemen by the capture of some of the rich Catholic cities in Guyenne, to form a junction with the army of Montgomery, then to march across to the Rhône, and there to meet the forces of the south, which would by that time be ready to take the field again; then to march north to Lorraine, there to gather in the Germans whom William of Orange would have collected to meet him; and then to march upon Paris, and to end the war by giving battle under its walls.   The Queen of Navarre was to remain in La Rochelle, which city was placed under the command of La Rochefoucault, and the two young princes were to accompany the army, where they were to have small commands.   They would thus become inured to the hardships of war, and would win the affection of the soldiers.

François de Laville had with his own troop ridden off to his chateau from Parthenay on the morning after the battle, Coligny advising him to take his mother at once to La Rochelle, as the chateau would speedily be attacked, in revenge for the sharp repulse that the Catholics had suffered there.   On his arrival the countess at once summoned all the tenants, and invited those who chose to accompany her, pointing out that the Catholics would speedily ravage the land. Accordingly the next day all the valuables in the chateau were packed up in carts, and the place entirely abandoned.   The whole of the tenants accompanied her, driving their herds before them, as they would find a market for these in the city. As they moved along they were joined by large numbers of other fugitives, as throughout the whole country the Protestants were making for refuge to the city.

When the Admiral marched away Philip rode with a young French officer, for whom he had a warm friendship, named De Piles.

The latter had been appointed governor of St. Jean d'Angely, which was now the sole bulwark of La Rochelle, and he had specially requested the Admiral to appoint Philip to accompany him.   The place was scarcely capable of defence, and the Admiral had only decided to hold it in the hope that the Duc d'Anjou, instead of following him with his whole army, would wait to besiege it.   This decision was, in fact, adopted by the Royalists, after much discussion among the leaders. Several of them wished to press on at once after Coligny, urging that the destruction of the remnant of his army would be a fatal blow to the Huguenot cause.   The majority, however, were of opinion that it was of more importance to reduce La Rochelle, the Huguenots' stronghold in the west, and in order to do this St. Jean d'Angely must first be captured.   Their counsel prevailed, and just as the siege of Poitiers had proved fatal to the plans of Coligny, so that of St. Jean d'Angely went far to neutralize all the advantages gained by the Catholic victory at Moncontour.

Scarcely had De Piles taken the command than the army of the Duc d'Anjou appeared before the walls, and at once opened fire. The garrison was a very small one, but it was aided by the whole of the inhabitants, who were, like those of La Rochelle, zealous Huguenots. Every assault upon the walls was repulsed, and at night the breaches made by the cannon during the day were repaired, the inhabitants, even the women and children, bringing stones to the spot, and the soldiers doing the work of building. On the 26th of October, after the siege had continued for a fortnight, the king himself joined the Catholic army, and summoned the place to surrender. De Piles replied that, although he recognized the authority of the king, he was unable to obey his orders, as he had been appointed to hold the city by the Prince of Navarre, the royal governor of Guyenne, his feudal superior, and could only surrender it on receiving his orders to do so. The siege, therefore, recommenced. The walls were so shaken that De Piles himself, after repulsing a furious attack upon them, came to the conclusion that the next assault would probably be successful, and he therefore caused a breach to be made in the wall on the other side of the town, to afford a means of retreat for his troops. His supply of ammunition, too, was almost exhausted.

"What do you think, Fletcher?" he said gloomily. "If we could but hold out for another ten days or so, the Admiral would have got so fair a start that they would never overtake him. But I feel sure that another twenty-four hours will see the end of it."

"We might gain some time," Philip replied, "by asking for an armistice. They probably do not know the straits to which we are reduced, and may grant us a few days."

"They might do so; at any rate it is worth trying," De Piles agreed; and an hour later Philip went with a flag of truce to the royal camp. He was taken before the Duc d'Anjou.

"I am come with proposals from the governor," he said.

"He will not surrender the town without orders from the
Prince of Navarre. But if you will grant a fortnight's armistice, he will send a messenger to the prince; and if no answer
arrives, or if no succour reaches him at the end of that time,
he will surrender on condition that the garrison shall be permitted to retire with their horses and arms, and that religious
liberty shall be granted to all the inhabitants."

The Duc consulted with his generals. The losses in the
attacks had been extremely heavy, and disease was raging in
the army, and, to Philip's inward surprise and delight, an
answer was made that the conditions would be granted, but
that only ten days would be given. He returned with the
answer to De Piles, and the armistice was at once agreed
upon, six hostages for its proper observance being given on
both sides. On the ninth day Saint Surin, with forty horsemen, dashed through the enemy's lines and rode into the town,
thus relieving De Piles from the necessity of surrendering.
The hostages were returned on both sides and the siege
recommenced.

Attack after attack was repulsed with heavy loss, several of
the bravest royalist officers, among them the governor of
Brittany, being killed. The town was valiantly defended
until the 2d of December, when De Piles, satisfied with having
detained the royal army seven weeks before the walls, and
seeing no hope of relief, surrendered on the same conditions
that had before been agreed on. Its capture had cost the Duc
d'Anjou 6000 men, about half of whom had fallen by disease,
the rest in the assaults, and the delay had entirely defeated
the object of the campaign. The gates were opened and the
little body of defenders marched out with colours flying. One
of the conditions of surrender had been that they should not
serve again during the war.

The Duc d'Aumale and other officers endeavoured to ensure
the observance of the condition of their safe conduct through
the Catholic lines; but the soldiers, furious at seeing the
handful of men who had inflicted such loss upon them going
off in safety, attacked them, and nearly a hundred were killed
—a number equal to the loss they had suffered throughout the
whole siege. De Piles with the rest were, by their own exer-

tions and those of some of the Catholic leaders, enabled to make their way through, and rode to Angoulême. There De Piles sent a letter demanding the severe punishment of those who had broken the terms of surrender, but no attention having been paid to his demand, he sent a herald to the king to declare that, in consequence of the breach of the conditions, he and those with him considered themselves absolved from their undertaking not to carry arms during the war, and he then rode away with his followers to join the Admiral.

The French army rapidly fell to pieces. With winter at hand it was in vain to attempt the siege of La Rochelle. Philip of Spain and the pope ordered the troops they had supplied to return home, alleging that the victory of Moncontour, of which they had received the most exaggerated reports, had virtually terminated the war. The German and Swiss troops were allowed to leave the service, and the nobles and their retainers were granted permission to do the same until the spring. Thus the whole fruits of the victory of Moncontour were annihilated by the heroic defence of St. Jean d'Angely.

In the meantime the Admiral had been moving south. In order to cross the rivers he had marched westward, and so made a circuit to Montauban, the stronghold of the Huguenots in the south. Moving westward he joined the Count of Montgomery at Aiguillon, and returned with him to Montauban, where he received many reinforcements until his army amounted to some twenty-one thousand men, of whom six thousand were cavalry. At the end of January they marched to Toulouse, a city with an evil fame as the centre of persecuting bigotry in the south of France. It was too strong to be attacked; but the country round it was ravaged, and all the country residences of the members of its parliament destroyed. Then they marched westward to Nismes, sending marauding expeditions into the Catholic districts, and even into Spain, in revenge for the assistance the king had given the Catholics. De Piles and his party had joined the Admiral at Montauban, and the former commanded the force that penetrated into Spain. Coligny turned north, marched up the Rhone, surmounting every obstacle of mountain and river until he reached

Burgundy, arriving at St. Etienne-sur-Loire on the 26th of May.

Here they were met by messengers from the court, which was in a state of consternation at the steady approach of an enemy they had regarded as crushed, and were ready in their alarm to promise anything. The Admiral fell dangerously ill, and at the news the king at once broke off the negotiations. He recovered, however, and advancing met the royal army, under Marshal Cossé, in the neighbourhood of the town of Arnay de Duc. Coligny's army had dwindled away during its terrible march, and it consisted now of only two thousand horsemen and two thousand five hundred arquebusiers, the cannon being all left behind. Cossé had ten thousand infantry, of whom four thousand were Swiss; three thousand cavalry, and twelve cannon. The armies took post on the hills on opposite sides of a valley through which ran a stream fed by some small ponds. The Royalists commenced the attack, but after fighting obstinately for seven hours were compelled to fall back with heavy loss. A fresh body was then directed against an intrenchment the Huguenots had thrown up near the ponds. Here again the fighting was long and obstinate, but at last the Catholics were repulsed.

The next morning both armies drew up in order of battle; but neither would advance to the attack, as the ground offered such advantages to those who stood on the defensive, and they accordingly returned to their camps. The Admiral being unwilling to fight till he received reinforcements marched away to La Charité, where he was reorganizing his force when a truce of ten days was made. At the end of that time he again marched north, and distributing his soldiers in the neighbourhood of Montargis took up his quarters at his castle of Chatillon-sur-Loing, where he remained while negotiations were going on.

CHAPTER XVIII

WHILE Coligny had been accomplishing his wonderful march round France, La Notie, who had been exchanged for Strozzi, had betaken himself to La Rochelle. He forced the Catholics, who were still languidly blockading that place, to fall back, defeated them near Lucon, and recaptured Fontenay, Niort, the Isle of Oléron, Brouage, and Saintes. At Fontenay, however, the brave Huguenot leader had his left arm broken, and was obliged to have it amputated.

Negotiations were now being carried on in earnest. Charles IX. was weary of a war that impoverished the state, diminished his revenues, and forced him to rely upon the Guises, whom he feared and disliked. Over and over again he had been assured that the war was practically at an end and the Huguenots crushed, but as often fresh armies rose. The cities that had been taken with so much difficulty had again fallen into their hands, and Paris itself was menaced.

The princes of Germany wrote begging him to make peace, and although the terms fell far short of what the Huguenots hoped and desired, the concessions were large, and could they have depended upon the good faith of the court their lives would have at least been tolerable. A complete amnesty was granted, and a royal command issued that the Protestants were to be exposed to neither insults nor recriminations, and were to be at liberty to profess their faith openly. Freedom of worship was, however, restricted within very small proportions. The nobles of high rank were permitted to name a place belonging to them where religious services could be performed. As long as they or their families were present these services could be attended by all persons in their jurisdiction.

Other nobles were allowed to have services, but only for their families and friends, not exceeding twelve in number. Twenty-four towns were named, two in each of the principal provinces, in which Protestant services were allowed, the privilege being extended to all the towns of which the Huguenots had possession at the signature of the truce. All property, honours, and offices were restored, and judicial decisions against their holders annulled. The four towns, La Rochelle, Montauban, Cognac, and La Charité, were for two years to remain in the hands of the Huguenots to serve as places of refuge. The edict in which the king promulgated the terms of peace stated the conditions to be perpetual and irrevocable. The Huguenots had the more hope that the peace would be preserved, since Montmorency, who was an opponent of the Guises, and had done his best to bring about peace, was high in favour with the king, and, indeed, held the chief power in France.

There can be little doubt that at the time the king was in earnest. He ordered the parliament of Paris to annul a declaration they had made declaring the Cardinal Chatillon, the Admiral's brother, deprived of his bishopric, and as it hesitated, he ordered its president to bring the records to him, and with his own hand tore out the pages upon which the proceedings were entered.

The priests throughout France threw every obstacle in the way of the recognition of the edict, and in several places there were popular disturbances and wholesale massacres. Paris, as usual, set the example of turbulence and bigotry.

As soon as the peace was concluded Philip prepared to return for a while to England. In the three years which had elapsed since he left home he had greatly changed. He had been a lad of sixteen when he landed in France, he was now a tall powerful young fellow. Although still scarcely beyond the age of boyhood, he had acquired the bearing and manners of a man. He stood high in the confidence of Coligny and the other Huguenot leaders, was a special favourite with the young Prince of Navarre and his cousin Condé, and had received the honour of knighthood at the hands of one of the greatest captains of his age.

"You had better stay, Philip," his cousin urged. "You may be sure that this peace will be as hollow as those which preceded it. There will never be a lasting one until we have taken Paris, and taught the bloodthirsty mob there that it is not only women and children who profess the reformed religion but men who have swords in their hands and can use them."

"If the troubles break out again I shall hasten back, François; indeed, I think that in any case I shall return for a while ere long. I do not see what I could do at home. My good uncle Gaspard has been purchasing land for me, but I am too young to play the country gentleman."

"Nonsense, Philip. There have been plenty of young nobles in our ranks, who, if your seniors in years, look no older than you do, and are greatly your inferiors in strength. They are feudal lords on their estates, and none deem them too young."

"Because they have always been feudal nobles, François. I go back to a place where I was, but three years ago, a boy at school. My comrades there are scarcely grown out of boyhood. It will seem to them ridiculous that I should return Sir Philip Fletcher, and were I to set up as a country squire they would laugh in my face. Until I am at least of age I should not dream of this, and five-and-twenty would indeed be quite time for me to settle down there. Here it is altogether different. I was introduced as your cousin, and as a son of one of noble French family, and to our friends here it is no more remarkable that I should ride behind Coligny and talk with the princes of Navarre and Condé than that you should do so. But at home it would be different; and I am sure that my father and mother, my uncle and aunt will agree with me that it is best I should not settle down yet. Therefore, I propose in any case to return soon. I agree with you there will be troubles again here before long. If not, there is likely enough to be war with Spain, for they say Philip is furious at toleration having been granted to the Huguenots; and in that case there will be opportunities for us, and it will be much pleasanter fighting against Spaniards than against Frenchmen. If there are neither fresh troubles here nor war with Spain I shall go and join the Dutch in their struggle against the Spaniards. Prince Louis of Nassau told me that he would willingly have me to ride behind him, and the Prince of Orange, to whom the Admiral presented me, also spoke very kindly. They, like you, are fighting for the reformed faith and freedom of worship, and cruel as are the persecutions you have suffered in France, they are as nothing to the wholesale massacres by Alva."

"In that case, Philip, I will not try to detain you; but at any rate wait a few months before you take service in Holland, and pay us another visit before you decide upon doing so."

Philip journeyed quietly across the north of France, and took passage to Dover for himself and his horses. Pierre accompanied him, taking it so greatly to heart when he spoke of leaving him behind that Philip consented to keep him, feeling, indeed, greatly loath to part from one who had for three years served him so well. The two men-at-arms were transferred to François' troop, both being promised that if Philip rode to the wars again in France they and their comrades now at Laville should accompany him. From Dover Philip rode to Canterbury. He saw in the streets he passed through many faces he knew, among them some of his former schoolfellows, and he wondered to himself that these were so little changed while he was so altered that none recognized in the handsomely-dressed young cavalier the lad they had known, although several stopped to look at and remark on the splendid horses ridden by the gentleman and his attendant. He drew rein in front of Gaspard Vaillant's large establishment, and dismounting, gave his reins to Pierre and entered. He passed straight through the shop into the merchant's counting-house.

Gaspard looked up in surprise at the entry of a gentleman unannounced, looked hard at his visitor and then uttered his name, and rushing forward embraced him warmly.

"I can hardly believe it is you," he exclaimed, holding Philip at arm's-length and gazing up in his face. "Why, you have grown a veritable giant, and as fine a man as your father was when I first knew him; and you have returned Sir Philip,

GASPARD VAILLANT GETS A SURPRISE.

too. I don't know that I was ever so pleased as when you sent me the news. I gave a holiday to all the workmen and we had a great fête. But of course you cannot stop now, you will be wanting to go up to your father and mother. Run upstairs and embrace Marie. We will not keep you at present, but in an hour we will be up with you."

In a minute or two Philip ran down again.

"*Pardieu*, but you are well mounted, Philip," the merchant said as he sprang into the saddle. "These are the two horses, I suppose, you told us about in your letters. And is this Pierre, who saved your life when you were captured at Agen?"

"And a good many other times, uncle, by always managing to get hold of a fat pullet when we were pretty near starving. I was always afraid that sooner or later I should lose him, and that I should find him some morning or other dangling from a tree to which the prevost-marshal had strung him up."

"Then I shall see you in an hour." And Philip galloped off to the farm.

The delight of Philip's parents as he rode up to the house was great indeed. Philip saw before he had been at home an hour that they were animated by somewhat different feelings. His mother was full of gratitude at his preservation through many dangers, and was glad that he had been able to do some service to her persecuted co-religionists—the fact that he had won great personal credit and had received the honour of knighthood at the hands of Coligny himself weighed as nothing in her eyes. It was otherwise with his father; he was very proud that his boy had turned out a worthy descendant of the fighting Kentish stock, and that he had shown, in half-a-dozen fights against heavy odds, a courage as staunch as that which his forefathers had exhibited at Cressy, Poitiers, and Agincourt.

"Good blood tells, my boy," he said; "and you must have shown them a rare sample of what an Englishman can do, before they knighted you. I would rather you had won it in an English battle, but all admit that there is no more capable chief in Europe than the Huguenot Admiral. Certainly there are no English commanders of fame or repute to compare with him, though if we ever get to blows with the Spanish we shall soon find men, I warrant me, who will match the best of them. There was a deal of talk in Canterbury, I can tell you, when the news came home, and many refugees who came through the town declared that they had heard your name among those of the nobles who rode with the Admiral and the brave La Noüe; indeed, there are two families settled here who fled from Niort, and these have told how you and your cousin saved them from the Catholics.

"I warrant you they have told the tale often enough since they have come here, and it has made quite a stir in Canterbury, and there is not a week passes without some of your old school friends, who used to come up here with you, running up to ask the last news of you and to hear your letters read; and it has been a pleasure to me to read them, lad, and to see how they opened their eyes when they heard that the Queen of Navarre and her son had given you presents, and that you often rode with the young prince and his cousin Condé. You have changed, Philip, mightily; not in your face, for I see but little alteration there, but in your manner and air. The boys did not seem to understand how you, whom they looked on as one of themselves, could be riding to battle with nobles and talking with princes, but I think they will understand better when they see you. You look almost too fine for such simple people as we are, Philip, though I do not say your clothes are not of sombre hues, as might be expected from one fighting in the Huguenot ranks."

"I am sure, father," Philip laughed, "there is nothing fine about me. I have gained knighthood, it is true; but a poorer knight never sat in saddle, seeing that I have neither a square yard of land nor a penny piece of my own, owing everything to the kindness of my good uncle and yourself."

"I must go out to-morrow morning, Philip, and look at those horses of yours, they must be rare beasts from what you say of them."

"That are they, father. Methinks I like the one I bought at Rochelle even better than that which the Queen of Navarre bestowed upon me; but I grieved sorely over the death of Victor, the horse François gave me. I was riding him at the fight of Moncontour, and he was shot through the head with a ball from a German arquebus."

Pierre had, as soon as they arrived, been welcomed and made much of by Philip's mother, and was speedily seated in the post of honour in the kitchen, where he astonished the French servants with tales of his master's adventures, with many surprising additions which had but slight basis of fact. Gaspard Vaillant and his wife thought that Philip's parents would like to have him for a time to themselves, and did not come up for two or three hours after he had arrived.

"You will admit, John, that my plan has acted rarely," the merchant said when he was seated, "and that, as I prophesied, it has made a man of him. What would he have been if he had stayed here?"

"He would, I hope, brother Gaspard," Lucie said gravely, "have been what he is now—a gentleman."

"No doubt, Lucie, he promised as much as that before he went, but he is more than that now. He has been the companion of nobles and has held his own with them, and if he should go to court now he would do honour to your family and his though he rubbed shoulders with the best of them. And now, what are you thinking of doing next, Philip? You will hardly care to settle down among us here after such a life as you have led for the last three years."

Philip repeated the views he had expressed to François de Laville, and his plans were warmly approved by his uncle and father, though his mother folded her hands and shook her head sadly.

"The lad is right, Lucie," the merchant said; "he is lord now of the Holford estates—for the deeds are completed and signed, Philip, making them over to you. But I agree heartily with your feeling that you are too young yet to assume their mastership. I have a good steward there looking after things, seeing that all goes well, and that the house is kept in order. But it is best, as you say, that a few years should pass before you go to reside there. We need not settle for a time whether you shall return to France or go to see service with those sturdy Dutchmen against the Spaniards. But I should say that it is best you should go where you have already made a name and gained many friends. There is no saying yet how matters will go there.

"Charles is but a puppet in the hands of Catherine de Medici; and with the pope, and Philip of Spain, and the Guises always pushing her on, she will in time persuade the king, who at present earnestly wishes for peace, to take fresh measures against the Huguenots. She is never happy unless she is scheming, and you will see she will not be long before she begins to make trouble again."

The news spread quickly through Canterbury that Philip Fletcher had returned, and the next day many of his old friends came up to see him. At first they were a little awed by the change that had come over him, and one or two of them even addressed him as Sir Philip. But the shout of laughter with which he received this well-meant respect showed them that he was their old school-fellow still, and soon set them at their ease with him.

"We didn't think, Philip," one of them said, "when you used to take the lead in our fights with the boys of the town, that you would be so soon fighting in earnest in France, and that in three years you would have gained knighthood."

"I did not think so myself, Archer. You used to call me Frenchie, you know, but I did not think at the time that I was likely ever to see France. I should like to have had my old band behind me in some of the fights we had there. I warrant you would have given as hard knocks as you got, and would have held your own there as well as you did many a time in the fights in the Cloisters. Let us go and lie down under the shade of that tree there, it used to be our favourite bank, you know, in hot weather, and you shall ask as many questions as you like, and I will answer as best I can."

"And be sure, Philip, to bring all your friends in to supper," John Fletcher said; "I warrant your mother will find plenty for them to eat. She never used to have any difficulty about that in the old times, and I don't suppose their appetites are sharper now than they were then."

Philip spent six months at home. A few days after his return many of the country gentry, who had not known John Fletcher, called on Philip as one who had achieved a reputation that did honour to the county—for every detail of the Huguenot struggle had been closely followed in England, and more than one report had been brought over by *emigrés* of the bravery of a young Englishman who was held in marked consideration by Admiral Coligny, and had won a name for himself even among the nobles and gentlemen who rode with that dashing officer De La Noüe, whose fame was second only to that of the Admiral. Walsingham, the English ambassador at Paris, had heard of him from La Noüe himself when he was a prisoner there, and mentioned him in one of his despatches, saying that it was this gentleman who had been chosen by Coligny to carry important despatches both to the Queen of Navarre and the Duc de Deux-Ponts, and had succeeded admirably in both these perilous missions; and that he had received knighthood at the hands of the Admiral for the valour with which he had covered the retreat at the battle of Jarnac.

Philip was at first disposed to meet these advances coldly.

"They have not recognized you or my mother, father, as being of their own rank."

"Nor have we been, Philip. I am but a petty land-owner, while it is already known that you are the owner of a considerable estate, and have gained consideration and credit, and as a knight have right to precedence over many of them. If you had intended to settle in France you could do as you like as to accepting their courtesies; but as it is, it is as well that you should make the acquaintance of those with whom you will naturally associate when you take up your residence on the estate your uncle has bought for you.

"Had your mother and I a grievance against them it might be different; but we have none. We Fletchers have been yeomen here for many generations. In our own rank we esteem ourselves as good as the best, but we never thought of pushing ourselves out of our own station; and in the ordinary course of things you would have lived and died as your fathers have done. The change has come about first through my marrying a French wife of noble blood, though with but a small share of this world's goods; secondly through her sister's husband making a large fortune in trade and adopting you as his heir; and thirdly, through your going out to your mother's relations and distinguishing yourself in the war. Thus you stand in an altogether different position to that which I held. You are a man with an estate; you are noble on your mother's side; you are a knight, and have gained the approval of great captains and princes. Therefore it is only meet and right that you should take your place among the gentry; and it would be not only churlish to refuse to accept their civilities now, but altogether in opposition to the course which your uncle planned for you."

Philip therefore accepted the civilities offered to him, and was invited to entertainments at many of the great houses in that part of the county; where indeed he was made a good deal of, his fine figure, the ease and courtesy of his bearing, and the reputation he had gained for bravery, rendering him a general favourite.

At the end of six months he received a letter from his cousin urging him to return. "Spring has now begun, Philip. At present things are going on quietly, and the king seems determined that the peace shall be kept. The Constable Montmorency is still very high in favour, and the Guises are sulking on their estates. The Huguenot nobles are all well received at court, where they go in numbers, to pay their respect to the king and to assure him of their devotion. I have been there with my mother, and the king was mightily civil and congratulated me on having been knighted by Coligny. We were present at his majesty's marriage with the daughter of the Emperor of Germany. The show was a very fine one and everything pleasant.

"There is a report that, in order to put an end to all further troubles, and to bind both parties in friendship, the king has proposed a marriage between his sister Marguerite and Henri of Navarre. We all trust that it will take place, for it will indeed be a grand thing for us of the reformed faith. It is rumoured that Queen Jeanne is by no means eager for the match, fearing that Henri, once at Paris, will abandon the simple customs in which he has been brought up, and may even be led away by the influence of Marguerite and the court to abandon his faith. Her first fear, I think, is likely enough to he realized; for it seems to me that he has been brought up somewhat too strictly, and being, I am sure, naturally fond of pleasure, he is likely enough to share in the gaieties of the court of Paris. As to her other fear, I cannot think there is foundation for it. Henri is certainly ambitious and very politic, and he has talked often and freely with me when we have been alone together. He has spoken once or twice of his chances of succeeding to the throne of France. They are not great, seeing that three lives stand between it and him, and now that the king has married they are more remote than before.

"Still there is the chance; and he once said to me, 'One thing seems to me to be certain, François: supposing Charles of Valois and his two brothers died without leaving heirs, France would not accept a Huguenot king. There would be the Guises, and the priests, and the papacy, and Spain all thrown in the scale against him.' 'That is likely enough, prince,' I said; 'and methinks your lot would be preferable as King of Navarre to that of King of France. However, happily there is no reason for supposing that the king and his two brothers will die without heirs.' He did not speak for some time, but sat there thinking. You know the way he has. Methinks, Philip, that when he comes to man's estate, and is King of Navarre, the Guises will find in him a very different opponent to deal with than the leaders of the Huguenots have been so far.

"The Admiral is so honest and loyal and truthful himself that he is ill fitted to match the subtlety of the queen-mother or the deceit and falsehood of the Guises. The Queen of Navarre is a heroine and saint, but although a wise woman, she is no match for intriguers. Condé was a gallant soldier, but he hated politics. Henri of Navarre will be an opponent of another sort. When I first knew him I thought him the frankest and simplest of young princes, and that is what most think him still. But I am sure he is much more than that. Having been about his person for months, and being the youngest of his companions—most of whom were stern, earnest Huguenot nobles—he was a great deal with me, and talked with me as he did not with the others. It seems to me that he has two characters, the one what he seems to be—light-hearted, merry, straightforward, and outspoken; the other thoughtful, astute, ambitious, and politic, studying men closely and adapting himself to their moods.

"I don't pretend to understand him at all—he is altogether beyond me; but I am sure he will be a great leader some day. I think you would understand him better than I should, and I know he thinks so too. Of course you had your own duties all through the campaign and saw but little of him, but more than once he said: 'I wish I had your English cousin with me. I like you much, Laville; but your cousin is more like myself, and I should learn much of him. You are brave and merry and good-tempered, and so is he; but he has a longer head than you have,'—which I know is quite true—'you would be quite content to spend your life at court, François, where you would make a good figure and would take things as they come. He would not. If he did not like things he would intrigue, he would look below the surface, he would join a party, he would be capable of waiting, biding his time. I am only seventeen, François; but it is of all things the most important for a prince to learn to read men and to study their characters, and I am getting on.

"'Your cousin is not ambitious, he would never conspire for his own advantage; but he would be an invaluable minister and adviser to a prince in difficulties. The Admiral meant well, but he was wrong in refusing to let me have Philip Fletcher. When I am my own master I will have him if I can catch him; but I do not suppose that I shall, because of that very fault of not being ambitious. He has made his own plans, and is bent, as he told me, on returning to England, and nothing that I can offer him will, I am sure, alter his determination. But it is a pity, a great pity.' By all this you see, Philip, that those who think the Prince of Navarre merely a merry, careless young fellow, who is likely to rule his little kingdom in patriarchal fashion, and to trouble himself with nothing outside so long as his subjects are contented and allowed to worship in their own way, are likely to find themselves sorely mistaken. However, if you come over soon, you will be able to judge for yourself.

"The Queen of Navarre saw a great deal of the countess, my mother, when they were at La Rochelle together, and has invited her to pay her a visit at Béarn, and the prince has requested me to accompany her. Of course if you come over you will go with us, and will be sure of a hearty welcome from Henri. We shall have some good hunting, and there is no court grandeur, and certainly no more state than we have at our chateau. In fact, my good mother is a much more important personage there than is Jeanne of Navarre at Béarn."

This letter hastened Philip's departure. The prospect of hunting in the mountains of Navarre was a pleasant one. He liked the young prince, and had, in the short time he had been his companion, perceived that there was much more in him than appeared on the surface, and that, beside his frank *bonhomie* manner, there was a fund of shrewdness and common sense. Moreover, without being ambitious, it is pleasant for a young man to know that one who may some day be a great prince has conceived a good opinion of him. He took Francois' letter down to his uncle Gaspard and read portions of it to him. Gaspard sat thoughtful for some time after he had finished.

"It is new to me," he said at last. "I believed the general report that Henri of Navarre was a frank, careless young fellow, fond of the chase, and, like his mother, averse to all court ceremony; likely enough to make a good soldier, but without ambition and without marked talent. If what François says is true—and it seems that you are inclined to agree with him—it may make a great difference in the future of France. The misfortune of the Huguenots hitherto has been that they have been ready to fall into any trap that the court of France might set for them, and on the strength of a few hollow promises to throw away all the advantages they had gained by their efforts and courage, in spite of their experience that those promises were always broken as soon as they laid down their arms.

"In such an unequal contest they must always be worsted, and honest and straightforward themselves, they are no match for men who have neither truth nor conscience. If they had but a leader as politic and astute as the queen-mother and the

Guises, they might possibly gain their ends. If Henri of Navarre turns out a wise and politic prince, ready to match his foes with their own weapons, he may win for the Huguenots what they will never gain with their own swords. But mind you, they will hardly thank him for it. My wife and your mother would be horrified were I to say that, as a Catholic, Henri of Navarre would be able to do vastly more to heal the long open sore and to secure freedom of worship for the Huguenots than he ever could do as a Huguenot. Indeed, I quite agree with what he says, that as a Huguenot he can never hold the throne of France."

Philip uttered an exclamation of indignation.

"You cannot think, uncle, that he will ever change his religion?"

"I know nothing about him beyond what you and your cousin say, Philip. There are Huguenots and Huguenots. There are men who would die at the stake rather than give up one iota of their faith; there are men who think that the reformed faith is better and purer than the Catholic, but who nevertheless would be willing to make considerable concessions in the interest of peace. You must remember that when princes and princesses marry they generally embrace the faith of their husbands, and when lately Queen Elizabeth was talking of marrying the Prince of Anjou, she made it one of the conditions that he should turn Protestant, and the demand was not considered to be insurmountable. It may be that the time will come when Henri of Navarre may consider the throne of France, freedom of worship, and a general peace, cheaply purchased at the cost of attending mass. If he does so, doubtless the Huguenots would be grieved and indignant, but so far as they are concerned it would be the best thing. But of course we are only talking now of what he might do should nought but his religion stand between him and the throne of France. As King of Navarre simply his interest would be all the other way, and he would doubtless remain a staunch Huguenot. Of course, Philip, I am speaking without knowing this young prince. I am simply arguing as to what an astute and politic man in his position, not over-earnest as to matters of faith, would be likely to do."

Three days later Philip rode to London with Pierre and embarked for La Rochelle. His uncle had amply supplied him with funds, but his father insisted upon his taking a handsome sum from him.

"Although you did not require much money before, Philip —and Gaspard told me that you did not draw from his agent at La Rochelle a third of the sum he had placed for you in his hands—it will be different now. You had no expenses before save the pay of your men and the cost of their food and your own, but in time of peace there are many expenses, and I would not that you should be in any way short of money. You can place the greater portion of it in the hands of Maître Bertram, and draw it as you require. At any rate it is better in your hands than lying in that chest in the corner. Your mother and I have no need for it, and it would take away half her pleasure in her work were the earnings not used partly for your advantage."

The ship made a quick run to La Rochelle, and the next morning Philip rode for Laville. He had not been there since the battle of Moncontour, and although he knew that it had been burnt by the Royalists shortly afterwards, it gave him a shock to see, as he rode through the gate, how great a change had taken place. The central portion had been repaired, but the walls were still blackened with smoke. The wings stood empty and roofless, and the ample stables, storehouses, and buildings for the retainers had disappeared. His aunt re ceived him with great kindness, and François was delighted to see him again.

"Yes, it is a change, Philip," the countess said, as she saw his eyes glancing round the apartment. "However, I have grown accustomed to it, and scarce notice it now. Fortunately I have ample means for rebuilding the chateau, for I have led a quiet life for some years, and as the count my husband, being a Huguenot, was not near the court from the time the troubles began, our revenues have for a long time been accumulating, and much of it has been sent to my sister's husband, and has been invested by him in England. There François agrees with me that it should remain. There is at present peace here, but who can say how long it will last?

One thing is certain, that should war break out again it will centre round La Rochelle, and I might be once more forced to leave the chateau at the mercy of the Royalists; it would, then, be folly to spend a crown upon doing more than is sufficient for our necessities. We only keep such retainers as are absolutely necessary for our service; there are but eight horses in the stables, the rest are all out on the farms, and should the troubles recommence we shall soon find riders for them."

"You have just arrived in time, Philip," François said presently, "for we start at the end of this week for Béarn, and although you could have followed us, I am right glad that you have arrived in time to ride with us. All your men are still here."

"I saw Eustace and Henri as I rode in," Philip said.

"The other two work in the garden. Of course their days for fighting are over. They could doubtless strike a blow in defence of the chateau, but they have not recovered sufficiently from their wounds ever to ride as men-at-arms again. However, two will suffice for your needs at present. I shall take four of my own men, for the country is still far from safe for travelling. Many of the disbanded soldiers have turned robbers, and although the royal governors hunt down and string up many, they are still so numerous that travellers from one town to another always journey in strong parties for protection. How did Pierre get on in England?"

"He was glad to return here again, François, although he got on well enough, as our house servants are French, as are also many of those on the farm, and he became quite a favourite with every one. But he is of a restless nature, and grew tired of idleness."

Three days later the party set out from Laville. The countess rode on horseback, and her female attendant *en croupe* behind one of the troopers. They journeyed by easy stages, stopping sometimes at hostelries in the towns, but more often at chateaux belonging to gentlemen known to the countess or her son. They several times came upon groups of rough-looking men, but the two gentlemen, their servants, and the six fully-armed retainers were a force too formidable to be meddled with, and they arrived safely at Béarn. The royal abode was a modest building, far less stately than was Laville before its ruin. It stood a short distance out of the town, where they had left the men-at-arms, with instructions to find lodgings for themselves and their horses. As they arrived at the entrance Prince Henri himself ran down the steps in a dress as plain as that which would be worn by an ordinary citizen.

"Welcome to Béarn," he said. "It is a modest palace, countess, and I am a much less important person here than when I was supposed to be commanding our army."

He assisted her to alight, and then rang a bell; a man came round from the back of the house and took the horse from Pierre, who was holding it, while Henri entered the house with the countess. A minute later he ran out from the house again.

"Now that I have handed over the countess to my mother I can speak to you both," he said heartily. "I am pleased to see you, François, and you too, Monsieur Philip."

"My cousin insisted on my coming with him, prince, and assured me that you would not be displeased at the liberty. But, of course, I intend to quarter myself in the town."

"You will do no such thing," the prince said. "We are poor in Béarn, as poor as church mice, but not so poor that we cannot entertain a friend. Your bed-room is prepared for you."

Philip looked surprised.

"You don't suppose," the prince said, laughing, "that people can come and go in this kingdom of ours without being noticed. We are weak, and for that very reason we must be on our guard. Half the people who come here come for a purpose; they come from the king, or from Philip of Spain, or from the Guises, and most of them mean mischief of some sort, so you see we like to know beforehand, and unless they ride very fast we are sure to get twenty-four hours' notice before they arrive. Then, you see, if we want a little more time a horse may cast its shoe, or some of the baggage may be missing, or perhaps an important paper somehow gets mislaid. It is curious how often these things happen. Then, when they arrive here they find that I have, as usual, gone off

for a fortnight's hunting among the mountains, and that, perhaps, my mother has started for Nérac. We heard yesterday
morning that you had crossed the frontier, and that the countess had with her her son and a big young Englishman, whose
identity I had no difficulty in guessing."

"And we met with no misfortunes by the way, prince,"
François said smiling.

"No," the prince laughed, "these things do not happen
always."

They had so far stood on the steps chatting; the two servants had followed the lackey with their own and their masters'
horses. The prince led the way indoors, and they were heartily
welcomed by the queen, who kept no more state at Béarn than
would be observed by any petty nobleman in France.

On the following day the two friends started with the prince
for the mountains, and were away for three weeks, during which
time they hunted the wild boar, killed several wolves, and shot
five or six wild goats. They were attended only by two or
three huntsmen and their three personal servants. They slept
sometimes in the huts of shepherds or charcoal-burners, sometimes in the forest, in spite of the cold, which was often severe.

"What do you say about this marriage which is being
arranged for me?" the prince asked suddenly one night as
they were sitting by a huge fire in the forest.

"It ought to be a great thing for the reformed religion, if
it is agreeable to your highness," François said cautiously.

"A politic answer, Monsieur de Laville. What say you,
Philip?"

"It is a matter too deep for me to venture an opinion,"
Philip said. "There is doubtless much to be said on both
sides. For example—you are a fisherman, prince?"

"Only moderately so, Philip; but what has that to do with
it?"

"I would say, sir, that when a fisherman hooks an exceedingly large fish it is just possible that, instead of landing it,
the fish may pull him into the water."

The prince laughed.

"You have hit it exactly, Monsieur Philip. That is just
the way I look at it. Marguerite of Valois is indeed a very

big fish compared with the Prince of Béarn, and it is not only she who would pull, but there are others, and even bigger fish, who would pull with her. My good mother has fears that if I once tasted the gaieties of the court of France I should be ruined body and soul. Now I have rather an inclination for the said gaieties, and that prospect does not terrify me as it does her. But there are things which alarm me more than gaieties. There is the king, who, except when he occasionally gets into a rage, and takes his own course, is but a tool in the hands of Catharine de Medici. There is Anjou, who made a jest of the dead body of my uncle Condé. There are Lorraine and the Guises; there are the priests; and there is the turbulent mob of Paris. It seems to me that, instead of being the fisherman, I should be like a very small fish enclosed in a very strong net." And he looked thoughtfully into the fire. "The king is at present with us, but his plighted word is worth nothing."

"But once married," François said, "you would have the princess on your side, and being then brother-in-law to the king, you would be safe from attack."

"The king has no great love for his own brothers," Henri said; "but I am not supposing that even Charles would lay hands on me after inviting me to his court to marry his sister. He would not venture upon that before the eyes of all Europe. It is the strain and the pressure that I fear. A girl who is sent to a nunnery, however much she may hate becoming a nun, can no more escape than a fly from the meshes of a spider. I doubt not that it seems to all the Huguenots of France that for me to marry Marguerite of Valois would be more than a great victory won for their cause; but I have my doubts. However, in a matter like this I am not a free agent. The Huguenot lords are all delighted at the prospect. My mother is still undecided. You see I am practically as much in a net here as I shall be at Paris if this marriage is made. I am rather glad the decision does not rest with me. I shall simply go with the stream; some day perhaps I shall be strong enough to swim against it. I hope that, at any rate, if I ride to Paris to marry Marguerite of Valois, you will both accompany me."

CHAPTER XIX

IN A NET

AFTER their return from hunting they remained for another fortnight at Béarn, and then started, the countess and François to return home, and Philip to pay a visit to the Count de Valecourt at his chateau in Dauphiny, in accordance with the promise he had given him to visit him on his return to France. Here he remained for a month. The count treated him with the warmest hospitality, and introduced him to all his friends as the saviour of his daughter. Claire had grown much since he had seen her, when he had ridden over with her father to Landres a year before. She was now nearly sixteen, and was fast growing into womanhood. Philip was already acquainted with many of the nobles and gentry of Dauphiny who had joined the Admiral's army, and after leaving Valecourt he stayed for a short time at several of their chateaux, and it was autumn before he joined François at Laville.

The inhabited portion of the chateau had been enlarged and made more comfortable, for the king was still firm in his decision that peace should be preserved, and showed marked favour to the section of the court that opposed any persecution of the Huguenots. He had further shown his desire for the friendship of the Protestant powers by the negotiations that had been carried on for the marriage of the Duke of Anjou to Queen Elizabeth.

"I have news for you," François said. "The king has invited the Admiral to visit him. It has, of course, been a matter of great debate whether Coligny should trust himself at court, many of his friends strongly dissuading him; but he deems it best in the interests of our religion that he should accept the invitation, and he is going to set out next week for Blois, where the king now is with the court. He will take only a few of his friends with him. He is perfectly aware of the risk he runs, but to those who entreat him not to trust himself at court he says his going there may be a benefit to the cause, and that his life is as nothing in the scale. However, he has declined the offers that have been made by many gentlemen to accompany him, and only three or four of his personal friends ride with him."

"No doubt he acts wisely there," Philip said. "It would be well-nigh destruction to our cause should anything befall him now; and the fewer of our leaders in Charles's hands the less temptation to the court to seize them. But I do think it possible that good may come of Coligny himself going there. He exercises wonderful influence over all who come in contact with him, and he may be able to counterbalance the intrigues of the Catholic party and confirm the king in his present good intentions towards us."

"I saw him two days ago, and offered to ride in his train," François said, "but he refused decidedly to let me. 'The friends who will accompany me,' he said, 'have, like myself, well-nigh done their work. The future is for you and those who are young. I cannot dream that the king would do wrong to invited guests; but should aught happen, the blow shall fall upon none of those who should be the leaders of the next generation.'"

The news of the reception of the Admiral at Blois was anxiously awaited by the Huguenots of the west, and there was great joy when they heard that he had been received most graciously by the king, who had embraced him and protested that he regarded it as one of the happiest days in his life, as he saw in his return to his side the end of trouble and an assurance of future tranquillity. Even Catharine de Medici received the Admiral with warmth. The king presented him from his private purse with the large sum of a hundred thousand livres to make good some of the great losses he had suffered in the war. He also ordered that he should receive for a year the revenues of his brother the cardinal, who had lately died, and appointed him guardian of one of the great estates during the minority of its heir—a post which brought with it considerable profits.

At Coligny's suggestion Charles wrote to the Duke of Savoy interceding for the Waldenses, who were being persecuted cruèlly for having assisted the Huguenots of France. So angered were the Guises by the favour with which the king treated the Admiral that they retired from court, and the king was thus left entirely to the influence of Montmorency and Coligny. The ambassador of Spain, who was farther angered by Charles granting interviews to Louis of Nassau, and by his holding out hopes to the Dutch of assistance in their struggle against Alva, also left France in deep dudgeon and with threats of war. The result was naturally to cause a better state of feeling throughout France. Persecutions everywhere ceased, and the Huguenots for the first time for many years were able to live in peace, and without fear of their neighbours.

The negotiations for the marriage between the Prince of Navarre and Marguerite de Valois continued. The prince was now eighteen and a half, and the princess twenty. The idea of a marriage between them was of old standing, for it had been proposed by Henry II. fifteen years before, but at the outbreak of the Huguenot troubles it had been dropped. Marshal Biron was sent by the king with the royal proposals to the Queen of Navarre, who was now at La Rochelle. The queen expressed her gratitude for the honour offered to her son, but prayed for time before giving a decided answer, in order that she might consult the ministers of her religion as to whether such a marriage might be entered into by one of the reformed religion.

The news of the proposed marriage, and also of the negotiations that had been opened for a marriage between Elizabeth of England and the Duc d'Alençon, created the greatest alarm throughout the Catholic world. A legate was sent to Charles by the pope to protest against it. Sebastian, King of Portugal, who had refused the hand of Marguerite when it had before been offered to him, reopened negotiations for it, while

Philip of Spain did all in his power to throw obstacles in the way of the match.

The ministers of the reformed religion, consulted by the queen, considered that the marriage of Henri to Marguerite would be of vast benefit to the Huguenot cause, and declared that a mixed marriage was lawful. The English ambassador gave his strongest support to it, and the Queen of Navarre now entered upon the negotiations in earnest and went to Blois for the purpose.

The differences were entirely religious ones, the court insisting that Henri, while living at Paris with his wife, should consent to be deprived of all means of worshipping according to his own religion, while Marguerite, while in Béarn, should be guaranteed permission to have mass celebrated there.

The king would have been ready to waive both conditions, but Catharine, who, after at first favouring the match now threw every obstacle in its way, was opposed to any concession. She refused to permit the Queen of Navarre to have any interview with either Charles or Marguerite unless she was also present, and hesitated at no falsehoods however outrageous in order to thwart the efforts of Jeanne and her friends. The pious queen, however, was more troubled by the extreme and open profligacy of the court than by the political difficulties she encountered, and in her letters implored her son to insist upon residing at Béarn with his wife, and on no account to take up his abode at Paris.

However, at last the difficulties were removed, the court abandoned its demand that Marguerite should be allowed to attend mass at Béarn, and the Queen of Navarre, on her part, consented that the marriage should take place at Paris, instead of at Béarn as she had before desired. She then went to Paris to make preparations for the wedding. The great anxiety she had gone through told heavily upon her, and a few days after her arrival at the capital she was seized with a fever, which, in a very short time, terminated her life, not without considerable suspicions being entertained that her illness and death had been caused by poison administered by an agent of Catharine. She was, undoubtedly, one of the noblest women of her own or any other time. She was deeply religious, ready to incur all dangers for the sake of her faith, simple in her habits, pure in her life, unconquerable in spirit, calm and confident in' defeat and danger, never doubting for a moment that God would give victory to his cause, and capable of communicating her enthusiasm to all around her—a Christian heroine, indeed. Her death was a terrible blow to the reformed religion. She died on the 9th of June, and the marriage was, in consequence, deferred until August.

The Admiral had not been present at Blois during the negotiations for the marriage, for after remaining there for three weeks he had retired to his estate at Chatillon, where he occupied himself with the work of restoring his ruined chateau. The Countess Amelie had accompanied the Queen of Navarre to Blois and also to Paris, and had been with her at the time she died. She had sent a message to François and Philip to join her there when she left Blois, accompanying her letter with a safe-conduct signed by the king. On the road they were met by the news of the death of the Queen of Navarre. It was a severe blow to both of them, not only from the effect it would have upon the Huguenot cause, but from the affection they personally felt for her.

The king being grievously harassed by the opposite counsels he received, and his doubts as to which of his advisers were honest, wrote to Coligny begging him to come and aid him with his counsel and support.

The Admiral received many letters imploring him not to go to Paris, where, even if the friendship of the king continued, he would be exposed to the danger of poison, to which, it was generally believed, his brothers and the Queen of Navarre had succumbed; but although fully aware of the danger of the step, he did not hesitate. To one of his advisers he wrote fearlessly:

"As a royal officer I cannot in honour refuse to comply with the summons of the king, but will commit myself to the providence of Him who holds in His hands the hearts of kings and princes, and has numbered my years, nay, the very hairs of my head."

One reason of the king's desire for the counsels of the Admiral was that he had determined to carry out his advice, and that of Louis of Nassau, to assist the Protestants of Holland, and to embark in a struggle against the dangerous predominance of Spain.

As a first step he had already permitted Louis of Nassau to recruit secretly in France five hundred horse and a thousand infantry from among his Huguenot friends, and to advance with them into the Netherlands, and with these Louis had on the 24th of May captured Mons, the capital of Hainault. The Huguenot leaders did their best to persuade Charles to follow up this stroke by declaring war against Spain; and the king would have done so, had it not been that Elizabeth of England, who had before urged him to this course, promising him her aid, now drew back with her usual vacillation, wishing nothing better than to see France and Spain engaged in hostilities from which she would without trouble or expense gain advantage. Meanwhile Catharine, Anjou, and the Guise faction all did their best to counteract the influence of the Huguenots.

Elizabeth's crafty and hesitating policy was largely responsible for the terrible events that followed. Charles saw that she had been fooling him, both in reference to his course towards Spain, and in her negotiations for a marriage with one or other of his brothers. These matters were taken advantage of by his Catholic advisers, and disposed him to doubt the wisdom of his having placed himself in the hands of the Huguenots. While Elizabeth was hesitating a blow came that confirmed the king in his doubts as to the prudence of the course he had taken. Alva laid siege to Mons. A Huguenot force of some three thousand men, led by the Sieur de Genlis, marched to its relief, but was surprised and utterly routed within a short distance of the town; 1200 were killed on the field of battle, some 1900 fugitives were slain by the peasantry, barely a hundred reached Mons.

Coligny, who was preparing a much larger force for the assistance of Louis of Nassau, still strove to induce the king to throw himself heart and soul into the struggle against Spain, and even warned him that he would never be a true king until he could free himself from his mother's control and the influence of his brother Anjou. The queen-mother, who had spies everywhere, was not long in learning that Coligny had given this advice, and her hatred against him was proportionately increased. She at once went in tears to Charles, and pointed out to him that it was to her counsel and aid alone that he had owed his success against the Huguenots, that they were now obtaining all the advantages for which they had fought in vain, and that he was endangering the safety of his throne by angering Spain, relying only on the empty promises of the faithless Queen of England. Charles, always weak and irresolute, succumbed at once to her tears and entreaties, and gave himself up altogether to her pernicious counsels.

After the death of the Queen of Navarre, the countess travelled back to Laville escorted by her son and Philip. The young men made no stay there, but returned at once to Paris, where, now that Coligny was in the king's counsels, there was no ground for fear, and the approaching nuptials of the young King of Navarre would be attended by large numbers of his adherents. They took a lodging near that occupied by the Admiral. De la Noüe was not at court, he being shut up in Mons, having accompanied Louis of Nassau in his expedition. The court was in deep mourning for the Queen of Navarre, and there would be no public gaieties until the wedding. Among the Huguenot lords who had come to Paris were the Count de Valecourt and his daughter, who was now seventeen, and had several suitors for her hand among the young Huguenot nobles.

François and Philip were both presented to the king by the Admiral. Charles received them graciously, and learning that they had been stopping at Béarn with the Prince of Navarre, presented them to his sister Margaret.

"These gentlemen, Margot, are friends of the King of Navarre, and will be able to tell you more about him than these grave politicians can do."

The princess, who was one of the most beautiful women of her time, asked them many questions about her future husband, of whom she had seen so little since his childhood, and about the place where she was to live; and after that time when they went to court with the Admiral, who on such occasions was always accompanied by a number of Huguenot gentlemen, the young princess always showed them marked friendliness. As the time for the marriage approached, the king became more and more estranged from the Admiral. Queen Elizabeth, while professing her friendship for the Netherlands, had forbidden English volunteers to sail to the assistance of the Dutch, and had written to Alva offering in token of her friendship to hand over Flushing to the Spaniards. This proof of her duplicity, and of the impossibility of trusting her as an ally, was made the most of by Catharine, and she easily persuaded the weak-minded king that hostilities with the Spaniards would be fatal to him, and that, should he yield to the Admiral's entreaties, he would fall wholly into the power of the Huguenots. The change in the king's deportment was so visible that the Catholics did not conceal their exultation, while a feeling of uneasiness spread among some of the Huguenot gentlemen at Paris.

"What are you doing, Pierre?" Philip said one day when he found his servant occupied in cleaning up the two pairs of heavy pistols they carried in their holsters.

"I am getting them ready for action, master. I always thought that the Huguenots were fools to put their heads into this cage, and the more I see of it the less I like it."

"There can be no reason for uneasiness, Pierre. The king himself has over and over declared his determination to maintain the truce, and even did he harbour ill designs against us he would not mar his sister's marriage by fresh steps against the Huguenots. What may follow after we have all left Paris I cannot say."

"Well, sir, I hope it may be all right, but since I got a sight of the king's face the other day I have no faith in him; he looks like one worried until well-nigh out of his senses—and no wonder. These weak men, when they become desperate, are capable of the most terrible actions. A month since he would have hung up his mother and Anjou had they ventured to oppose him, and there is no saying now upon whom his wrath may fall. At any rate, sir, with your permission I mean to be prepared for the worst, and the first work is to clean these pistols."

"There can be no harm in that anyhow, Pierre, but I have no shadow of fear of any trouble occurring. The one thing I am afraid of is, that the king will keep Coligny near him, so that if war should break out again we shall not have him for our general. With the Queen of Navarre dead, the Admiral a prisoner here, and De la Noüe a captive in the hands of Alva, we should fight under terrible disadvantages, especially as La Rochelle, La Charité, and Montauban have received royal governors in accordance with the conditions of the peace."

"Well, we shall see, master. I shall feel more comfortable if I have got ready for the worst."

Although Philip laughed at the fears of Pierre, he was yet impressed by what he had said, for he had come to rely very much upon the shrewdness of observation of his follower. When, however, he went that evening to the Count de Vale-court's, he saw that there was no tinge of such feeling in the minds of the Huguenots present. The only face that had an unusual look was that of Claire. Apparently she was gayer than usual, and laughed and talked more than was her wont; but Philip saw that this mood was not a natural one, and felt sure that something had happened. Presently when he passed near her she made room for him on the settee beside her.

"You have not heard the news, Monsieur Philip?"

"No, mademoiselle, I have heard no particular news."

"I am glad of it. I would rather tell you myself. My father has to-day laid his commands on me to marry the Sieur de Pascal."

Philip could not trust himself to speak. He had never acknowledged to himself that he loved Claire de Valecourt, and had over and over again endeavoured to impress upon his mind the fact that it would be ridiculous for him even to think of her, for that her father would never dream of giving her, a rich heiress, and the last of one of the proudest families of Dauphiny, to a simple English gentleman.

As he did not speak the girl went on after a pause. "It is not my wish, Monsieur Philip; but French girls do not choose for themselves. My father stated his wishes to me three months ago in Dauphiny; I then asked for a little time, and now he has told me that it is to be. He is wise and good, and I have nothing to say against the Sieur de Pascal, who, as you know, is our near neighbour, a brave gentleman, and one whom I have known since my childhood. It is only that I do

"YOU HAVE NOT HEARD THE NEWS, MONSIEUR PHILIP?"

not love him.   I have told my father so, but he says that it is
not to be expected that a young maid should love until after
marriage."

"And you have promised?" Philip asked.

"Yes, I have promised," she said simply.   "It is the duty
of a daughter to obey her father, especially when that father is
as good and kind as mine has always been to me.   There, he
is beckoning to me;" and rising, she crossed the room.

Philip, a few minutes later, took his departure quietly.
François de Laville came in an hour afterwards to their
lodgings.

"Well, Philip, I did not see you leave the count's.   Did
you hear the news before you left?   The count announced it
shortly after you had gone."

"His daughter told me herself," Philip said.

"I am sorry, Philip.   I had thought, perhaps—but it is of
no use talking of that now."

"Not the least in the world, François.   It is natural that
her father should wish her to marry a noble of his own province.   She has consented, and there is no more to be said.
When is Henri to arrive?   We are all to ride out to meet him
and to follow him into Paris.   I hope that it will all pass off
well."

"Why, of course it will.   What is to prevent it?   The
wedding will be the grandest ever known in Paris.   I hear
that Henri brings with him seven hundred Huguenot gentlemen, and a hundred of us here will join him under the
Admiral.   It will be a brave sight."

"I wish it was all over."

"Why, it is not often you are in low spirits, Philip.   Is
it the news that has upset you, or have you heard anything
else?"

"No; but Pierre has been croaking and prophesying evil,
and although I in no way agree with him, it has still made me
uneasy."

"Why, what is there to fear?" François said laughing;
"not the mob of Paris; surely they would never venture to
brave the king's anger by marring the nuptials by disorder;
and if they did, methinks that eight hundred of us, with

Coligny at our head, could cut our way through the mob of Paris from one end of the city to the other."

The entrance of the King of Navarre into Paris was indeed an imposing sight. Coligny with his train had joined him outside the town, and the Admiral rode on one side of the young king and the Prince of Condé on the other. With them rode the Dukes of Anjou and Alençon, who had ridden out with a gay train of nobles to welcome Henri in the king's name, and escort him into the city. The Huguenots were still in mourning for the late queen, but the sumptuous materials of their dress set off by their gold chains and ornaments made a brave show even by the side of the gay costumes of the prince's party.

The betrothal took place at the Louvre on the 17th of August, and was followed by a supper and a ball; after the conclusion of the festivities Marguerite was, in accordance with the custom of the princesses of the blood, escorted by her brothers and a large retinue to the Bishops' Palace adjoining the Cathedral, to pass the night before her wedding there. The ceremony upon the following day was a most gorgeous one. The king, his two brothers, Henri of Navarre, and Condé were all dressed alike in light yellow satin embroidered with silver, and enriched with precious stones. Marguerite was in a violet velvet dress embroidered with *fleurs de lis*, and she wore on her head a crown glittering with gems. The queen and the queen-mother were dressed in cloth of gold.

Upon a lofty platform in front of the Cathedral of Notre Dame, Henri of Navarre with his train of Protestant lords awaited the coming of the bride, who was escorted by the king and all the members of his court. The ceremony was performed in sight of an enormous concourse of people by the Cardinal Bourbon, who used a form that had been previously agreed upon by both parties. Henri then led his bride into the Cathedral, and afterwards with his Protestant companions retired to the Episcopal Palace while mass was being said. When this was over the whole party sat down to dinner in the Episcopal Palace.

In the evening an entertainment was given in the Louvre to the notabilities of Paris, and after supper there was a masque of the most lavish magnificence. On Tuesday, Wednesday, and Thursday there was a continuation of pageants and entertainments. During these festivities the king had shown marked courtesy to the Admiral and the Huguenot lords, and it seemed as if he had again emancipated himself from his mother's influence, and the hopes of the Protestants that he would shortly declare war with Spain were raised to the highest point.

Although the question was greatly debated at the time, and the belief that the massacre of the Protestants was deliberately planned long beforehand by the king and queen-mother is still generally entertained, the balance of evidence is strongly the other way.

What dark thoughts may have passed through the scheming brain of Catharine de Medici none can say, but it would certainly appear that it was not until after the marriage of Henri and Marguerite that they took form. She was driven to bay. She saw that in the event of a war with Spain the Huguenots would become all-powerful in France. Already the influence of the Admiral was greater than her own, and it had become a battle of life and death with her, for Coligny, in his fearless desire to do what was right, and for the service of France, was imprudent enough over and over again to warn the king against the evil influence of the queen-mother and the Duke d'Anjou, and Charles in his fits of temper did not hesitate to divulge these counsels. The Duke d'Anjou and his mother, therefore, came to the conclusion that Coligny must be put out of the way. The duke afterwards did not scruple to avow his share in the preparations for the massacre of Saint Bartholomew.

The Duchess of Nemours, her son Henry of Guise, and her brother-in-law the Duc d'Aumale, were taken into their counsels, and the plan was speedily settled. Few as were the conspirators taken into the confidence of the queen-mother, mysterious rumours of danger reached the ears of the Huguenots. Some of these taking the alarm left Paris and made for their estates, but by far the greater portion refused to believe that there could be danger to those whom the king had invited to be present upon such an occasion. In another week,

Coligny would be leaving, having, as he hoped, brought the king entirely round to his views, and the vast majority of the Huguenot gentlemen resolved to stay until he left.

Pierre grew more and more serious. François had left the lodgings, being one of the Huguenot gentlemen whom Henri of Navarre had chosen to lodge with him at the Louvre.

"You are getting quite unbearable, Pierre, with your long face and your grim looks," Philip said to him on the Friday morning, half in joke and half in earnest. "Why, man, in another week we shall be out of Paris and on our way south."

"I hope so, Monsieur Philip, with all my heart I hope so; but I feel just as I used to do when I was a boy living in the woods, and I saw a thunder-cloud working up overhead. I cannot tell you why I feel so, it is something in the air. I wish sir, oh, so much! that you would leave at once."

"That I cannot do, Pierre. I have no estates that demand my attention, no excuse whatever for going. I came here with my cousin, and shall leave with him."

"Well, sir, if it must be, it must."

"But what is that you fear, Pierre?"

"When one is in a town, sir, with Catharine de Medici, and her son Anjou, and the Guises, there is always something to fear. Guise is the idol of the mob of Paris, who have always shown themselves ready to attack the Huguenots. He has but to hold up his finger and they would be swarming on us like bees."

"But there are troops in the town, Pierre, and the king would punish Paris heavily were it to insult his guests."

"The king is a weathercock and goes whichever way the wind blows, monsieur—to-day he is with the Admiral, to-morrow he may be with the Guises. At any rate I have taken my precautions. I quite understand that if the danger is foreseen you will all rally round the Admiral and try to fight your way out of Paris. But if it comes suddenly there will be no time for this. At any hour the mob may come surging up the streets shouting, as they have often shouted before, 'Death to the Huguenots!' Then, monsieur, fighting would not avail you. You would be unable to join your friends, and you

would have to think first of your own life. I have been examining the house, and I find that from an upper window one
can gain the roof. I got out yesterday evening after it was
dark, and found that I could easily make my way along.
The tenth house from here is the one where the Count de Valecourt lodges, and it is easy to gain access to it by a window
in the roof. There will be some of your friends there, at any
rate. Or we can pass down through any of the intervening
houses. In the three before we reach that of the count Huguenots are lodged. The others belong to Catholics, but it
might be possible to pass down through them and to go into
the street unobserved. I have bought for myself some rags
such as are worn by the lowest of the mob, and for you a
monk's gown and hood. These I have placed securely against
a chimney on our roof. I have also, monsieur," and Pierre's
eyes twinkled, "bought the dress of a woman of the lower
class, thinking that there might be some lady you might be
desirous of saving."

"You frighten me, Pierre, with your roofs and your disguises," Philip said, looking with wonder at his follower.
"Why, man, this is a nightmare of your own imagination."

"It may be so, master. If it is, no harm is done; I have
laid out a few crowns uselessly, and there is an end of it. But
if it should not be a nightmare, but a real positive danger,
you would at least be prepared for it, and those few crowns
may be the saving of our lives."

Philip walked up and down the room for some time.

"At any rate, Pierre, you have acted wisely. As you say
the cost is as nothing; and though my reason revolts against
a belief in this nightmare of yours, I am not such a fool as to
refuse to pay any attention to it. I know that you are no
coward, and certainly not one to indulge in wild fancies.
Let us go a step farther. Suppose that all this should turn
out true, and that you, I, and—and some lady are in disguise
in the midst of a howling mob shouting, 'Death to the
Huguenots!' What should we do next? Where should we
go? It seems to me that your disguise for me is a badly
chosen one. As a monk, how could I keep with you as a
beggar, still less with a woman?"

"When I bought the monk's robe I had not thought of a woman, monsieur; that was an after-thought. But what you say is just. I must get you another disguise. You shall be dressed as a butcher or a smith."

"Let it be a smith, by all means, Pierre; besides, it would be safer. I would smear my face with dirt. I should get plenty on my hands from climbing over the roofs. Let us suppose ourselves, then, in the mob. What should we do next?"

"That would all depend, sir, whether the soldiers follow the Guises and take part with the mob in their rising. If so Paris would be in a turmoil from end to end, and the gates closed. I have thought it all over again and again, and while your worship has been attending the entertainments I have been walking about Paris. If it is at night I should say we had best make for the river, take a boat and drift down, or else make for the walls and lower ourselves by a rope from them. If it is in the day we could not do that, and I have found a hovel, at present untenanted, close to the walls, and we could wait there until night."

"You will end by making me believe this, Pierre," Philip said angrily, as he again walked up and down the room with impatient steps. "If you had a shadow of foundation for what you say, even a rumour that you had picked up in the street, I would go straight to the Admiral. But how could I go and say, 'My servant, who is a faithful fellow, has taken it into his head that there is danger from an attack on us by the mob.' What think you the Admiral would say to that? He would say that it was next door to treason to imagine such things, and that if men were to act upon such fancies as these they would be fit only for hospitals for the insane. Moreover, he would say that even if you had evidence, even if you had something to show that treachery was meant, he would still, in the interest of France, stay at his post of duty."

At this moment the door opened, and François de Laville entered hurriedly.

"What is the matter, François?" Philip exclaimed, seeing that his cousin looked pale and agitated.

"Have you not heard the news?"

"I have heard nothing. I have not been out this morning."

"The Admiral has been shot."

Philip uttered an exclamation of horror. "Not killed, François; not killed, I trust?"

"No; two balls were fired, one took off a finger of his right hand, and another has lodged in his left arm. He had just left the king, who was playing at tennis, and was walking homewards with two or three gentlemen, when an arquebus was fired from a house not far from his own. Two of the gentlemen with him assisted him home, while some of the others burst in the door of the house. They were too late; only a woman and a man-servant were found there. The assassin had fled by the back of the house, where a horse was standing in waiting. It is said that the house belongs to the old Duchess of Guise. It is half an hour since the news reached the palace, and you may imagine the consternation it excited. The king has shut himself up in his room, Navarre and Condé are in deep grief, for they both regard the Admiral almost as a father; as for the rest of us, we are furious. There is a report that the man who was seen galloping away from the house from which the shot was fired was that villain Maurevel, who so treacherously shot De Mouy, and was rewarded by the king for the deed. It is also said that a groom in the livery of Guise was holding the horse when the assassin issued out. Navarre and Condé have gone to Coligny; the king's surgeon is dressing his wounds."

CHAPTER XX

THE TOCSIN

AS soon as François had finished his account of the attempted assassination of the Admiral, he and Philip sallied out, the latter having hastily armed himself.

"I must go back to the Louvre," François said, "and take my place by the King of Navarre. He is going to see the king, and to demand permission to leave Paris at once. Condé and La Rochefoucault are going to see the king as soon as they return from the Admiral's, for the same purpose, as it is evident their lives are not safe here."

Philip made his way to the Admiral's house in the Rue de Bethisy. Numbers of Huguenot gentlemen were hurrying in that direction, all, like himself, armed, and deeply moved with grief and indignation, for Coligny was regarded with a deep affection as well as reverence by his followers. Each as he overtook others eagerly inquired the news, for as yet most of them had learned nothing beyond vague rumours of the affair. Philip's account of it increased their indignation. So it was no act of a mere fanatic, but the work of the Guises, and probably of Catharine and Anjou. In a short time between two and three hundred gentlemen were gathered in the courtyard and ante-chamber of Coligny's house. Some walked up and down silent and stern; others gathered in groups and passionately discussed the matter. This was an attack not only upon the Admiral but upon the Huguenots in general. It was the work of the Guises, ever the deadliest foes of the reformed faith, the authors of every measure taken against them, the cause of all the blood that had been shed in the civil wars. One thing was certain, all must leave Paris and prepare for a renewal of the war; but it was equally certain they could not leave until the Admiral was fit to be moved.

"Truly he is a saint," said one of the gentlemen who had come down from the room where Coligny was lying. "He suffered atrociously in the hands of the surgeon, for he had come without his instruments, and amputated Coligny's fingers with a dagger so blunt that it was only on the third attempt that he succeeded. Merlin, his minister, was by his side, with several of his most intimate friends. We were in tears at the sight of our noble chief thus traitorously struck down. He turned to us and said calmly, 'My friends, why do you weep? As for me I deem myself happy at having thus received wounds for the sake of God.' Then he said that most sincerely he forgave the man who wounded him and those who had instigated him to make the attack, knowing for certain that it was beyond their power to hurt him, for even should they kill him death would be a certain passage to life."

An hour later François arrived.

"The prince has seen the king, Philip. He is furious, and has sworn that he will inflict the most signal punishment upon the authors and instigators of the crime: Coligny had received the wound, but he himself most felt the smart. The King of Navarre told me he was sure that Charles was deeply in earnest. He feels it in a threefold sense: first, because it is the renewal of the troubles that he had hoped had been put an end to; in the second place, because Coligny is his guest; and, lastly, because he has the greatest respect and confidence in him, not only believing in his wisdom, but knowing that his counsel is always sincere and disinterested. He is coming to visit the Admiral himself this afternoon, Philip. It is no use our staying here. There is nothing to be done and no prospect of seeing the Admiral."

As they moved towards the entrance to the courtyard the Count de Valecourt joined them.

"I have just left the Admiral," he said; "he is easier, and the king's surgeon is of opinion that he will recover from his wounds, and possibly may be fit to travel in a litter in another week."

"That is good news indeed," François said, "for the sooner we are all out of Paris the better."

"There is no doubt of that," the count agreed; "but as all say that the king is furious at this attack upon the Admiral, I do not think the Guises dare strike another blow for some time. Still, I shall be glad indeed when we can set forth. It is certain we cannot leave the Admiral here. The villains who are responsible for the attempt will be furious at its failure, and next time they may use the weapon to which they are most accustomed—poison. Even if the king himself begged him to stay at the Louvre until cured, Catharine de Medici is there, and I would not trust him under the same roof with her for all my estates. We have been talking it over, and all agree that we must wait until he can be moved. Inconstant as Charles is, there can be no fear of a change in his friendly intentions now. He has already closed all the gates of Paris save two, and everyone who goes in or out is closely questioned and has to show his papers."

By this time they had arrived at the door of the count's dwelling.

"Come in, monsieur," he said; "my daughter is terribly upset at this attack upon the Admiral, for whom she has a profound reverence, and, were she a Catholic, would, I doubt not, make him her patron saint."

"How is he, father?" Claire asked eagerly, as they entered the room.

"He is better, Claire; the king's physician thinks he has every chance of recovering."

"God be praised!" she said earnestly; "it would indeed have been a terrible day for us all had the assassin taken his life, and it would have seemed a mark of Heaven's anger at this marriage of the Protestant king with a Catholic princess. What says King Charles?"

"He is as angry as any of us, and declares that the assassin and those who abetted him shall be punished in the severest manner. He has visited the Admiral and expressed his grief and indignation to him."

"I shall be glad to be back in Dauphiny, father. This city with its wickedness and its violence is hateful to me."

"We shall go soon, dear. The doctor hopes that in a week the Admiral will be well enough to be moved in a litter, and we shall all accompany him."

"A week is a long time, father; so much may happen in a week."

"There is no fear of anything happening, Claire. You must not let this sad business affect your nerves. The anger of the king is so great that you may be sure none will attempt to repeat this stroke. What think you, Monsieur de Laville?"

"I agree with you altogether, count."

"And you, Monseur Philip?"

"I see no cause for fear, count, and yet I feel sure that it would be well to take every precaution. I acknowledge that I have no grounds whatever for my fear: I have been infected by my lackey, who is generally the lightest-hearted and most reckless fellow, but who has now turned croaker and fears a sudden rising of the mob of Paris, instigated thereto by the Guises."

"Has he heard anything to favour such an idea, or is it merely born of to-day's outrage?"

"No, I think he has heard nothing specific, though he may have caught up vague threats in wandering through the streets."

"Why, that is not like you," the count said smiling, "who have been through so many fights and dangerous adventures, to be alarmed at a shadow."

"No, count, I do not think that I am given, any more than is my lackey, to sombre thoughts; but I own that he has infected me, and I would that some precautions could be taken."

"Precautions of what kind, Monsieur Philip?"

"I have not thought them out," Philip said; "but were I the next in rank to the Admiral I would enjoin that a third of our number should be under arms night and day, and should at night patrol our quarters; secondly, that a rallying-place should be appointed, say at the Admiral's, to which all should mount and ride directly an alarm is given."

"The first part could hardly be managed here," the count

said gravely. "It would seem that we doubted the royal assurances of good faith and his promises of protection. We have enemies enough about the king's ear, and such a proceeding would be surely misrepresented to him. You know how wayward are his moods, and that it would need but a slight thing to excite his irritation and undo all the good that the Admiral has effected."

Two or three other Huguenot gentlemen now entered, and a general conversation on the state of affairs took place. Philip was standing a little apart from the others when Claire came up to him.

"You really believe in danger, Monsieur Philip?"

"Frankly I do, mademoiselle. The population hate us. There have been Huguenot massacres over and over again in Paris. The Guises are doubtless the instigators of this attack on the Admiral; they are the idols of the Paris mob, and if they gave the word it would at once rise against us. As I told your father, I have no real reason for uneasiness, but nevertheless I am uneasy."

"Then the danger must be real," the girl said simply. "Have you any advice to give me?"

"Only this. You have but a week to stay here in Paris. During that time make excuses so as not to stir abroad in the streets more than you can help; and in the second place I would say, lie down in your clothes at night, so as to be in readiness to rise instantly."

"I will do that," she said. "There is nothing else?"

"Nothing that I can think of. I hope and trust that the emergency will not come; but at any rate, until it does come, we can do no more."

A few minutes later Philip and his cousin took their leave; the former went back to his lodgings, the latter to the Louvre. Philip was surprised at not finding Pierre, and sat up later than usual expecting his return, but it was not till he was rising next morning that the man made his appearance.

"Why, where have you been all night?" Philip asked angrily. "This is not the time for pleasure."

"I have been outside the walls, master," Pierre said.

"What in the world did you go there for, Pierre?"

"Well, sir, I was here when M. de Laville brought in the news of the shooting of the Admiral. This seemed to me to bear out all that I have said to you. You hurried away without my having time to speak to you, so I took it upon myself to act."

"In what way, Pierre?"

"I went straight to the stables, sir, and took one of your honour's chargers and my horse, and, riding one and leading the other, passed out through the gate before the orders came about closing. I rode them to a village six miles away, and put them up at a small inn there and left them in the landlord's charge. I did not forget to tell the stable-boy that he should have a crown for himself if on my return I found the horses in as good condition as I left them. Then I walked back to Paris, and found a crowd of people unable to enter, and learned that the gates had been closed by the king's order. I went off to St. Denis, and there bought a long rope and an iron hook; and at two in the morning, when I thought that any sentries there might be on the walls would be drowsy, came back again to Paris, threw up my hook, and climbed into one of the bastions near the hut we had marked. There I slept until the morning, and now you see me. I have taken out the horses, so that, should you be obliged to fly, there would be means of escape. One charger will suffice for your wants here, and to ride away upon if you go out with the Huguenot company, whether peacefully or by force of arms. As for me, I would make my way there on foot, get the horses, and rejoin you."

"It was a good idea, Pierre, and promptly carried out. But no one here has much thought of danger, and I feel ashamed of myself at being the only one to feel uneasy."

"The wise man is uneasy while the fool sleeps," Pierre said. "If the Prince of Condé had been uneasy the night before Jarnac he would not have lost his life, and we should not have lost a battle. No harm has been done. If danger does come, we at least are prepared for it."

"You are quite right, Pierre. However surely he may count upon victory, a good general always lays his plans in case of defeat. At any rate, we have prepared for everything."

Pierre muttered something to himself.

"What do you say, Pierre?"

"I was only saying, master, that I should feel pretty confident of our getting away were there only our two selves to
think of. What with our disguises, and what with your honour's strong arm—and what I can do to back you—and what
with our being on our guard, it would be hard if we did not
make our way safe off. But I foresee that, should there be
trouble, it is not of your own safety you will be thinking."

"Mademoiselle de Valecourt is engaged to the Sieur de
Pascal," Philip said gravely.

"So I heard from one of the count's lackeys; but there is
many a slip between the cup and the lip, and in such days as
these there is many an engagement that never becomes a marriage. I guessed how it would be that night after you had
saved Mademoiselle Claire's life, and I thought so still more
when we were staying at Valecourt."

"Then your thoughts ran too fast, Pierre. Mademoiselle
de Valecourt is a great heiress, and the count should, of course,
give her in marriage to one of his own rank."

Pierre shrugged his shoulders almost imperceptibly.

"Your honour is doubtless right," he said humbly; "and
therefore, seeing that she has her father and Monsieur de
Pascal to protect her, we need not trouble more about those
articles of attire stowed away on the roof above, but shall be
able to concern ourselves solely with our own safety, which
puts a much better complexion on the affair."

"The whole matter is ridiculous, Pierre," Philip said
angrily, "and I am a fool to have listened to you. There,
go and see about breakfast, or I shall lose my patience with
you altogether."

There were several consultations during the day between
the leading Huguenots. There was no apparent ground for
suspicion that the attack upon the Admiral had been a part of
any general plot, and it was believed that it was but the outcome of the animosity of the Guises and the queen-mother
against a man who had long withstood them, who was now
higher than themselves in the king's confidence, and who had
persuaded him to undertake an enterprise that would range

France on the side of the Protestant powers. The balance of evidence is all in favour of the truth of this supposition, and to the effect that it was only upon the failure of their scheme against the Admiral that the conspirators determined upon a general massacre of the Huguenots. They worked upon the weak king's mind until they persuaded him that Coligny was at the head of a plot against himself, and that nothing short of his death and those of his followers could procure peace and quiet for France. At last, in a sudden access of fury, Charles not only ranged himself on their side, but astonished Catharine, Anjou, and their companions by going even farther than they had done, and declaring that every Huguenot should be killed.

This sudden change, and his subsequent conduct during the few months that remained to him of life, seem to point to the fact that this fresh access of trouble shattered his weak brain, and that he was not fairly responsible for the events that followed, the guilt of which rests wholly upon Catharine de Medici, Henry of Anjou, and the leaders of the party of the Guises.

Philip spent a considerable portion of the day at the Louvre with Henri of Navarre, François de Laville, and a few of the young king's closest followers. There was no shadow of disquiet in the minds of any of them. The doctors reported that the Admiral's state was favourable; and although all would have been glad to be on their way south, they regarded the detention of a few days as a matter of little importance.

Listening to their talk about the court entertainments and pleasures, Philip quite shook off his uneasiness, and was angry with himself for having listened to Pierre's prognostications of evil. "All these Huguenot lords know France and the Parisians better than I do," he said to himself. "No thought of danger occurs to them. It is not even thought necessary that a few of them should take up their abode at the Admiral's. They have every faith in the king's protestations and pledges for their safety." Philip dined at the Louvre, and it was ten o'clock before he returned to his lodging. He was in excellent spirits, and saluted Pierre with the laughing inquiry:

"Well, bird of ill omen, what fresh plottings have you discovered?"

"You do not believe me, master, when I tell you," Pierre said gravely.

"Oh, then, there is something new?" Philip said, seating himself on a couch. "Let me hear all about it, Pierre, and I will try not to laugh."

"Will you descend with me to the door, Monsieur Philip?"

"Assuredly I will if it will please you, though what you are going to show me there I cannot imagine."

Pierre led the way downstairs and out through the door.

"Do you see that, sir?"

"Yes, I see that, Pierre."

"What do you take it to be, sir?"

"Well, it is not too dark to see what it is, Pierre. It is a small white cross that some urchin has chalked on the door."

"Will you please to walk a little farther, sir? There is a cross on this door. There is none here, neither on the next. Here you see another, and then a door without one. Now, sir, does not that strike you as curious?"

"Well, I don't know, Pierre. A boy might very well chalk some doors as he went along and leave others untouched."

"Yes, sir. But there is one very remarkable thing; I have gone on through several streets, and it has always been the same—so far as I can discover by questioning the concierges —at every house in which Huguenots are lodging there is a white cross on the door, in the houses that are not so marked there are no Huguenots."

"That is strange, certainly, Pierre," Philip said, struck alike by the fact and by the earnestness with which Pierre expressed it. "Are you quite sure of what you say?"

"I am quite sure, sir. I returned here at nine o'clock and saw this mark on our door. I did not pay much heed to it, but went upstairs. Then, as I thought it over, I said to myself, Is this a freak of some passer-by, or is it some sort of signal? Then I thought I would see whether our house alone was marked, or whether there were crosses on other doors. I went to the houses of several gentlemen of our party, and on each of their doors was a white cross. Then I looked farther and found that other houses were unmarked. At some of these I knocked and asked for one or other of your friends. In each

"THAT CROSS IS PLACED THERE BY DESIGN."

case I heard that I was mistaken, for that no Huguenots were lodging there. It is evident, sir, that this is not a thing of chance, but that these crosses are placed there by design."

Philip went down the street and satisfied himself that Pierre had spoken correctly, and then returned to his lodgings, pausing, however, before the house of the Count de Valecourt, and erasing the cross upon it. He entered his own door without touching the mark, but Pierre, who followed him in, rubbed the sleeve of his doublet across it unnoticed by his master, and then followed him upstairs. Philip seated himself thoughtfully.

"I like not these marks, Pierre. There may be nothing of importance in them; some fanatic may have taken the trouble to place these crosses upon our doors, cursing us as he did so. But at the same time I cannot deny that they may have been placed there for some set purpose, of which I am ignorant. Hitherto there has been nothing whatever to give any foundation to your fancies, but here is at least something tangible, whatever it may mean. What is your own idea?"

"My own idea is, sir, that they intend to arrest all the Admiral's followers, and that the king, while speaking us fair, is really guided by Catharine, and has consented to her plans for the capture of all the Huguenot lords who have come into this trap."

"I cannot believe that such an act of black treachery can be contemplated, Pierre. All Europe would cry out against the king who, inviting numbers of his nobles to the marriage of his sister, seized that occasion for imprisoning them."

"It may not be done by him, sir. It may be the work of the Guises' agents among the mob of Paris, and that they intend to massacre us as they did at Rouen and a score of other places, and as they have done here in Paris more than once."

"That is as hard to believe as the other, Pierre. My own supposition is by far the most probable, that it is the work of some fanatic; but at any rate we will be on the watch to-night. It is too late to do anything else, and were I to go round to our friends they would mock at me for paying any attention to such a trifle as a chalk mark on a door. I own that I think it serious, because I have come, in spite of my reason, to believe somewhat in your forebodings; but no one else seems to entertain any such fears." Opening the casement, Philip seated himself there. "Do you lie down, Pierre. At two o'clock I will call you; and you shall take my place."

Pierre went out, but before lying down he again went quietly downstairs, and with a wet cloth entirely erased the mark from the door, and then placing his sword and his pistols ready at hand lay down on his pallet. At one o'clock Philip aroused him.

"There is something unusual going on, Pierre. I can see a light in the sky as of many torches, and can hear a confused sound as of the murmur of men. I will sally out and see what it is."

Placing his pistols in his belt and taking his sword he wrapped himself in his cloak, and followed by Pierre, also armed, went down into the street. As he went along he overtook two men. As he passed under a lamp one of them exclaimed, "Is that you, Monsieur Fletcher?" He turned. It was the Sieur de Pascal.

"It is I, Monsieur de Pascal. I was going out to learn the meaning of those lights over there."

"That is just what I am doing myself. As the night is hot, I could not sleep, so I threw open my window and saw those lights, which were, as it appeared so me, somewhere in the neighbourhood of the Admiral's house, and I thought it was as well to see what they meant."

As they went along they came upon men with lighted torches, and saw that in several of the streets groups of men with torches were silently standing.

"What is taking place?" the Sieur de Pascal asked one of the men.

"There is going to be a night masque and a mock combat at the Louvre," the man said.

"It is strange I heard nothing about it at the Louvre," Philip said as they proceeded on their way. "I was with the King of Navarre up to ten o'clock, and had anything been known of it by him or the gentlemen with him I should have been sure to have heard of it."

They were joined by two or three other Huguenot gentle-men, roused by the unusual light and talking in the street, and they proceeded together to the Louvre. Large numbers of torches were burning in front of the palace, and a body of soldiers was drawn up there.

"The man was right," the Sieur de Pascal said. "There is evidently some diversion going on here."

As they approached they saw a movement in front, and then three or four men ran towards them.

"Why, De Vignes," De Pascal exclaimed as the first ran up, "what is the matter?"

"That I do not know," De Vignes said. "I was roused half an hour ago by the lights and noise, and came down with De la Rivière, Maurepas, Castellon, and De Vigors, who lodges with me, to see what it was about. As we approached the soldiers they began to jeer at us in a most insolent manner. Naturally we replied, and threatened to report them to their officers, when the insolent varlets drew and ran at us. Maure-pas has, as you see, been wounded by a halbert, and as we five could not give battle to that crowd of soldiers we ran for it. I shall lay the matter before La Rochefoucauld, and request him to make a complaint to the king. What can we do now, gentlemen?"

"I see not that we can do anything," De Pascal said. "We have heard that these torch-light gatherings are part of a plan for a sham attack on a castle, or something of that sort, for the amusement of the king. Doubtless the soldiers are gathered for that purpose. We cannot arouse La Rochefoucauld at this hour of the night, that is certain; so I see nothing to do but to go home and wait till morning."

"You do not think," Philip said, "that there is any possi-bility of a general attack upon us being intended."

"What! an attack got up at the Louvre under the very eyes of the king, who is our firm friend? You are dreaming, Mon-sieur Fletcher."

"I have one suspicious fact to go upon," Philip said quietly, and then related the discovery of the crosses upon the doors.

The others, however, were absolutely incredulous that any

treachery could be intended, and after talking for a short time longer, they returned to their lodgings.

"What is to be done now, Pierre?"

"I should say we had better search farther, sir. If there is any harm intended, the mob of Paris will be stirring. Let us go down towards the Hôtel de Ville; that is always the centre of mischief. If all is quiet there, it may be that this story is correct, and that it is really only a court diversion. But that does not explain why the street should be lighted up near the Admiral's."

"It does not, Pierre."

After they had passed another group of men with torches, Pierre said, "Did you notice, sir, that each of those men had a piece of white stuff bound round his arm, and that it was the same with those we passed before? If there is any mischief intended, we should be more likely to learn what it is if we were to put on the same badge."

"The idea is a good one, Pierre;" and Philip took out his handkerchief, tore it in two, and handing half of it to Pierre, fastened the other round his arm. As they went along they met men with torches or lanterns, moving in the same direction as themselves. All wore white handkerchiefs or scarves round their arms. Philip became more and more anxious as they went on, and regretted that he had not returned to his lodgings and renewed his watch there. However, a few minutes' walking took them to the Hôtel de Ville. The square in front of the building was faintly illuminated by a few torches here and there, and by large cressets that blazed in front of the Hôtel. The light, however, was sufficient to show a dense body of men drawn up in the square, and the ruddy light of the flames flashed from helmet, lance-point, and axe.

"What think you now, Monsieur Philip? There must be eight or ten thousand men here, I should say all the city bands under their captains."

As they paused a citizen officer came up to them. "All is ready, your excellency. I do not think that a man is absent from his post. The orders remain unchanged, I suppose?"

"Quite unchanged," Philip said briefly, seeing that in the faint light he was mistaken for someone else.

"And the bell is to be the signal for beginning?"

"I believe there has been a change in that respect," Philip said; "but you will hear that later on. I am only here to see that all is in readiness."

"Everything has been done as ordered, your excellency. The gates are closed, and will not be opened except to one bearing special orders under the king's own seal. The boats have all been removed from the wharves. There will be no escape."

Philip repressed a strong impulse to run the man through the body, and only said:

"Good. Your zeal will not be forgotten."

Then he turned and walked away. They had gone but a few paces when, in the distance, the report of a pistol was heard.

"Too late!" he exclaimed in passionate regret. "Come, Pierre," and he broke into a rapid run. Several times groups of men came out from bye-streets at the sound of the rapid footsteps, but Philip exclaimed, "Away there! I am on urgent business for Anjou and Guise." The men fell back at once in each case, not doubting from the badges on the arms, which they could make out in the darkness, that Philip was bearing some important order.

"To the Admiral's first," he said to Pierre. "It is there they will surely begin." But as they entered the Rue de Bethisy, he saw a number of men pouring out from the Admiral's house with drawn swords and waving their torches over their heads. By the light Philip could make out Henry of Guise and Henry of Valois with their attendants and soldiers.

"We are too late here, Pierre. The Admiral has doubtless been murdered; his confidence in the king's word has undone him." Coligny, indeed, had refused the offer of many Protestant gentlemen to spend the night in the house, and even Teligny his son-in-law had gone to his own lodgings a short distance away. He had with him only his chaplain Merlin, the king's surgeon, three gentlemen and four or five servants; while in the court below were five of the King of Navarre's Swiss guards. The Admiral had been awakened by the increasing noise without, but entertained no alarm whatever. Suddenly a loud knocking was heard at the outer gate, and a demand for entrance in the king's name.

The Admiral directed one of the gentlemen named Le Bonne to go down and unbar the gate. As he did so, Cosseins, an officer of Anjou's household, rushed in, followed by fifty soldiers, and stabbed Le Bonne to the heart. The soldiers had been despatched by the king himself under pretence of guarding the Huguenots, and twelve hundred arquebusiers had also been posted under the same pretext in the neighbourhood. The faithful Swiss defended the inner door, and when driven back, defended for a time a barricade hastily thrown upon the stairs. One of the Huguenot gentlemen rushed into the Admiral's room with the news that the gate had been forced. The Admiral calmly replied, "I have kept myself for a long time in readiness for death. Save yourselves if you can. It would be hopeless for you to attempt to save my life."

In obedience to his orders, all who were with him, save a German interpreter, fled to the roof and made their escape in the darkness. The barricade was carried, and a German named Besme, a follower of the Duke of Guise, was the first to rush into the Admiral's room. Coligny was calmly seated in a chair, and Besme struck him two blows with his sword, while those following despatched him.

Guise was waiting in the courtyard below; when he heard that the Admiral was killed he ordered the body to be thrown out of the window. When he recognized that it was indeed the body of the Admiral, he gave it a brutal kick, while one of his followers cut off the head, and then Guise called upon the soldiers to follow him, saying, "We have begun well, let us now see to the others, for so the king commands."

As Philip turned from the spot the bell of the church of Saint Germain l'Auxerrois peeled forth, and shouts instantly rose from all quarters. As he reached the street in which he lodged Philip saw that it was already half full of armed men, who were shouting "Death to the Huguenots!" and were hammering at many of the doors. He fell at once into a walk and made his way through them unmolested, the white badge on his arm seeming to guarantee that he was a friend. He passed his own door and made for that of the Count de Valecourt. A combat was going on in front of it, and by the light of the torches Philip saw De Pascal defending himself bravely against a host of enemies. Sword in hand, Philip sprang forward. But before he could make his way through the soldiers a musket shot rang out and De Pascal fell dead. Philip drew back.

"To our own house, Pierre," he exclaimed to his lackey, who was keeping close behind him; "we can do nothing here, and the door may resist for a few minutes." There was no one in front of the entrance, though at all the doors marked with a white cross the soldiers were hammering with the butts of their arquebuses. They slipped in, pushed the bars across, ran upstairs and made their way on to the roof and climbed along it until they reached the window of the house in which De Valecourt lodged; felt their way across the room till they discovered the door, issued out, and as soon as they found the staircase ran down. Already there was a turmoil below. A light streamed out from a door of the count's apartments on the first floor. Philip ran in. Claire de Valecourt was standing with one hand resting on the table deadly pale but quiet. She was fully dressed.

"Where is your father?" Philip exclaimed.

"He has gone down with the servants to hold the stairs."

"I will join him," Philip said. "Pierre will take care of you; he knows what to do. We will follow you. Quick, for your own sake and your father's."

"I cannot go and leave him."

"You will do him no good by staying, and delay may cost us all our lives. You must go at once, if you do not, at the risk of your displeasure I must carry you."

"I will go," she said. "You saved me before, and I trust you."

"Trust Pierre as you would trust me," he said. "Now, Pierre, take her hand and hurry her upstairs." The clash of swords mingled with shouts and oaths were heard below, and Philip, as he saw Pierre turn with Claire de Valecourt, ran down. On the next landing the count with four serving men was defending himself against the assault of a crowd of armed men who were pushing up the staircase.   Others behind them held torches, while some of those engaged in the fray held a torch in one hand and a sword in the other.

"Ah, is it you, Monsieur Fletcher?" the count said as Philip placed himself beside him, felling one of the foremost of the assailants as he did so with a sweeping blow.

"It is I, count.   My house is not attacked, and I have sent off your daughter in charge of my man to gain it along the roofs.   We will follow them as soon as we can beat back these villains."

"The king's troops must arrive shortly," the count said.

"The king's troops are here," Philip said.   "This is done by his orders, and all Paris is in arms.   The Admiral has already been murdered."

The count gave a cry of fury and threw himself upon his assailants.   His companions did the same, and step by step drove them backward down the stairs.   There was a cry below of "Shoot them down!" and a moment later three or four arquebuses flashed out from the hall.   The count, without a word, pitched forward among the soldiers, and two of the retainers also fell.   Then the crowd surged up again.   Philip fought desperately for a time.   Another shot rang out, and he felt a sudden smart across his cheek.   He turned and bounded up the stairs, paused a moment at the top and discharged his two pistols at the leaders of the assailants, pulled to the door of the count's chamber, leaving the corridor in darkness, and then sprang up the stairs.   When he reached the door of the unused room by which they had entered he fastened it behind him, got through the window and closed it after him, and then rapidly made his way along the roofs until he reached his own.   Closing and fastening the casement he ran down to his room.   Claire was standing there with Pierre by her side. She gave a low cry as he entered alone.

"My father!" she exclaimed.

"God has taken him," Philip said, "as He has taken many others to-night.   He died painlessly, mademoiselle, by a shot from below."

Claire sank into a chair and covered her face with her

hands. "His will be done," she said in a low but firm voice as she looked up a minute later. "We are all in His hands and can die but once. Will they soon come?"

"I trust not," Philip said; "they may follow along the roof when they cannot find us in any of the rooms, but they will have no clue as to which house we have entered."

"I will remain here and wait for them," she said.

"Then, mademoiselle, you will sacrifice our lives as well as your own, for assuredly we shall not leave you. Thus far we have escaped, and if you will follow my directions we may all escape together. Still, if you wish it we can die here together."

"What is to be done?" she asked, standing up.

Pierre handed Philip a bundle.

"I brought them down as I passed," he said.

"This is a disguise," Philip said, handing it to the girl. "I pray you to put it on at once. We also have disguises, and will return in them in a few minutes."

CHAPTER XXI

ESCAPE

"THIS is awful, Pierre," Philip said, as he hurriedly assumed the disguise the latter had prepared. The clamour outside was indeed terrible. The bell of St. Germain l'Auxerrois was still sounding its signal, but mingled with it were a thousand sounds of combat and massacre, the battering of hammers and axes upon doors, the discharges of arquebuses and pistols, the shouts of men and the loud screams of women. Pierre glanced out of the window. With the soldiers were mingled a crowd from the slums of Paris, who, scenting carnage from the movements of the citizen troops, had waited in readiness to gather the spoil, and had arrived on the spot as if by magic as soon as the first signal of alarm told them that the work of slaughter had begun.

"Can we get out behind, think you, Pierre?" Philip asked as he joined him.

"I will see, sir. One could scarce sally out here without being at once seized and questioned. Doubtless a watch was placed in the rear at first, but the soldiers would be likely to make off to join in the massacre and get their share of plunder as soon as the affair began. You will do, sir, as far as the dress goes, but you must smear your face and arms; they are far too white at present, and would be instantly noticed."

Philip rubbed is hands, blackened by his passage across the roofs, over his face and arms, and then joined Claire, who started as he entered.

"I did not know you," she said. "Come; are we ready?

PHILIP, CLAIRE, AND PIERRE DISGUISE THEMSELVES.

it were surely better to die at once than to listen to these dreadful sounds."

"One moment. Pierre will return directly; he has gone to see whether the lane behind the houses is clear. Once fairly away, and our course will be easier."

Pierre returned almost immediately. "The way is clear."

"Let us go, then, mademoiselle."

"One moment, monsieur. Let us pray before we start; we may have no time there." And standing with upturned face she prayed earnestly for protection.

"*Lead us, O God,*" she concluded, "*through the strife and turmoil, as Thou didst the holy men of old through the dangers of the lions and the furnace. But if it be Thy will that we should die, then do we commend our souls to Thee, in the sure faith that we are but passing through death into life.*—Now I am ready," she said, turning to Philip.

"You cannot go like this, Mademoselle Claire," Pierre said reverently. "Of what good would that disguise be to you when your face would betray you in the darkest street. You must ruffle your hair, and pull that hood over your face so as to hide it as much as possible."

The girl walked across to a mirror.

"I would I could take my sword, Pierre," said Philip.

"Take it, sir; strap it boldly round your waist. If anyone remarks on it, laugh, and say it was a Huguenot's half an hour ago. I will carry mine stuck under my arm. Use as few words as may be, if you have to speak, and speak them gruffly, or they will discover at once that you are no smith. I fear not for ourselves. We can play our parts—fight or run for it. It is that angel I fear for."

"God will protect her, Pierre. Ah! They are knocking at the door, and the women of the house may be coming down to open it."

"Not they, sir. You may be sure they are half-mad with terror. Not one has shown herself since the tumult began. The landlord and his two sons are doubtless with the city bands. Like enough they have led some of their fellows here, or why should they attack the door, as it is unmarked?"

Claire joined them again. They hurried downstairs and

then out by the back entrance into a narrow lane. Philip carried a heavy hammer on his shoulder. Pierre had a large butcher's knife stuck conspicuously in his girdle. He was bare-headed and had dipped his head in water, so that his hair fell matted across his face, which was grimy and black.

Day was now breaking, but the light was as yet faint. "Keep close to me, Claire," Philip said as they reached the street, which was ablaze with torches. "Above all things do not shrink or seem as if you were afraid."

"I am not afraid," she said. "God saved me before from as great a peril, and will save me again if it seems good to Him."

"Keep your eyes fixed on me; pay no attention to what is going on around you."

"I will pray," she said simply.

Just as they entered the street the crowd separated, and the Duke of Guise, followed by several nobles of his party, rode along, shouting:

"Death to all Huguenots! it is the king's command."

"It is the command you and others have put into his mouth, villain!" Philip muttered to himself.

A roar of ferocious assent rose from the crowd, which was composed of citizen soldiers and the scum of Paris. They danced and yelled, and uttered ferocious jests at the dead bodies lying in the road. Here the work of slaughter was nearly complete. Few of the Huguenots had offered any resistance, although some had fought desperately to the last. Most of them, however, taken by surprise, and seeing resistance useless, had thrown down their arms, and either cried for quarter or had submitted themselves calmly to slaughter. Neither age nor sex had availed to save them; women and children, and even infants had been slain without mercy.

The soldiers, provided with lists of the houses inhabited by Huguenots, were going round to see that none had escaped attack. Many in the crowd were attired in articles of dress that they had gained in the plunder. Ragged beggars wore cloaks of velvet or plumed hats. Many had already been drinking heavily. Women mingled in the crowd, as ferocious and merciless as the men.

"Break me in this door, friend," an officer, with a list in his hand and several soldiers standing beside him, said to Philip.

The latter did not hesitate; to do so would have brought destruction on himself and those with him, without averting for more than a minute or two the fate of those within. Placing himself in front of the door, he swung his heavy hammer and brought it down upon the woodwork. A dozen blows and the door began to splinter. The crack of a pistol sounded above, and the officer standing close to him fell dead. Four or five shots were fired by the soldiers at the window above. Another two or three blows and the door gave way. Philip went aside, as the soldiers, followed by a crowd, rushed in, and returned to Claire, who was standing by the side of Pierre a few paces away.

"Let us go on," he said.

A few yards further they were at the entrance of a lane running north. As Philip turned into it a man caught him by the arm.

"Where are you going, comrade?" he said. "There is plenty of work for your hammer yet."

"I have a job elsewhere," Philip said.

"It is rare work, comrade. I have killed five of them with my own hand, and I have got their purses too," he chuckled. "Hello! who is this girl you have with you?" And he roughly caught hold of Claire.

Philip's pent-up rage found a vent; he sprang upon the man, seized him by the throat, and hurled him with tremendous force against the wall, whence he fell a senseless mass on to the ground.

"What is it?" cried half a dozen men rushing up.

"A Huguenot in disguise," Philip said. "You will find his pockets are full of gold."

They threw themselves upon the fallen man, fighting and cursing to be the first to ransack his pockets, while Philip with his two companions moved up the lane unnoticed. Fifty yards farther Claire stumbled and would have fallen had not Philip caught her. Her head had fallen forward, and he felt at once that she was insensible. He placed her on a door-step and supported her in a sitting position, Pierre standing by. A minute later a group of men came hurrying down the street.

"What is it?" one of the group asked as he stopped for a moment.

"It is only a woman squeamish," Pierre said in a rough voice. "She would come with us, thinking she could pick up a trinket or two; but, *ma foi*, it is hot down there, and she turned sick. So we are taking her home."

Satisfied with the explanation the men hurried on.

"Shall I carry her, Pierre? Her weight would be nothing."

"Better wait a few minutes, Monsieur Philip, and see if she comes round. Our story is right enough as long as we stop here, but people might want to know more if they were to meet you carrying a woman."

Some minutes passed, and then, finding that Claire remained unconscious, Philip lifted her on to his shoulder.

"We will risk it, Pierre. As long as we only meet them coming along in twos or threes we can go on safely, for if they are inquisitive I can set her down and speedily silence their questioning. If we see a large body coming we can either turn down a side street, or if there is no turning at hand can set her down again and answer as before. Every step we get farther away from the quarter we have left the better."

He had carried Claire but a few hundred yards when he felt her move. He at once set her down again on a door-step. In a few minutes she was able to stand, and, assisted by Philip, she presently continued her course at a slow pace. Gradually the movement restored her strength, and she said, speaking for the first time, "I can walk alone."

An hour later they reached the hut that they had marked out as their place of refuge. Pierre went to a corner and drew out from under a heap of rubbish a large bundle.

"Here is your cloak and mine," he said, "and a change of clothes for each of us. We could not wander about the country in this guise."

Philip laid the cloaks down to form a sort of couch, and placed the bundle with the rest of the things in as a pillow.

"Now, mademoiselle," he said, "you will be safe here until nightfall. First, you must drink a glass of wine and try and eat something; Pierre brought some up here two days ago. Then I hope you will lie down. I will watch outside the door, Pierre will go down into the town to gather news."

"I will take something presently," she said. "I could eat nothing now."

But Pierre had already uncorked a bottle, and Philip advised her to drink a little wine.

"You will need all your strength," he said, "for we have a long journey before us." She drank a few drops.

"Do not go yet," she said; "I must speak to you." Philip nodded to Pierre, who left the hut. Claire sat on the cloaks for some minutes in silence.

"I have been thinking, Monsieur Philip," she said at last, "and it seems to me that it would not be right for me to go with you. I am the promised wife of the Sieur de Pascal, and that promise is all the more sacred since he to whom I gave it"—and she paused—"is gone. It would not be right for me to go with you. You shall take me to the Louvre, where I will crave the protection of the King and Queen of Navarre. Do not think me ungrateful for what you have done for me. Twice now you have saved my life, and, and—you understand me, Philip?"

"I do," he said, "and honour your scruples. One of my objects in sending Pierre down into the town again is to learn what has taken place at the Louvre. It may be that this fiendish massacre has extended there, and that even the King of Navarre and the Huguenot gentlemen with him have shared the fate of the others. Should it not be so, it would be best in every way that what you suggest should be carried out. As for the Sieur de Pascal, it may be that the blow that has bereft you of your good father may well have fallen upon him also."

"But many will surely escape as we have done. It cannot be that all our friends—all those who rode in with the princes —can have been murdered."

"Some have doubtless escaped; but I fear that the massacre will be almost universal, for it has evidently been carefully planned, and once begun will extend not only to the followers of Navarre, but to all the Protestants within the walls of Paris."

"Do you know aught concerning the Sieur de Pascal?" Claire asked, looking up. Something in the tone of his voice struck her.

"I saw him fall, mademoiselle. He had made for the door of your house, doubtless with the intention of joining your father in defending it to the last, but the murderers were already there. He was attacked on the door-step, and was surrounded and well-nigh spent when I saw him. I tried to reach him through the crowd, but before I could do so he fell. Then, seeing that it would be but throwing away my life and destroying all chance of saving yours, I hurried away to carry out the plan I had before formed of making my way along the roofs, and so entering your house. Monsieur de Pascal fell, mademoiselle, as a brave soldier, fighting against a host of foes, and in defence of yourself and your father. It was an unfortunate, though noble impulse, that led him there, for I had rubbed out the mark upon your door that served as a guide for the soldiers, and you and the count might have escaped over the roof before any attack was made, had not his presence aroused their suspicions."

Claire had hidden her face in her hands as he began to speak, and he had kept on talking in order to give her time to collect her feelings; but as she was now crying unrestrainedly, he went quietly out of the hut and left her to herself, glad that tears had come to her relief for the first time. An hour later the door opened behind him, and Claire called him in.

"I am better now," she said, "I have been able to cry. It seemed that my heart was frozen, and I was like one in a terrible nightmare. Now I know that it is all true, and that my dear father is dead. As for Monsieur de Pascal, I am sorry that a brave soldier has been killed; but that is all. You know that I received him as my affianced husband simply in obedience to my father's commands, and that my heart had no part in it; God has broken the tie, and for that, even in this time of sorrow, I cannot but feel relief." At this moment there was a knock at the door, then the latch was lifted, and Pierre entered.

"What is the news, Pierre?"

"It is bad, sir. The king has in truth put himself at the

head of the massacre, and even in the Louvre itself several Huguenot gentlemen have been slain, though I could not learn their names. It is said that some of them were slain in the presence of the young Queen of Navarre in spite of her entreaties and cries. The young king and his cousin Condé are close prisoners, and it is said that they too will be slain unless they embrace the Catholic faith. The massacre has spread to all parts of the town, and the Huguenots are every-where being dragged from their homes and killed, together with their wives and children. It is said that the bodies of Coligny and other Huguenot leaders have been taken to the Louvre, and that the king and the queen-mother and the ladies, as well as the gentlemen of the court, have been down to view them and make a jest of them. Truly, sir, Paris seems to have gone mad. It is said that orders have been sent to all parts of France to exterminate the Huguenots."

Philip made a sign to Pierre to leave the hut. "This is terrible news," he said to Claire, "and it is now clear that the Louvre will afford you no protection. In these days no more mercy is shown to women than to men, and at best, or at worst, you could but save your life by renouncing your faith."

"I had already decided," she said quietly, "that I would not go to the Louvre. The death of Monsieur de Pascal has altered everything. As his affianced wife, with the consent of my father, the king would hardly have interfered to have forced me into another marriage; but being now free he would treat me as a ward of the crown, and would hand me and my estates to one of his favourites. Anything would be better than that. Now, of course, it is out of the question. Estates I have none, for, with the extermination of our people, their estates will be granted to others."

"As to that, mademoiselle, they have been trying to mas-sacre the Huguenots for years, and though, doubtless, in the towns many may fall, they will not be taken so readily in the country, and may even yet rally and make head again. Still, that does not alter the present circumstances, and I see no other plan but that I had first formed, for you to accompany me and my servant in disguise."

The girl stood hesitating, twining her fingers over each

other restlessly. "It is so strange, so unmaidenly," she murmured.

"Then, Claire," Philip said, taking her hands in his, "you must give me the right to protect you. It is strange to speak of love at such a time as this, but you know that I love you. As a rich heiress, and altogether above my station, even had you been free I might never have spoken; but now, standing as we do surrounded by dangers, such distinctions are levelled. I love you with all my heart, and it seems to me that God Himself has brought us together."

"It is surely so, Philip," she said, looking up into his face. "Has not God sent you twice to save me? Some day I will tell you of my heart, but not now, dear—not now. I am alone in the world save you. I am sure that my father if he now sees us must approve; therefore, Philip, henceforth I am your affianced wife, and am ready to follow you to the end of the world." Philip stooped down and kissed her gently, then he dropped her hands and she stood back a little apart from him.

"It were best that I called Pierre in," he said; "even in this lonely quarter some one might pass, and, seeing him standing at the door, wonder who he might be." So saying he opened the door and called Pierre in.

"Pierre," he said gravely, "Mademoiselle de Valecourt is now my affianced wife."

"That is as it should be, master," Pierre said; and then stepping up to Claire, who held out her hand to him, he reverently pressed it with his lips.

"Mademoiselle," he said, "my life will henceforth be at your disposal as at that of my master. We may have dangers to face, but if anyone can get you through them, he can."

"Thank you, Pierre," the girl said; "it is well, indeed, that we should have with us one so faithful and attached as yourself."

In the hours that passed before nightfall, Philip related to Claire how Pierre's warnings had excited his uneasiness, and how the discovery of the chalk marks on the doors had confirmed him in his conviction that some evil was intended, and explained the steps they had taken for providing for an escape from the city.

"I have been wondering vaguely, Philip," she said when he had told the story, "how it was that you should have appeared so suddenly, and should have a disguise in readiness for me. But how could you have guessed that I should be ready to go with you?" and for the first time a slight tinge of colour came into her cheeks.

"It was scarcely a guess, Claire, it was rather a despairing hope. It seemed to me that amid all this terror and confusion I might in some way be able to rescue you, and I made the only preparation that seemed possible. I knew that you were aware that I loved you. When you told me of your engagement I felt that you were saying farewell to me. When I thought of saving you, it was for him and not for myself, for I knew that you would never oppose your father's wishes. I did not dream of such a general calamity as it has been; I thought only of a rising of the mob of Paris, and that perhaps an hour or two in disguise might be sufficient until the king's troops restored order."

"It is very wonderful," Claire said earnestly; "it seems beyond all doubt that it is God Himself who has thus given me to you, and I will not doubt that, great as the dangers may seem to be before us, He will lead us safely through them. You will make for La Rochelle?"

"Yes, once there we shall be safe. You may be sure that there at least the cruel orders of the king will be wholly disregarded, as we may hope they will be in many other towns in which the Huguenots are numerous; but at La Rochelle certainly, were all the rest of France in flames, the people would remain steadfast. But I do not believe that the power of the Huguenots will be broken. It may be that in the northern towns the orders of the king will be carried out, but from thence we have obtained no aid in our former struggles. Our strength in the south will still remain, and though the loss of so many leaders and nobles here in Paris will be a heavy blow, I hope that the cause of the faith will speedily rally from it and make head again, just as it did when all seemed lost after the battle of Moncontour."

So they talked until night fell, with Pierre sitting discreetly in the corner as far away as possible, apparently sleeping most

of the time.   As soon as it became perfectly dark the bundle
of clothes was taken from the hiding-place, and going outside
the hut Philip and Pierre put on their ordinary attire.   Claire
had simply slipped on the dress prepared for her over her own,
and had but to lay it aside.   After partaking of a meal they
made their way to the nearest steps leading to the top of the
wall.   One end of the rope was fastened to the parapet, the
other was tied round Claire, and she was carefully lowered to
the ground.   Philip and Pierre slid down the rope after her,
and they at once started across the country.   After three hours'
walking they reached the farm where Pierre had left the horses.
They left Claire a short distance away.   As Pierre had seen
the horses put into the stables he knew exactly where they
were.   He had, on leaving them there, paid for a week's keep,
saying that he might come for them in haste, and perhaps at
night, and if so he would saddle and take them off without
waking the farmer.

The horses whinnied with pleasure when Philip spoke to
them.   The saddles and bridles were found hanging on a beam
where Pierre had placed them, and in two or three minutes
the horses were led out ready to start.   Philip had arranged
his cloak behind his saddle for Claire to sit upon, and led the
horse to the place where she was awaiting them.

"All has passed off well," he said.   "No one in the farmhouse seems to have heard a sound."

He leapt into the saddle.   Claire placed her foot on his
and he swung her up behind him, and they then started at a
brisk trot.

Avoiding all large towns, and stopping only at village inns,
they made their way south, making long journeys each day.
In the villages there was little of the religious rancour that
animated the people in the towns, and after the first two days
Philip found that the news of what had occurred at Paris had
not as yet spread.   Eager questions were asked Pierre as to
the grand wedding festivities at Paris, and there was everywhere a feeling of satisfaction at a union that seemed to
promise to give peace to France.   Claire was generally supposed to be Philip's sister, and the hostesses always did their
best to make the girl with her pale sad face as comfortable as

possible. Fearing that a watch might have been set at the bridges they avoided these, crossing either by ferry-boats or at fords. The Loire was passed above Orleans, and as that city, Blois, and Tours all lay on the northern bank, they met with no large towns on their way until they approached Chatellerault. They bore to the south to avoid that city and Poitiers, and on the eighth day after leaving Paris they reached the chateau of Laville, having travelled upwards of two hundred miles. As they crossed the drawbridge Philip's four retainers met them at the gate and greeted him most warmly.

"Is the countess in?" he asked as he alighted.

"She is, Monsieur Philip; she has been for some days at La Rochelle and returned yesterday. There are rumours, sir, that at Poitiers and Niort the Catholics have again, in spite of the edicts, fallen upon the Huguenots, and though the countess believes not the tale we had a guard posted at the gate last night."

"I am afraid it is true, Eustace," Philip said. "Take the horses round to the stables and see to them well, they have travelled fast." Taking Claire's hand he led her up the steps, and just as he entered the hall the countess, to whom the news of his approach had been carried, met him.

"Aunt," he said, "I confide this lady to your loving care. It is Mademoiselle de Valecourt, now my affianced wife. I have bad news to tell you; but I pray you lead her first to a chamber, for she is sore wearied and in much grief."

"François is not dead?" the countess exclaimed in a low voice, paling to the lips.

"I trust not, aunt. I have no reason for believing that he is."

"I will wait here, Philip, with the countess's permission," Claire said. "It is better that you should not keep her in suspense even for a moment on my account."

"I thank you, mademoiselle," the countess said as she led the girl to a couch. "This is but a poor welcome that I am giving you, but I will make amends for it when I have heard what Philip has to tell me. Now, Philip, tell me the worst, and let there be no concealment."

Philip related the whole story of the massacre, his tale being interrupted by frequent exclamations of horror by the countess.

"It seems incredible," she cried, "that a king of France should thus dishonour himself alike by breaking his vows, disregarding his own safe-conduct, and massacring those who had accepted his hospitality. And François, you say, was at the Louvre with the King of Navarre and Condé, and even there within the walls of the royal palace some of the king's guests were murdered; but more than this you know not?"

"That is the report that Pierre gathered in the street, aunt; it may have been exaggerated. Everyone eagerly seized and retailed the reports that were current. But even if true it may well be that François is not among those who fell. To a certain extent he was warned, for I told him the suspicions and fears that I entertained, and when he heard the tumult outside he may have effected his escape."

"I do not think so," the countess said, drawing herself up to her full height. "My son was one of the prince's gentlemen of the chamber, and he would have been unworthy of his name had he thought first of his personal safety and not of that of the young king."

Philip knew that this was so, and the knowledge had from the first prevented his entertaining any great hopes of his cousin's safety. However he said, "as long as there was a hope of his being of service to the prince I am sure that François would not have left him. But from the first, aunt, resistance was in vain and would only have excited the assailants. Pierre heard that in few cases was there any resistance whatever to the murderers. The horror of the thing was so great that even the bravest, awakened thus from their sleep, either fell without drawing sword or fled."

"What a day for France!" the countess exclaimed; "the Admiral, our bravest soldier, our greatest leader, a Christian hero, slaughtered as he lay wounded! And how many others of our noblest and best! And you say orders have been sent over all France to repeat this horrible massacre? But enough for the present; I am forgetting my duties as hostess. Mademoiselle de Valecourt, we are alike mourners—you for your noble father, I for my son, both of us for France and

for our religion. Yet I welcome you to Laville. For you
brighter days may be in store. My nephew is a gallant gentleman, and with him you may find a home far away from this
unhappy country. To me, if François has gone, Philip will
stand almost in the light of a son. François loved him as a
brother, and he has grown very dear to me, and gladly shall I
welcome you as his wife. Now, come with me. Philip, I
leave it to you to send round the news to the tenants, and to
see that all preparations are made to leave the chateau once
again to the mercy of our foes, and to retire to La Rochelle,
where alone we can talk with safety. See that the bell is rung
at once. The tenants know the summons, and though little
expecting danger will quickly rally here."

Philip at once went out into the courtyard, and in a minute
the sharp clanging of the bell told the country round that
danger threatened. The retainers of the chateau ran hastily
out, arming themselves as they went, and exclamations of
horror and fury broke from them as Philip told them that the
order for the massacre of the Huguenots throughout France
had gone forth, and that already most of those who rode to
Paris with the King of Navarre had fallen. Then he repeated
the countess's order, that upon the following morning the
chateau should be abandoned and all should ride to La
Rochelle, and he despatched half a dozen mounted men to
warn all the Huguenot gentry in the district.

In a few minutes the tenants began to flock in. Although
the tale that they heard involved the destruction of their
newly-built houses, and the loss of most of their property,
this affected them but slightly in comparison with the news
of the murder of Coligny and of so many Huguenot leaders,
and of the terrible fate that would befall the Huguenots in
every town in France. Some wept, others clenched their
weapons in impotent rage, some called down the curses of
Heaven upon the faithless king, while some stood as if completely dazed at the terrible news. Philip spoke a few cheer-
ing words to them.

"All is not lost yet, my friends. Heaven will raise up fresh
leaders for us. Many may fall, but the indignation and rage
that you feel will likewise animate all who, dwelling in the

364 ST. BARTHOLOMEW'S EVE

country, may escape, so that ere long we shall have fresh
armies in the field. Doubtless the first blow will be struck at
La Rochelle, and there we will meet these murderers face to
face, and will have the opportunity of proving to them that
the men of the reformed religion are yet a force capable of
resisting oppression and revenging treachery. There is one
thing: never again shall we make the mistake of laying down
our arms, confiding in the promises and vows of this perjured
king, never again shall we be cozened into throwing away
the results of our victories. Gather your horses and cattle as
you did before. Take your household goods in carts, and at
daybreak send in here the waggons that you have to provide
in case of necessity."

At noon the next day the whole of the occupants of the
chateau started for La Rochelle. The tenants, with their
cattle and horses and all their portable property, had left at
daybreak, and at nightfall the countess and her party came
up with them. The encampment was a large one. The
women and children slept under the waggons, the men lay
down by fires they had kindled, while a portion were told off
to keep watch over the animals. The train had swollen considerably since they had started. Most of the inhabitants of
the villages were Huguenots, and as soon as these heard of
the massacres in Paris and elsewhere they collected their animals, loaded up their carts, and took the road to the city of
refuge. After four days' travelling they entered La Rochelle.

The news had arrived before them, being brought by some
of those who had escaped the massacre by being lodged without the walls of Paris. The countess and Claire were received at the house of Monsieur Bertram. Philip found lodgings near them, and the whole of the inhabitants vied with
each other in their hospitable reception of the mass of fugitives. Claire was completely prostrated by the events through
which she had passed, and Monsieur Bertram's daughter devoted herself to her, tending her with unwearied care, until,
after a week in bed, she began again to gather strength. The
time of the countess was entirely occupied in filling the part
that had before been played by Jeanne of Navarre, holding
consultations with the town-councillors, going down to the

walls and encouraging the men who were labouring there, and urging on the people to make every sacrifice in defence of their religion and homes. She herself set the example by pawning her jewels and selling her horses and devoting the proceeds to the funds raised for the defence.

She worked with feverish activity, as if to give herself no time for thought. She was still without news of François. Henri of Navarre and the Prince of Condé had, as was soon known, been compelled to abjure their religion as the price of their lives. She was convinced that her son would have refused to buy his life upon such conditions. Philip, who had come to regard François as a brother, was equally anxious, and two days after his arrival at the city he took Pierre aside.

"Pierre," he said, "I cannot rest here in ignorance of the fate of my cousin."

"That I can see, master. You have eaten no food the last two days. You walk about at night instead of sleeping, and I have been expecting every hour that you would say to me, 'Pierre, we must go to Paris.'"

"Will you go with me, Pierre?"

"How can you ask such a question?" Pierre said indignantly. "Of course if you go I go too. There is not much danger in the affair, and if there were, what then? we have gone through plenty of it together. It will not be now as when we made our escape. Then they were hunting down the Huguenots like mad dogs. Now they think they have exterminated them in Paris, and will no longer be on the look-out for them, it will be easy enough to come and go without being observed, and if we find Monsieur François we will bring him out with us. The young count is not like you, monsieur. He is brave, and a gallant gentleman, but he is not one to invent plans of escape, and he will not get away unless we go for him."

"That is what I think, Pierre. We will start at once; but we must not let the countess know what we are going for. I will get the chief of the council openly to charge me with a mission to the south, while telling them privately where I am really going, and with what object. I am known to most of them, and I doubt not they will fall in with my plans. We will ride my two best horses and lead a spare one. We will leave them a few miles outside Paris and then go in disguised as countrymen. At any rate we shall soon be able to learn if my cousin is among those who fell; if not, he must be in hiding somewhere. It will not be easy to discover him, but I trust to you to find him."

Accordingly the next day the countess heard that Philip had been requested by the council to proceed on a mission to the south, where the Huguenots were everywhere in arms.

CHAPTER XXII

PHILIP took clothes with him in his saddle-bags of gayer colours than those worn by the Huguenots, and as soon as they were beyond the district where the Protestants were in the ascendant, he put these on instead of those in which he had started. They rode fast, and on the fifth day after leaving La Rochelle they entered Versailles. No questions had been asked them by the way, and they rode into the courtyard of the principal inn, and there stabled their horses.

"Your animals look as if they needed rest, sir," the landlord said, as they dismounted.

"Yes, we have come from the south, and have pressed them too much. I have business in Paris which will occupy me for a few days, therefore I will leave them here for a rest. I suppose you can furnish me with two horses to take me as far as St. Cloud, and a man to bring them back again."

"Certainly I can, sir, and your horses shall be well looked after here."

"Then we will go on the first thing in the morning. Have the horses ready by that time."

The next morning they rode to St. Cloud, dismounted there, and handed over the horses to the man who had ridden behind them. Then they crossed by the bridge over the river, and entering the wood that bordered the Seine, put on the disguises they had brought with them, concealing their clothes among some thick bushes, and then walked on into Paris. They put up at a small inn, and as they partook of a meal, listened to the talk of those around them. But it was not here that they could expect to gather the news they required. They heard the names of many of those who had been killed, but these were all leaders of distinction; and as soon as they had finished their food they started for the Louvre. "I don't see how we are to find out what we want, now we are here, Pierre," Philip said after they had stood for some time looking at the gate through which numbers of gentlemen entered or left the palace. "It will take some little time, sir," Pierre said. "I think the best plan will be for me to purchase some clothes suitable for the lackey of a gentleman of rank. I can get them easily enough, for the shops will be full of garments bought of those who took part in the massacre. Then I shall make acquaintance with one of the lackeys of the court, and with plenty of good wine I shall no doubt be able to learn all that he knows as to what took place at the Louvre." At that moment a gentleman passed them.

"That is Count Louis de Fontaine, the cousin of the man I killed in that duel. I am sure it is he. By what I saw of him, he is a gentleman and a man of honour, and by no means ill-disposed towards us. I will speak to him; do you stay here till I return."

Pierre was about to protest, but Philip had already left him, and was following the count. He waited until they were in a comparatively quiet place, and then walked on and overtook him.

"Count Louis de Fontaine," he said.

The nobleman turned in surprise at being addressed by this big countryman. Philip went on: "Our acquaintance was a short one, count. It was some four years ago at Agen that I met you, and had the misfortune to have trouble with your cousin, Count Raoul, but short as it was, it was sufficient to show me that you were a gentleman of heart, and to encourage me now to throw myself on your generosity."

"Are you the gentleman who fought my cousin, and afterwards escaped from the castle?" the count asked in surprise.

"I am, count. I am here upon no plot or conspiracy, but simply to endeavour to ascertain the fate of my cousin, François de Laville, who was with the King of Navarre on that fearful night a fortnight since. His mother is distracted at hearing no news of him, while to me he is as a brother. I effected my own escape, and have, as you see, returned in disguise to ascertain his fate. I am unable to obtain a list of those who were murdered, and seeing you, I felt that it would be safe to rely upon your honour, and to ask you to give me the news I require. I will fall back now, for it might be thought strange that a noble should be talking to a peasant, but I pray you to lead the way to some quiet spot where I can speak with you unnoticed."

"My lodging is in the next street. Follow me, and I will take you up to my room."

As soon as they had entered the lodging the count said, "You are not deceived, I am incapable of betraying a trust imposed upon me. I bear you no malice for the slaying of my cousin, for indeed the quarrel was not of your seeking; still less do I feel hostility toward you on the ground of your religion, for I doubt not from what you say, that you are of the reformed faith. I lament most deeply and bitterly the events that have taken place—events which dishonour our nation in the eyes of all Europe. I have not the pleasure of knowing your name."

"I am the Chevalier Philip Fletcher, an Englishman by birth, though related on my mother's side to the family of the Count de Laville."

"I have heard your name, sir, as that of one of the bravest gentlemen in the following of Admiral Coligny. Now, as to your cousin; his fate is uncertain. He was certainly cut down by the hired wretches of the Guises. They passed on in search of other victims, believing him to be dead; but his body was not afterwards found, and the general opinion is that he either recovered and crawled away, and is still in some hiding-place, or that he is concealed somewhere in the palace itself. Search was made next day, but without success. Some think he may have reached the streets, and been there killed, and his body, like so many others, thrown into the Seine. I trust that this is not the case, but I have no grounds for bidding you hope."

"At any rate you have given me cause to hope, sir, and I

thank you heartily. It is something to know that he is not certainly dead. Can you tell me on which side of the palace was his chamber? I saw him there frequently, but did not on any occasion go with him to his room."

"It was on the side facing the river; it was near that of the King of Navarre."

"Thank you, count; it is but a small clue with which to commence my search, but it is at least something. You say that the palace itself has been searched?"

"Yes; on the following morning it was thoroughly searched for fugitives in hiding, but for all that he may be concealed there by some servant whose good-will he had gained. Is there anything else that I can tell you? I may say that I have personally no influence whatever at court. I have never failed to express myself strongly in reference to the policy of persecution, and I am only here now in obedience to the royal orders to present myself at court."

"There is nothing else, count. I thank you most sincerely for having thus respected my disguise, and for the news you have given me."

Philip returned to the Louvre and joined Pierre, who was impatiently waiting.

"I followed you for some distance, sir, but when I saw you address the count, and then follow quietly behind him, I saw you were right, and that he was to be trusted, and so returned to await your coming. Have you obtained any sure news from him?" Philip repeated his conversation with the count.

"I will wager he is hidden somewhere in the palace," Pierre said. "Badly wounded as he must have been, he could not have hoped to make his escape through the streets, knowing no one who would have dared to give him refuge. It is far more likely that some of the palace servants came upon him just as he was recovering, and hid him away. He was always bright and pleasant, fond of a jest, and it may well be that some woman or other took pity on him. The question is, How are we to find out who she is?"

"It is as likely to be a man as a woman, Pierre."

"No," Pierre said positively. "Women are wonderfully tender-hearted, and are not so afraid of consequences as men are. A man might feel some pity at seeing a gentleman so sorely wounded; but he would not risk his own life to shelter him, while any woman would do it without hesitation. It may be a lady of noble family, or a poor kitchen wench, but that it is a woman I would wager my life."

"It seems hopeless to try to find out who it is," Philip said despondently.

"Not hopeless, sir, though doubtless difficult. With your permission I will undertake this part of the task. I will get myself up as a workman out of employment—and there are many such—and will hang about near that little gate; it is the servants' entrance, and I shall be able to watch every woman that comes out."

"But what good will watching do?"

"It may do no good, sir, but yet it may help. A woman with such a secret as that on her mind will surely show some signs of it upon her face. She will either have a scared look or an anxious look; she will not walk with an easy step."

"Well, there is something in what you say, Pierre. At any rate I can think of nothing better."

The next morning Pierre took up his position opposite the gate, but had no news that night to report to his master, nor had he on the second or third, but on the fourth he returned radiant. "Good news, master. The count is alive, and I have found him."

Philip sprung from his settle and grasped his faithful follower by the hand. "Thank God for the news, Pierre. I had almost given up hope. How did you discover him?"

"Just as I expected, sir. I have seen in the last three days scores of women come out, but none of them needed a second look. Some were intent on their own finery, others were clearly bent on shopping. Some looked up and down the street for a lover who ought to have been waiting for them. Not one of these had a secret of life and death on her mind. But this afternoon there came out a young woman with a pale face and an anxious look. She glanced nervously up and down the street, not as one expecting to meet a friend, but as if she feared an enemy. After a moment's hesitation she crossed the road, and walked along with an indecisive air, more than once glancing behind her as if afraid of being followed.

"'This is my lady,' I said to myself, and keeping some distance behind and on the opposite side of the road I followed her. She soon turned off into a side street. Once or twice she paused, looked into a shop, hesitated, and then went on again. You may be sure I marked the spots, and was not surprised to find that in each case it was an apothecary's before which she had hesitated. At last, after looking round again timidly, she entered one; and when I came up I also went in. She gave a nervous start. I asked to be supplied with a pot of salve for a wound, and the man helped me from one he had just placed on the counter before him. I paid for it and left. Two or three minutes later I saw her come out. Whatever she had bought she had hidden it under her cloak. Up to this time she had walked fast, but she now loitered and looked at the wares displayed on the stalls.

"'You are in no hurry to go back,' I said to myself. 'You have got what you wanted, and you do not wish to attract attention by returning to the palace after so short an absence.' At last, when she was in a quiet spot, I walked quickly up to her. 'Mademoiselle,' I said, taking off my hat, 'I am a friend of the gentleman for whom you have bought that salve and other matters.' She became very white, but she said stoutly: 'I don't know what you are talking about, sir; and if you molest a modest young woman in the streets I shall appeal to the town constables for protection.' 'I repeat,' I said, 'that I am a friend of the gentleman for whom you have just bought the materials for dressing his wounds. I am the servant of his cousin, the Chevalier Fletcher, and the name of your patient is Count François de Laville.'

"She looked at me stupefied with astonishment, and stammered: 'How do you know that?' 'It is enough, mademoiselle, that I know it,' I said. 'My master and I have come to Paris expressly to find Monsieur de Laville, and when we have found him to aid him to make his escape. Do not hesitate to confide in me, for only so shall we succeed in the object of our journey.' 'What is your master's Christian name?' she asked, still doubtful. 'It is Philip,' I said. She clasped her hands together. 'The good God be praised!' she exclaimed. 'It was of Philip he spoke when he was so ill. He was unconscious. Surely it is He that has sent you to me. It has been terrible for me to bear my secret alone.' 'Let us walk farther,' I said, 'before you tell me more. There are too many people passing here; and if they notice the tears on your cheeks they may suspect me of ill-treating you, and may ask troublesome questions.' After a few minutes' walk we came to a quiet square. 'Let us sit down on this stone seat,' I said. 'We can talk freely here. Now, tell me all about it.'

"'I am one of the bed-makers of the palace, and it fell to me to sweep the room occupied by the Count de Laville. Once or twice he came in while I was there and spoke pleasantly; and I thought what a handsome fellow he was, and said to myself what a pity it was that he was a heretic. When that terrible night came we were all aroused from our sleep, and many of us ran down in a fright to see what was the matter. We heard shouts and cries and the clashing of swords. As I passed Monsieur de Laville's room the door was open. I looked in. Three soldiers lay dead on the floor, and near them the count, whom I thought was also dead. I ran to him and lifted his head, and sprinkled water on his face from a flagon on the table. He opened his eyes and made an effort to get to his feet. I was frightened out of my life at it all, and I said to him: "What does it all mean, monsieur?"

"'"It is a massacre," he said faintly. "Do you not hear the firing in the streets and the din in the palace? They will return and finish me. I thank you for what you have done, but it is useless." Then I thought for a moment. "Can you walk, monsieur?" "Barely," he replied. "Lean on my shoulder, monsieur," I said. "I will help you up the stairs. I know of a place where you may lie concealed." With great difficulty I helped him up a staircase that was but little used, and got him to the top. Several times he said: "It is of no use; I am wounded to death!" but he still held on. I slept in a little garret in the roof with two other servants, and at the end of the passage was a large lumber-store. It was into this that I took him. Nobody ever went there, and it was safe except in case of special search. I laid him down and then moved some of the heavy cabinets and chests at the farther end, a short distance from the wall, so that there would be space enough for him to lie behind them. Here I made a bed with some old cushions from the couches, got him into the place, first bandaging his wounds as well as I could in the faint light that came in through a dormer-window. I fetched a jug of water from my room and placed it beside him, and then moved the furniture so as to close up the spot at which he had entered. Against it I piled up tables and chairs, so that to anyone who did not examine it very closely it would seem that the heavy furniture was against the wall. There he has been ever since.

"'Two or three times a day I have managed to steal away from my work to carry him water and food that I brought from the kitchen when we went down to our meals. For a time I thought he would die; for four days he did not know me. He talked much to himself, and several times he mentioned the name of Philip, and called upon him to aid him against the murderers. Fortunately he was so weak that he could not speak much above a whisper, and there was no fear of his voice being heard. The day after I hid him the whole palace was searched to see if any Huguenots were concealed. But up in the attics they searched but carelessly, seeing that we slept three or four in each room, and no one could well be hidden there without all knowing it. They did enter the lumber-room. But I had carefully washed the floor where he had lain, and as I could not get out the stains of blood I pushed some heavy chests over them. I was in my room when they searched the lumber-room, and my heart stood still until I heard them come out and knew that they had found nothing.

"'For the last ten days the count has gained strength; his wounds are still very sore and painful, but they are beginning to heal. I have bought wine for him, and can always manage to conceal enough food from the table to suffice for his wants. He can walk now, though feebly, and spoke to me but to-day about making his escape. It would be easy enough to get him out of the palace if I had a lackey's attire for him. I could lead him down private staircases till near the door from which we come out of the palace. But I had little money, for I had sent off most of my wages to my mother only a day or two before the royal wedding. Still we might have managed that; I could have borrowed some on some pretence or other. He is however too weak to travel, and the effort to do so might cause his wounds to burst out afresh; but now that his cousin has come all will be well.'

"'Where is he wounded?' I asked.

"'He has four wounds: one is on the head, another on the neck, one is a stab in the body, that must have narrowly missed his heart; and the other is a sword-thrust through his arm. But how, monsieur, did you know,' she asked, 'that it is I who have hidden the count?' I told her that I had been watching for four days, feeling sure that the count was hidden in the palace; but hers was the first face that showed anxiety, and that when I saw her buying salve at the apothecary's I felt sure that it was she who was sheltering the count."

"And have you arranged anything, Pierre?" Philip asked anxiously.

"Only this much, sir, that to-morrow evening, as soon as it is dark, she will leave the palace with Monsieur François. That will give us plenty of time to make our plans, which will be easy enough. We have but to take an apartment and bring him up into it. No one need know that there are more than ourselves there, and we can nurse him for a few days until he is fit to ride. Then we have only to get him a disguise like that in which we entered. We can hide him in the wood, go on to where we hid our clothes, put them on instead of our disguises, enter St. Cloud, go on to Versailles, fetch the three horses, and return to him—with, of course, a suit of clothes for himself."

There was no difficulty in hiring two rooms in a quiet street. Suits of clothes suitable for a court lackey were purchased, and these were given by Pierre to the girl when she came out in the afternoon. Philip had accompanied Pierre to meet her.

"My good girl," he said, "I cannot tell you how deeply I feel the kindness that you have shown my cousin. You have risked your life to save him; and that, I am sure, without the smallest thought of reward. Still so good an action must not pass without acknowledgment, though no money can express the amount of our gratitude to you."

"I do not want to be paid, sir," she said. "I had no thought of money."

"I know that," Philip replied; "but you must allow us to show our gratitude in the only way we can. In the first place, what is your name?"

"Annette Riolt, sir."

"Well, Annette, here are fifty crowns in this purse. It is all that I can spare at present; but be assured the Countess de Laville will send you, at the first opportunity, a sum that will be a good *dot* for you when you find a husband. If the messenger by whom it is sent asks for you by your name at the door of the palace by which you usually leave it, will he obtain access to you?"

"Yes, sir. The porter at the door knows me; and if he should be changed, whoever is there will inquire of the maids, if he asks for Annette Riolt, one of the chamber-women in the north wing of the palace."

"Very well, Annette. You may rely that a messenger will come. I cannot say how soon; that must depend on other circumstances. Where do you come from?"

"From Poitiers, sir; my parents live on a little farm called La Machoir, two miles north of the city."

"Then, Annette, the best thing for you to do is to leave your present employment and to journey down home. It will be easy to send from La Rochelle to Poitiers, and unless the place is besieged, as it is likely to be before long, you will soon hear from us. Probably the messenger will have visited the farm before you reach it."

"I will do that, sir," the girl said gratefully. "I never liked this life, and since that terrible night I have scarcely had any sleep. I seem to hear noises and cries just as they say the king does, and shall be indeed glad to be away. But I cannot come out with the count this evening. We only get out once in five days, and it was only as a special favour I have been let out now. I will come with him to the door talking with him as if he were a lackey of my acquaintance."

At the hour agreed upon Philip and Pierre, stationed a few yards from the door, saw a man and woman appear. The girl made some laughing remark and then went back into the palace. The man came out. He made two quick steps and then stumbled, and Philip ran forward and grasped him firmly under the arm.

"You were just in time, Philip," François said with a feeble laugh, "another step and I should have been down. I am weaker than I thought I was, and the fresh air is well-nigh too much for me. I have had a close shave of it, Philip, and have been nearer death in that attic up there than I ever was on a field of battle. What a good little woman that was! I owe my life to her. It is good of you coming here to find me, old fellow, you are always getting me out of scrapes. You remember that affair at Toulouse. Thank you, Pierre, but mind, that arm you have got hold of is the weak one. Now, how far have we got to go, Philip? for I warn you I am nearly at the end of my strength."

"We will get into a quiet street first, François, and there you shall have a drink from a flask of excellent wine I have here, then we will help you along. You can lean as heavily as you like upon us, you are no great weight now; and anyone who notices us helping you will suppose that we are conveying a drunken comrade to his home."

But in spite of all the assistance they could give him François was terribly exhausted when he reached the lodging. Here Philip and Pierre bandaged his wounds far more securely and firmly than his nurse had been able to do, and the next morning when he awoke he declared himself ready to start at once. It was a week, however, before Philip would hear of his making such an effort; but by that time good eating and drinking had done so much for him that he thought he would be able to stand the fatigue of the journey, and the next morning they started. Disguised as peasants they passed out through the gates unquestioned. François was left in the wood with the clothes they had purchased for him. The others then went on and found their bundles undisturbed, obtained their three horses at Versailles, and riding back soon had François mounted. The wound on his head was so far healed that it was no longer necessary to bandage it, and although he looked pale and weak there was nothing about him to attract special notice. They journeyed by easy stages south, lengthening the distances gradually as François gained strength, and riding fast towards the end so as to reach La Rochelle before an army under Marshal Biron sat down before it. It was evening when they arrived, and after putting up their horses they made their way to Monsieur Bertram's. Philip mounted the stairs, leaving François to follow him slowly.

"I shall not take more than two or three minutes to break the news, but I must prepare your mother a little, François.— She has not said much, but I know she had but little hope though she bore up so bravely."

The countess was sitting with Claire and the merchant's daughter. It was the first time Philip had seen Mademoiselle de Valecourt since they first arrived at La Rochelle. She was dressed now in deep mourning. A flush of bright colour spread over her face as Philip entered. As in duty bound he turned first to the countess and saluted her affectionately, and then turned to Claire and would have kissed her hand, but the countess said, "Tut, tut, Philip, that is not the way to salute your betrothed;" and Philip, drawing her to him, kissed her for the first time since they had betrothed themselves to each other in the hut in Paris, and then saluted Mademoiselle Bertram.

"We have been under no uneasiness respecting you, Philip," the countess said; "for Claire and myself both look upon you as having a charmed life. Has your mission been successful?"

"It has, aunt, beyond my hopes. And first I must ask your pardon for having deceived you."

"Deceived me, Philip! In what way?"

"My mission was an assumed one," Philip said; "and in reality Pierre and I journeyed to Paris."

A cry broke from the countess's lips.

"To Paris, Philip! And your mission has been successful? You have heard something?"

"I have done more, aunt, I have found him."

"The Lord be praised for all His mercies!" burst from the lips of the countess, and she threw herself on Philip's neck and burst into a passion of tears, the first she had shed since he brought the news from Paris.

"Courage, aunt," Philip whispered. He glanced towards the door; Claire understood him and ran to open it. François came quietly in.

"Mother," he said, and the countess, with a cry of joy, ran into his arms.

The French army appeared before the town on the following day, and the siege was at once commenced. With Marshal Biron were the dukes of Anjou and Alençon, the King of Navarre, and the Prince of Condé, who had been compelled to accompany him. The siege made little progress. The defences were strong, and the Huguenots were not content only to repel assaults, but made fierce sallies, causing a considerable loss to the besiegers. To the surprise of the defenders they heard that the Count de la Noüe had arrived in camp with a mission from the king. He had remained a captive in the camp of the Duke of Alva after the surrender of Mons, and so had happily escaped the massacre of St. Bartholomew. He had then been released, and had gone to France to arrange his ransom. The king, who was now tormented with remorse, sent for him and entreated him as a personal favour to go as his Commissioner to La Rochelle, and to endeavour to bring about a cessation of hostilities, authorizing him to grant almost any terms.

De la Noüe undertook the task unwillingly, and only upon condition that he would be no party to inducing them to surrender unless perfectly satisfied with the guarantees for the observance of any treaty that might be made. When a flag of truce came forward and announced that Monsieur de la Noüe had arrived on the part of the king, the news was at first received with incredulity. Then there was a burst of indignation at what was considered the treachery of the count. He was refused permission to enter the town, but after some parleying a party went out to have an interview with him outside the gate. The meeting was unsatisfactory; some of the citizens pretended that they did not recognize De la Noüe, saying that the person they knew was a brave gentleman, faithful to his religion, and one who certainly would not be found in a Catholic camp.

A few days later, however, the negotiations were renewed. The count pointed out that they could not hope finally to resist the whole force of France, and that it would be far better for them to make terms now than when in an extremity. But he was able to give no guarantees that were considered acceptable by the citizens. De la Noüe's position was exceedingly difficult. But at last the citizens perceived that he was still loyal to the cause; and as he had beforehand received the king's authority to accept the governorship of the town, the people of La Rochelle agreed to receive him in that position, provided that no troops entered with him.

The negotiations fell through and the siege was renewed with vigour, De la Noüe now taking the lead in the defence, his military experience being of immense assistance. Very many of the nobles and gentlemen in the Catholic army were present as a matter of duty; they fought with the usual gallantry of their race, but for the most part abhorred the massacre of St. Bartholomew, and were as strongly of opinion as were the Huguenots of France and the Protestants throughout Europe that it was an indelible disgrace upon France. Their feeling was shown in many ways. Among others, Maurevel, the murderer of De Mouy, and the man who had attempted the assassination of the Admiral, having accompanied the Duke of Anjou to the camp, no one would associate with him or suffer him to encamp near, or even go on guard with him into the trenches, and the duke was in consequence obliged to appoint him to the command of a small fort which was erected on the sea-shore.

Incessant fighting went on, but the position was a singular one. The Duke of Alençon had been an unwilling spectator of the massacre of St. Bartholomew. He was jealous of Anjou, and restless and discontented, and he contemplated going over to the Huguenots. The King of Navarre and his cousin Condé, and the Huguenot gentlemen with him, were equally anxious to leave the camp, where they were closely watched; and De la Noüe, while conducting the defence, occasionally visited the royal camp and endeavoured to bring about a reconciliation.

He was much rejoiced on his first arrival at the city to find both François and Philip there, for he had believed that both had fallen in the massacre. He took great interest in Philip's love affair, and made inquiries in the royal camp, where he learned that Mademoiselle de Valecourt was supposed to have perished with her father in the massacre, and that the estates had already been bestowed by the king on one of his favourites.

"I should say that if our cause should finally triumph a portion at least of her estates will be restored to her; but in that case the king would certainly claim to dispose of her hand."

"I care nothing for the estates, nor does she," Philip said. "She will go with me to England as soon as the fighting here is over, and if things look hopeless we shall embark and endeavour to break through the blockade by the king's ships. Even had she the estates she would not remain in France, which has become hateful to her. She is now fully restored to health, and we shall shortly be married."

When De la Noüe next went out to the French camp he sent a despatch to the king saying that Mademoiselle de Valecourt had escaped the massacre and was in La Rochelle. He pointed out that as long as she lived the Huguenots would, if at any time they became strong enough to make terms, insist upon the restoration of her estates, as well as those of others that had been confiscated. He said that he had had an interview with her, and had learned that she intended, if a proper provision should be secured for her, to retire to England. He therefore prayed his majesty, as a favour to him and as an act of justice, to require the nobleman to whom he had granted the estates to pay her a handsome sum, when she would make a formal renunciation of the estates in his favour.

A month later he received the royal answer, saying that the king had graciously taken the case of Mademoiselle de Valecourt into his consideration, that he had spoken to the nobleman to whom he had granted her estate, and to the Duke of Guise, whose near relative he was, and that these noblemen had placed in his hands the sum of ten thousand livres, for which was enclosed an order payable by the treasury of the army upon the signatures of M. de la Noüe and Mdlle. de

Valecourt, and upon the handing over of the document of renunciation signed by her.

M. de la Noüe had told Philip nothing of these negotiations, but having obtained from Claire the necessary signature, he, one evening, on his return from the royal camp, came into the room where they were sitting, followed by two servants carrying small, but heavy bags.

"Mademoiselle," he said, when the servants had placed these on the table and retired, "I have pleasure in handing you these. Philip, Mademoiselle de Valecourt will not come to you as a dowerless bride, which indeed would be a shame for a daughter of so old and noble a family. Mademoiselle has signed a formal renunciation of her rights to the estates of her late father, and by some slight good offices on my part his majesty has obtained for her from the man to whom he has granted the estates of Valecourt the sum of ten thousand livres—a poor fraction indeed of the estates she should have inherited, and yet a considerable sum in itself.

A week later Sir Philip Fletcher and Claire de Valecourt were married in the principal church of La Rochelle. The Count de la Noüe, as a friend and companion-in-arms of her father, gave her away, and all the Huguenot noblemen and gentlemen in the town were present. Three weeks later a great assault upon the bastion of L'Evangile having been repulsed, the siege languished, the besieging army having suffered greatly both from death in the trenches and assaults, and by the attacks of fever. The Count of Montgomery arrived from England with some reinforcements. De la Noüe resigned to him the governorship and left the city. The Prince of Anjou shortly afterwards received the crown of Poland, and left the camp with a number of nobles to proceed to his new kingdom, and the army became so weakened that the siege was practically discontinued, and the blockading fleet being withdrawn Philip and his wife took passage in a ship for England, Pierre accompanying them.

"I may come some day with François, Philip," the countess said, "but not till I see that the cause is altogether lost. Still I have faith that we shall win tolerance. They say that the king is mad. Anjou has gone to Poland. Alençon is still unmarried. I believe that it is God's will that Henri of Navarre should come to the throne of France, and if so, there will be peace and toleration in France. So long as a Huguenot sword is unsheathed I shall remain here."

Philip had written to acquaint his father and mother of his marriage and his intention to return with his wife as soon as the siege was over. There was therefore but little surprise, although great joy, when he arrived. He had sent off Pierre on horseback as soon as the ship dropped anchor at Gravesend, and followed more leisurely himself. They were met a few miles out of Canterbury by a messenger from his uncle telling them to ride straight to his new estate, where he would be met by his mother and father, the latter of whom had started the day before in a litter for the house, and that his uncle and aunt would also be there.

Upon Philip and Claire's arrival they were received with much rejoicing. Monsieur Vaillant had sent round messengers to all the tenantry to assemble, and had taken over a number of his workmen, who had decorated the avenue leading to the house with flags, and thrown several arches across it.

"It is a small place in comparison to Valecourt, Claire," Philip said as they drove up to the house.

"It is a fine chateau, Philip; but now that I have you it would not matter to me were it but a hut. And oh, what happiness to think that we have done with persecution and terror and war, and that I may worship God freely and openly! He has been good to me indeed, and if I were not perfectly happy I should be the most ungrateful of women."

Claire's dowry was spent in enlarging the estate, and Philip became one of the largest landowners in the county. He went no more to the wars, save that, when the Spanish armada threatened the religion and freedom of England, he embarked as a volunteer in one of Drake's ships, and took part in the fierce fighting that freed England for ever from the yoke of Rome, and in no small degree aided both in securing the independence of Protestant Holland, and of seating Henri of Navarre firmly upon the throne of France. Save to pay two or three visits to Philip and her sisters, the Countess de Laville and her son did not come to England. François

fought at Ivry and the many other battles that took place before Henri of Navarre became undisputed King of France,
and then became one of the leading nobles of his court.

Philip settled a small pension on the four men-at-arms who
had followed his fortunes and shared his perils, and they returned to their native Gascony, where they settled down, two
being no longer fit for service, and the others having had
enough fighting for a lifetime.

The countess had, soon after François returned to La
Rochelle, sent a sum of money to the girl who had saved his
life, that sufficed to make her the wealthiest heiress in her
native village in Poitou, and she married a well-to-do farmer,
the countess herself standing as godmother to their first child,
to their immeasurable pride and gratification.

Pierre remained to the end of his life in Philip's service,
taking to himself an English wife, and being a great favourite
with the children of Philip and Claire, who were never tired
of listening to the adventures he had gone through with their
father and mother in the religious wars in France.

THE END.

"Wherever English is spoken one imagines that Mr. Henty's name is known. One cannot enter a schoolroom or look at a boy's bookshelf without seeing half-a-dozen of his familiar volumes. Mr. Henty is no doubt the most successful writer for boys, and the one to whose new volumes they look forward every Christmas with most pleasure."—*Review of Reviews.*

A LIST OF BOOKS

FOR YOUNG PEOPLE

By

G. A. HENTY,

KIRK MUNROE, JAMES WHITCOMB RILEY,
ERNEST THOMPSON SETON, and Others

Published by

CHARLES SCRIBNER'S SONS

153 to 157 Fifth Avenue

New York

A LIST OF BOOKS

FOR

YOUNG PEOPLE

By G. A. HENTY

BY CONDUCT AND COURAGE

A Story of Nelson's Days. Illustrated. $1.20 *net* (postage, 16c.).

This, the last of the celebrated Henty Books ever to be published, is a rattling story of the battle and the breeze in the glorious days of Parker and Nelson. The hero is brought up in a Yorkshire fishing village, and enters the navy as a ship's boy.

In the course of a few months after joining he so distinguishes himself in action with French ships and Moorish pirates that he is raised to the dignity of midshipman. His ship is afterward sent to the West Indies. Here his services attract the attention of the Admiral, who gives him command of a small cutter. In this vessel he cruises about among the islands, chasing and capturing pirates, and even attacking their strongholds. He is a born leader of men, and his pluck, foresight, and resource win him success where men of greater experience might have failed. He is several times taken prisoner: by mutinous negroes in Cuba, by Moorish pirates who carry him as a slave to Algiers, and finally by the French. In this last case he escapes in time to take part in the battles of Cape St. Vincent and Camperdown. His adventures include a thrilling experience in Corsica with no less a companion than Nelson himself.

WITH THE ALLIES TO PEKIN

A Tale of the Relief of the Legations. Illustrated by WAL PAGET. $1.20 *net*.

In this book the writer re-tells the story of the Siege of Pekin in a way that is sure to grip the interest of his young readers. The experience of Rex Bateman, the son of an English merchant at Tientsin, and of his cousins, two girls whom Rex rescues from the Boxers just after the first outbreak, offer a variety of heroic incident sufficient to fire the loyalty of the most indifferent lad.

THROUGH THREE CAMPAIGNS

A Story of Chitral, Tirah, and Ashanti. Illustrated by WAL PAGET. $1.20 *net*.

The exciting story of a boy's adventures in the British Army. Lisle Bullen, left an orphan, is to be sent home by the colonel of the regiment on the eve of the Chitral campaign. The boy's patriotism compels him, instead, to secretly join the regiment. He early distinguishes himself for conspicuous bravery. His disguise is discovered and his promotions follow rapidly.

By G. A. HENTY

"Among writers of stories of adventures for boys Mr. Henty stands in the very first rank."—*Academy* (London).

THE TREASURE OF THE INCAS

A Tale of Adventure in Peru. With 8 full-page Illustrations by WAL PAGET, and Map. $1.20 net.

Peru and the hidden treasures of her ancient kings offer Mr. Henty a most fertile field for a stirring story of adventure in his most engaging style. In an effort to win the girl of his heart, the hero penetrates into the wilds of the land of the Incas. Boys who have learned to look for Mr. Henty's books will follow his new hero in his adventurous and romantic expedition with absorbing interest. It is one of the most captivating tales Mr. Henty has yet written.

WITH KITCHENER IN THE SOUDAN

A Story of Atbara and Omdurman. With 10 full-page Illustrations. $1.20 net.

Mr. Henty has never combined history and thrilling adventure more skillfully than in this extremely interesting story. It is not in boy nature to lay it aside unfinished, once begun; and finished, the reader finds himself in possession, not only of the facts and the true atmosphere of Kitchener's famous Soudan campaign, but of the Gordon tragedy which preceded it by so many years and of which it was the outcome.

WITH THE BRITISH LEGION

A Story of the Carlist Uprising of 1836. Illustrated. $1.20 net.

Arthur Hallet, a young English boy, finds himself in difficulty at home, through certain harmless school escapades, and enlists in the famous "British Legion," which was then embarking for Spain to take part in the campaign to repress the Carlist uprising of 1836. Arthur shows his mettle in the first fight, distinguishes himself by daring work in carrying an important dispatch to Madrid, makes a dashing and thrilling rescue of the sister of his patron, and is rapidly promoted to the rank of captain. In following the adventures of the hero the reader obtains, as is usual with Mr. Henty's stories, a most accurate and interesting history of a picturesque campaign.

STORIES BY G. A. HENTY

"His books have at once the solidity of history and the charm of romance."—*Journal of Education.*

TO HERAT AND CABUL

A Story of the First Afghan War. By G. A. HENTY. With Illustrations. 12mo, $1.20 net.

The greatest defeat ever experienced by the British Army was that in the Mountain Passes of Afghanistan. Angus Cameron, the hero of this book, having been captured by the friendly Afghans, was compelled to be a witness of the calamity. His whole story is an intensely interesting one, from his boyhood in Persia; his employment under the Government at Herat; through the defense of that town against the Persians; to Cabul, where he shared in all the events which ended in the awful march through the Passes from which but one man escaped. Angus is always at the point of danger, and whether in battle or in hazardous expeditions shows how much a brave youth, full of resources, can do, even with so treacherous a foe. His dangers and adventures are thrilling, and his escapes marvellous.

WITH ROBERTS TO PRETORIA

A Tale of the South African War. By G. A HENTY. With 12 Illustrations. $1.20 net.

The Boer War gives Mr. Henty an unexcelled opportunity for a thrilling story of present-day interest which the author could not fail to take advantage of. Every boy reader will find this account of the adventures of the young hero most exciting, and, at the same time a wonderfully accurate description of Lord Roberts's campaign to Pretoria. Boys have found history in the dress Mr. Henty gives it anything but dull, and the present book is no exception to the rule.

AT THE POINT OF THE BAYONET

A Tale of the Mahratta War. By G. A. HENTY. Illustrated. 12mo, $1.20 net.

One hundred years ago the rule of the British in India was only partly established. The powerful Mahrattas were unsubdued, and with their skill in intrigue, and great military power, they were exceedingly dangerous. The story of "At the Point of the Bayonet" begins with the attempt to conquer this powerful people. Harry Lindsay, an infant when his father and mother were killed, was saved by his Mahratta ayah, who carried him to her own people and brought him up as a native. She taught him as best she could, and, having told him his parentage, sent him to Bombay to be educated. At sixteen he obtained a commission in the English Army, and his knowledge of the Mahratta tongue combined with his ability and bravery enabled him to render great service in the Mahratta War, and carried him, through many frightful perils by land and sea, to high rank.

BY G. A. HENTY

"Mr. Henty might with entire propriety be called the boys' Sir Walter Scott."—*Philadelphia Press.*

IN THE IRISH BRIGADE

A Tale of War in Flanders and Spain. With 12 Illustrations by CHARLES M. SHELDON. 12mo, $1.50.

Desmond Kennedy is a young Irish lad who left Ireland to join the Irish Brigade in the service of Louis XIV. of France. In Paris he incurred the deadly hatred of a powerful courtier from whom he had rescued a young girl who had been kidnapped, and his perils are of absorbing interest. Captured in an attempted Jacobite invasion of Scotland, he escaped in a most extraordinary manner. As aid-de-camp to the Duke of Berwick he experienced thrilling adventures in Flanders. Transferred to the Army in Spain, he was nearly assassinated, but escaped to return, when peace was declared, to his native land, having received pardon and having recovered his estates. The story is filled with adventure, and the interest never abates.

OUT WITH GARIBALDI

A Story of the Liberation of Italy. By G. A. HENTY. With 8 Illustrations by W. RAINEY, R.I. 12mo, $1.50.

Garibaldi himself is the central figure of this brilliant story, and the little-known history of the struggle for Italian freedom is told here in the most thrilling way. From the time the hero, a young lad, son of an English father and an Italian mother, joins Garibaldi's band of 1,000 men in the first descent upon Sicily, which was garrisoned by one of the large Neapolitan armies, until the end, when all those armies are beaten, and the two Sicilys are conquered, we follow with the keenest interest the exciting adventures of the lad in scouting, in battle, and in freeing those in prison for liberty's sake.

WITH BULLER IN NATAL

Or, A Born Leader. By G. A. HENTY. With 10 Illustrations by W. RAINEY. 12mo, $1.50.

The breaking out of the Boer War compelled Chris King, the hero of the story, to flee with his mother from Johannesburg to the sea coast. They were with many other Uitlanders, and all suffered much from the Boers. Reaching a place of safety for their families, Chris and twenty of his friends formed an independent company of scouts. In this service they were with Gen. Yule at Glencoe, then in Ladysmith, then with Buller. In each place they had many thrilling adventures. They were in great battles and in lonely fights on the Veldt; were taken prisoners and escaped; and they rendered most valuable service to the English forces. The story is a most interesting picture of the War in South Africa.

BY G. A. HENTY

"Surely Mr. Henty should understand boys' tastes better than any man living."—*The Times.*

WON BY THE SWORD

A Tale of the Thirty Years' War. With 12 Illustrations by CHARLES M. SHELDON, and four Plans. 12mo, $1.50.

The scene of this story is laid in France, during the time of Richelieu, of Mazarin and Anne of Austria. The hero, Hector Campbell, is the orphaned son of a Scotch officer in the French Army. How he attracted the notice of Marshal Turenne and of the Prince of Conde; how he rose to the rank of Colonel; how he finally had to leave France, pursued by the deadly hatred of the Duc de Beaufort—all these and much more the story tells with the most absorbing interest.

A ROVING COMMISSION

Or, Through the Black Insurrection at Hayti. With 12 Illustrations by WILLIAM RAINEY. 12mo, $1.50.

This is one of the most brilliant of Mr. Henty's books. A story of the sea, with all its life and action, it is also full of thrilling adventures on land. So it holds the keenest interest until the end. The scene is a new one to Mr. Henty's readers, being laid at the time of the Great Revolt of the Blacks, by which Hayti became independent. Toussaint l'Overture appears, and an admirable picture is given of him and of his power.

NO SURRENDER

The Story of the Revolt in La Vendée. With 8 Illustrations by STANLEY L. WOOD. 12mo, $1.50.

The revolt of La Vendée against the French Republic at the time of the Revolution forms the groundwork of this absorbing story. Leigh Stansfield, a young English lad, is drawn into the thickest of the conflict. Forming a company of boys as scouts for the Vendéan Army, he greatly aids the peasants. He rescues his sister from the guillotine, and finally, after many thrilling experiences, when the cause of La Vendée is lost, he escapes to England.

UNDER WELLINGTON'S COMMAND

A Tale of the Peninsular War. With 12 Illustrations by WAL PAGET. 12mo, $1.50.

The dashing hero of this book, Terence O'Connor, was the hero of Mr. Henty's previous book, "With Moore at Corunna," to which this is really a sequel. He is still at the head of the "Minho" Portuguese regiment. Being detached on independent and guerilla duty with his regiment, he renders invaluable service in gaining information and in harassing the French. His command, being constantly on the edge of the army, is engaged in frequent skirmishes and some most important battles.

BY G. A. HENTY

"Mr. Henty is the king of story-tellers for boys."—*Sword and Trowel.*

AT ABOUKIR AND ACRE

A Story of Napoleon's Invasion of Egypt. With 8 full-page Illustrations by WILLIAM RAINEY, and 3 Plans. 12mo, $1.50.

The hero, having saved the life of the son of an Arab chief, is taken into the tribe, has a part in the battle of the Pyramids and the revolt at Cairo. He is an eye-witness of the famous naval battle of Aboukir, and later is in the hardest of the defense of Acre.

BOTH SIDES THE BORDER

A Tale of Hotspur and Glendower. With 12 full-page Illustrations by RALPH PEACOCK. 12mo, $1.50.

This is a brilliant story of the stirring times of the beginning of the Wars of the Roses, when the Scotch, under Douglas, and the Welsh, under Owen Glendower, were attacking the English. The hero of the book lived near the Scotch border, and saw many a hard fight there. Entering the service of Lord Percy, he was sent to Wales, where he was knighted, and where he was captured. Being released, he returned home, and shared in the fatal battle of Shrewsbury.

WITH FREDERICK THE GREAT

A Tale of the Seven Years' War. With 12 full-page Illustrations. 12mo, $1.50.

The hero of this story while still a youth entered the service of Frederick the Great, and by a succession of fortunate circumstances and perilous adventures, rose to the rank of colonel. Attached to the staff of the king, he rendered distinguished services in many battles, in one of which he saved the king's life. Twice captured and imprisoned, he both times escaped from the Austrian fortresses.

A MARCH ON LONDON

A Story of Wat Tyler's Rising. With 8 full-page Illustrations by W. H. MARGETSON. 12mo, $1.50.

The story of Wat Tyler's Rebellion is but little known, but the hero of this story passes through that perilous time and takes part in the civil war in Flanders which followed soon after. Although young he is thrown into many exciting and dangerous adventures, through which he passes with great coolness and much credit.

BY G. A. HENTY

"No country nor epoch of history is there which Mr. Henty does not know, and what is really remarkable is that he always writes well and interestingly."—*New York Times.*

WITH MOORE AT CORUNNA

A Story of the Peninsular War. With 12 full-page Illustrations by WAL PAGET. 12mo, $1.50.

Terence O'Connor is living with his widowed father, Captain O'Connor of the Mayo Fusiliers, with the regiment at the time when the Peninsular war began. Upon the regiment being ordered to Spain, Terence gets appointed as aid to one of the generals of a division. By his bravery and great usefulness throughout the war, he is rewarded by a commission as colonel in the Portuguese army and there rendered great service.

AT AGINCOURT

A Tale of the White Hoods of Paris. With 12 full-page Illustrations by WALTER PAGET. Crown 8vo, olivine edges, $1.50.

The story begins in a grim feudal castle in Normandie. The times were troublous, and soon the king compelled Lady Margaret de Villeroy with her children to go to Paris as hostages. Guy Aylmer went with her. Paris was turbulent. Soon the guild of the butchers, adopting white hoods as their uniform, seized the city, and besieged the house where our hero and his charges lived. After desperate fighting, the white hoods were beaten and our hero and his charges escaped from the city, and from France.

WITH COCHRANE THE DAUNTLESS

A Tale of the Exploits of Lord Cochrane in South American Waters. With 12 full-page Illustrations by W. H. MARGETSON. Crown 8vo, olivine edges, $1.50.

The hero of this story accompanies Cochrane as midshipman, and serves in the war between Chili and Peru. He has many exciting adventures in battles by sea and land, is taken prisoner and condemned to death by the Inquisition, but escapes by a long and thrilling flight across South America and down the Amazon.

ON THE IRRAWADDY

A Story of the First Burmese War. With 8 full-page Illustrations by W. H. OVEREND. Crown 8vo, olivine edges, $1.50.

The hero, having an uncle, a trader on the Indian and Burmese rivers, goes out to join him. Soon after, war is declared by Burmah against England and he is drawn into it. He has many experiences and narrow escapes in battles and in scouting. With half-a-dozen men he rescues his cousin who had been taken prisoner, and in the flight they are besieged in an old, ruined temple.

BY G. A. HENTY

"Boys like stirring adventures, and Mr. Henty is a master of this method of composition."—*New York Times.*

THROUGH RUSSIAN SNOWS

A Story of Napoleon's Retreat from Moscow. With 8 full-page Illustrations by W. H. OVEREND and 8 Maps. Crown 8vo, olivine edges, $1.50.

The hero, Julian Wyatt, after several adventures with smugglers, by whom he is handed over a prisoner to the French, regains his freedom and joins Napoleon's army in the Russian campaign. When the terrible retreat begins, Julian finds himself in the rear guard of the French army, fighting desperately. Ultimately he escapes out of the general disaster, and returns to England.

A KNIGHT OF THE WHITE CROSS

A Tale of the Siege of Rhodes. With 12 full-page Illustrations by RALPH PEACOCK, and a Plan. Crown 8vo, olivine edges, $1.50.

Gervaise Tresham, the hero of this story, joins the Order of the Knights of St. John, and proceeds to the stronghold of Rhodes. Subsequently he is appointed commander of a war-galley, and in his first voyage destroys a fleet of Moorish corsairs. During one of his cruises the young knight is attacked on shore, captured after a desperate struggle, and sold into slavery in Tripoli. He succeeds in escaping, and returns to Rhodes in time to take part in the defense of that fortress.

THE TIGER OF MYSORE

A Story of the War with Tippoo Saib. With 12 full-page Illustrations by W. H. MARGETSON, and a Map. Crown 8vo, olivine edges, $1.50.

Dick Holland, whose father is supposed to be a captive of Tippoo Saib, goes to India to help him to escape. He joins the army under Lord Cornwallis, and takes part in the campaign againt Tippoo. Afterwards he assumes a disguise, enters Seringapatam, and at last he discovers his father in the great stronghold of Savandroog. The hazardous rescue is at length accomplished, and the young fellow's dangerous mission is done.

IN THE HEART OF THE ROCKIES

A Story of Adventure in Colorado. By G. A. HENTY. With 8 full-page Illustrations by G. C. HINDLEY. Crown 8vo, olivine edges, $1.50.

The hero, Tom Wade, goes to seek his uncle in Colorado, who is a hunter and gold-digger, and he is discovered, after many dangers, out on the Plains with some comrades. Going in quest of a gold mine, the little band is spied by Indians, chased across the Bad Lands, and overwhelmed by a snowstorm in the mountains.

BY G. A. HENTY

"Mr. Henty is one of the best story-tellers for young people."
—*Spectator.*

WHEN LONDON BURNED

A Story of the Plague and the Fire. By G. A. HENTY. With
12 full-page Illustrations by J. FINNEMORE. Crown 8vo,
olivine edges, $1.50.

The hero of this story was the son of a nobleman who had lost his
estates during the troublous times of the Commonwealth. During the
Great Plague and the Great Fire, Cyril was prominent among those
who brought help to the panic-stricken inhabitants.

WULF THE SAXON

A Story of the Norman Conquest. By G. A. HENTY. With
12 full-page Illustrations by RALPH PEACOCK. Crown
8vo, olivine edges, $1.50.

The hero is a young thane who wins the favor of Earl Harold and
becomes one of his retinue. When Harold becomes King of England
Wulf assists in the Welsh wars, and takes part against the Norsemen
at the Battle of Stamford Bridge. When William of Normandy in-
vades England, Wulf is with the English host at Hastings, and stands
by his king to the last in the mighty struggle.

ST. BARTHOLOMEW'S EVE

A Tale of the Huguenot Wars. By G. A. HENTY. With 12
full-page Illustrations by H. J. DRAPER, and a Map.
Crown 8vo, olivine edges, $1.50.

The hero, Philip Fletcher, has a French connection on his mother's
side. This induces him to cross the Channel in order to take a share
in the Huguenot wars. Naturally he sides with the Protestants, distinguishes himself in various battles, and receives rapid promotion for
the zeal and daring with which he carries out several secret missions.

THROUGH THE SIKH WAR

A Tale of the Conquest of the Punjaub. By G. A. HENTY.
With 12 full-page Illustrations by HAL HURST, and a
Map. Crown 8vo, olivine edges, $1.50.

Percy Groves, a spirited English lad, joins his uncle in the Punjaub,
where the natives are in a state of revolt. Percy joins the British
force as a volunteer, and takes a distinguished share in the famous
battles of the Punjaub.

BY Q. A. HENTY

"The brightest of the living writers whose office it is to enchant the boys.—*Christian Leader.*

A JACOBITE EXILE

Being the Adventures of a Young Englishman in the Service of Charles XII. of Sweden. By G. A. HENTY. With 8 full-page Illustrations by PAUL HARDY, and a Map. Crown 8vo, olivine edges, $1.50.

Sir Marmaduke Carstairs, a Jacobite, is the victim of a conspiracy, and he is denounced as a plotter against the life of King William. He flies to Sweden, accompanied by his son Charlie. This youth joins the foreign legion under Charles XII., and takes a distinguished part in several famous campaigns against the Russians and Poles.

CONDEMNED AS A NIHILIST

A Story of Escape from Siberia. By G. A. HENTY. With 8 full-page Illustrations. Crown 8vo, olivine edges, $1.50.

The hero of this story is an English boy resident in St. Petersburg. Through two student friends he becomes innocently involved in various political plots, resulting in his seizure by the Russian police and his exile to Siberia. He ultimately escapes, and, after many exciting adventures, he reaches Norway, and thence home, after a perilous journey which lasts nearly two years.

BERIC THE BRITON

A Story of the Roman Invasion. By G. A. HENTY. With 12 full-page Illustrations by W. PARKINSON. Crown 8vo, olivine edges, $1.50.

This story deals with the invasion of Britain by the Roman legionaries. Beric, who is a boy-chief of a British tribe, takes a prominent part in the insurrection under Boadicea; and after the defeat of that heroic queen (in A. D. 62) he continues the struggle in the fen-country. Ultimately Beric is defeated and carried captive to Rome, where he is trained in the exercise of arms in a school of gladiators. At length he returns to Britain, where he becomes ruler of his own people.

IN GREEK WATERS

A Story of the Grecian War of Independence (1821–1827). By G. A. HENTY. With 12 full-page Illustrations by W. S. STACEY, and a Map. Crown 8vo, olivine edges, $1.50.

Deals with the revolt of the Greeks in 1821 against Turkish oppression. Mr. Beveridge and his son Horace fit out a privateer, load it with military stores, and set sail for Greece. They rescue the Christians, relieve the captive Greeks, and fight the Turkish war vessels.

BY G. A. HENTY

"No living writer of books for boys writes to better purpose than Mr. G. A. Henty."—*Philadelphia Press.*

THE DASH FOR KHARTOUM

A Tale of the Nile Expedition. By G. A. HENTY. With 10 full-page Illustrations by JOHN SCHÖNBERG and J. NASH. Crown 8vo, olivine edges, $1.50.

In the record of recent British history there is no more captivating page for boys than the story of the Nile campaign, and the attempt to rescue General Gordon. For, in the difficulties which the expedition encountered, in the perils which it overpassed, and in its final tragic disappointments, are found all the excitements of romance, as well as the fascination which belongs to real events.

REDSKIN AND COW-BOY

A Tale of the Western Plains. By G. A. HENTY. With 12 full-page Illustrations by ALFRED PEARSE. Crown 8vo, olivine edges, $1.50.

The central interest of this story is found in the many adventures of an English lad, who seeks employment as a cow-boy on a cattle ranch. His experiences during a "round-up" present in picturesque form the toilsome, exciting, adventurous life of a cow-boy; while the perils of a frontier settlement are vividly set forth in an Indian raid.

HELD FAST FOR ENGLAND

A Tale of the Siege of Gibraltar. By G. A. HENTY. With 8 full-page Illustrations by GORDON BROWNE. Crown 8vo, olivine edges, $1.50.

This story deals with one of the most memorable sieges in history—the siege of Gibraltar in 1779–83 by the united forces of France and Spain. With land forces, fleets, and floating batteries, the combined resources of two great nations, this grim fortress was vainly besieged and bombarded. The hero of the tale, an English lad resident in Gibraltar, takes a brave and worthy part in the long defence, and it is through his varied experiences that we learn with what bravery, resource, and tenacity the Rock was held for England.

NOTE.—For a list of Henty Books at popular prices, see the following page.

A List of Books ❊
❊ for Young People

... BY ...

KIRK MUNROE

A SON OF SATSUMA
Or, With Perry in Japan
BY KIRK MUNROE

With twelve Illustrations by HARRY C. EDWARDS. $1.00 net.

THIS absorbing story for boys deals with one of the most interesting episodes in our National history. From the
beginning Japan has been a land of mystery. Foreigners were
permitted to land only at certain points on her shores and nothing
whatever was known of her civilization and history, her romance
and magnificence, her wealth and art. It was Commodore Perry
who opened her gates to the world, thus solving the mystery of
the ages, and, in this thrilling story of an American boy in
Japan at that period, the spirit as well as the history of this great
achievement is ably set forth.

MIDSHIPMAN STUART

Or, the Last Cruise of the Essex. A Tale of the War of 1812.
Illustrated. 12mo, $1.25.

This is an absorbing story of life in the American Navy during
the stirring times of our war of 1812. The very spirit of the
period is in its pages, and many of the adventures of the Essex
are studied from history.

IN PIRATE WATERS

A Tale of the American Navy. Illustrated by I. W. TABER.
12mo, $1.25.

The hero of the story becomes a midshipman in the navy just at the
time of the war with Tripoli. His own wild adventures among the
Turks and his love romance are thoroughly interwoven with the stirring history of that time.

BY KIRK MUNROE

THE "WHITE CONQUERORS" SERIES

WITH CROCKETT AND BOWIE

Or, Fighting for the Lone Star Flag. A Tale of Texas. With 8 full-page Illustrations by VICTOR PÉRARD. Crown 8vo, $1.25.

The story is of the Texas revolution in 1835, when American Texans under Sam Houston, Bowie, Crockett and Travis, fought for relief from the intolerable tyranny of the Mexican Santa Aña. The hero, Rex Hardin, son of a Texan ranchman and graduate of an American military school, takes a prominent part in the heroic defense of the Alamo, and the final triumph at San Jacinto.

THROUGH SWAMP AND GLADE

A Tale of the Seminole War. By KIRK MUNROE. With 8 full-page Illustrations by V. PÉRARD. Crown 8vo, $1.25.

Coacoochee, the hero of the story, is the son of Philip the chieftain of the Seminoles. He grows up to lead his tribe in the long struggle which resulted in the Indians being driven from the north of Florida down to the distant southern wilderness.

AT WAR WITH PONTIAC

Or, the Totem of the Bear. A Tale of Redcoat and Redskin. By KIRK MUNROE. With 8 full-page Illustrations by J. FINNEMORE. Crown 8vo, $1.25.

A story when the shores of Lake Erie were held by hostile Indians. The hero, Donald Hester, goes in search of his sister Edith, who has been captured by the Indians. Strange and terrible are his experiences ; for he is wounded, taken prisoner, condemned to be burned, but contrives to escape. In the end all things terminate happily.

THE WHITE CONQUERORS

A Tale of Toltec and Aztec. By KIRK MUNROE. With 8 full-page Illustrations. Crown 8vo, $1.25.

This story deals with the Conquest of Mexico by Cortez and his Spaniards, the "White Conquerors," who, after many deeds of valor, pushed their way into the great Aztec kingdom and established their power in the wondrous city where Montezuma reigned in splendor.

CHARLES SCRIBNER'S SONS

153-7 Fifth Avenue   New York

JEB HUTTON, A GEORGIA BOY

By JAMES B. CONNOLLY. Illustrated. $1.20 net. (Postage, 13 cents.)

A thoroughly interesting and breezy tale of boy-life along the Savannah River by a writer who knows boys, and who has succeeded in making of the adventures of Jeb and his friends a story that will keep his young readers absorbed to the last page.

KING MOMBO

By PAUL DU CHAILLU. Author of "The World of the Great Forest," etc. With 24 illustrations. $1.50 net. (Postage, 16 cents.)

The scene is the great African forest. It is a book of interesting experiences with native tribes, and thrilling and perilous adventures in hunting elephants, crocodiles, gorillas and other fierce creatures among which this famous explorer lived so long.

A NEW BOOK FOR GIRLS

By LINA BEARD and ADELIA B. BEARD. Authors of "The American Girl's Handy Book." Profusely Illustrated.

An admirable collection of entirely new and original indoor and outdoor pastimes for American girls, each fully and interestingly described and explained, and all designed to stimulate the taste and ingenuity at the same time that they entertain.

SEA FIGHTERS FROM DRAKE TO FARRAGUT

By JESSIE PEABODY FROTHINGHAM. Illustrations by REUTERDAHL. $1.20 net. (Postage, 14 cents.)

Drake, Tromp, De Reuter, Tourville, Suffren, Paul Jones, Nelson and Farragut are the naval heroes here pictured, and each is shown in some great episode which illustrates his personality and heroism. The book is full of the very spirit of daring and adventurous achievement.

BOB AND HIS GUN

By WILLIAM ALEXANDER LINN. With 8 Illustrations.

The adventures of a boy with a gun under the instruction of his cousin, an accomplished sportsman. The book's aim is to interest boys in hunting in the spirit of true sport and to instruct in the ways of game birds and animals.

BY ROBERT LEIGHTON

"Mr. Leighton's place is in the front rank of writers of boys' books."
—*Standard.*

THE GOLDEN GALLEON

Illustrated, crown 8vo, olivine edges, $1.50.

This is a story of Queen Elizabeth's time, just after the defeat of the Spanish Armada. Mr. Leighton introduces in his work the great sea-fighters of Plymouth town—Hawkins, Drake, Raleigh, and Richard Grenville.

OLAF THE GLORIOUS

With 8 full-page Illustrations by RALPH PEACOCK. Crown 8vo, olivine edges, $1.50.

This story of Olaf, King of Norway, opens with his being found living as a bond-slave in Esthonia, and follows him through his romantic youth in Russia. Then come his adventures as a Viking, his raids upon the coasts of Scotland and England, and his conversion to Christianity. He returns to Norway as king, and converts his people to the Christian faith.

WRECK OF "THE GOLDEN FLEECE"

The Story of a North Sea Fisher-boy. With 8 full-page Illustrations by FRANK BRANGWYN. Crown 8vo, olivine edges, $1.50.

The hero is a parson's son who is apprenticed on board a Lowestoft fishing lugger. The lad suffers many buffets from his shipmates, while the storms and dangers which he braved are set forth with intense power.

THE THIRSTY SWORD

A Story of the Norse Invasion of Scotland (1262-63). With 8 full-page Illustrations by ALFRED PEARSE, and a Map. Crown 8vo, olivine edges, $1.50.

This story tells how Roderick Mac Alpin, the sea-rover, came to the Isle of Bute; how he slew his brother in Rothesay Castle; how the earl's eldest son was likewise slain; how young Kenric now became king of Bute, and vowed vengeance against the slayer of his brother and father, and finally, how this vow was kept, when Kenric and the murderous sea-rover met at midnight and ended their feud in one last great fight.

THE PILOTS OF POMONA

A Story of the Orkney Islands. With 8 full-page Illustrations by JOHN LEIGHTON, and a Map. Crown 8vo, olivine edges, $1.50.

Halcro Ericson, the hero, happens upon many exciting adventures and hard experiences, through which he carries himself with quiet courage. The story gives a vivid presentation of life in these far northern islands.

www.ingramcontent.com/pod-product-compliance
Lightning Source LLC
Chambersburg PA
CBHW021339110726
47900CB00005B/1540